An Une[xpected Gentleman]

"Johnson returns to [...] ht readers once again w[...] and a sensible and spirited heroine." —*Publishers Weekly*

"I loved the story and the characters in *An Unexpected Gentleman*. This was an emotional roller-coaster of a story with a sigh-worthy ending." —*Rakehell*

"There's a merging of humor with poignancy, a delightful cast of characters, and just enough sensuality and emotional intensity to bring the story out of the ordinary, something Johnson does quite well." —*RT Book Reviews*

"Alissa Johnson takes some historical romance tropes and gives them new life, delivering a satisfying romance." —*Romance Junkies*

"I loved this book . . . Very touching and romantic." —*Night Owl Reviews*

"Great characters, believable and engrossing conflict, a powerful and tender romance, a stunning transformation and redemption of the hero, an easy-to-read pace, and overall just a really good story." —*TwoLips Reviews*

"Alissa Johnson brings wit, romance, sexy and charming characters, and laugh-out-loud humor to the reader . . . I would highly recommend the read." —*The Season*

continued . . .

Praise for

Nearly a Lady

"A delightfully witty gem . . . . A courageous, hilarious heroine, laugh-out-loud humor, and a true hero who will steal your heart." —Jennifer Ashley, *USA Today* bestselling author

"High on believable, witty characters and emotional honesty."
—*Publishers Weekly*

"This book was perfect for me. Seriously, *perfect*."
—*Fiction Vixen*

"*Nearly a Lady* is a fun and utterly charming book."
—*Rakehell*

"Highly recommended!" —*Fresh Fiction*

"Johnson beautifully tells a rags-to-riches tale."
—*Booklist*

"I plan to revisit this story for years to come."
—*All About Romance*

More praise for
the novels of Alissa Johnson

"Alissa Johnson strikes the perfect tone between romantic humor, suspense, drama, and just good old-fashioned hijinks between two charismatic characters."
—*Night Owl Reviews*

"Spiced with razor-sharp wit with a perfect touch of comic jest, Alissa Johnson has served up a hot and passionate Regency romance like a seasoned pro."   —*Fresh Fiction*

"[This book] has everything that I look for in a romance novel! I cannot wait to pick up another of her books."
—*Romance Reader at Heart*

"If you're a lover of historical romance—even if you aren't—and you haven't read Ms. Johnson's books yet, you should remedy that immediately."
—*The Good, The Bad and The Unread*

"With wit and whimsy, Johnson crafts tales filled with charming original characters, captivating readers seeking the unusual, the imperfect, and the most endearing heroines since Jill Barnett."   —*RT Book Reviews*

"Funny, charming, heart-wrenching, majorly romantic, and sexy as hell . . . Destined to become a keeper."
—*Rakehell*

Berkley Sensation titles by Alissa Johnson

NEARLY A LADY
AN UNEXPECTED GENTLEMAN
PRACTICALLY WICKED

Practically Wicked

Alissa Johnson

BERKLEY SENSATION, NEW YORK

THE BERKLEY PUBLISHING GROUP
Published by the Penguin Group
Penguin Group (USA) Inc.
375 Hudson Street, New York, New York 10014, USA

Penguin Group (Canada), 90 Eglinton Avenue East, Suite 700, Toronto, Ontario M4P 2Y3, Canada
(a division of Pearson Penguin Canada Inc.) • Penguin Books Ltd., 80 Strand, London WC2R 0RL,
England • Penguin Group Ireland, 25 St. Stephen's Green, Dublin 2, Ireland (a division of Penguin
Books Ltd.) • Penguin Group (Australia), 250 Camberwell Road, Camberwell, Victoria 3124, Australia
(a division of Pearson Australia Group Pty. Ltd.) • Penguin Books India Pvt. Ltd., 11 Community
Centre, Panchsheel Park, New Delhi—110 017, India • Penguin Group (NZ), 67 Apollo Drive,
Rosedale, Auckland 0632, New Zealand (a division of Pearson New Zealand Ltd.) • Penguin Books
(South Africa) (Pty.) Ltd., 24 Sturdee Avenue, Rosebank, Johannesburg 2196, South Africa

Penguin Books Ltd., Registered Offices: 80 Strand, London WC2R 0RL, England

This is a work of fiction. Names, characters, places, and incidents either are the product of the author's
imagination or are used fictitiously, and any resemblance to actual persons, living or dead, business
establishments, events, or locales is entirely coincidental. The publisher does not have any control over
and does not assume any responsibility for author or third-party websites or their content.

PRACTICALLY WICKED

A Berkley Sensation Book / published by arrangement with the author

PUBLISHING HISTORY
Berkley Sensation mass-market edition / October 2012

Copyright © 2012 by Alissa Johnson.
Cover art by Judy York.
Cover design by George Long.
Interior text design by Laura K. Corless.

ISBN: 978-0-425-25803-3

BERKLEY SENSATION®
Berkley Sensation Books are published by The Berkley Publishing Group,
a division of Penguin Group (USA) Inc.,
375 Hudson Street, New York, New York 10014.
BERKLEY SENSATION® is a registered trademark of Penguin Group (USA) Inc.
The "B" design is a trademark of Penguin Group (USA) Inc.

PRINTED IN THE UNITED STATES OF AMERICA

10 9 8 7 6 5 4 3 2 1

ALWAYS LEARNING   **PEARSON**

For Bryan and Hillery Johnson, with love.

Chapter 1

❧

*L*ife was best experienced through a thick layer of fine drink.

Inferior drink might do in a pinch, but Maximilian Dane was certain that nothing accompanied an evening of debauchery with the demimonde quite so well as several goblets of excellent wine at dinner, followed by a glass, or two, of expensive port in the billiards room, followed by a liberal tasting of superb brandy in the card room, followed by any number of flutes of champagne in Mrs. Wrayburn's ballroom, followed by . . . whatever it was he had poured in the library. He recalled an amber hue and delicate bite. He also recalled forgoing the actual pour and drinking straight from the bottle.

In hindsight, that may have been a mistake.

Because at some point following that final drink, he left the library in search of . . . something or other, and rather than finding his way back to the ballroom where this something was most likely to be found, he had landed here—in a quiet, unfamiliar room illuminated by only a spattering of candles, and seated in a plain wooden chair before a plain wooden table, which had both initially appeared to be adequately sized for a man of five-and-twenty, but upon his sitting, had proved to be entirely too near to the floor. His legs were bent at an angle he suspected would be impossible were it not for the limbering quality of all those glasses.

"What in God's name is the matter with this furniture?"

"Lord Highsup cut the legs off for me when I was six," a woman's voice explained. He liked the sound of it, lower than one expected from a woman and warm like the fine drink from the library.

He looked up from the golden wood grain of the table and squinted until the form sitting across from him came into focus. His companion wore a night rail and wrap. They were white, ruffled, and provided a sharply contrasting background to the dark braid of hair that fell over her shoulder and ended just below a well-formed breast.

"You're not six."

"Indeed, I am not. How astute of you to ascertain."

"Plenty tart, though, I see. Who are you?" He threw up a hand, narrowly avoiding a thumb to the eye. "No . . . No, wait. I know. I never forget a lady." Leaning closer, he took in the young woman's pale gray eyes and delicate features, along with her rigid posture and indifferent expression. "You . . . are Miss Anna Rees, The Ice Maiden of Anover House."

There was a slight pause before she spoke. "And you are Mr. Maximilian Dane, the Disappointment of McMullin Hall."

"Ah . . . *Not*," he informed her with a quick jab of his finger at the ceiling, "*anymore*. At half past seven this morning, or somewhere . . . thereabouts, I became *Viscount* Dane . . . the Disappointment of McMullin Hall."

"Oh." Her tone softened as the meaning of his words set in. "Oh, I am sorry."

"'S neither here nor there," he assured her with a clumsy sweep of his hand. "Speaking of which . . . Where is here, love?"

"Anover House."

"Yes, I know. Lovely party. Where in Anover House?"

"The nursery."

"Ah. That would explain the miniature furniture, wouldn't it?" He shifted a bit and grimaced when he caught the side of his ankle on the table leg. "Bit long in the tooth for the nursery, aren't you?"

"It was the nearest room, my lord. You—"

"Don't," he cut in sharply. "Don't call me that. I've hours yet."

"Hours?"

"Until everyone hears, until everyone knows I am Lord Dane." He curled his lip in disgust. "Until I have to be a bloody viscount."

"Very well. Mr. Dane, then. If you would—"

Something about the way she said his name sparked a memory.

"Mrs. Carring," he said suddenly and made a failed effort at snapping his fingers. *"That's* why I came upstairs." The reasonably attractive and exceptionally accommodating widow Carring had invited him to her guest chambers. He'd stopped in the library for that last drink, something to further blur the face of his brother, and then . . . He'd become a bit turned around. He gave Miss Rees a quizzical look. "Came down the wrong hall, did I?"

"If you were after Mrs. Carring, yes. She is a floor below."

"I climbed an extra set of steps?" Strange, he'd not have thought himself capable. His legs felt like pudding. "Huh. And how is it I came to be in your company?"

"I was in the hallway. You waved, tripped, and landed at my feet."

He closed his eyes in thought, found it made the room

spin unpleasantly, and let his gaze drift over Miss Rees's face instead. He recalled now, smiling at the pretty lady, losing his feet, and finding them again with the lady's assistance. She smelled sweet and flowery, like sugar biscuits and roses. "So, I did. What the devil did I trip on?"

"I couldn't say," Miss Rees replied and rose smoothly from her chair.

In a display of coordination that surprised him, he reached forward and took hold of her wrist without falling out of his seat. "Where are you going?"

"To ring for assistance." She tugged at her wrist, but he held on with a gentle grasp. He liked the way the heat of her skin seeped through the cotton and warmed his palm.

"Don't. I don't want help. I don't need it." And the moment she rang for it, she'd leave. He wanted that least of all. The ballroom below was filled with ladies like the widow Carring—worldly women clad in silk, rubies, and the promise of sin-filled nights. But it was the prim little creature before him now who intrigued him. "You've a different sort of promise."

"I beg your pardon?"

He shook his head, lightly so as not to lose it entirely. "Never mind. Don't ring for help."

"You cannot stay here in the nursery, my lord, and—"

"Mr. Dane," he reminded her. "Why not? Are there children about?"

Surely not. Surely no one, not even the most depraved of Mrs. Wrayburn's friends, would be so ridiculous as to bring a child to one of the woman's parties.

"No, but—"

"Then we'll stay. Sit," he pressed again. He considered and rejected the idea of tugging her back onto her seat. His current level of coordination was unpredictable at best. He wasn't looking to do the woman an injury. "Talk with me."

"I can't. It isn't proper."

He snorted a little in response. As far as good society

was concerned, the words "proper" and "Anover House" were mutually exclusive. "What do we care for proper, you and I?"

"I care," she replied, and he watched with fascination as her already rigid back straightened just a hair further. "My mother would most assuredly care."

"Then she ought to have had the sense to move you out of the house by now."

If he remembered correctly, rumor had it Mrs. Wrayburn had, in fact, tried to marry her daughter off on more than one occasion, but Miss Rees was content to stay as she was—a reclusive and spoiled young woman, and a burden on her overindulgent mother.

Well, the little darling could indulge someone else for a change.

"I want you to stay," he informed her. "And now that I'm a viscount, I'm fairly certain you have to do as I say. Sit. Talk."

Unless he was very much mistaken, her lips twitched with amusement. "No."

This time, when she pulled at her wrist he had no choice but to grant her freedom or risk being yanked from his seat.

He squinted at her willowy arms. "Stronger than you look."

That dubious compliment earned him a bland expression. "I daresay a kitten would give you trouble in your current condition, which is why I need to ring—"

"That's insulting." Quite possibly true, but nonetheless insulting. "Unless you are referring to one of those giant breeds of cats? Tigers and such? They have exceptionally large kittens."

"Cubs, Mr. Dane. And no, I was not."

"Then I'm insulted." He made a show of slumping in his chair, but when that failed to lure out a smile, he tried another tack. "Before passing along your next barb, you might consider taking into account the sad, *sad* nature of events that has led to my weakened state."

"I beg your pardon?"

He wondered if he was, perhaps, not expressing himself as clearly as he imagined. "There's been a death in the family, you'll recall."

It was unforgivable to make mention of his brother's passing in such a careless manner, and he might have felt a little guilty for it, were he not so damnably angry with his brother just now. And so gratified to see Miss Rees's expression soften once again. And so stupendously drunk.

But softened or not, Miss Rees appeared implacable in her resolve to leave. "Please understand, Mr. Dane, I am most sorry for the loss of your father. However—"

Baffled, he straightened in his chair. "My father?"

"The gentleman from whom you've inherited the viscounty."

"Ah, no. My elder brother, Reginald. My father shuffled off the mortal coil years ago." He gave that additional thought. "Maybe only two. Strange, seems longer. And not long enough." The viscount's baritone voice had grown happily dim in his memory.

"I am truly sorry for the loss of your brother," Miss Rees corrected patiently. "However, I cannot continue to keep company with you in here, like this. I may not come from good ton, but I am an unmarried young woman, and as a gentleman, you—"

"Good Lord, child, where did you acquire the impression I was a gentleman?"

"Very well," she conceded. "As a *viscount*, you are expected, at the very least, to make a show of adhering to the strictures governing a gentleman's behavior, and as such, you *must* respect my wish to not risk being seen in—"

"Oh, for God's sake," he groaned, "just *go*."

A lecture of what he *must do* was the last thing he wanted to listen to at present. He'd done nothing but follow the mandates of others for the first three-and-twenty years of his life. It had been an appalling experience. He had discovered in the two years since that it was far better to be a disappointment than a pawn. Better still if he didn't have to suffer through someone else's long-winded opinion on the matter.

Miss Rees glanced at the bellpull, then back to him. "Will you allow me to ring for—?"

"No." If he couldn't sit with the pretty lady, he'd sit alone for a bit and find his own way back downstairs.

"As you like," she murmured and turned and walked away with the flowing grace that had helped cement her nickname as the Ice Maiden.

"Like gliding on ice," he mumbled. "'Snot natural."

Giving no indication of having heard the comment, she reached the door, paused with her hand on the handle, and looked back with a pleading expression. "*Please* allow me to ring for assistance."

"No."

"But I—"

"No."

A small crease formed between the dark arcs of her brows. "You can't mean to—"

"Unaccustomed to hearing the word 'no,' aren't you?"

Her lips thinned. "I ought to have left you in the hall."

"Regrets are like mistresses," he informed her.

"I . . ." Her hand dropped from the handle. "What?"

"Good men don't have them."

She blinked at that, then broke into a soft laughter that sent pleasant chills along his skin. "That is the most ridiculous adage I have ever heard."

"I'm foxed," he pointed out and shrugged. "I'm cleverer when . . . cleverer? Is it cleverer? Or is it more clever? Whichever. I'm brilliant when I'm sober."

"And less inclined to announce it, one might hope." With a resigned sigh, she reached for the door handle again, but this time, she locked the door and dropped the key in her pocket.

"You move like a queen," he said quietly as she crossed the room and resumed her seat in front of him. "On ice skates. What did you just do?"

"I locked the door."

"Yes, I know." He was drunk, not blind. "Why?"

"To avoid another inebriated guest stumbling in upon us by accident."

"You mean to stay?" he asked, not quite believing it.

Avoiding his gaze, she brushed a smoothing hand down the sleeve of one arm. "You won't allow me to call for some-one else."

"And you aren't willing to leave me sitting here all alone? That is . . . unexpected." He leaned in for a closer inspection of her features. "Aren't you supposed to be frigid and uncaring?"

She looked at him, her eyes narrowing just a hair. "Aren't you supposed to be charming?"

He grinned at her, appreciating the sharp retort. "I'll have you know, I could talk the devil out of his tail."

"I'm not a devil, Mr. Dane."

"No . . . I believe you might be an angel."

"And I believe the reports of your charm have been grossly exaggerated."

"It was trite, wasn't it?" He propped his elbow on the table, rested his chin in his hand, and studied her features at leisure. "There *is* something . . . otherworldly about you. The eyes, I think. But they're not angelic. They're fae."

"They're merely sober."

"Equally disconcerting. Why is it you never come down-stairs with your mother? She throws wonderful parties. You'd enjoy yourself, I think."

"I doubt it."

"You're enjoying yourself now, with me," he pointed

out. Reasonably, to his mind. "The ballroom is brimming with fellows just like myself."

"Inebriated?"

"Yes," he allowed. "Also, exciting and charming."

She eyed him with frank curiosity. "Is that what you're doing coming to parties like these? Dedicating your life to being exciting and charming?"

"I don't dedicate myself to anything," he assured her, lifting his chin from his hand. "Entirely too much work."

"Being a member of the demimonde isn't work? Drink and women and scandals." She shook her head lightly. "Seems prodigiously taxing to me. Why do you do it?"

"Because I can," he replied with a careless lift of one shoulder. "Because I'm not supposed to."

She digested that quietly a moment before speaking. "A viscounty comes with many responsibilities, I imagine. Will you change your ways now?"

"I have changed my ways, sweet. That is how I landed here. And I must say, misshapen furniture notwithstanding, I rather like where I am at present." He smiled at her and watched the faintest of blushes bloom on her cheeks. "How is it you knew of my nickname, but not that my brother was the viscount?"

To her credit, she merely blinked at the sudden change of subject. "When one spends little time outside one's rooms, one gains information in bits and pieces. I encountered your name and reputation in passing."

"Everything you do is in passing. A moment in the ballroom, a mere peek out of the opera box. I've never met the man to have spent more than thirty seconds in your company."

A flicker of unease crossed her features, but it was gone almost the instant it arrived. "Do you mean to brag to your friends to have been the only one?"

"And be banished from your mother's home?" He made

a scoffing noise. "I'll keep the accomplishment to myself, though it will cost me. You're the subject of considerable speculation, you know."

"Am I?" She digested that behind a shuttered expression. "One would think people would have something more compelling to discuss than a woman of whom they know nothing."

"It's the mystery of the thing," he explained. "What will become of the spoiled, reclusive daughter of the notorious Mrs. Wrayburn? Will she follow in her mother's footsteps and become a member of the demimonde, will she marry a tradesman with the fortune to keep her in silk and diamonds?"

"Perhaps I'm not as spoiled as people seem to think," she countered softly. "Perhaps I'll marry a pauper and reside in a cottage in the countryside."

"And live off your dowry?" He considered that. "Do you have dowry?"

"You'd have to ask my mother."

"Hardly matters," he decided. "Who are you going to meet, peeking into ballrooms and parlors long enough to give us all a glimpse of your fae eyes and fine feathers, and hiding away upstairs for the rest of the night?"

"I don't hide," she replied, a whisper of defensiveness creeping into her voice. "And I've met you."

"I hope you're not expecting a proposal."

Her lips curved. "You're shortsighted to not consider the notion. You could do your duty to the viscounty and shock good society in one fell swoop."

"That is an *excellent* point." Leaning toward her, he offered a lovelorn expression. "Will you marry me, Miss Anna Rees?"

"No, Lord Dane. I will not."

The quick rejection surprised him into sitting up. There wasn't a single unmarried woman of his acquaintance who would refuse an offer, even a drunken one, from a peer. "You would turn down the opportunity to be a viscountess?"

"Gladly."

He pressed his lips together in thought before asking, "Is it because I'm the viscount?"

"No, it is because I have no interest in being a member of either the demimonde or the beau monde. Or being married to either." There was a short hesitation before she spoke again. "I want the cottage in the countryside."

"Do you? Truly?" He'd never have guessed it. No one who had caught a glimpse of Miss Rees in her exquisite gowns and sparkling jewels, or listened to Mrs. Wrayburn wax lovingly on about her daughter's adorable demands for exquisite gowns and sparkling jewels, would have entertained the idea for even a moment. Miss Rees was more of an enigma than any of them had realized. "Fascinating. What else do you want?"

"From my life, do you mean?" One dark brow winged up. "Why on earth would I share my dreams with you?"

"You just told me of the cottage," he reminded her. "And I'm not out to have your secrets. Merely your interests. It's a way to pass the time. Unless you'd care to sit here in silence?"

"I don't . . ." She trailed off, looked away, and was quiet for so long, Max thought perhaps she had chosen to sit in silence after all. Which was all the same to him. There were worse ways to spend the evening than sitting quietly with Miss Anna Rees. He liked looking at her—the high plane of her cheekbones, the soft curve of her jaw. He wanted to reach out and trace the outline of her ear, maybe draw his finger down the length of her pale neck.

"I want a hound," Miss Rees said suddenly, and even with the layers of drink blurring his senses, he instantly recognized the twin notes of uncertainty and determination in her voice. It took him a moment more, however, to push through those layers and remember what they'd been talking about.

"A hound. Right. You want a hound. Like your mother's pug?"

"No, not a lapdog. A *hound*," she emphasized with a hint of excitement. "I want a sturdy sort of dog I can stroll with through a forest or have run beside me when I ride. Something not apt to disappear into a well or be trampled under a carriage."

He was suddenly reminded of the Newfoundland he'd had as a boy. Brutus. A hulking, slobbering beast of a thing. "I *adored* that dog."

"I'm sorry?"

He shook his head. "Nothing. Won't your mother purchase a dog for you?"

"A town house is no place for a large animal," she said quietly and began to trace a narrow scratch in the wood of the table with a long, elegant finger.

"Not some dogs, certainly. But something like one of those spotted coach hounds. They'd be happy chasing you and your mother through Hyde Park." He couldn't recall having ever seen the lady at the park, but surely she went out for fresh air now and again.

"I'll wait for a cottage."

"Why should you?" When she refused to answer, he dipped his head to catch her eye. "Your mother won't purchase one for you, will she?"

"It is her home," she said by way of answer and went back to tracing the scratch.

"I see," he said carefully, straightening. Perhaps Mrs. Wrayburn and her daughter were not as close as Mrs. Wrayburn had led others to believe. "I think . . . You're not at all what you seem, are you?"

Her eyes drifted up from the table. "Beg your pardon?"

"Am I slurring?" he asked and smacked his lips experimentally.

"Considerably, but it's the yawning that renders you unintelligible."

"Ah." He closed his eyes briefly and discovered the room still spun around him but at a more reasonable speed than before. "God, I am tired."

"Is there no one I could fetch to take you home?"

The few friends he would trust inside his home were not the sort of men who attended parties thrown by Mrs. Wrayburn. He opened his eyes and gave her what he hoped was a wink but, under the circumstances, might well have been a slow blink. "No one whose company I should enjoy so much as yours. Are you quite certain you won't marry me?"

"Yes."

"Pity," he replied and meant it. Once his position as Lord Dane became public knowledge, the freedom he'd enjoyed as a less-than-desirable match would disappear. No one was interested in marrying the dissolute younger brother of a perfectly healthy viscount. But a dissolute viscount . . . that was another matter. He was to be prime game for the unwed ladies of the respectable set until he chose a bride. What fun it would be to disappoint them all by eloping with the lovely, fascinating, and entirely unsuitable Miss Rees. "If you should change your mind—"

"I'll not."

"But if you should, I promise you that cottage in the country."

A small smile curved her lips. "And the hound?"

"And the hound."

"And why would you do that, Lord Dane?"

"Everyone should have at least a piece of what they want." And the longer he sat there, staring into Miss Rees's fae eyes, the more he realized that what he wanted most at the moment was her. "I like the way you smile. It's tremendously sweet. And that little eyetooth, there on the right. It's a bit crooked. I find that beguiling."

"Beg your pardon?"

He realized he was yawning again. "Beguiling. Your tooth is beguiling."

"An entire ballroom of charmers just like yourself, did you say? I'd no idea what delights I was missing."

Suddenly, he didn't like the idea of her mingling with other gentlemen. Particularly not the sort of gentlemen to be found downstairs. "I may have exaggerated the allure of the ballroom. You're far better off up here."

"I have always suspected."

"You're best off in my company." He wanted to prove it, but it seemed too much of a challenge at present. "I shall call on you tomorrow."

"You may have other duties to attend to tomorrow, my lord."

"Right. Next week, then. I'll call on you next week."

She made a humming noise in the back of her throat that he easily recognized as the sound of a woman humoring a man. His sister had been fond of employing it when they'd been younger and he would air his intent to defy their father.

"Got round to it eventually," he heard himself mumble.

"What was that?"

"I'll get round to it," he stated more clearly. "After this business with my brother."

Another noise, this time accompanied by a patronizing smile and slight inclination of the head. It mattered little to his mind. Next week would be soon enough to prove himself. Just now, he was too exhausted to even think about attempting to prove something. And too drunk. And much, much too angry at his brother for *his* last attempt at trying to prove something to someone.

"Do you know how he died, Miss Rees? My brother?"

She shook her head.

"A duel. A damned duel. And not even over a woman. Some ridiculous puppy accused him of cheating during a game of cards, and my idiot brother called him out. He's left a wife and four daughters alone, and the estate to a ne'er-do-well. And they'll say he died with honor . . . Or defending his honor, I've forgotten which. At any rate, honor will be bandied about like a child's ball while the puppy abandons his ailing mother to run off to the continent, my nieces wail into their pillows, and the Dane estate crumbles into ruin." He tried lifting his hand for a toast before realizing he hadn't a glass, or the energy to lift it.

"To honor," he muttered.

"Lives are ruined in less savory pursuits than honor."

"No." He sighed and leaned back in his tiny chair. His head was so damnably heavy. "No, I don't think they are."

"Haven't you honor?" Miss Rees asked quietly.

He allowed his tired eyes to close, just for a moment, and sighed heavily. "To be honest, Miss Rees . . . I don't much care."

Chapter 2

❧

It was a little known fact that Miss Anna Rees was unaware of her true age.

According to Mrs. Wrayburn, her only daughter would turn nineteen come April. However, Anna clearly recalled repeating the ages of seven and nine, and her fifteenth year had been celebrated three times—twice in the summer and once in the fall. At best guess, she was near to four-and-twenty and her birthday fell somewhere between July and November.

Once, she had inquired after her true birthday only to be told by her mother that a date of birth was of no consequence. What mattered was how old one appeared.

"And I cannot appear a young woman if I have a daughter grown," Mrs. Wrayburn had said. "Be a darling and play along."

Anna had outwardly conceded, inwardly doubted they were fooling anyone, and secretly wondered if her mother had simply forgotten the date.

It hardly signified now, she thought. At one-and-twenty or four-and-twenty, she was an adult. And not just any sort of adult, but one possibly teetering on the verge of becoming an Old Maid. Worse, an old maid that was at once both the most disreputable old maid in all of Christendom, and the dullest.

Here she was, a grown woman living in Anover House, where the most notorious of the demimonde's widows threw the most depraved parties in all of London, and yet she'd not engaged in a conversation of any length with a gentleman before tonight. She'd scarcely conversed with anyone other than her mother, her governess, and her mother's staff.

Her experiences with society were very much as Mr. Dane described them—sporadic in nature and brief of duration. She had been to the theater twice in her life and had spent both evenings hidden away in a box. So well hidden, in fact, that she'd not been able to see but half the stage. She'd never been to someone else's ball or been invited to a dinner party. At her mother's gatherings, she was dressed in finery and made to stand for a half hour or so on a private, second-level balcony in the ballroom. This was the limited extent of her participation at Anover House, and her loathing of it knew no bounds.

Lord, how she hated being on that balcony, hated standing there alone and silent while the crowd looked her over like a curiosity in a museum. Some chose to stare openly, some glanced at her in passing on their way to the terrace or refreshment table, still others pretended complete indifference, but took surreptitious peaks from behind fans or over shoulders.

It seemed everyone was whispering.

And all the while, Mrs. Wrayburn could be heard in the crowd below, exclaiming over her daughter's attributes like a doting parent. "La, isn't she simply beautiful? Isn't my darling girl the most exquisite of gems?"

Anna knew herself to be reasonably pretty, not beautiful. But thanks to her clever mother, she was unattainable, and there was nothing more captivating, more alluring than that.

Occasionally, if a guest of great consequence requested an introduction, or if her mother was simply feeling generous and playful, a short visit to the balcony was permitted. Bows and curtsies were exchanged, along with a few pleasantries if the guest was a woman, but any attempt to engage Anna in a true conversation was immediately thwarted, particularly if the guest was a gentleman.

Despite her mother's penchant for providing excuses that painted Anna in an unflattering light—*My darling girl has quite insisted on remaining apart from the festivities tonight. You will forgive her eccentricities, I'm sure*— Anna had been content with the interference in the past. She had no interest in becoming acquainted with her mother's gentlemen friends.

At least, not until now.

Anna studied the man before her. She'd never have imagined it could be so pleasant spending time with a gentleman. It was foolish, of course, to be taken in by the questionable charm of an inebriated libertine, but she couldn't seem to help herself.

She was fascinated by Max Dane. And not simply because he was handsome, though that detail had not escaped her notice. He seemed such a contradiction to her, at once both playful and dangerous.

His mischievous charm delighted her. His deep-set, hazel eyes held the unmistakable light of humor, and the loose curl in his tousled hair of rich brown lent him an endearingly boyish look. Though she imagined he'd not be pleased to hear it, there was something about the man that struck her as being just a little bit adorable.

But Max Dane was no boy. It was difficult to assess his height while he was sitting, but he was larger than her uncommonly tall governess, Mrs. Culpepper, which would put him at a minimum of six feet. And while he might appear harmless enough in his slouched and disheveled state, there was no mistaking the wide breadth of his shoulders and outline of muscle beneath his formal evening attire.

Max Dane was a man grown.

Anna leaned a little closer and watched the flickering candlelight cast moving shadows across his handsome face.

This man was unattainable in every sense of the word. And she did so find him captivating.

She wondered what he would say if she told him that tonight was shaping up to be the single most exciting, enchanting night of her life. Probably, he would call her a callous fool, as it was also the night he was grieving the loss of his brother.

Poor boy.

Without thought, she leaned forward and brushed a lock of his hair from his forehead. She'd never known a loss such as his.

Realizing what she was about, she snatched her hand back, fully expecting for him to comment on her forward behavior. As well he might. What on earth had she been thinking?

But he didn't move. His eyes remained closed. His breathing was deep and steady.

She swallowed hard. "Mr. Dane?"

Still nothing. He was fast asleep.

Anna glanced from her guest to the door. She could leave now or call for help.

Her eyes tracked back to Max. She could sit and stare at his handsome features if she wanted, and for as long as she liked.

Slowly, her gaze dipped to his mouth and settled there.

She could do most anything she cared to, really.

It was folly, what she was considering. If someone had told her earlier in the day that, in a few hours' time, she would be considering taking advantage of a gentleman in his sleep, she would have pronounced the notion, and the individual, ridiculous.

And now here she was, leaning just a little closer . . . And closer still . . .

It was the strangest sensation, as if she were watching herself at a distance and quite enjoying the view.

Dreams of freedom and country cottages were all well and good, but Anna rather thought that she was nothing, if not practical. She would likely never have that cottage, never have true freedom. And she would almost certainly never have a chance such as this again.

Let them call her the Ice Maiden of Anover House, she thought. She would know differently. She, and no one else.

But just to be sure on that score, she whispered, "Mr. Dane, are you . . . ?"

There was no response, no hint that he'd heard her.

And suddenly the room took on a surreal quality. The scent of candles grew strong and the creak of her chair as she leaned forward those last few inches sounded inordinately loud.

And then she was kissing him. Or, more accurately, she was holding her lips lightly against his. Whether or not this constituted a real kiss was unclear. It rather seemed as if one or the both of them ought to be moving.

In fact, she was certain at least one of them ought to be moving, but she couldn't seem to get the job done. For some reason, pressing her lips to his while he slept seemed a natural, albeit decidedly wicked, thing to do. Moving felt more wicked than natural, like it might push her over the line that separated inexcusably forward from outright wanton.

With a mental sigh, she realized a small advantage was all it could be. She lingered a moment longer, wanting to savor the experience. If this was to be her only kiss, it would at least be of respectable duration.

Keeping her eyes shut, she concentrated on every detail. Max's lips were soft, but firm. His breath light and sweet against her skin. The scent of whatever he'd been drinking earlier tickled her nose pleasantly. She wanted to reach out and touch him, feel the texture of his hair, but that, too, felt like too much.

With regret that it could not be more, she began to pull away.

And then the unimaginable happened. One of them began to move.

Max shifted, and a warm hand slipped around her neck, pulling her gently but firmly back into place.

Her eyes flew open, her hands came up to his chest, and her heart made a valiant effort to leap from her chest. For a moment, she forgot to breathe.

Max didn't seem to mind. He held her in place as his lips explored hers in lazy sweeps and brushes. Shock and fear lingered but for a heartbeat, just until Anna realized that his grip was coaxing, not implacable, and that his mouth moved over hers in invitation, not demand.

Your only chance. Your only kiss.

She relaxed, leaned forward once more, and kissed him back.

And, heavens, she'd been a fool to think she'd been kissing him before. That had been a meeting of lips, nothing more. This . . . this was . . .

This was extraordinary. Wonderful. Fantastical. Words could not adequately describe the array of sensations that washed over her. She felt as if she were both sinking and floating. It seemed as if the world were spinning and only the two of them were grounded. She felt heated and anxious as he sampled the corner of her mouth, impatient when the tip of his tongue slipped between her lips for just a taste. She wanted to do more, so much more. And she wanted to do it quickly. Yet she was content as well. Happy to stay exactly as she was, doing exactly what they were doing.

The first feeling she knew to be arousal. And had someone told her it would be so magical, she might have sought out an inebriated man with a handsome face before now.

Only, it wouldn't have been the same. It would have been someone else's hands on her, someone else's lips moving over hers. Perhaps that was why she wanted to stay exactly where she was, *as* she was—because she was with Max Dane.

But not only was it impossible for her to stay, it was highly unlikely she would ever return. There was no reason to hope she would ever have another opportunity to indulge in a stolen kiss. And so she memorized every second of sliding lips and heated breath, cataloged every leap of her heart, every spark of desire, every flitting sensation. She didn't want a single instant of the experience to slip from her memory.

But all too soon, the memory ended. Max gently separated them, and one twinkling hazel eye slowly opened.

"Am I asleep?" he said softly, and it took her a minute to realize he was recalling her question from earlier. A small, wicked smile formed. "No."

"I . . ." Words failed her. She was leaning over the man, panting like a common doxy, and had nothing to say for herself.

He caught her gaze and held it. "Well, that was a pleasant surprise."

"I don't . . . I don't know what possessed me," she managed at last. She touched shaky fingers to her lips, saw his eyes darken as they followed the movement, and dropped her hand. "I beg your pardon."

"I believe that's my duty. To beg for pardon."

"Is it? . . . Well . . . I see." She remained as she was a moment more before coming back to herself with a small start. Good Lord, what was she *doing*? She straightened quickly and nodded once. "Pardon granted, then. Do excuse me."

"What? . . . Wait." He caught her arm when she would have stood and made the dash for the door that she ought to have made some time ago. "Don't go."

"Lord Dane, please—"

"Mr. Dane." He shook his head impatiently. "Never mind, call me Max. Then we needn't worry over misters and lords."

"No, I can't—"

"Why not?" He gave her a teasing smile. "You've already kissed me. Seems a minor breach of etiquette in comparison."

"I should not have done so." She really, really should not have done so. "I typically do not give such free rein to my curiosity, but it would seem that tonight was an exception—"

"Curiosity?" He let go of her arm. "That's why you kissed me?"

That, and a thousand other reasons a man like him would misinterpret or simply not understand. "Yes. Why else?"

His lips twitched. "Why else, indeed. Well, did I at least satisfy?"

"My curiosity? Yes, quite, thank you."

"You're entirely welcome," he replied with a dry tone that set her nerves on edge.

She felt a fool. Why, *why* had she thought this was a good idea? What had made her think she could get away with such outrageous behavior? Of course he would wake up. Of course he'd not really been asleep. And now here she was, without the foggiest notion of how to handle the situation. Without the foggiest notion of how to handle *him*.

She cast a longing glance at the door. "I've offended you. I'm sorry. I'll go—"

"No, no," Max cut in with an impatience that seemed mostly self-directed. "You've not offended me. I'm unaccustomed to honesty, that's all. Sit down, love."

She knew she'd somehow pricked his pride, and she

suspected he might be mocking her a little, but there was a gentleness to the teasing, an invitation to play along, as if the entire experience was but a harmless bit of silliness. It did more to temper her embarrassment and desire to flee than a hundred polite assurances might have accomplished.

Perhaps she shouldn't have kissed him, but there was no reason the memory of it needed to end with her running out of the room in mortification.

"You . . . You should make new friends," she said carefully. "One shouldn't grow used to hearing lies." She thought of her own life and felt something of a hypocrite. "One should not approve of them, at any rate."

"Oh, I approve. I prefer my friends dishonest. That way, I'm never left guessing when it's wise to trust them and when it's not."

"Wouldn't it be better that they always be honest?"

"No one is honest all the time. Not even my sainted brother. Devil take him."

"You don't mean that," she argued gently, resuming her seat. "He was your brother."

"He's a ridiculous bastard."

She noticed his use of the present tense and a pang of sympathy settled in her chest. How hard it would be to remember to speak of a family member in the past tense. How painful.

"But you loved him."

He leaned back in his chair once more and closed his eyes as he had before, but he no longer seemed a cavalier man to her, just a heartbroken boy.

"Yes," he admitted softly. "God, yes. I loved him."

She sought for a way to comfort but didn't know where to begin. She'd no experience in such matters. She had already said sorry. What came after that?

Max lifted a shoulder, let it drop. "We cannot always help who we love, I suppose."

"Or like who it is we love," she added, simply because she felt she ought to say *something*.

"True." He tilted his head at her. "Do you like your mother?"

Not in the least, she thought, but what she said was, "We get on well enough."

Which was true, provided she kept as much distance from her as the confines of Anover House, and her mother's desperate need to be the center of everyone's attention, allowed.

"Most people find her quite likable," Max commented.

"Most people are not required to live with her."

"Family," he said and bobbed his head with his eyes still closed. "They can be the hardest to love . . . or not love . . . Whichever was our original point." A furrow appeared across his brow. "I seem to have lost track."

Anna hadn't, but the talk of her highly likable mother prompted a sudden, terrible, sickening notion.

She licked lips suddenly gone dry. "Mr. Dane—"

"Max," he corrected.

"Right. Max. You've not . . . with Madame?"

One bleary eye opened. "I've not what with who, now?"

"My mother. You've not . . . ? Er . . ." She couldn't say it. She just couldn't. She hated even thinking it. ". . . Courted her? Or—"

"Oh. *Oh.*" Both eyes snapped wide. "Good God, no." He made a clumsy effort to straighten in his chair. "Lovely woman, your mother. Beautiful, clever, all that, but . . . No. Absolutely not." He gave her a smile designed to charm. "I prefer a woman who's a bit . . . warmer. Such as yourself."

A wash of pleasure heated her skin. "That was very kind."

"No. It wasn't," he countered, slumping in his chair once more. "Kind would have been to remake your furniture. Who is Lord Hiccup? He must be quite fond of you."

"Lord Highsup," she corrected, amused. "I don't remember him well. He passed not long after gifting me this table set. Mrs. Culpepper says he was a friend of Captain Wrayburn's." Of whom she could recall very little and could learn nothing from her mother other than that he'd left an inconveniently meager inheritance upon his equally inconvenient death. Anna liked to assume the best of the man, as it wasn't every gentleman who was willing to wed a fallen woman with a bastard child on her hip.

"Captain Wrayburn," he repeated on another yawn. "Not your father. That would be Mr. Rees."

"Rees was the name of my maternal grandmother," she mumbled and looked for a quick way to change the subject. She didn't wish to have a conversation on her illegitimacy. "Mr. Dane, you are but a hairbreadth from falling out of that chair. May I ring for help now?"

"No."

She opened her mouth to speak but was cut short by the sound of creaking floorboards as someone walked past the nursery door.

Another lost guest, or a maid or footman on an errand.

Or perhaps Mrs. Culpepper had come looking for her, Anna thought with a pang of guilt. The woman would be in a state if she discovered her charge missing at this time of night.

"I must go, Mr. Dane."

"Max."

"I must go, Max. My absence will be noted eventually." And should his role in her adventure be discovered, there was a very real possibility Mrs. Wrayburn would ban him from the house.

He sighed heavily and closed his eyes. "Yes, all right. Call on you tomorrow."

"Next week," she reminded him softly.

His eyes remained closed but his lips curved. "Next week."

She was silent a moment, debating. He was drunk. He

was part of a world she despised and sought to escape. He was everything her mother and, more convincingly, Mrs. Culpepper had ever warned her about.

In that moment, he was all she wanted.

She took a deep breath, and then the second-biggest chance of her life.

"Do you promise?" she asked on a whisper.

"Promise," he mumbled. "Next week."

A moment later, a soft snore issued forth from his lips.

Anna stayed just a minute more, studying his handsome face and the steady rise and fall of his chest. When she took her leave at last, it was with a secret, wicked smile, and a hope for the future she'd never known before.

Chapter 3

Four years later

Mrs. Wrayburn did not ruin her life in the pursuit of honor. Rather, she temporarily marred it in pursuit of Mr. Richard Templeton, who, after one too many drinks, had suggested a game of midnight equestrian hide-and-seek through the streets of London. In between protectors, and willing to oblige the young, wealthy, and dimwitted Mr. Templerton, the equally inebriated (and arguably dimwitted) Mrs. Wrayburn had scarcely made it out of the mews before falling from her horse and breaking her leg.

According to the physician, the injury would heal in a few months' time. According to Mrs. Wrayburn, life as she knew it was *over*.

"I am ruined, Anna. *Ruined*."

Anna shifted slightly in the seat next to her mother's bed and calmly placed another stitch in her sampler. "So you say, Madame."

And so Mrs. Wrayburn had been saying—or wailing,

to be precise—for the better part of forty-eight hours. Madame's ever loyal housekeeper, butler, and lady's maid had all found urgent matters to attend to outside the home after the first twenty-four. Anna couldn't blame them. Had she not, shortly thereafter, convinced her mother to finally take the laudanum the physician had left, she would have followed suit.

That convincing had been no mean feat. Her mother had a particular distaste for opiates. She rarely partook and never supplied it at her parties. She claimed it was both the expense and the danger of addiction that kept her free of the drug. But Anna suspected it was because the effects of the drug on her mother were unflattering. On the rare occasions she ingested laudanum for medicinal purposes, Madame became loud, loose of tongue, and prone to slurring for a half hour or more before suddenly dropping into a long slumber, during which she drooled rivers and snored with enough volume to wake the dead.

Anna was most eager for the snoring to commence. She glanced at the clock on the mantel. The last dose had been given twenty minutes ago. Ten long minutes to go.

"Weeks!" Her mother wailed. "Months! The season will be over and I have nothing to show for it but . . . *this.*" She waved a hand at her bound leg in disgust. "Oh, that damned Mr. Templerton."

"He sent roses this morning."

Madame scowled at her. "One cannot pay the butcher with roses."

"One might consider selling a diamond necklace or two," Anna suggested, knowing full well her mother would never consent to such drastic measures. Madame did not relinquish her personal possessions for any reason. Ever. When something had outlived its usefulness, it was stored away, even if that something was torn, or broken, or hopelessly out of fashion. Even if she'd never cared for the item to start, Madame kept it . . . because it was *hers*. Templer-ton's roses would be hung to dry before the day was out.

Madame gave her a disgusted look. "I cannot believe you would even suggest such a thing."

"And how else to you propose to settle your accounts?"

"You are missing the point, girl. It isn't about what I must do now. It is my future of which I speak."

Lord, the woman was dramatic. "It is a minor break, Madame. You'll be fit to dance again before you know it. A few weeks—"

"*Weeks*, she says," Madame cut in with a disgusted and graceless wave of her arm, "as though it's but a trifle to dis-appear from society for such a time. As though that grasp-ing Mrs. Markhouse isn't plotting to dispossess me of my hard-earned popularity as we speak, and here I am, power-less to stop her. What do you suppose will become of me when she succeeds, hmm?"

"I suppose you will become the second most notori-ous woman in London." Anna pulled her needle through fabric. "I shall try to hold my head up through the shame of it."

"She mocks me. My own daughter mocks me in my grief." Madame jabbed a shaking, bejeweled finger at her. "You've your father's cold heart."

"And his plain eyes," Anna added for her. Madame did so despair of her only daughter's drab eyes.

"Nothing of the kind," Madame slurred. "Engsly had beautiful eyes. Not so bright as my own, mind you, but a lovely blue in their own right. I don't know where the devil you acquired that dreadful gray."

"Engsly now, is it?" Anna inquired with a small smile. Her mother had named her father countless times. Without, to Anna's best recollection, having ever used the same name twice. Engsly was but one more gentleman in a long list of sires. "I am a biological wonder."

"You're an ungrateful little monster, is what you are."

Accustomed to her mother's sharp tongue and unpredictable temper, Anna registered the sting of the words and set them aside in the blink of an eye. "Yes, you ought to send me packing to my father's. Let him stomach me. Better yet, allow me the dowry you promised when I was a girl and you may be free of me—"

"Dowry?" Madame stared round-eyed at Anna as if she'd grown a second head. "I did no such thing."

"Five hundred pounds," Anna reminded her, just as she had reminded her at least once a month since the estimated age of sixteen.

"Nonsense. What would you do with such a sum, anyway? Hide yourself away in the countryside? Good God, what would people say if Mrs. Wrayburn's daughter was left to such a fate?"

For a woman who had spent her entire adult life bucking convention, Madame was inordinately sensitive to the opinions of others. And for a woman so keen on acquiring the good opinion of others, she was lamentably stubborn in her ways. Anna knew she had as much chance of convincing her mother to hand over the five hundred pounds as she did convincing her to sell a piece of jewelry. Which is to say, no chance at all.

She glanced at the clock. Five minutes. "Tell me of this Mr. Engsly. Is he a gentleman, a tradesman, a—?"

"Oh, for . . ." Madame threw her a disgusted look. "It is not Mr. Engsly. It is *Lord* Engsly. Phillip Michael Haverston, the fifth Marquess of Engsly. Don't be deliberately stupid, girl."

"I beg your pardon, Madame," Anna replied calmly. "In the future, I shall endeavor to separate my stupidity from my gullibility."

"See that you . . . What the devil does that mean?"

"Nothing."

One finely arched eyebrow winged up. "You don't believe me, is that it?"

Not a single word. "Of course I believe you, Madame. Why would you lie?"

"Oh, I lie for all sorts of reasons," Madame replied with a breezy wave of her hand. "Mostly for my own amusement."

"That, I believe," Anna murmured.

Her mother appeared not to hear her. "But Engsly . . . I lied about Engsly for your own good." She sniffed dramatically and adopted a tragic expression. "I'm not so terrible a mother, you know. I don't look to hurt you."

"I'm certain you don't." That would require an expenditure of time and energy Madame had never appeared inclined to spend on her only child.

"You'd have sought him out," Madame explained. "I didn't want that."

"And why not?" Anna inquired without even a remote interest in what answer her mother might care to offer. Lord Engsly was not her father and there was only one reason Madame wouldn't want Anna to seek out other family . . . She didn't want to share.

"Coldhearted, just as I said. *He* would have looked for ways to hurt you."

Anna tugged on her thread, completing a tight French knot. "Then I am grateful for your protection."

Her mother made an unpleasant noise in the back of her throat that Anna hoped indicated she was nearer to sleep and snoring. "Don't believe me. No one ever believes me."

Only those with sense. "That is not—"

"I've proof, you know."

The hand holding the needle stilled.

This was new.

Her mother had given her plenty of names over the years, and a variety of fantastical stories attached to those names. Her father was Robert Henry, the courageous officer killed in battle whilst defending Wellington himself. He was Charlie Figg, the sweet son of a vicar who met with a tragic fate at the end of a highwayman's pistol. He was

Raphael Moore, the dashing highwayman who'd met his somewhat less tragic fate at the end of the gallows' rope.

Anna had taken the stories with a grain—or bucket, as need be—of salt, but never before had her mother offered proof.

Curious but skeptical, Anna narrowed her gaze. "What sort of proof?"

"A contract," Madame replied with an airy smugness. "Made him sign one, same as the others."

"You had a contract with my father?" She'd never considered that a possibility. She'd been born before her mother had married Captain Wrayburn and, shortly after his death, become the *Notorious Mrs. Wrayburn*. It had never been clear (nor of particular interest) to Anna whether or not her mother had made official arrangements with men in the distant past.

"Much good it did me," Madame grumbled, her voice becoming notably more slurred. The glaze over her eyes grew thicker.

"Where is it?" Anna demanded, but her mother's gaze had tracked to a corner of the room where it remained, unfocused and unseeing. Anna tossed her embroidery loop aside and reached out to give the woman a quick shake. "Madame, where is it?"

"What?" Madame blinked at her like a sleepy, irritated owl. "Where is what?"

"The contract you had with my father, where do you keep it?"

"With the others, of course. Must you be so loud?" She pushed away Anna's hands. "Let me be."

Anna flicked her gaze at the ceiling. The others were no doubt in the locked sitting room off the master bedchambers. Madame liked to keep her most prized possessions nearby.

"I want to see it. I want . . . Madame?" Anna watched in frustration as her mother's eyes slid closed. *"Madame."*

It was no use, Mrs. Wrayburn had succumbed to the laudanum at last.

Damn it.

She scowled in defeat at the sleeping form.

Damn, damn, damn it.

"*Now* you give me peace?" she groused. "Confounded, disagreeable—"

"I wish to see that contract."

Anna started at the husky voice that sounded behind her. Turning in her seat, she found her companion, and one-time governess, standing in the open door of the room.

A remarkably large-boned woman of advancing years who towered over Anna by more than half a foot, Mrs. Culpepper possessed hands that looked strong enough to crack walnuts, shoulders broad enough to be mistaken for a man's, and unbeknownst to most, an enviable mane of thick black hair she kept tightly bound beneath a frilly cap.

Anna had heard the nickname "Ogress" whispered by a gentleman once. It was the only occasion in which she had requested her mother remove a specific guest from the house. The request had been denied, but she'd felt the better for trying.

Mrs. Culpepper was no ogress. She was a friend and confidante, a woman of uncommon intelligence and admirable character. Had the offending idiot troubled to set down his drink and look beyond what was merely different, he'd have seen she was also quite handsome, with a well-proportioned nose, large brown eyes, and full lips that were more often to be found smiling than not.

Anna gave her mother one last look of disgust, then left her seat to meet with Mrs. Culpepper in the hall.

"Were you eavesdropping just now?" Anna teased, pulling the door shut behind her.

"Nothing of the sort. I overheard the two of you speaking whilst passing in the hall."

"You overheard an entire conversation in passing?"

"Indeed." Mrs. Culpepper took her arm and ushered them both down the hall at a clipped pace. "Come along, dear."

"What? No." She took a fretful glance over her shoulder, half expecting her mother to come stalking out the sick room. "We cannot go snooping about Madame's chambers."

"Why not?"

"Because it's wrong." She'd have thought that fairly obvious.

Mrs. Culpepper threw her a bland look without slowing her pace. Right and wrong were primarily academic considerations in Anover House.

"Very well," Anna conceded, "because Madame will hear of it and rain hell upon our heads."

"By locking you up like a princess in a castle?" She pulled Anna up a back stairwell. "Yes, we should hate to see that happen."

"She might ban me from the library."

"The marvelous thing about libraries is that their contents can be easily moved."

"But what if she—?"

Mrs. Culpepper stopped at the top of the stairs, turned, and took Anna by the shoulders. "Now you look at me, and you listen carefully. Your mother is on another level of this house, where she will remain unconscious for the next eight hours, thank you, heavenly Father. Anyone else who might give a fig is out of the house and fully occupied devising the means that will allow them to *remain* out of the house for as long as possible. Everyone else can be bought off. You are not likely to see this opportunity again."

All valid points, but before Anna could nod agreement, Mrs. Culpepper turned and marched resolutely down the hall. Anna followed cautiously, casting furtive looks behind her, then watched in awe as the woman who'd once been paid to be a child's moral compass slid a key into the lock of the most sacred, most forbidden of rooms at Anover House.

"Where did you get that?" Anna demanded in a whisper as her friend opened the door.

"Never you mind. Suffice it to say . . . Oh . . ." Mrs. Culpepper went still at the sight of the sitting room. "Oh, saints preserve us."

Anna peeked around Mrs. Culpepper and sucked in a quick breath. "Good Lord."

The room was filled, positively filled, with . . . *everything.*

Boxes and chests, furniture and clothing. There were crates and trunks, and odds and ends—some odder than others, and some of them unidentifiable—covering the crates and trunks. An épée peeked out from behind an armoire, the familiar glitter of diamonds spilled out of a hat box, and everywhere one looked, there were piles upon piles of paper.

Some women used their sitting rooms to write correspondence and receive friends. Mrs. Wrayburn used hers as a vault. These were the items she considered too valuable to be stored in the attic. These were her most meaningful, most treasured possessions.

Anna's eyes widened at the sight of an old-fashioned gentleman's nightcap perched atop a fraying parasol sticking out of a boot.

Shaking her head in wonder, she said the only words that came to mind. "My mother is *most* odd."

"Indeed," Mrs. Culpepper agreed with feeling. "Well, no use in dillydallying. Older paperwork is over here."

Anna dragged her eyes away from the bizarre assemblage and watched Mrs. Culpepper pick her way expertly across the room. "You've been in here?"

"I have. Madame likes to have things dusted out and

reorganized every now and then. With careful oversight, mind you." She lifted her skirts to step over a stack of books. "But it was not so filled as this the last time I was allowed access."

Anna glanced nervously over her shoulder at the door. "We ought not be doing this."

Mrs. Culpepper calmly opened a small wooden chest and began to extract stacks of letters and papers. "Breaking into your mother's sitting room? Too late, I'm afraid. But if needs must, I shall blame this escapade on you. Dragged me straight inside, you did."

"I have been told I can be heartless."

Mrs. Culpepper flicked her a stern look. "You shouldn't repeat such nastiness, even in jest. It gives the words a weight they do not deserve. Now come along and help, dear."

Poking fun at her mother's sentiments seemed the very thing to lighten their sting, but experience told Anna that this was not an argument she was likely to win.

With a shrug, she forged her way through the room to Mrs. Culpepper and picked a mound of papers to dig through. She found receipts, correspondence to her long-deceased great-aunt, a number of invitations to balls and dinner parties, and what looked to be pages that had been removed from at least two ledgers. All of it more than a decade old. She found much the same in the next pile, and the next, and the one after that.

"This could take days," Anna muttered after what felt like hours of searching.

"I may have something," Mrs. Culpepper announced, and Anna looked up to see her opening an oversized, unmarked book. "It's a journal. It's . . . Oh my." Mrs. Culpepper's eyebrows winged up as she turned one page, then another. "It is a most explicit journal. She names her paramours, the generalities of their contracts, her opinions of their particular . . . er, charms and . . . and . . ." Mrs. Culpepper tilted her head and grimaced. "Good heavens, did you know your mother can sketch?"

"No." Anna leaned forward for a look, but Mrs. Culpepper drew the book away. "I suppose the value in such a book would be in blackmail."

Mrs. Culpepper shook her head and gingerly turned another page. "Any gentleman in search of a discrete affair would keep well away from your mother. Although, some of them might be willing to pay to have these sketches destroyed. Particularly Mr. Hayes." She squinted a little at the page and tsked in sympathy. ". . . That poor man."

Anna had been introduced to Mr. Hayes two years ago. She recalled a rail-thin man with dull amber eyes who had introduced himself to her bust. "May I see?"

Mrs. Culpepper yanked the journal away again and pressed the open pages against her chest. "Certainly not."

"Oh, for pity's sake," Anna groaned, dropping her hand. "I am the grown, illegitimate daughter of *the* Mrs. Wrayburn. Who the deuce will know or care if I see another naughty drawing?"

"I do, and so would your mother."

"Have you gone daft?" At the estimated age of ten, Anna had been given a detailed accounting of what went on between men and women behind closed doors. The lesson had been delivered at her mother's orders and had included a variety of visual aids. According to Mrs. Wrayburn, carnal innocence was but a silly euphemism for ignorance, and ignorance was but an open door for curiosity and its many unpleasant consequences. It was rare for Anna to be in agreement with her mother on anything, but in this matter, they were in complete accord.

Anna reached for the journal again. "I've seen dozens—"

"There are several self-portraits."

"Oh." She winced and drew her hand away. "Oh, *ick*."

Mrs. Culpepper sniffed. "Indeed."

Wrinkling her nose, Anna waved her hand in the general direction of the offending book. "Look at the older entries."

Mrs. Culpepper flipped through page after page of the journal. "The earliest is well after you would have been born. I think . . ." At last, her eyes landed on a page and stayed. "Wait . . . Wait a . . . Here it is. Good heavens, here it is. Listen to this . . . 'Anna's birthday approaches. I sent word to her father but naught will come of it. There will be no response or visit from Engsly.' "

Mrs. Culpepper caught Anna's gaze over the book in the ensuing silence. "Well," she said at length. "It would seem you really are the daughter of the late Lord Engsly."

"It would seem I am," Anna agreed. Pushing aside an old cloak and a pair of half boots, she took a seat on one of the trunks and waited for a feeling of excitement or recognition, or even anger, but nothing came. She felt strangely detached from the news, as if she were hearing of someone else's lineage. "Is there anything else?"

Mrs. Culpepper scanned the page. "Let us see . . . 'no word or visit from Engsly,' " she repeated, " 'though perhaps it is best, as the child grows uncommonly . . .' " Mrs. Culpepper trailed off, lifted her eyes from the page, and cleared her throat. "There's no need to read this. We have the information we need."

Annoyed, Anna jumped up and snatched the book away before Mrs. Culpepper could close it.

. . . the child grows uncommonly fat and I daresay stupider with each passing day. Were the marquess to visit now, he would most certainly leave again with all due haste.

"You were an exceedingly clever child, Anna," Mrs. Culpepper said loyally.

"And fat, apparently. I don't remember that."

Mrs. Culpepper waved the comment away with pursed lips. "You might have been going through something of an awkward stage when I first came to Anover House, but you were beautiful."

"I was fortunate," Anna said, tossing the journal aside. "To have had you." Taking a deep breath, she looked about the room and suddenly felt at a loss of what to do next. "Do you suppose the marquess believed Madame's claim that I was his?"

"It would have made little difference one way or the other, to my understanding. The late lord Engsly was not the sort to take notice of his parental duties. I remember your mother speaking of him a time or two."

"Poorly, I assume." Her mother spoke poorly of everyone, provided the individual in question was out of earshot.

"She referred to him once as a fickle, untrustworthy cad, or something along those lines. I took that to mean he failed to honor their contract."

Anna nodded, remembering her mother's earlier words. *Much good it did me.* That was the trouble with being dependent upon the wealth and power of nobility. They had the wealth and power to do as they pleased.

Mrs. Culpepper turned and began to shuffle through the papers she'd removed from the chest once more. "I wonder how much was left owing?"

"Why? The man's passed, hasn't he? One can't expect a dead man to honor his debts."

"By all accounts, one couldn't have expected it from him alive. His sons, however . . ."

"Sons," Anna repeated slowly. "I may have brothers. How strange."

"You've brothers with considerable fortunes and reputations for honoring familial debts. The late marquess left the estate in something of a mess, made worse by the perfidy of his second marchioness. It was all the talk last year." As was her wont when there was great gossip to be shared, Mrs. Culpepper leaned forward a hair and lowered her voice. "It is said that the late Lady Engsly, the marquess's second wife, conspired with her husband's man of business to bilk the Engsly estate out of a fortune. I've no idea if it is true, but it *is* known that Lady Engsly amassed a veritable mountain of debt and enemies, and she was forced to flee to the continent when her stepson gained the title and discovered her betrayal. She died not long after and your brothers have been about for the last year making amends and settling her debts. If the new marquess would do that for his stepmother, you can be certain he'd do the same for his father.

You might . . . Oh!" Mrs. Culpepper exclaimed suddenly. She spun about and began searching the papers once more. "Do you know, I might have seen . . . Yes, here they are. Letters from the marquess himself. I'd not thought anything of them at first, but . . ."

Anna watched her friend quickly open the first missive and begin to read. "Did you see him, ever? The late marquess?"

"Not that I recall," Mrs. Culpepper replied without looking up. "Certainly not here."

"What of the current marquess?"

"He is not the sort to move in Madame's circle."

"Well then, I am inclined to like him already."

"He is also a dear friend to Lord Dane."

The name, so unexpected, caused the air to catch in Anna's lungs.

Max Dane. Good heavens, there was a man she'd not given thought to in some time. She'd made a point of it. Well, she'd made a point of *trying* not to dwell on him, at any rate.

She'd had no other choice. Max had not come back to call on her as promised after their encounter in the nursery. In fact, he'd ceased visiting Anover House altogether. She'd never heard from him again, and after a brief bout of heartache and self-pity, Anna had come to the conclusion that she had been a silly, shortsighted girl to have expected differently. She'd seen her mother deep in her cups often enough to know that plans made in the thick of drink were rarely seen to fruition, generally to the benefit of everyone involved.

A viscount and the illegitimate daughter of a courtesan with nothing more in common than a shared kiss. What future could there have been for them, really? None at all, and it had been the height of naïveté to believe otherwise.

Anna took pains to keep her voice and expression neutral. "Is he? Well, there is no accounting for taste, I am told."

"There is no accounting for your stubbornness," Mrs. Culpepper countered. "Pretend it means nothing to you, if you like, but I know he captured your fancy that night."

"I should never have told you of it," Anna mumbled. She'd held out for two days, all but bursting at the seams with the secret and the hope it had sparked. In the end, however she'd succumbed to excitement and given Mrs. Culpepper a lengthy, albeit slightly modified, retelling of the night. Anna had wisely chosen to edit out any mention of kissing.

Mrs. Culpepper gave her a gentle pat on the shoulder. "Not everything is meant to be kept secret, poppet."

"Not everything need come to light." She contemplated that statement as it pertained to current circumstances and ran a thumb over the binding of the journal on the floor. "What am I to do with this information?"

"Make use of it," Mrs. Culpepper said, picking up the next page in her stack of letters from the marquess.

"Approach Engsly?" She wrinkled her nose at the idea. "I don't know that I wish to do that. I don't care for the idea of visiting the father's sins upon the sons."

"Better they be visited upon his daughter?"

That seemed a mite melodramatic. "They've not—"

"He ought to have provided for you," Mrs. Culpepper cut in with a quick, sharp look over her letter.

Anna shrugged. "He may very well have. Or perhaps he

knew full well I was someone else's bastard. Who's to say Madame doesn't lie to herself, same as everyone else?"

There was a brief pause before Mrs. Culpepper answered. "The marquess himself."

"Beg your pardon?"

Mrs. Culpepper offered the pages of the letter. "See for yourself."

Anna snatched the papers and scanned the contents. It didn't take long before she found the passage that held her name. The marquess expressed all due pleasure at the news of his infant daughter's continued good health. The tone of the letter struck Anna as one of mild irritation rather than pleasure, but that hardly registered in the grand scheme of things.

"He acknowledged me?"

Stunned, she shared a look of wonder with her friend before returning her attention to the letter.

"Why on earth would Madame keep that a secret?" she mumbled, going on to the next page, hoping to find a date, at the very least. "What could she possibly stand to gain? Why would he admit paternity and then . . ." She trailed off as the mention of a contract and a number on the last page caught her eye. "Good heavens."

"What is it?"

Anna held the page up for Mrs. Culpepper to see. "He says he does not owe fifty pounds per annum for my care; the contract clearly states he must only provide forty."

"The contract he did not fulfill," Mrs. Culpepper added and began to rub her hands together and chortle. "The Engsly estate owes *you* three-and . . . er . . . eight-and . . . Well, let us say six-and-twenty years of allowance. Well over a thousand pounds."

Over a thousand pounds. It was a fortune. Nowhere near enough to cover the cost of a place like Anover House, but more than ample to procure a cottage in the countryside. More than enough to procure her freedom.

"The Engsly estate is financially well off?"

"Flush these days, by all accounts."

Then Lord Engsly would scarce note the loss of a thousand pounds. A hard resolve settled over her. "And the current marquess is a man of honor, you say?"

"My dear, he is renowned for it." A smug smile spread over Mrs. Culpepper's face. "Oh, sneaking into this room was quite the smartest thing we have ever done. Now, let us see if we might find the contract itself."

Chapter 4

✢

Max's arrival at Caldwell Manor played out much as his arrivals always did. He was greeted with polite smiles and commendable efficiency from the staff, and promptly escorted into the small sitting room off the library, where Mrs. Webster, the housekeeper, offered refreshments. Ginger biscuits, his favorite. Max politely declined. The biscuits were brought, anyway.

It was a routine Max took pleasure in, despite its formality. He had been six the first time his family visited Caldwell Manor, and though much had changed over the years, there were some things on which he could always rely. He would always be welcomed, there would never be a shortage of ginger biscuits, and hell would freeze solid before Mrs. Webster took "no, thank you" for an answer.

Feeling more relaxed by the moment, Max tugged free an already loose cravat, leaned back in his third-favorite chair, and mused that *this* was why he would always agree to visit Caldwell, even when a summons came in the

middle of the London season. He would come for the comfort of its routines and the consistency of its inhabitants.

"What the devil are you doing here?"

Max looked up to find Lucien Haverston, the Marquess
of Engsly, standing in the doorway. He looked disheveled
and wild-eyed, his dark hair sticking up in several places.

Max returned the greeting with a blank stare. "Well . . .
this is new."

"Why aren't you in London?"

"Because I'm answering your summons."

Black brows lowered on a handsome face that had broken the hearts of many a maiden. Or so Lucien had liked to
claim in his youth. "What?"

"I was invited. You invited me. You insisted I visit, in
fact. You said your wife would be in Scotland. I was spending too much time in London. You promised a bit of fishing, a little revelry with the lasses at the tavern, fine weather
and clean country air—"

"Oh, hell, I *did*," Lucien cut in with a groan. "Last
month, was it?" He shook his head suddenly and waved his
hand about as if to erase the thought. "Doesn't matter. You
have to go."

"What? Why?"

"I have guests."

"Yes," Max returned pointedly. "Me."

"You're not a guest. You're . . . you." Lucien blinked at
that statement, then began snapping his fingers repeatedly
in the manner of someone slowly arriving at a solution to a
particularly vexing dilemma. "You *are* you." He stopped
snapping to point. "You have to stay."

Max rubbed the back of his hand under his chin. "Are
you catching?"

"I'm not sick. I'm . . . I'm in need of a drink."

Lucien spun about on his heel and marched across the
room toward a set of crystal decanters on a fine old walnut

sideboard, then stopped suddenly and whirled about with a blank expression. "I never promised revelry at the tavern."

Max shrugged and stretched out his legs before him. "Can't blame a man for trying."

"Of course you can. My wife would."

And Lucien would rather face the gallows than cause Lilly one moment's consternation. The Marquess and Marchioness of Engsly were famously besotted with each other.

"Do you want one?" Lucien inquired, pouring from a decanter.

Max shook his head, and watched in fascination as his friend swallowed down a finger-full of spirits. Lucien had never been one for drink. He took wine at meals, the occasional brandy after dinner and ale during travel, that was all.

"Are you going to tell me what's—?"

"My sister is coming." Lucien blew out a hard breath after the drink. "Any minute now."

"Winnefred? Brilliant."

"No, not my brother's wife." Lucien flicked a longing glance at the brandy bottle but didn't refill his glass. "My father's daughter. My sister."

Max straightened in the chair, intrigued and wary. "You don't have a sister."

"Apparently, I do."

"I see." He took a closer look at his friend's face and for the first time noticed shadows beneath his eyes. Lucien wasn't merely out of sorts. He was well and truly worried. "When did you learn of it?"

"A fortnight ago," Lucien replied, setting down his glass. "She wrote to my solicitor in London. He verified her claim of proof. God, this is discomforting. Gideon and I have always known this sort of thing might happen, of course. Our father was a faithless bastard. It's a miracle we're not lousy with half siblings. But the reality of facing a sister . . ."

Was something his friend didn't have to do alone, Max finished silently. "I'm happy to stay."

Lucien bobbed his head and took a seat on the very edge of the settee across from Max. "Excellent. Excellent. She's from your world. Your presence might well put her at ease."

"We live in the same world, Lucien," Max drawled. "I just know more interesting people. Who is this girl?"

"Miss Anna Rees. The daughter of Mrs. Rebecca Wrayburn."

"Anna . . ." The name came out a little strangled. Max cleared his throat and tried again. "Anna Rees? *The* Miss Anna Rees?"

Oh, hell. Oh, holy hell.

The light of memory washed over Lucien's worried face. "That's right, didn't you tell me that you know the girl personally?"

"No, I told you I'd met her." Once it had become clear that Anna Rees wanted nothing to do with him, he saw no particular reason to keep secret the fact that they'd met. He'd also seen no particular reason to advertise the fact that she wanted nothing more to do with him, and had therefore limited his accounting of the evening to Lucien and Gideon.

"What is she like?" Lucien inquired.

"I don't know. She's . . ." She was Anna Rees. Beautiful, alluring, captivating. Cold and unattainable. Max shook his head and resisted the urge to shift in his seat. "I don't know."

He'd only imagined he'd known.

"Come on, man," Lucien pressed. "You're one of precious few people to have ever spoken with the girl."

"My memory of the occasion is a bit foggy round the edges, for a contingent of reasons."

"You were drunk?"

"It was four years ago. Naturally, I was drunk." Max shrugged, unashamed and unrepentant. Many men went through a period of unruliness. His had come a mite later than some, that was all. He'd since tempered his drinking. The remainder of his habits continued to garner the disapproval of good society, but he no longer felt the need to drink himself into oblivion on a regular basis. "I was also grieving the unexpected acquisition of the viscounty."

"Hell. How did that meeting proceed, exactly? You didn't behave badly toward her, did you?"

"Do you know, I have wondered that very thing—" He grinned when Lucien's face took on a dark cast. "Settle your feathers, Your Lordship. I was in no position to have taken advantage of the girl. I fell asleep in creation's most uncomfortable chair. Little minx left me there."

Just like the first time he'd mentioned the meeting to Lucien, Max wisely left out that he'd proposed to the woman in a drunken stupor. That he'd returned a week later, as she'd made him promise, only to be told by Mrs. Wrayburn that her daughter was not receiving visitors. That he'd returned again and again, and had written, twice, before finally accepting the fact that Miss Rees wanted nothing to do with him.

Lucien rose from his seat yet again and stabbed a finger at Max. "By God, if I hear a different story from her . . . Maybe you should leave."

Max decided he wasn't going anywhere. The last thing Lucien needed was more time alone with his worries. A bit of distraction, that's what he needed. "You're going to be unbearable as an older brother."

"I'm already an older brother."

"Not to a sister. It's different." He thought of his own sister, Beatrice. Often when he pictured her in his mind, he saw not the grown woman with a child of her own, but the mischievous little girl who used to follow him about the house, begging him to play at dolls or some equally inconvenient and embarrassingly female game, and generally having her way. It was near impossible to deny Beatrice anything . . . or should have been. "Trust me."

"You're right." Lucien speared his fingers through his hair. "I know you're right. What the devil do I know of sisters?"

"You've a sister-in-law," Max pointed out.

Lucien sent him a bland look. "Have you met Freddie?"

The fiercely independent and oft times wild Winnefred was hardly representative of what some preferred to think of as the weaker sex.

"You have a wife," he tried instead. "I should think that comparable on some level."

"Well, it's not. I don't know what to do with the woman, what to say to her. Should I apologize? Should I have gone to her instead of insisting she come here? Do I embrace her? Do I welcome her to my home or to our home?" He swore under his breath and began to pace between the settee and the fireplace. "It should have been her home before now. It should have been available to her at the very least. Hell, I will need to apologize."

Or she would, Max thought darkly, if he discovered she was playing the Haverstons false and turning his friend inside out in the process. "For pity's sake, man, sit down. You're making this into more than it is. You'll have a conversation with the woman and she'll be on her way." And he could get down to the business of investigating her claim on the Haverstons. "You can manage that—"

"I invited her for a visit," Lucien cut in. "Not a conversation."

"You don't mean to have her stay on at Caldwell." By the look of Lucien's expression, he did. Oh, bloody hell. "Lucien, you don't know this woman. I'm not sure anyone knows this woman, not even her own mother."

"I know enough. We share a bond. We share blood."

"The blood of a faithless bastard," he reminded Lucien. "And her mother, you'll recall, is Mrs. Wrayburn. A woman many might call a faithless bitch, though I've yet to meet the man careless enough to do so within earshot—"

"You've never believed blood would out," Lucien said, clearly taken aback, but not so much that he slowed his determination to wear a hole in the carpet.

"It doesn't. It can't. Blood doesn't do much of anything." And the mere claim of blood shouldn't grant one unfettered access to Caldwell Manor.

"It makes family," Lucien countered.

"No, it makes lineage." Max shook his head and held up a hand to forestall further argument. A serious debate wasn't going to help Lucien at present. "Just . . . be cautious in your dealings with Miss Rees."

"Of course."

There was no "of course" about it. "What proof did Miss Rees provide?"

"Correspondence between our father and her mother, along with a contract and a journal."

"A contract?"

"She was his mistress. Naturally, there was a contract." Lucien's lips twisted. "And naturally, his lordship failed to fulfill his obligations."

The sliver of unease and suspicion that had been working on Max's skin began to grow at an exponential rate.

"And Miss Rees has requested you do so in his stead," he guessed. "Those obligations amount to how much, exactly?"

"A thousand pounds or so." Lucien dismissed the number with an impatient wave of the hand. "Immaterial, she'll have whatever she needs. Settling the contract is not the purpose of having her visit. She's my sister. I want to meet her."

Max said nothing aloud, but he was swearing profusely in his head. Anna wasn't coming to Caldwell Manor to meet with family, or even to collect that thousand pounds. She was after what Lucien's reputation guaranteed—the very thing he had just agreed to provide . . . *whatever she needs.*

It was no secret the marquess and his brother had been actively making retributions for the financial crimes committed by their stepmother before her death. And it would be a fairly simple thing for a woman as diversely connected as Mrs. Wrayburn to find a competent forger in London.

Max debated how much opposition it was wise to put forward at present. Just a little to start, he decided. It was too late to rethink the invitation, but not too late to encourage that bit of caution once the woman arrived.

"You don't find it peculiar that there's been no mention of Miss Rees or Mrs. Wrayburn amongst your father's papers?" he asked.

"I've not gone through them all. I'm not sure we've found them all. My stepmother made a mess of things before her departure. Boxes in the attic, in the cellar, even in the stable. Some things have been lost for good, I'm sure." Lucien grimaced and shrugged. "To be honest, finding and reading my father's personal letters has not been a priority."

Max nodded in reluctant understanding. He'd just as soon not learn the contents of his father's mail. He was, however, determined to learn of Anna's intentions in attaching herself to the Haverstons.

"She's here," Lucien announced suddenly, his gaze riveted to the windows overlooking the front of the house.

Rising from his seat, Max saw the small black dot of a carriage that was slowly making its way down Caldwell's long, winding drive. A spark of anticipation began to mingle with his unease and suspicion. There she was, he thought, Miss Anna Rees.

Bloody hell.

He'd not thought of the woman in years . . . not voluntarily. She did have a habit of sneaking into his mind at the oddest times. The smell of roses and baking biscuits had brought her to mind once or twice, and he'd caught himself staring at a terrier of some sort in Hyde Park a few months back and recalling her dream of owning a hound. And there'd been that brief and unexpected burst of fear two weeks back when he'd heard someone from Anover House had been injured in a fall from her horse. It passed mere seconds later when the injured party was revealed to be Mrs. Wrayburn, but in that moment before . . .

Max cut off his line of thought with a scowl. Clearly, he'd thought of her more often and more recently than he'd cared to admit.

"I cannot believe the Ice Maiden of Anover House might be your sister," he murmured.

"*Is*," Lucien corrected as he made a failed effort at flattening his hair with his hands. "*Is* my sister. And you'll not call her that."

"Everyone calls her that," Max countered. He craned his neck to watch as key members of Caldwell staff began to line up on the portico. "And for good reason."

"No longer. Let your London acquaintances know she's a member of this family now, and she'll be afforded the proper respect."

"It's gossip amongst the ton, Engsly," Max replied dryly. "No one is afforded the proper respect." He threw up a hand to forestall an argument. "I'll do my best to be of use to you."

Lucien nodded, satisfied in the way only those who assumed the best of everyone could be. He shot his sleeves and straightened his cravat. "How do I look? Presentable?"

Good enough for the likes of Anna Rees. "You look like the Marquess of Engsly." Max gestured toward the door and studiously ignored the sudden urge to fuss with his own appearance. "Let's go greet the woman."

Chapter 5

This is lunacy.

Anna glanced out the carriage window at the passing front lawn of Caldwell Manor, with its lush green grass and towering hardwoods, and wondered at what size a lawn and drive ceased being a lawn and drive, and became a tidy field and well-tended road.

She looked over at Mrs. Culpepper, who was slumped against the side of the carriage, face covered by a bonnet gone askew. Her companion's skin had taken on a peculiar green tint over the course of their half-day journey, the result of Mrs. Culpepper's susceptibility to carriage sickness.

They were cracked, the pair of them.

What on earth had they been thinking, sneaking out of Anover House in the dead of night to come here? What if her mother took it in her head to send someone after them? They'd run off with her third-best carriage, after all.

What if the Marquess of Engsly was a complete loon

and had taken it into *his* head to retract the invitation to
Caldwell Manor before they'd even arrived?

What if the invitation had been sent merely as a means
to lure her away from the safety of Anover House, and the
moment she did arrive they were swept off to the continent,
or Australia or the Americas, or to wherever the devil it
was the Haverstons swept their unwanted bastard children.
God, she hoped it wasn't to the bottom of a local lake.

The morbid thought was just ridiculous enough to snap
her back to her senses. For goodness sake, she wasn't going
to suffer violence at the hands of the marquess. Her screaming nerves and wild imagination were naught more than an
overreaction to the strains of the past fortnight.

They hadn't slipped away in the dead of night; they'd
left at dawn. And her exchanges with the marquess over the
last week had been perfectly civil. There was no reason to
believe the man was an ogre in person.

Really, all she needed to concern herself over was how
to make herself agreeable to a perfectly courteous man,
which shouldn't be too terribly difficult. She'd had a lifetime of facing the judgment of strangers, courteous and
otherwise, and she'd muddled along well enough.

Surely she could muddle along just as well for an hour
or two at Caldwell Manor. She could smile and curtsy and
swallow her fear and pride this one last time, and then she
would be free.

Probably . . . Maybe . . . Blast it, this was different. Vastly
different. Smiles and curtsies were, most often, all that had
been expected of her at Anover House. The marquess would
expect her to speak. He would expect her to *converse*.

In the whole of her life, she had conversed with only one
other gentleman. And he'd not sought the experience out a
second time.

A bubble of nervous laughter escaped before she could
tamp it down. "This is *madness*."

Next to her, Mrs. Culpepper stirred, pushing her bonnet out of her face. "What is it, dear?"

"Nothing, I . . ." Anna trailed off as she glanced over and saw that her companion's skin had gone from green to gray sometime in the last hour. "Mrs. Culpepper, are you all right?"

Mrs. Culpepper waved a large hand. "Quite. Good heavens, have we arrived?"

As if to answer the question, the carriage rolled to a stop. "It would appear we have."

"For pity's sake, child," Mrs. Culpepper gasped and began a frantic bid to right her appearance, "why did you not wake me earlier?"

As there was little to be gained in explaining that she had, in fact, attempted to rouse Mrs. Culpepper on two separate occasions, Anna turned her attention out the window instead and came to the startling realization that Caldwell Manor was rather lovely up close.

She'd not expected a peer's country estate to be lovely. She'd expected grand and imposing. The house may have laid some claim to the first, particularly at a distance, with its stone façade and impressive size, but she could see now that the severe lines of its three stories were softened by gently arched windows, cheerful blue shutters, and the somewhat awkward and whimsical addition of a small turret at the back corner of the house. What might have been an austere entrance was brightened by the inclusion of potted plants at the front doors and colorful flowers along the base of the portico.

Almost, it appeared inviting. *Almost.*

Waiting on that portico was Lucien Haverston, the Marquess of Engsly . . . along with a goodly number of his staff, which was most odd.

"Why on earth would he—?"

Anna snapped her mouth closed when the carriage door swung open and a footman appeared, ready to assist her down.

She blinked at him, at the harsh sunlight beyond the carriage, and at the almost-but-not-quite-welcoming front portico.

And suddenly, she wished the front lawn had been a little larger, the drive a little longer.

"Chin up," Mrs. Culpepper advised in a whisper. "Shoulders back and eyes straight ahead."

It was the advice Mrs. Culpepper always delivered before Anna was forced to make an appearance for her mother. The familiarity of it gave her the courage to step from the carriage.

After a moment's adjustment to the bright light, her eyes landed on the unfamiliar gentleman standing in the center of the portico. Tall and lean, in a finely tailored suit, the Marquess of Engsly looked very much as Anna had expected, with the notable exception of his hair being a little messy and his deep-set eyes being rather dark. She had pictured the marquess with the *lovely* blue eyes of his father.

Their father, she reminded herself as she assisted Mrs. Culpepper out of the carriage and up the steps of the portico. The late marquess was *their* father.

"Miss Rees." Engsly bowed low as they approached. "Welcome to Caldwell Manor."

And this man was her brother, standing right before her, and still it didn't feel real to her.

"My lord." She curtsied smoothly, relieved when her knees of pudding held. "It was most kind of you to invite us. May I present my companion, Mrs. Culpepper?"

Engsly bowed again but straightened with a slight frown. His eyes flicked from Anna and back to Mrs. Culpepper. "I . . . Forgive my bluntness, Mrs. Culpepper, but are you unwell?"

Observant, Anna noted. And interested in the well-being of someone a man of his rank might consider well beneath his notice.

Or fearful his guests had brought a plague to Caldwell Manor. It was difficult to say.

Mrs. Culpepper inclined her head briefly. If she was impressed by a man of Lord Engsly's stature, it didn't show. But then, Mrs. Culpepper had witnessed any number of peers engaging in any number of unflattering behaviors at Anover House. The nobility's thin layer of charm had no doubt worn away long ago.

Or it might have been the carriage sickness. Also difficult to determine.

"Quite, my lord," Mrs. Culpepper replied. "It is only that travel does not agree with me."

"I understand. My sister-in-law is much the same." He made a subtle motion with his hand and two maids in crisp white aprons immediately stepped forward. "Allow Faith and Mary to escort you upstairs. Would you have me send for the physician?"

"Thank you, my lord, but no. I shall be quite well now that I've feet on solid ground once more. And I shall be well enough for the time being to remain here with Miss Rees—"

"Nonsense," Anna pressed. "You must have a rest."

"Well . . ." Mrs. Culpepper glanced at the maids, and Anna knew the woman was in more discomfort than she had let on, to even be considering the suggestion. "If you are certain?"

Anna nodded and, not trusting herself to speak again, lest the selfish sentiment *I take it back, don't leave me alone with these people* should come spilling out, pressed her lips together in what she hoped was some facsimile of a confident smile.

Evidently, it was good enough for the ailing Mrs. Culpepper. She sent Anna a sickly and grateful look, along with a weak pat on the shoulder Anna assumed was meant to be bolstering, then allowed the maids to lead her away.

Feeling cut adrift, Anna watched the line of staff shuffle a bit as the trio passed. A footman stepped aside to allow them entrance into the house . . .

And that was when she saw him, standing bold as you please next to one of the pretty potted flowers.

Lord Maximilian Dane.

Oh, hell. Oh, holy hell.

For the first time in her life, Anna knew what it meant to have the air stolen from one's lungs. It felt, she discovered, very much as the phrase described, as if someone had reached inside her and snatched away her breath.

She'd truly believed she'd never see him again, and his sudden presence before her now felt, if not like a blow, then an impossibly hard shove. She had the ridiculous urge to step back and call out for Mrs. Culpepper, or turn about and head straight back to the carriage. At the very least, she wanted to swear loud and long.

This was dreadful. This was inconceivably awful.

In the days and weeks following the realization that Max Dane would not be returning to Anover House, Anna had indulged in a daydream or two (or several dozen) of what it might be like should they meet in passing sometime in the future.

The exact content of those daydreams had varied, but on the whole she had envisioned herself to be surrounded by a bevy of friends and admirers. She'd been flawless in appearance, composed in manner, and eloquent of speech. In short, her dreams had been flights of extreme fancy in which Max Dane had come to the realization that not returning to Anover House had been a judgment error of *colossal* proportions.

Now here she was, dusty and rumpled from travel, alone for all intents and purposes, and stunned speechless.

Oh, how she wanted to get back into the carriage.

Fortunately, a lifetime of keeping her chin up, shoulders

back, and eyes straight ahead stopped her from making a complete cake of herself. She even managed after a moment to school her features into a serene expression.

Coherent speech, however, remained elusive.

"I . . . Er . . ."

Max did not appear to be similarly affected. He quickly stepped forward and executed a smart bow.

"Miss Rees. All of this has come as something of a surprise to me as well."

This wasn't a surprise. A surprise was finding an unexpected gray hair at one's temple, leaving one to wonder if one was a trifle older than previously estimated.

Seeing Max Dane at Caldwell Manor was an outright shock. And seeing him close up prompted the immediate and entirely useless thought that he'd grown more handsome. Probably it was merely that he was (presumably) sober. There were no shadows beneath his hazel eyes, no sallowness to the skin that spoke of too much drink and insufficient sleep. Lord Dane didn't look like the dissolute rake she'd met at Anover House four years ago, the dashing but inebriated young man whose sensual mouth and captivating charm had tempted her into initiating the most wicked moment of her life. That man had been fascinating and charismatic and, at times, in very real danger of losing his seat.

The Lord Dane before her now had bowed with an easy grace and restrained strength. He looked strong and hale and . . . and not particularly pleased to see her. His handsome face was set in hard lines, his mouth unsmiling.

Was he angry with her?

Surely not. He had no call to be. *Surely*, he was simply taken aback, as she was.

Anna managed a credible curtsy, caught between an involuntary thrill at seeing him again, and the ardent desire to be somewhere, anywhere, else at present.

She had kissed this man. She had leaned forward and

pressed her lips to *those* lips. And then she'd never seen him again.

"Lord Dane . . ." She began, and then, to her mortification, found she was unable to add anything more substantial than, ". . . Hello."

She watched him smirk a little, which both confused and annoyed her. Of course *he* wasn't out of sorts. He'd obviously had some warning of her arrival.

"Hello," he echoed. "Your journey was uneventful, I trust?"

They'd become stuck in a rut for two hours. She'd almost turned the carriage around a half dozen times. Mrs. Culpepper's illness had required they stop repeatedly. One stop had come too late.

"Quite."

"We are all happy to hear it, I'm sure."

"Thank you, my lord."

Go away, she begged silently. *Please, please go away.* She could face her new brother, or she could face the man who'd broken her heart. She couldn't face them both together.

Engsly cleared his throat, drawing her attention. "Dane's estate of McMullin Hall is but twenty miles away," he explained. "Our families have been friends for generations."

"How lovely." *Please do make him go away.*

"Miss Rees may wish to hear of our history another time," Max suggested, and then, as if he'd heard her thoughts and had a care for her discomfort—both of which she highly doubted—he bowed and added, "If you will excuse me, I'll leave the two of you to become better acquainted."

Anna watched him walk away and felt marginally better when he disappeared inside the house.

Lord Engsly cleared his throat again. "Lord Dane has been a true friend to the Haverstons for many years. His presence here doesn't make you uneasy, I hope? I'd thought—"

"Not in the least," Anna lied. Because, really, what else could she possible say? *Your dearest friend makes me exceedingly uneasy. Please do remove him from your home for the few hours I am here.*

"Excellent. Excellent. I should like for the two of you to be friends as well."

"I'm sure that would be lovely."

She was sure there was scarcely a chance in hell of that occurring. But as Lord Dane had clearly not seen fit to inform his dearest friend of their history, she thought it might be best to keep her peace on the matter as well.

She remained mostly silent while Engsly introduced her to the staff—a formality that confused her—and as she was ushered into the front hall with its soaring ceiling, sweeping twin staircases, and marble balustrades. And she was quiet still as she was led down a wide hall lined with windows that let in broad beams of sunlight to warm the air.

Engsly was saying something about the front of the manor being an addition made in the last century, and the rear of the manor retaining many of its Elizabethan charms. But all the while, she kept thinking, *My brother. This man is my brother.*

And willing herself to feel something other than concern for Mrs. Culpepper, continued unease at the presence of Max Dane, and the desire to be done with Caldwell Manor and on her way as quickly as possible.

"Here we are," Engsly announced, gesturing her through an open set of doors. "The family parlor."

He'd brought her to the parlor rather than his study? Anna hadn't expected that, but after a moment's thought, decided to take it as a promising sign that he viewed her as something more than a distasteful matter of business. Which, incidentally, and less promising, was an indication that he didn't intend to give her the thousand pounds straight away.

There would be a discussion.

"Please," Engsly encouraged, gesturing toward a settee. "Make yourself comfortable."

"Thank you. It is a lovely room." Anna had the overall impression of sturdy, old-fashioned, but well-kept furniture and muted colors on the walls and carpet, but the details of the room escaped her. She kept her eyes on the marquess as she settled on the edge of a seat.

He, in turn, kept his eyes on her as he took up position in a chair across from her.

A lengthy silence followed.

"Well," she tried, and brushed a hand down her skirt.

"Well," he countered.

The eyeing continued until a maid, whose name had already escaped Anna, brought refreshments into the room.

Anna snatched up a biscuit the moment they were within reach and took a small bite. "These are quite good."

They could have tasted of mud and she'd not have cared. She was just grateful to have something to discuss.

"I'm glad they please you," Lord Engsly said, taking one for himself as the maid disappeared again. "They're orange and spice. One of Gideon's favorites. He'll be arriving soon. And my wife. They're traveling from Scotland."

"It will be a pleasure to make their acquaintance," she replied and hoped it was true.

At least she'd not been expected to greet the family all at once. Perhaps the experience would be less traumatic if her exposure to the Haverstons was done slowly, bit by bit.

Or perhaps it would be like amputating a limb with a butter knife.

"Acquaintance," Lucien repeated, and a small furrow worked into his brow. "Yes. I had hoped you might meet with my brother's wife as well. Unfortunately, Winnefred also finds long trips to be unpleasant. I am told she is learning to ride, which should make travel easier for her."

"That seems wise." She fiddled with the biscuit in her hand until it began to crumble, forcing her to stop. "Well," she said and would have kicked her own shin if she'd been able. Surely they'd moved beyond "well" by now.

Engsly cleared his throat. "Yes . . . Well."

Or perhaps not.

She put the remainder of the biscuit in her mouth, smiled politely around the food, and chewed slowly. If she couldn't say something intelligent, she might as well have an excuse for it.

Engsly reached for another himself but paused with his hand halfway to the plate. Suddenly, he swore under his breath, rose from his seat, and stalked to the fireplace and back whilst vigorously scrubbing his hand over his head.

The last went a long ways toward explaining the peculiar state of his hair. The rest made Anna distinctly nervous.

He didn't strike her as friendly and welcoming now. He struck her as agitated.

"Allow me to be frank, Miss Rees." He stopped before her and blew out a short breath while her stomach tightened into a knot. "I haven't the foggiest notion of how to go about this . . . this . . ." He waved his hand about in an indecipherable manner. "This business of having a sister. I've no experience with sisters. I feel overwhelmed. And a little idiotic. I am not generally so inept at making conversation."

To her surprise, she felt a small smile form on her lips. What a relief it was to acknowledge the awkwardness of the situation rather than making things worse by trying to dance about it; and what a relief to know he wasn't about to inform her that he'd booked her passage on a ship to the Americas.

"I've no experiences with brothers," she offered. "I've no siblings of any sort."

She also felt like an idiot, but she was willing to take commiseration only so far.

Evidently, it was far enough for Engsly. His shoulders visibly relaxed and the hint of a smile touched his lips. "I quite like my sister-in-law, mind you."

"But it is not the same," she guessed and reached for a second biscuit. Perhaps this one would taste like oranges and spice, after all.

"No, it is not." He resumed his seat and took his second biscuit. "I like to think, however, that we will become every bit as comfortable with each other over time. A few weeks here and—"

"A few weeks?" Anna nearly choked on her food. "You wish for me to stay a few weeks?"

He couldn't be serious.

"Or longer, if it suits you." He gave her a bemused look. "How else are we to come to know each other?"

Why on earth would you wish to know me?

"I . . . had not anticipated a protracted visit. I thought . . . a day or two"—or an hour or two—"and Mrs. Culpepper and I would be on our way. She has a sister in the north." She stopped awkwardly, and with the realization that she'd not answered his question. "I had hoped, of course, that we might develop an ongoing correspondence."

She hadn't really. She hadn't allowed herself to hope or expect anything beyond a few hours of his time and the thousand pounds.

He digested that quietly before responding. "Miss Rees, it will be several days yet before Gideon arrives. You must stay here until then, at the very least. He is most eager to meet you."

"Several days?" She swallowed hard. She hadn't translated "soon" into "days."

"You'll be perfectly comfortable here, I assure you."

The devil she would. There was a very long list of

reasons why she would most certainly not be comfortable staying on. And at the top of that list, written in bold and underlined lettering, was the name Lord Maximilian Dane. Good God, she had to find a way out of this.

"I am honored by the request, my lord, and Codridgeton is a lovely village, I'm sure, but—"

"Codridgeton? No, you'll stay here."

"Here? At Caldwell Manor?" She realized she was parroting almost everything he said, but couldn't seem to stop herself. Stay a few weeks? At Caldwell Manor? Was the man unhinged? "There is a perfectly serviceable inn in the village. The Bear's Rest, I believe? I saw—"

She cut off with the realization that they had jumped from whether or not she would be staying, to where she would be staying. How on earth had that happened?

"A fine establishment," he allowed, "but I'd just as soon not be obliged to saddle a horse every time we wished to have a word. I would prefer for you to stay at Caldwell."

Anna was beginning to wonder if she might prefer a voyage to the Americas. "Do you think that wise, my lord?"

His lips curved in a smile she could only describe as a little bit smug. "I'm not in the habit of offering suggestions I think unwise."

She doubted he was in the habit of offering suggestions at all. He was a marquess. He commanded. She wished he would command himself into using a little common sense. Perhaps he simply wasn't comfortable acknowledging the obvious, but it needed to be done.

"I shouldn't be in your home at all. You know what I am," she said quietly. "What my mother is."

It was inconceivable that he should want her under his roof for a single night, let alone weeks.

"Yes," he replied evenly. "You are my sister. Your mother is the mother of my sister."

"There will be talk." There would be *endless* talk, even

in a village distanced from London, like Codridgeton. Just the thought of it made her skin crawl.

It appeared not to bother the marquess one whit. He lifted a slightly amused and highly arrogant brow. "Do you know who *I* am, Miss Rees?"

Baffled, she shook her head and made her best guess. "My half brother?"

"I am the sixth Marquess of Engsly. Our father was the fifth Marquess of Engsly." He leaned forward a little and tried another reassuring smile. "Let them talk."

She wished she could smile back. The intended sentiment was appreciated. He meant to acknowledge her in a way their father had not, and he could well afford any consequences. The talk of neighbors would not bring down the house of a marquess.

What Engsly seemed not to understand was that she was not a marquess, or a marchioness. She wasn't even a Haverston. Unlike the legitimate members of the family, she was vulnerable to the censure and disdain.

At worse, he would be branded a naïve fool.

At best, she'd be branded a grasping interloper.

Unfortunately, those appeared to be her only options. Returning to Anover House was out of the question and going anywhere else required more than the half pound she had left in her reticule. Mrs. Culpepper's sister had not agreed to take in a pauper, and Anna refused to become a financial burden on Mrs. Culpepper.

She needed the thousand pounds. And unless she suddenly found the temerity to demand he hand over those pounds *this very instant*, grasping interloper it would have to be.

She pasted on a pleasant smile. "I shall direct the driver to unload our trunks."

His smile was likewise amiable and, she very much hoped, far more sincere.

"It's already been taken care of."

Of course it had been. He was, as he had so aptly pointed out, the sixth Marquess of Engsly. There'd never really been any question of her staying.

T he remainder of Anna's meeting with the marquess was kept mercifully brief. Engsly gave her an abbreviated tour of the manor, pointing out the doors to the dining room, the music room, and his study. The library, billiards room, and orangery were down another hall and she was encouraged to explore all of the house and grounds to her heart's delight.

"I had thought to share a dinner downstairs," he told her as a pair of maids followed them to her chambers, "but with your companion out of sorts, perhaps the two of you would prefer I sent your meals upstairs?"

He really was a thoughtful sort, Anna mused. Pity he'd not thought to let her leave, or stay at the inn or, at a minimum, evict the other houseguest before her visit. "I would be most grateful, thank you."

"Here we are then," he chimed, as they stopped outside her chambers. "Your Mrs. Culpepper is across the hall, just there." He pointed to the exact door, which was unnecessary, really, as a steady and familiar stream of snores could be heard emanating from the other side of the door.

She looked into her own chambers. It seemed a fine room, complete with its own little balcony. Not so large or opulent as some of the guest chambers in Anover House, but that could only be counted as a mark in its favor, as her mother's taste in fashion had always been more fashionable than tasteful. The bed appeared to be in the more ornate style that was popular more than fifty years past. The walnut armoire and chest of drawers predated the bed by another twenty years. The wood of each gleamed with the polishing of decades. These were items of quality that were meant to be used and enjoyed, not present merely to impress.

Mrs. Culpepper would no doubt pronounce the room "well appointed." Anna thought comfortable a better description.

"It's a lovely room," she murmured. "Thank you."

"It is my pleasure to have you here," he said softly. "If there is anything else you need or want, please don't hesitate to ask."

She wanted to ask for her blasted thousand pounds, *if it's not too much trouble*, but, in the end, she put on her pleasant smile once again, thanked him for his hospitality, and wished him, and the hovering maids, good evening.

Then she stepped into the room and closed the door.

For a moment, Anna stood where she was, staring at the back of the door in something of a daze. Eventually, she forced herself to walk to the bed, where she took a seat on the mattress and began the arduous task of sorting through the tangled web of her thoughts.

Problems were much easier to address when approached methodically. Emotions were simpler to define and manage when one didn't attempt to define and manage all of them at once. Particularly on a day like today.

In just under eleven hours, she'd left London, and possibly her own mother, for good. She'd met a brother she'd not known existed a month ago. Somehow, she'd been coerced into staying at Caldwell Manor for at least several days (which was going to be interesting to explain to Mrs. Culpepper, who was no doubt surprised to have had her trunk delivered to her room) so that she could meet the other brother she'd not known existed a month ago. And to top it all off, she was, for the first time in four years, under the same roof as Max Dane.

Every one of those developments was monumental, any one of them would have made the day unforgettable, but it was the last that sent her heart racing the fastest.

Damn the man, why could he not have grown thicker round the middle and developed a bald pate?

Why did he have to be so handsome still, so appealing? She couldn't possibly face him, let alone carry on a polite conversation, without remembering all the reasons she'd been taken with him four years ago. She'd certainly not be able to look at him without thinking of their kiss. How could she, when she'd been so damnably careful to capture every detail of it as it happened? Every taste and sound and dizzying sensation had been permanently etched in her mind.

As were a thousand other particulars of that night—the way he'd made her laugh, made her feel clever and interesting, lovely and desirable. And hopeful. She'd never been so hopeful as she had for those few weeks after they'd met.

Though she'd not liked admitting it, even to herself, the truth was that she'd never been so heartbroken as the day she'd realized and accepted that Max Dane wasn't coming back.

The blighter.

He ought to have at least written a letter explaining why, instead of leaving her to wonder what she'd done wrong.

"I didn't do a damned thing wrong," she muttered to herself, not so much because she believed it, but because it helped to hear it said aloud.

"I'm not doing a damned thing wrong now," she added, because that, too, felt good to hear.

"I'll not be doing anything wrong when I take that thousand pounds and leave with Mrs. Culpepper. There is nothing unseemly in . . ." She trailed off and wrinkled her nose. Now she just felt silly.

But talking to herself had helped settle her nerves. Talking with Mrs. Culpepper would be even better, but it was hours yet before dinner, and it was possible Mrs. Culpepper might sleep straight through to morning, leaving Anna with nothing to do, and no one to do it with, for the remainder of the evening.

Anna frowned at the door. She wasn't fully comfortable taking advantage of the invitation to explore, no matter how sincerely offered, but she couldn't possibly spend the entire night dwelling on her change of circumstances.

She was in dire need of distraction. Her embroidery tools and the few books she'd taken from Anover House had been packed in Mrs. Culpepper's trunk, and Anna hadn't the heart to wake the woman. There was nothing else for it; she'd have to find diversion elsewhere.

The library, she decided. Surely she could seek out that room without mishap or, more importantly, running into Max Dane. Caldwell Manor was enormous and the hall with the library wasn't terribly far from where she was now. She could risk it.

Chapter 6

❦

*S*he shouldn't have risked it.

Anna swallowed past the dry lump in her throat. Almost, she'd made it to the library. In fact, she could see its double doors not twenty feet down the hall . . . Or, more notably, fifteen feet beyond where Max Dane stood, blocking her path.

He'd all but materialized before her like a ghost. One moment he'd not been there, then she'd turned her head for just an instant to peek into an open parlor, and when she'd looked back again, there he was, looming like a specter.

Only one might imagine a specter to be less substantial in appearance.

Also, they were unlikely to bow and say, "Miss Rees," in voice that sent pleasant shivers up one's spine.

He really did look handsome, Anna thought with a suppressed sigh. And she'd forgotten to so much as glance in the vanity mirror before leaving her chambers again. Her appearance had now gone from sadly road worn to slovenly. Lovely.

Fortunately, however unexpected and unwelcome this meeting was, it didn't come as quite the shock as their first. Perhaps it wouldn't go as poorly either.

Chin up, shoulders back, eyes straight ahead.

She managed a credible curtsy and when she spoke, her voice remained calm and steady. "Lord Dane, a pleasure to see you again. I—"

"Is it? A pleasure?"

The question, odd in and of itself, had a mocking quality to it, lending it the feel of an opening salvo.

Good heavens, he truly *was* angry.

Baffled, and a little irritated that he should feel he had the right to anger, she said the first thing that came to mind. "Well, no. Not entirely."

He smiled, an almost disdainful curve of the lips that held little humor. "Still honest, I see."

This was why it was so important for a person to think before speaking. And why it was sometimes better for a person to not speak at all. Particularly when that person had inadequate practice.

"I only meant that the circumstances are somewhat awkward," she tried.

"Awkward," he repeated slowly, as if tasting the word. "That is one way of putting it."

This wasn't going well at all. Between his cold manner and her missteps, the experience was growing painful. Better to end it before it became worse. They could try again tomorrow, if need be. Or never, if the good lord had any mercy to spare for her and sent Max packing back to London or his own estate sometime during the night.

She hesitated, uncertain if she should retreat back to her room or push onward to the library.

Onward, she decided, and stepped forward. He might

make her uncomfortable, but he'd not embarrass her into retreat.

I've done nothing wrong.

"If you will excuse me, Lord Dane, I was just on my way to—"

He stepped into her path and gestured at the open door of a nearby room. "I'd like a word, please, Miss Rees."

She glanced inside. "In a billiards room?"

"Unless you'd prefer to have this conversation in front of any passing staff?"

She didn't want to have a conversation at all—unless it was likely to end in his confession of unbearable remorse at having tossed her aside four years ago—but he was right, there were things that might be said that were best said in private.

"Very well," she agreed and stepped past him into the room.

He didn't offer her a seat once inside, and she wasn't inclined to take one. Instead, she watched him cross his arms over his chest and lean a hip against one of the two tables occupying the room.

"I'd never thought to see you outside of London," he said at length.

You never thought to see me at all.

"It has been quite an experience thus far," she replied, keeping her tone light. One of them needed to put an effort into making things easy between them.

"You came without your mother."

"She was unable to make the journey." Primarily because her mother not been informed of said journey, but now was not the time to mention it.

"I heard of her injury. Was it wise to leave her side at such a time?"

"The injury was not terribly serious," she assured him and silently congratulated herself for not allowing any hint of annoyance or defensiveness to enter her voice. "And she is recovering with all due speed."

"Nevertheless, your abandonment of her now might appear to some to be . . . a trifle cold."

She thought his comment, and the tone in which it was delivered, to be a *trifle cold*, but he continued on before she could respond.

"Strange business, this sudden connection of yours to the Haverstons."

"Not so very strange," she countered, growing increasingly impatient. "Illegitimate children are born every day. Presumably there has been but one immaculate conception."

"Oh, I don't doubt your secular origins, Miss Rees," he drawled. "I've met your mother, you'll recall."

Not a hint of emotion was allowed to touch her face. Why not just call the woman a whore and be done with it, she thought. He wasn't wrong, exactly, but that wasn't the point. "Is this why you wished to leave the hall, so you might impugn my mother's character in private?"

"Not at all. You'll also recall that I quite liked your mother." He offered a negligent lift of the shoulder. "I'm merely making conversation."

They weren't having a conversation. She wasn't certain what they were having—a thinly veiled battle, perhaps— but it wasn't a conversation.

If he wished to pretend otherwise, however, she could play along. But she'd be damned if she continued to go on as the defendant. "And what of you, my lord? What could possibly have drawn you from the bosom of your gambling hells and iniquitous dens?"

"London's dens of iniquity have done without my visitations for some time now. Which you might have heard if you'd left your sanctuary more often."

"You've given up the life of debauchery?" She didn't believe it for an instant.

"You misunderstand. Debauchery, when I care for it—and I generally do—now comes to me."

"You've become a depraved recluse. How delightful."

He acknowledged the barb with the lift of an eyebrow. "Still just as tart, as well, I see."

"There is something to be said for living up to expectations," she replied and, because she couldn't curl her fingers into her palms without him noticing, curled her toes inside her shoes instead.

"I wouldn't know." His gaze turned shrewd. "And what of your expectations? What is it you really want from Lucien?"

Had he not been told of the thousand pounds? Anna wondered. For two people reputed to be the closest of friends, there seemed to be a great many secrets between Engsly and Max. But maybe that was the way of it between gentlemen. She would have to ask Mrs. Culpepper.

"It is none of your concern." If Engsly wished to keep secrets from Max, it was none of *her* concern. "It is between Lord Engsly—"

Max leaned forward just a hair. "On the contrary, Miss Rees, the Haverstons, and anything that threatens them, are very much my concern. The thousand pounds you're demanding from them concerns me a great deal."

She shook her head, baffled and not a little frustrated. "If you knew of the thousand pounds, why did you just ask—?"

"That can't possibly be all you want."

She wasn't sure what all she wanted; she'd not hoped for or made plans around anything but the thousand pounds.

"But it is what's bothering you now," she countered and decided she was tired of dancing around the subject of his peculiar behavior. "Why is that?" she asked softly. "Why are you so angered by my presence here?"

He shook his head dismissively. "I'm not angry so much as I am, as I believe I mentioned, highly, *highly* suspicious."

"Well." She took a moment to consider the circum-stances, imagined herself in his place, and came to the con-clusion that his suspicion was both understandable and unlikely to be assuaged by anything she could say or do at present. "I suppose I would be as well."

Feeling at a loss, and inexplicably disappointed, she turned to leave. She would find her book in the library and return to her room, where she would stay until Lord Gideon arrived, or Max left, whichever came last.

"That's it?" Max called to her back, his voice an incon-gruent mix of annoyance and amusement.

She turned around, taking a deep breath for both patience and to steady frayed nerves. For pity's sake, what did he expect from her? "My apologies, I thought we were through."

"We've not resolved anything."

Resolution wasn't possible. How could he not see that? "Is there something I could say that would immediately put your suspicions to rest?"

"Immediately? No, but—"

"Then I see no point in pursuing this conversation any further. Now, if you'll excuse me, I am weary and wish to retire to my chambers."

"It's half past five."

That was all? It felt half past next week. "I am unaccus-tomed to travel."

"You're unaccustomed to having to explain your be-havior."

"If you like."

"If I like. How very accommodating. What if I should like for you to leave Caldwell Manor and never return?" He stepped closer, giving her the distinct impression he was making an attempt at intimidation.

Anger and insult spurred her into stepping forward in return and giving him her iciest stare. "Then you are bound for disappointment. I have every right to be here."

"That remains to be seen."

"It doesn't, in fact. I was invited by the marquess. That gives me the right. And you've no rational reason for suspecting my motives for accepting that invitation, *nor* my goals now that I've arrived." She understood the instinctual desire to protect, but this went beyond the natural desire to defend a friend.

"I've no reason to trust you either," he returned coldly. "I don't even have reason to like you."

Those words stung, even if the sentiment did not come as a surprise. "You liked my company well enough at Anover House," she reminded him.

He lifted a shoulder. "I am what is referred to as an amiable drunk. After a few too many glasses, I like *everyone*."

His accentuation of "everyone" was not lost on her. Nor was his meaning.

For titled men like Lord Dane, there were gentlemen and ladies of good breeding, and then there was everyone else. And *that*, Anna realized with a sinking heart, was likely at the heart of his belligerence toward her. It wasn't just that she might be lying, but that she didn't have the right to keep company with the Haverstons, regardless of whether she was telling the truth or not.

A woman like her was good enough to toy about with at Anover House, but she had no business pretending to be a lady at Caldwell Manor.

It was a similar argument to the one she'd presented to Lord Engsly not two hours earlier. But pointing out that there were those who held her in contempt, and it was therefore unwise for her to stay at Caldwell, was a far cry from being informed that she was, indeed, contemptible and therefore had no right to be at Caldwell.

Evidently, Max's proclamation four years ago of having no care for honor had not been mere hyperbole.

"Well, then . . ." Angry, disgusted, and frustrated because

both emotions were tainted with a hint of shame, she walked to a nearby sideboard and grabbed the largest, fullest decanter she saw. Resisting the urge to hurl it at his head, she carried it back and set it before him on the table. "If you must be sotted to withstand my presence here, then I suggest you have at it. I am not leaving."

He tilted his head and narrowed his eyes ever so slightly, as if she were some vaguely interesting species of bug. "Is that a spark of temper I see, Ice Maiden?"

She waited a pointed beat before responding.

"If you like," she replied, and with a regal lift on her chin, she spun on her heel and glided out of the room.

Devil take the library. She would keep herself occupied contemplating all the ways she could make Max Dane pay for his boorish behavior.

*B*etween gleaning what little information he could about Miss Rees from the staff, and distracting Lucien from the worry of having a new sister, Max was too occupied for the remainder of the evening to spare much thought for his behavior in the billiards room. He remained quite confident in his handling of the situation . . . Until the rest of the house found its way to bed.

There was, Max mused as he sat in his chambers, something about the dark isolation of night that forced a man's thoughts unhappily inward.

No doubt the phenomenon did much to contribute to the popularity of imbibing spirits as an evening pastime. He considered indulging in that pastime, but ultimately decided that the only thing worse than facing one's possible failings while sitting alone in the dark was facing them while drinking alone in the dark.

And so he was regrettably sober when he began to reconsider his treatment of Anna. After much time spent scowling at the dark walnut of his door and copious amounts of pacing, Max arrived at the conclusion that he was not handling things as well as he might.

As well as he *ought*.

Because, really, he ought not be acting so much like a mad man.

It bothered him not one whit that he wasn't comporting himself as a gentleman. It bothered him quite a bit, however, that he had failed to comport himself as a rational adult.

He thought he'd passed the age when emotion could unduly influence behavior. In fact, he could remember the last time he'd lost control to anger. At nine, he'd hurled a vase at Reginald's head for an offense now long forgotten. It may have had something to do with a broken toy, or possibly over sweetmeats. At any rate, an offense had been committed and a vase had been hurled. Max's punishment had been two lashes for the broken vase and ten lashings for endangering the heir apparent, whose head, incidentally—and much to Max's immediate regret—had escaped breakage.

It wasn't the first or last lashing he'd receive, but it had been the worst. One would think he'd not have forgotten the lesson.

Yet here he was, allowing resentment and suspicion to undermine control and common sense. All because of a rejection he'd received four years ago.

It was absurd, baffling, and not a little embarrassing.

Anna Rees was not the first woman to have declined his attentions. True, she was the only one to have seemingly encouraged those attentions for the sole purpose of spurning them, but even that didn't explain his severe reaction to her.

He wasn't sure he could explain it, except to say that everything was, and had been, different with Anna.

It had *felt* different when they'd been in the nursery, and not merely because he'd been drunk (which, in fact, had not been so very different), and it had felt different when he'd woken the next morning.

It had seemed bigger somehow, better, more significant.

The week following his brother's death had been a morass of misery. Reginald had been a self-important brat of a boy and a pompous, selfish coward of a man. Max could say without guilt or shame that he'd neither liked nor respected his brother past the age of ten. But he had loved him. Just as Anna had intuitively known, he had loved him. The loss of Reginald, and the monstrous stupidity surrounding his death, had throbbed like an open wound.

Filling his mind with the lovely Miss Anna Rees had been a welcomed balm, a necessary distraction. He'd thought of her face, her soft voice and low laughter, that long dark braid, and the way her lips had moved against his. He'd lost himself in the memory of her.

He'd even made plans—long-term plans, which was most definitely different. He would buy Anna that hound, and the cottage if she still wanted it after seeing McMullin Hall. She'd need to choose between special license or elopement. There was no purpose in waiting for the banns to be read, and forgoing marriage altogether was not an option. Any children they might have would be legitimate. Any questions of fidelity would be . . . Well, there would be no questions, that was the point.

By the time his last, unavoidable responsibility had been filled, he was near to climbing the walls, wanting to see Anna again. *His* Anna, as he had come to think of her. And bugger the rules of mourning. He'd looked forward to visiting a woman before, but he'd never felt like such an excited schoolboy, not even when he'd been an excitable schoolboy.

He'd all but bloody run to Anover House.

And when she'd refused him, refused even to speak with him, it had wounded more than his pride. It had destroyed a dream. A ridiculous dream constructed out of grief and erected on the foundation of a drunken memory, but a dream nonetheless.

In the dark of his chambers, Max ran a hand down his face.

It had become obvious very quickly that he had built the encounter into more than it was. He should have considered that he'd not just misinterpreted the situation but her intentions as well. Perhaps she'd not meant for things to progress as far as they had in the nursery and had simply regretted her impetuous behavior afterward.

She ought to have expressed her change of heart or disinterest in him in person rather than having him turned away at the door, but . . . it had been four years ago. They had been young and foolish . . . Younger and more foolish, at any rate. One might imagine they had altered for the better in the time since. He liked to think, the last twelve hours notwithstanding, he had. Perhaps she had as well.

It was possible that the wounded pride of four years ago, and a long-held sense of obligation to the Haverstons, who'd been more like brothers to him than friends, had made him a touch . . . imperious.

Or maybe Anna was a manipulative adventuress. Either way, he wasn't helping himself, or Lucien, by conducting open warfare with the woman.

Which meant they would need to cry pax.

Which meant, Max realized with a long, long look at the brandy bottle, he would need to apologize.

Chapter 7

❧

$\mathcal{A}$nna rose as the first hints of sunlight peeked around the edges of her light blue drapes. Grabbing her wrap from the foot of the bed, she stayed seated on the mattress for several moments, blinking in the semidarkness.

It was a strange sensation indeed, waking up in an unfamiliar room. There was something a little bit eerie about it, and a great deal exciting. She'd not spent a night of her adult life outside of Anover House. Now here she was, miles from London in the guest chambers of a marquess.

She wanted to explore, both the feeling and her surroundings, and after only the briefest hesitation, she denounced her plan to remain isolated in her chambers as both impractical and unacceptable.

She had more pride than that. She wasn't above removing herself from an unpleasant situation, mind you, but there was a difference between remaining above a fray and hiding from it. Max Dane would not intimidate her into hiding.

Anna slipped from the bed and set about dressing herself while her mind wrestled with how to deal with Max moving forward. As planned, she'd spent no small amount of time and energy the night before envisioning all manner of punishments for him. It hadn't been as rewarding as she'd hoped, but it had been preferable to dwelling on the other, less easily managed emotions that boiled just below the anger.

The level of animosity exhibited by Max had been unexpected and unwelcomed, but equally disquieting was how deeply his words had cut.

Anna had faced derision in the past. She'd seen it on the faces of many of her mother's guests. Disdain, ridicule, scorn, and even envy, these were no strangers to her. But while being the focus of such unpleasantness had never lost the power to cut, neither had it ever wounded quite like Max's behavior the night before.

She feared disappointment might be the cause. She may have decided long ago that it was best Max had not returned to Anover House for her (and given how deeply his behavior had wounded, she conceded the possibility that she'd not been entirely reconciled with that decision), but it had never occurred to her that his reason for doing so was simple, awful contempt. She felt like twice the fool now. How could she have been so blind to the man's true nature? To think of the time and energy she'd spent pining for him, imagining him as something he wasn't.

Anna paused in the buttoning of her gown and gave herself a mental shake. There was nothing to be gained by chastising herself. She'd misjudged a man's character, that was all. She was not the first woman to have done so and she would not be the last.

According to her mother, to ascribe any character to a man was to grossly misjudge his character, but Anna liked to think that saying had less to do with reality and more to do with her mother's penchant for hyperbole.

Anna put on a new pair of leather half boots she'd had made before leaving Anover House. The use of funds had been difficult, but necessary. One could not expect to reside in a country cottage without a single pair of leather boots.

And that was what she needed to concentrate on now— her cottage, her thousand pounds, and the man who currently controlled both.

Lord Engsly seemed to be the sort of man Madame failed to take into consideration when pronouncing all men lacking by design—a perfectly decent gentleman. Slightly high-handed in the way he'd maneuvered her into staying on at Caldwell, but decent all the same . . . Perhaps more than decent, now that she thought on it. It wasn't every peer of the realm who would invite his father's bastard into his home.

Without the exhaustion and nerves and frustration of the day before clouding her perspective, Anna began to see Engsly and her current circumstances in a new light.

She was a welcomed guest in a magnificent country estate. This was a dream come to life for many people. It wasn't her dream, but she'd be a true fool (and an ungrateful one to boot) to make it into an onus.

What had Mrs. Culpepper said as they'd left London?

What adventure awaits us, my dear. Let us make the most of it.

And so she would, Anna thought as she snatched up her bonnet, trimmed in pale blue to match her dress, and left her chambers. She would do whatever it took to make the best of things, with or without the approval of Max Dane.

Anna felt a renewed sense of hope and purpose as she made her way downstairs. There was, in her opinion, no better time of day than dawn.

At Anover House, she loved the hour around sunrise for its stillness. Her mother and any houseguests never rose before noon, and the staff, being required to spend a good portion of their nights at work for Mrs. Wrayburn's parties, were rarely expected to be up again before first light.

Often, Anna was the only person awake in the house. Sometimes it seemed as if she were the only person in residence, as if Anover House belonged to her and she could roam its halls and rooms as she pleased. For an hour or two a day, she could almost convince herself that she was free.

She didn't need to convince herself of anything at Caldwell, she realized with a dawning smile. She was a guest at a beautiful country estate on her way to having her own lovely country cottage. Things were fine quite as they were.

Things were also considerably more active at Caldwell Manor than she'd anticipated. The muted bang of pots and pans could be heard coming from the kitchen below. The shuffle of feet and the creek of floorboards sounded above. Apparently, life in a country manor began much earlier than life in a town house.

Well, no matter, she decided. A particular guest would certainly still be abed, and that was good enough.

Still, she avoided the hall with the library and billiards room, having had her fill of that part of the house for now. But she found a music room and orangery, a number of guest rooms, several rooms used for storage, and a half dozen rooms with purposes that eluded her.

She'd also discovered, through the windows of one such mysterious room, that the sun had fully risen on what looked to be a lovely morning. More notably, it hadn't risen over grimy roofs and chimneys, but a vast landscape of green.

No longer interested in remaining indoors, she found a back door at the end of a hall and stepped outside into the soft, warm air of a sunny morning.

Oh, how lovely.

Beyond the back lawn lay the rolling hills she wanted to explore. Nearly giddy with anticipation, Anna took a deep breath in, chose a direction at random, and headed off.

She had imagined, in the past, what a stroll about the countryside of a sunny morning might be like. There would be birdsong and the chatter of squirrels, a brisk breeze carrying the scent of hay and pine. Perhaps she would spy cattle in the distance, or maybe a drover taking his flock to market.

Peaceful, bucolic, ideal—these were the words she most often encountered in her books when reading about the English countryside. They were the words that came to mind when she'd fantasized about strolling across England's green fields.

In truth, she'd spent a considerable amount of her time fantasizing about countryside strolls.

When Anover House was asleep, that was when she wandered its halls. But when it was awake, and at its wildest and loudest, Anna had retreated into books and her own imagination. She had envisioned herself walking in the beautiful, peaceful fields surrounding her imaginary cottage more times than she could count.

Unfortunately, reality did not conform entirely to Anna's fantasies.

She stepped in manure within the first half hour, which, for obvious reasons, had not arisen as a possibility in her daydreams. Even after scraping off the worst of the muck against a rock, the smell remained pungent, and so it seemed only sensible to remedy the problem with an ankle-deep wade into the wide stream she came upon.

The water was colder than she anticipated, and the slick rocks along the bottom made any sort of movement rather precarious, but with a little effort, she was able to scrape the offending muck from her boots without taking an unexpected dive into the water.

The long soaking, however, allowed water to seep through the thin leather of her boots, saturating her stockings, and walking became less comfortable after leaving the stream. But Anna pushed the unpleasant feeling aside and headed for the nearest hill. Aching muscles would keep her mind off the condition of her feet.

The hill wasn't particularly steep, but it was tall, and the ground near the top was damp and loose. Her feet slid out beneath her repeatedly, resulting in the last ten minutes of her hike becoming more of a scramble than a climb. By the time she reached the top, her gown was torn at the hem and covered in soil from the knees down, her hands were filthy from seeking purchase in the dirt and grass, and, as expected, her legs were screaming.

But the view at the peak made it all worthwhile.

The beautiful countryside lay out before her, *exactly* as she had always dreamed: fertile fields and hills broken by stands of hardwoods and the occasional stone wall. A warm breeze brushed her face, and the scent of hay teased her nose. The sound of sheep and cattle echoed in the distance. It was a world apart from the sounds and smells of London and, in her estimation, a world improved.

Anna grinned and decided that, unfortunate manure encounter notwithstanding, and despite her aching muscles, wet shoes, torn gown, and what she was certain were colossal-sized blisters on her feet, this was shaping up to be a perfectly wonderful morning.

She enjoyed the vista a minute longer, then took a deep breath of the sweet air and headed off once more.

For the next hour, she walked through fields, through stands of trees, and over small hills, careful to move in a circle about the manor house rather than stray too far away. After a while, however, her feet began to ache and sting to the point where she was no longer able to ignore the discomfort. It was time to head back, she decided, as she reached the top of another rise. She could explore the next hill another morning, perhaps venture closer to the flock of sheep she could see in the distance.

Anna took a final look, turned, and found herself staring at small brown eyes at the end of a long canine muzzle.

"Well, my goodness," she whispered, delighted. "Who have we here?"

Black and tan with lopsided ears, a low-slung tail, and an intense stare, the dog didn't quite reach her knees, but its strength was apparent in its long, lean lines.

"Aren't you adorable," she crooned and stretched her hand out for the dog to smell. "Aren't you a beauty?"

The beauty lowered its head and issued a quiet snarl that showcased an impressive set of sharp, white teeth. Anna's heart leapt at the sight.

"Oh, my . . . Oh. All right. All right, then. Good dog." She withdrew her hand slowly and began to carefully back away. The dog crouched lower and followed, his snarl deepening into a long, low growl.

"Here now, no need for that." Fear formed a hard knot in her chest. It wasn't a great beast of an animal, no more than fifty pounds at a guess, but it appeared sufficiently agile (not to mention annoyed) to do considerable damage to her person. "No need at all. I quite like dogs."

The dog lunged, snapped at the air a few feet from her toes, and jumped back again, quick as lightning.

"No! Bad dog!" She wasn't able to keep the tremor out of her voice, but she compensated with volume, and by shaking her finger at the dog as if scolding a naughty child. The latter left her feeling equal parts ridiculous and terrified. "Very bad dog!"

Her lack of confidence must have shown because the dog lunged at her feet again, stopped short by a good distance, and jumped back once more.

She took a deep breath, intending another scold with the desperate notion that she might be able to keep things at a standoff until help arrived. But she wasn't given the opportunity to put her ill-conceived plan to the test.

A series of shrill whistles sounded behind her, and to her immense shock and greater relief, the dog spun about in the opposite direction and sprinted back to the flock, for all the world as if Anna had suddenly ceased to exist.

With her heart lodged stubbornly in her throat, Anna kept her eyes trained on the dog, fearful it might change its mind and come sprinting back for another go at her ankles. Even the sound of footsteps coming up swift behind her couldn't force her to turn around.

But the sound of Max Dane's voice could.

"Are you injured?"

Oh, damn and blast.

The thank-you Anna had fully intended to deliver to her rescuer died a swift and painful death when she turned about and saw Max—looking a bit winded, she noted, but otherwise neat and collected. From what she could tell, she looked as if she'd lost in a footrace through a briar patch in a wind storm.

He closed the distance between them and took in her disheveled appearance with a quick, thorough glance. "Are you hurt?"

Shaking her head, she gestured toward the dog, who had gone back to darting around the edges of its flock. "No. No, he didn't actually . . . He only . . . Engsly ought keep better control of his pets."

"Clover's not a pet, sweet. And she is a she."

She was too rattled to do more than blink at his use of an endearment. "Well, *she* could use a spot of training."

"She guards and herds the flock. A better-trained shepherd's dog you'll not find in England." He looked out over the field to the flock and his lips thinned to an annoyed line. "Pity the same can't be said for the shepherd."

She felt a bit thick for having assumed the animal was a pet. Of course it was a shepherd's dog. The flock was right before her. Evidently, the transition from city to country life did not come as naturally as she'd hoped.

"I didn't see him," she mumbled.

"My point exactly," he said under his breath before returning his attention to her. "Certain you're unharmed?"

"Yes." She shrugged but found she wasn't quite capable of being wholly nonchalant about the incident. "She tried to bite me."

"If she'd wanted a bite, she'd have taken one. She was nipping at your feet to move you along."

"I tried to move along," she replied, defensive. "She followed."

"She wanted you to move along faster." He gave her a small smile. "Gave you quite a scare, did she?"

The amusement in his voice grated just enough to steal her spine. "I have recovered."

"I am relieved to hear it."

"Are you?" she asked caustically.

Much to her surprise, he winced and offered what she might have taken for an apologetic expression, had he been anyone else. "I don't wish you ill, Anna."

"Merely my swift departure?" she asked, not believing him.

"On the contrary—" He made a show of turning about and holding out his elbow for her to take. "—it would be an honor to escort you back to the house."

He looked the perfect gentleman awaiting a lady's pleasure, but Anna knew better. He was no gentleman, and she was no lady. To refuse his offer would be petty, but when she took his elbow, it was with a cautious grasp and suspicious eye.

"I had hoped to find you this morning," he commented lightly as he started them off. "You are now fully recovered from your journey, I presume?"

"Yes," she replied warily. Coming to her rescue, playing the escort, asking after her general well-being . . . What game was he playing? And why the devil wasn't he still abed like every other self-respecting degenerate? "I thank you for inquiring."

"I'm not utterly without manners. Usually. Which leads us to why I sought you out this morning. I wanted . . ." He trailed off, slanted a sharp look at her skirts and brought them to an abrupt stop. "You said you weren't injured."

"Sorry?" She followed his gaze, baffled. Her gown was muddy, not bloody. "I'm not—"

"You're limping."

"Oh, that." She shrugged. "My boots are wet, that's all. I've a blister or two."

He gestured at an old tree stump a few feet away. "Sit down a moment."

"That won't be necessary," she assured him. "I am perfectly well."

"Sit," he repeated and gave her a gentle push in the direction of the stump.

"And when I am done, shall I retrieve a pheasant for you?" she asked tartly. "Curl about your feet to warm your toes? Run alongside your carriage?"

He held up a hand in surrender. "I apologize for my abruptness. If you would . . ." He trailed off, narrowed his eyes just a hair, and ran his tongue over his teeth, considering. "The toe-warming idea has some merit."

"Good day, Lord Dane." If he hoped to gain her cooperation by making a racy jest, he was to be sorely disappointed. She turned to resume her walk toward the house, alone, but he stopped her with a gentle hand on her arm.

"Stop. Just a moment. Please." He took a deep breath and flicked his eyes heavenward. "Miss Rees, I beg of you, humor my gentlemanly side, negligible and neglected though it may be, and have a seat."

He ended this small speech by stripping out of his coat and laying the fabric over the stump. It was a thoughtful, even chivalrous gesture, and one she couldn't argue against without appearing foolish.

"This really is unnecessary," she reiterated, but she

limped over, perched on the edge of the stump as it was too uneven to make a proper seat, and decided that she still felt foolish, only for different reasons.

"But harmless," he returned and knelt at her feet to untie her boots.

As he appeared quite intent on the task, she discarded the idea of insisting she do her own untying. Instead, she marveled at the deftness of his fingers as they worked the laces. When she'd first met Max, he'd been a man under the influence of drink. He'd been notably uncoordinated, unable to manage so much as a snap of the fingers. But this man . . . this man had decidedly agile fingers. She found them to be fascinating for reasons she chose not to acknowledge.

When he slipped a finger between the leather and her stockings, she thought it strange that his touch should feel familiar. Strange and awful, as he found her so distasteful, and she had fallen asleep the night before gleefully envisioning his forked tongue on a spit.

Discomforted, she made conversation merely to distract herself. "How did you know how to send Clover away?"

"I've watched the shepherd work with her now and again. Why are your boots sopping wet?" he inquired suddenly with a quick glance up. "What happened?"

"Hmm?" Her eyes snapped to his. There was nothing untoward in peering at one's own feet whilst a gentleman's hands just happened to be upon them . . . and yet she felt a warmth of embarrassment rise to her cheeks. "Oh. I . . . I stepped in something unpleasant and washed my boots in the stream."

His fingers came up to lightly brush across the mud at her knees. "And then . . . you fell on the banks?"

"No." She pushed his hand away. There was something very much untoward in allowing a man to handle one's knees. "I . . . knelt to pick a flower. I didn't realize the ground was so . . ."

"Dirty?"

She drew a hand down her sleeve, the picture of composure, and decided the best response to that was no response at all.

"Liar." He laughed softly and began to ease her boot from her foot. "Keep that secret, if you like. My imagination can fill in . . . Damn it, woman, what have you done?"

"I beg your pardon? I've done nothing wrong. I . . ." She trailed off when he moved his head and her foot became visible. "Oh, my."

Apparently, she'd done something wrong. On the inside of her ankle, the thin cotton of her stocking was worn and stained pink with blood. A large blister must have formed and opened, and the exposed skin beneath rubbed raw.

"How did you let it get to this point?" Max demanded.

She scowled at her bloody stocking. "I hadn't realized it was as bad as all that."

"You were limping," he reminded her, reaching for her other foot.

"I never said it didn't hurt, I said I hadn't realized it was quite so bad. Besides, I wasn't limping. I was stepping with caution. There is a difference."

If he had a particular reaction to that bit of nonsense, she'd never know it. He kept his head bent and refrained from comment.

The removal of the second boot revealed a stocking spotted pink at the heel and big toe. Two blisters, then. Both of them clearly less severe than the one on her first foot, but ghastly all the same. Anna sighed in defeat. Manure, mud, a mad dog, bloody blisters, and the presence of Max Dane. Her stroll about the countryside had now officially turned into a disaster.

Max cupped the heel of her first foot and gently turned it for inspection. "How long have you been stepping cautiously on these feet?"

"Not long."

"'Not long' being a relative phrase?" he inquired, glancing up. "Or just a lie?"

"Not long being the politest way of informing you to mind your own business. Might have known the effort was wasted. Now, if you are done pretending to be a gentleman, might I have my footwear back?"

He released her foot and handed her the boots. "By all means. Let's get you back to the house."

"Thank you." She accepted his hand and rose from the tree stump. The ground was cold and a little damp beneath her stockinged feet. "Now—"

"You're welcome," he cut in, and then, to her complete astonishment, he put an arm around her shoulders and bent in an attempt to put the other arm behind her knees.

She hopped away, quick as Clover. "What on *earth* do you think you are doing?"

"I'm going to carry you back," he replied, as if it was the most natural thing in the world.

She gripped her boots against her chest like a shield and took another step back. "The devil you are."

"You're injured."

"It's a *blister*, Lord Dane." One would think a bone was protruding. Carry her back, indeed.

"It's several," he countered, "and one is bleeding profusely."

"Yes, gushing blood, really," she replied dryly. "I do wonder if the physician will allow me to retain the limb."

He ignored her sarcasm. "It's a quarter mile back to the house."

"It's not half that."

He gestured impatiently at her feet. "You're practically barefooted."

"Yes," she agreed and took some pleasure in adopting a patronizing tone, "and no doubt I am in for a slow and uncomfortable return walk, but if you think for one moment I will allow you—"

"If *you* think for one moment I'm going to stand by while you hobble all the way back to the house, you are very much mistaken."

She'd heard men could be autocratic in their misguided attempts at chivalry, but she'd never experienced the phenomenon firsthand. It struck her as distinctly ridiculous under the circumstances, and more than a little aggravating.

"This is not your decision to make, Lord Dane. My blisters and my morning stroll need not and do not concern you."

"If that were true, I'd leave you to hobble, wouldn't I? Now come—" He stepped forward again, hand outstretched.

She stepped back.

He dropped his arm and gave her a bland look. "Are we really going to do this?"

"Argue?"

"Play catch-me like a pair of eight-year-olds?"

She'd rather not. She didn't think the scraps of her dignity could take the strain. But neither were they eager to accept another capitulation. She'd retreated from the billiards room and now she was retreating back to the house. Both were disheartening enough, but never let it be said she hadn't retreated on her own two, blistered feet.

Max offered his hand. "One of us needs to take the higher road, sweet."

Again, the use of an endearment. What the devil had changed in the last twelve hours? "Are you volunteering?"

His smile was slow, wicked, and filled with humor. "Darling, I wouldn't know where to begin looking for it."

She considered that statement and the light in which it had been offered. It was difficult to poke at a man who made jests out of his own sins and shortcomings. But, in this instance, she wasn't averse to the challenge.

"The paths you walk are low, indeed," she agreed. "But surely if I were to provide a long, long rope along with a climbing hook, and point you in the right direction, you might find your way if I held aloft a great light and—"

He let out a frustrated laugh. "For pity's sake—"

"You're the one who began the analogy," she reminded him smugly. "It's not my fault you chose a poor one."

"But it would be my fault if your injury worsened because of a long walk back to the house. Engsly would have my head."

"And if I allow you to carry me all the way back to the house, Mrs. Culpepper would have my head." Mrs. Culpepper would pronounce Lord Dane terrifically romantic, but Max couldn't know that, and Mrs. Culpepper was too loyal to mind the fib.

"However," she added, aware that some sort of compromise would need to be made. There was independence, and then there was unreasonable stubbornness. She hadn't the experience to know for certain where the line separating the two fell, but she suspected that an argument over a blister and an eighth-to-quarter-mile walk indicated that it wasn't far off, "the blistering does sting a bit and I would, of course, appreciate some assistance—"

"Excellent." He stepped forward once again as if to sweep her up.

"In the form of your *arm*, Lord Dane."

Max stopped and dropped his hands. He looked to the sky in the manner of one praying for patience, yet again, then looked to her in the manner of one sizing up his opposition, and then, at last, held out his elbow in the manner of one defeated.

"Very well, hobble it is."

She stepped forward slowly, transferring her boots to one hand, and took his arm just as she had earlier, with great care.

"I'll not bite," he promised, starting them off slowly.

"So you say now."

"And so you've little reason to believe," he added for her.

She cast him a sideways glance as she gritted her teeth in discomfort. The green grass of the English countryside, which had always looked so invitingly soft in the drawings of her books, was not, as it turned out, especially soft or inviting. "Your conduct toward me has altered considerably since yesterday."

"Indeed. The very reason I sought you out this morning, in fact." He steered her away from a rough patch of ground. "I wished to apologize for my behavior yesterday."

"Do you wish to apologize," she asked with skepticism, "or do you apologize?"

It was the most minor quibble of semantics, and one she felt no shame at all in making. She rather felt she deserved a proper apology.

"I apologize," he said in a clear, earnest voice. "I behaved badly and I am sorry for it."

He seemed sincere, but while his unexpected confession of remorse was welcome, what she couldn't understand was, "Why?"

"Beg your pardon?"

"Why are you sorry now, all of a sudden? What changed over the course of one night?"

"Perception," he offered. "A little time can effect a drastic change in perception . . . I can see by your expression you don't believe a word of it."

"A word here and there, certainly." Time could change a great many things, but she wasn't willing to accept that a single night had changed him. "But in this instance, I am uncertain of the sentiment."

"Would you allow me an explanation?"

"By all means." She rather felt she deserved that along with the apology. Perhaps a bit of groveling as well. His behavior really had been quite atrocious.

There was a brief pause before Max spoke. "I had not thought to see you again," he began at length. "I'd not realized I'd be seeing you again when I arrived at Caldwell yesterday. The news of your imminent arrival came as a considerable surprise."

"My arrival at Caldwell shocked you into behaving like an arse?"

"More or less," he replied with a slight shrug. "I said I had an explanation, not an excuse. If I had an excuse, I wouldn't need to be apologizing."

She considered that with pursed lips and silently conceded he had a fair point. "Do you always respond to surprise with anger and contempt?"

"Do you always respond to apologies with suspicion and criticism?"

She had no idea. The only other person she'd ever truly fought with was her mother, and the woman never apologized.

"I don't mean to be difficult." She reconsidered that. "Or perhaps I do. I daresay I've some call to be. Either way, I simply do not understand the why of it all. Why should seeing me again cause such an unpleasant reaction in you?"

"If you had asked me before last night, I'd have told you I was merely being protective of a friend. But the truth is, I used my affection for the Haverstons as an excuse to behave badly."

"Why did you want to behave badly at all?"

"Because . . . Our last meeting . . ." Looking uncomfortable, he rubbed a hand over the back of his neck and mumbled, "Never underestimate the awful power of wounded pride."

"Your pride?" What absurdity, she thought. "Why should *your* pride have been wounded?"

He stopped them both and dropped her arm as he turned to stare at her intently, his expression unreadable.

"What?" She demanded after a moment. "What is it?"

"I am trying to puzzle out if you're being deliberately mean or deliberately stupid."

"I beg your pardon?" She stiffened, inside and out. "I have never been either."

"Accidently stupid, then?"

"If this is how you issue apologies, I'll do without—"

"You refused to see me," he accused suddenly. He looked away, giving Anna the impression he was both angry and a little embarrassed. "You asked for a promise and then refused to see me."

"I . . . I don't understand. Last night? I retired early, and I'd no desire—"

"No, not last night," he bit off, still refusing to meet her eye. "At Anover House."

There was a moment of silence as she tried to wrap her head around his words. The moment didn't help. "I refused to see you at Anover House?"

"Yes, you . . ." Finally, his gaze came back to her. "Didn't you?"

"Just . . . Before? In London, you mean?" Of course in London, she thought with irritation. Was there a different Anover House? "You called on me?"

"I did. Repeatedly, in fact." He tilted his head, his hazel eyes studying her face. "You didn't know, did you?"

She shook her head. "I still don't understand. Did you call on me recently?"

"No. I came to see you a week or so after our meeting . . . As I said I would." The embarrassment and aggravation were gone from his features. In their stead was the light of dawning realization. "I was told you wished not to be disturbed, that you would not receive me. That wasn't the case, was it?"

She shook her head slowly, mutely.

He'd come? He'd called on her? A spark of excitement lit beneath her skin, but she was careful to keep it banked.

"Told by whom?" she asked, afraid she already knew the answer. There was really only one person it could have been.

"Your mother."

"Oh." A tight knot formed in her stomach. "Oh, I see."

She didn't see, not really. There was a swirling cloud of questions and fury and hope and she couldn't see much of anything past it. Why would her mother have done such a thing? No wonder he'd been less than eager to see her again.

He'd come. Just as he'd promised.

"There were letters as well," he told her.

"Letters," she repeated softly, stunned.

"A couple. May I presume you did not receive them?"

"I never saw them. I never heard . . ." She shook her head, feeling adrift. "You wrote to me. You came to see me."

"Yes." He tipped his head a little, studying her. "You truly had no idea?"

"No. None at all. I give you my word." She wished she had something better to offer. The word of a courtesan's daughter held little weight. Fortunately, in this case, it only had to hold more than the courtesan's.

He had to believe it was Madame who lied. He had to believe she'd not have treated him so callously.

"I believe you," he said.

Oh, thank heavens.

She offered a tentative smile. "And I believe you came as promised."

"Thank you."

For several long moments there was silence between them. Her smile wanted to waver, but she kept it firmly in place. What did she say now? What did they do?

"Would you have met with me?" he asked suddenly.

She hesitated in her response. Not because she was unsure of the answer, but because the question felt weighted. As if she might be admitting to something vastly more significant than *certainly I would have sat with you of a Saturday morning in my mother's parlor.*

"Yes," she said at last, though the answer was delivered

to her own feet. She'd never known such a strange mix of awkwardness and hope. "This is most uncomfortable."

"Is it? I find it . . ." He paused, considering, then landed on ". . . interesting."

That was certainly one word for it.

"I don't know what to say." She swallowed audibly. "I apologize for my mother's interference and any discomfort or—"

"Don't," he cut in gently. "If it wasn't your doing, then I don't want an apology from you."

What *did* he want from her? She may have found the courage to ask just that, but he spoke again before she could.

"I feel doubly foolish now, for my earlier behavior."

"I feel more inclined to forgive it."

"It isn't typical for me to be so ill-mannered," he assured her. "Well, yes, I suppose we both know it is. But I'm generally not so callous with it. I am sorry."

Anna considered whether or not she wished to accept the apology in full. She truly was more inclined to forgive him now that she understood the source of his animosity, but she hadn't fully made up her mind on the matter. Rejection was not an acceptable reason for treating a person poorly.

On the other hand, he appeared to have arrived at the same conclusion, apologizing to her whilst still under the impression that she had turned him away in London. That ought to count for something.

"Apology accepted," she said at last and prayed she wasn't making a terrible mistake.

He blew out a short breath of relief that Anna found most gratifying. "You're a patient and forgiving soul, Anna Rees."

"Am I?" Was she? She'd never been called so before, not even by Mrs. Culpepper, who was always quick to compliment. Her mother, who preferred to be quick with an insult, regularly accused her of being impatient, intolerant, and unfeeling. "You are the first to allege it."

"I find that difficult to believe," he countered, catching his hands behind his back. "Both times we have met, I have been inebriated with either drink or anger. And yet you are still willing to speak to me. Patient and forgiving."

"I'd not thought of it quite that way." Her lips twitched with amusement. "You have been uncommonly loutish in our encounters, haven't you?"

"A man does like to make a memorable first impression on a lady," he returned ruefully.

Her initial impression of him had been quite favorable, until her mother had ruined everything. And then, of course, he'd made everything worse. If only it was possible to go back and make everything right.

"Perhaps we might start again?" she suggested. It was never truly possible to start over, of course. One could no more erase the past than predict the future. But sometimes, a second chance could be had. Perhaps their meeting again, after so many years, was such a chance.

"I would like that."

"Well, then." Feeling better than she had in days, she dipped into a quick curtsy. "Lord Dane, I am delighted to make your acquaintance."

He returned the bow. "Miss Rees, the pleasure is entirely mine."

Anna held back an outright grin. Her spark of hope was fast growing into a small flame of cautious excitement. But there was one troubling matter left that she could not allow to pass without comment or clarification.

"Before we put all the disagreeableness behind us, might I ask you a question?"

"Am I going to like this question," Max asked warily, "or am I going to be apologizing again?"

"I'll not pretend to know what you will or will not like,

but there's no need to apologize a second time. Once was enough."

"Ask your question, then."

"Do you . . ." She stopped to find the right words. "Are you truly an amiable drunk?"

She couldn't possibly become friends with someone who viewed her as "less than," who thought she belonged to the class of "everyone," as he had applied the word the night before.

He winced, which was even more gratifying than seeing him relieved. "I feel like apologizing again."

"If it would help to clear your conscience, by all means, do so." Though it wasn't necessary, she was still amenable to a bit of groveling.

"I'm sorry. No, I don't . . . That is, I am not an amiable drunk . . . Well, I am, in truth. I'm quite good-natured when in my cups, in fact. But the implication made last night—"

She held up her hand. "I understood the implication, and I accept the apology."

"Excellent. Thank you." He let out a small puff of air, and his shoulders visibly relaxed. "Now then, I've a question for you. Are you truly Lucien and Gideon's half sister?"

"Yes, I am." And now that they were no longer at odds with each other, she no longer felt compelled to pretend she wasn't fazed by the sudden change in her circumstances. "I don't fault you for not believing it straight off. It is strange, as you said before. I can still scarce believe it myself. But I have the proof, if you'd like to see it—"

"I would."

"Oh." She blinked at that, felt the spark of hope dim a little. She'd only made the offer conversationally. "Right. Well."

Max had the decency to look a little sheepish. "Please understand, I am grateful for your forgiveness, of course, and happy to have peace between us. But the truth is, Miss Rees, I don't know you. Aside from your purported desire for a dog, and the fact that you've laid a claim on the Haverston family—a family to whom I owe a great deal—I know next to nothing about you."

She saw the sense in his argument and understood the reasoning behind it, but the words still pricked. After Mrs. Culpepper, Max probably knew more about her than any other person in her life. They were the only two people who knew of her dream to buy a country cottage. And he was the only one to know of her silly wish for a hound.

Which, now that she thought on it, was a sad state of affairs, indeed. She had no better claim to friendship outside of Mrs. Culpepper than a man with whom she'd spent such a nominal amount of time? And who had been ready to toss her bodily from Caldwell Manor only yesterday?

Surely she had more depth of character than what could be mined in the course of an evening. She did not begin and end with her dreams of a thousand pounds, a hound, and a home. She was vastly more complex, far more interesting than that. She had to be. The alternative was too depressing to entertain. Almost as depressing as never having known a friend who'd not been paid to keep her company. But that, at least, could be changed.

She had no intention of spending her visit defending herself to Max, but she could certainly spend her visit coming to know him and Engsly. She could at least try. There were a thousand reasons for why she might ultimately be unsuccessful—her lack of experience making friends being foremost in her mind—but that wasn't an acceptable excuse for not making the effort.

If she'd intended to be isolated and friendless for the rest of her life, she should have stayed at Anover House. And if showing Max the proof of her lineage would help create a foundation of trust between them—a necessary beginning to any friendship, surely—then she was willing to oblige.

She brushed her hand down her waist in a smoothing

manner. "The proof is in a contract, along with a journal and several correspondences between the late marquess and my mother. I presume Engsly's man of business still has the contract. You may ask to see it, if you like. I'll not oppose it."

"And the letters and journal?"

"I retain them, though Engsly's man has seen them and can verify the existence of the pertinent content. And no, you may not see them. There is much in them that is private."

"You wish to protect your mother?"

At the moment, she wished she could use the journal to beat her heartless mother about her scheming head.

"My mother is not the only person who would be adversely affected should the contents of her journal and letters be made public."

"I'm not going to make them public—"

"The answer is no, Lord Dane." It wasn't often that she felt compelled to put her foot down on a matter, and it was unfortunate that she had to do so with Max, so soon after determining that they might become friends, but there was no way around it. The journal and letters were filled with material she had no right to share.

Max's mouth turned down at the corners, but he nodded. "Fair enough. The contract will do. But tell me this— are the Haverstons counted amongst those who might be adversely affected?"

"The letters are from the late marquess to a woman who was not his wife," she pointed out. "If nothing else, it would be further insult to the late marchioness."

"I see," he said grimly. "Is there any chance I could convince you to destroy those letters?"

"Yes. I'll gladly do so at the first opportunity."

"Is immediately not an option?"

"They are proof of my parentage," she said by way of answer.

"And you need the proof to get the thousand pounds."

"Yes," she answered and lifted her chin. If he expected

her to apologize for the need to feed and house herself, he was in for quite a wait.

He bobbed his head. "Sensible."

"I . . . Yes." She'd not been expecting such ready agreement. "It is."

His lips twitched. "You were waiting for me to condemn you."

". . . Perhaps."

"As I said, we do not know each other well."

"No, we do not," she acknowledged. "Do you mean to stay on at Caldwell?"

"For a time," he replied.

It took all her courage and determination to meet his eyes. "Then we've time to know each other."

She'd issued exactly two invitations for friendship in her life, both of them to Max. God willing, this one would fare better than the last.

His smile was slow and perfect. "I do look forward to it."

This time, when he offered his elbow, Anna took it without suspicion or argument.

Chapter 8

$\mathcal{I}$n retrospect, it may have been wise for Anna to have put up a small argument because two minutes later, she stumbled when her foot met with a sharp rock and he immediately bent down, slipped an arm under her knees, and swung her up against his chest. Apparently without consideration as to whether or not she might appreciate the help.

She did not appreciate the help.

"Put me down," she demanded, even as her arms went around his neck to steady herself.

"So you can further injure yourself? Or trip, fall, grab at me in a blind panic, and injure us both?"

She sputtered at that bit of silliness. "I . . . Blind panic?"

"As I said, I don't know you all that well."

"Oh, this is ridiculous. If you would just—"

"If you continue to struggle," he told her casually, "I might well drop you."

"I highly doubt the fall would prove fatal."

"No." He shifted her weight in his arms. "Tremendously embarrassing, though."

She considered that. If he dropped her now and she wasn't able to get her feet under herself in time . . .

"Wise decision," Max murmured when she went perfectly still.

She wasn't certain it was wise, but it was preferable to being dropped on her backside. And, in truth, once she allowed herself to relax in his hold, she discovered that it wasn't an altogether unpleasant experience.

It reminded her of when she was little and, having fallen asleep in the library window seat or her favorite overstuffed chair, being scooped up by Mrs. Culpepper to be carried back to the nursery.

She'd felt warm and light in those moments, as if she'd been floating.

The rest was, of course, completely different. There had been unconditional love and security in Mrs. Culpepper's strong arms. Max's arms promised an entirely different kind of warmth. While she could admit that she found that promise as intriguing as she had the first night they'd met, she made the decision to put aside those feelings for now and concentrate on the simple, more manageable task of simply getting to know the man.

She could do that, she told herself. She wasn't her mother, to be guided blindly by passion. She could separate a carnal interest from an intellectual interest. They could be friends. With a mental nod of determination, she settled as comfortably as she might in Max's hold and studiously ignored the small voice in the back of her head that called her a liar and a fool.

Max shifted Anna in his arms and sidestepped an exposed root from a nearby walnut tree.

She felt good in his arms, a pleasant weight. At first.

After a solid ten minutes of walking and making polite small talk, however, the weight became less pleasant and more . . . weighty.

Her scent still teased him, roses and sugar biscuits, same as it had been in the nursery of Anover House. And the soft curves of her legs tempted his imagination toward all manner of ill-advised but delightful imagery. But nine stone was nine stone and the muscles in his arms began to protest the burden before too long. It was a fine reminder of the hidden costs of chivalry and the price of getting one's own way. It had, after all, been his idea to carry her back to the house.

With the slim remainder of his pride hanging in the balance, he ignored the strain in his arms and back and focused on the pleasurable details of holding Anna Rees— that teasing scent and those soft curves, and the amusing way she held herself stiff and still, pulling away from him as far as her confined situation allowed. To ease aching muscles—and, admittedly, to please himself—he shifted her in his arms, drawing her closer.

Her features remained utterly passive, but he could feel the tension in her body increase threefold. While he found her primness entertaining, he wasn't looking to make her miserably uncomfortable.

"Enjoying your first visit to the country?" he inquired in an effort to put her at her ease.

The question was so patently absurd under the circumstances that it immediately drew a laugh from her. The sound of it set his skin alight. He'd forgotten how much he'd liked that laugh.

"It has been . . ." She tilted her head, searching for the right word. "Enlightening."

It was the perfect word.

Four years he'd spent believing a lie. For four years, he'd thought the worst of her.

But Anna hadn't refused to see him. She'd not ignored his letters.

There was the possibility of her lying, of course, but he didn't believe it. There was too little to be gained by the subterfuge. She already had Engsly. She didn't need his good opinion.

She had it nonetheless.

You've been uncommonly loutish in our encounters.

He'd been a lout and more. Their first meeting at Anover House didn't trouble him overmuch. While he'd not count it amongst his finest hours, he was by no means ashamed of his behavior. It had been a good night and, if it hadn't been for Mrs. Wrayburn, would have made for one happy memory in the midst of misery. But most importantly, Anna hadn't complained. She'd begged his promise to return. She would have met with him again.

Without doubt, there was nothing wrong in what had passed between them at Anover House.

Yesterday, however . . .

Max was thoroughly ashamed of his behavior in the billiards room. More so when he held it up against Anna's in comparison. He'd thought she'd played him for a fool and he had treated her with derision and scorn. She'd thought he'd broken his promise and she'd remained perfectly polite . . . until he'd become a boor, but she could scarce be blamed for that.

It occurred to him as they reached the edge of the back lawn that Anna was, by far, a greater lady than he was a gentleman. He'd have liked to tell her so but feared it would sound disingenuous so soon after their row.

Forgiving and patient would have to do for now. They weren't, in his opinion, the defining characteristics of a lady, but they seemed to please her, and he couldn't ask for more.

Well, he could, and likely would in time. But for the duration of their walk—

"Oh, no," Anna gasped suddenly, jerking in his arms. "Set me down. Set me down this—"

"Easy." He tightened his grip. "I thought we'd been through this."

"They're watching. Set me—"

"Stop squirming. Who's watching?"

"Someone in the house, of course." She unwound an arm from his neck to point. "Didn't you see the curtains move?"

There were, at best guess, thirty sets of curtains visible from the back side of the house. "No. I confess I did not."

"Well, I did. Now—"

"What difference does it make if someone sees?"

"They'll talk."

His eyes widened in mock amazement. "Discuss the marquess's recently discovered and only just arrived half sister who is purported to be the daughter of *the* Mrs. Wrayburn? Never say."

She merely sniffed at that. "The fact that there is substantial talk already occurring is not a reason to encourage even more—"

"We're not encouraging anything. Unless it's a muscle spasm of crippling proportions," he amended. "You're not as light as you look."

There was a long, weighted pause before she responded. "Charming."

He wasn't concerned with charm so much as distraction. It was a good deal easier to carry the woman when she wasn't struggling. "At least you're not wearing one of your bejeweled gowns."

She was visibly taken aback by that comment. "I . . . What? I haven't any bejeweled gowns."

"The diamond dress?"

"The what?" she asked with a small, surprised laugh.

"The ball gown with the diamonds sewn into the sleeves." That gown had been all the talk for weeks.

"The . . ." A small line formed between her brows as

she searched her memory. "That light blue bit of nonsense with the cream ribbons along the hem?"

"If it had diamonds sewn into the sleeves, then yes, that one."

"What nonsense. They were paste, of course. Who told you they were diamonds?"

"I don't recall if I was told, exactly. It was simply assumed as the truth." He was confident it had been Mrs. Wrayburn who'd spread the rumor, but Max rather thought Anna had heard enough about her mother lying for one day.

"By everyone?" she asked.

"Was there a jeweler in attendance who was allowed a closer inspection?"

"No."

"Then yes, everyone."

She slumped a little in his arms. "Diamonds sewn into the sleeves. Good Lord, the demimonde is gullible. I wish I could have brought that gown along. I'd have worn it to Bond Street before leaving London and sold it to the first idiot who called it the diamond dress."

He sidestepped a muddy patch of ground. "Why couldn't you bring it along?"

"It's not mine. It's my mother's."

Mrs. Wrayburn was both taller and notably more ample in the bust than her daughter. "You shared gowns with your mother?"

"I suppose one might call it that. She had ball gowns made for me to wear but not to keep. She took them back."

"To reuse the material," he guessed.

"One would assume."

Clearly, she had her doubts. "But you—?"

She gave him a patronizing look. "Don't think I've not recognized your attempt at distraction, Lord Dane."

"Max," he encouraged. "And I wasn't attempting to distract you so much as occupying your mind until we reached the house."

"That is the very definition of distraction."

He bit the inside of his cheek to keep a straight face. "No, it's not."

"It . . ." She opened her mouth, closed it. "Yes, it is—"

"Not at all."

"How can you—?"

"Not the least bit alike."

Her eyes narrowed. "You're just being—"

"Care to put a wager on it?"

"You may stop now. I'll not ask you to set me down again." She looked up at the house. "Not much point to it now."

"None at all," he agreed. They'd already reached the steps of the back terrace.

"But you'll not be carrying me inside."

"Certainly not," he agreed, but only because opening the door with his hands full would be an exercise in physical comedy.

Instead, he climbed the steps and set her down in front of the door, keeping one hand at her waist longer than was strictly necessary. He hadn't intended to draw the moment out, he just couldn't seem to stop himself. He felt compelled to retain that simple connection with her, his hand one tantalizing inch above the gentle curve of her hip.

"Will you require assistance to your chambers?"

"I didn't require assistance to the house," she reminded him and took a step back, disconnecting from him entirely.

Because he wanted to reach for her again, he caught his hands behind his back. "You're welcome."

She accepted the lighthearted reprimand with good grace. "I thank you for coming to my aide."

"It was my pleasure." His arms would be sore for it tomorrow.

"Well." Her eyes shifted to the door and back. "I should . . ."

"You've plans for the remainder of the day?" he asked quickly. He didn't want her to leave. Not quite yet.

"To be honest, Lord Dane—"

"Max," he encouraged again. "Please."

"Max, then," she agreed with a smile. "To be honest, I'd planned on being well on my way to Mrs. Culpepper's sister. It was not my original intention to stay on at Caldwell. I'd thought . . . Well . . ."

"You thought you'd take your thousand pounds and go."

She squared her shoulders defensively. "I had assumed that would be the marquess's preference."

"And I assumed that would be your assumption. I meant no offense."

"I . . ." She blew out a small breath. "It will take some effort, this coming to know each other."

"It's not the knowing, I think. It's the trusting."

And trust, once lost, even through no—or, in his case, partial—fault of one's own, could be difficult to regain. For reasons he wasn't yet ready to look at too closely, Max wanted that trust back, for both of them. But it was going to have to wait a little longer.

"So you've no plans . . ." he prompted.

"I believe I shall keep my companion company for the morning and tend to my wounds, grievous as they are. And you?"

"I'm for Codridgeton," he lied. "With any luck, I'll conclude my business before dinner."

"Well then . . ." Her eyes traveled back to the door. "Until this evening, I suppose."

"This evening," he agreed, unable to think of another way to stall her departure. Or his.

He watched her walk through the door, then spun about and headed straight to the stables. Only, he wasn't for Codridgeton. He was for London, to visit with Engsly's man.

Max knew that, generally speaking, lying wasn't the

most effective means by which to regain trust. But now and again, telling the truth was equally unhelpful. He believed Anna in so far as *she* knew herself to be the daughter of the late marquess. But with the only evidence having originated from the something-less-than-believable Mrs. Wrayburn, he remained unconvinced.

Journals could be fabricated. Letters and contracts might be forged. One would hope Lucien's man would recognize when he'd been presented with a fake, but it was always better to ensure for oneself.

Why Mrs. Wrayburn would set up such a ruse, Max couldn't begin to guess. There were no rumors of financial instability, no indications that the woman was interested in attaching herself to the respectable set. But after what he'd learned today, he'd not rule out pure spleen as a motive.

Whatever Mrs. Wrayburn's rationale, if the contract was false, he'd find a way to extract Anna from the mess. It was the least he could do. And Engsly would help. He'd not blame the daughter for the sins of the mother.

If the contract appeared valid, well then, he'd feel like an arse . . . or more of an arse, to be precise. But better he be uncomfortable with having done too much than someone else be miserable because he'd failed to do enough. He'd experienced the repercussions of the latter once before. He'd not make the same mistake again.

Chapter 9

❦

*A*nna kept to the impromptu plan she'd given Max on the terrace. She changed out of her muddy gown and into a slighted dated but clean dress of ivory muslin with eyelet trim. Then she saw to the care of her blisters and went to check on Mrs. Culpepper. She found her friend awake, dressed, and eager for both company and a spot of breakfast.

Happy to see to both, Anna had trays brought up to the room. While they worked their way through a well-prepared meal of eggs and fish, Anna explained the changes in their circumstances. To Anna's great relief, Mrs. Culpepper had already ascertained for herself what was going on and took the news of their unexpected stay at Caldwell quite well. She was, she professed, in no hurry to be inside that dreadful carriage once more.

Mrs. Culpepper then proceeded to ask a seemingly endless number of questions about Engsly, and Anna spent the next hour doing her best to answer them all. But not once did Mrs. Culpepper mention Max, leaving Anna to believe that no one had yet mentioned Lord Dane to her. Not eager to be the first, Anna said nothing of him during their meal and conversation, nor afterward when they fell into the easy midmorning habit of settling in with their books of choice.

As familiar and comforting as the routine was, it failed to put Anna in a settled state. She had difficulty concentrating on anything but her morning walk with Max. Her mind went back to certain moments, over and over again. A look here, a touch there. An eighth-to-quarter mile in his arms. It was all terribly exciting. More so, no doubt, because it was a kind of excitement of which she had very little past experience.

She was interested in a man. It was likely irrational and ill-advised given their history, but there it was . . . She still rather liked Max Dane. And it felt marvelous. There were, after all, many kinds of adventure. This was but one.

One highly distracting adventure, she mused after reading the same paragraph for the third time and realizing she would need to read it a fourth.

Giving up, Anna traded her book for her embroidery, but as the day stretched on, she found herself no more engaged by her sampler than she had been by her story. She stuck herself twice, both times a direct result of her looking out the window to the front drive rather than at her work.

She knew Max had claimed he'd not be back until evening, but one could never be entirely certain of these things. The village wasn't far, and if his business was completed very quickly, then . . . then he would return early and she would still be keeping company with her friend. What difference did it make where the man was just now?

In a few hours, of course, it would make all the difference, but—

"If it's not too much trouble, dear, might you hand me my tea?"

Pulled from her musings, Anna looked to where Mrs. Culpepper sat in a chair by the window, a cream shawl about her shoulders and her book of poetry in her hands.

"You are looking much improved," she commented, reaching over to give Mrs. Culpepper the cup. Her friend's gray coloring had been replaced with a healthier, albeit still pale, pink.

"As are you," Mrs. Culpepper commented.

Anna frowned, confused. "I wasn't ill."

"Dread can lend an unfortunate pallor." Mrs. Culpepper took a sip and wrinkled her nose a little at what had to be very cold tea. "I trust you've stopped fearing Lord Engsly might set upon you with daggers at any moment?"

"It wasn't daggers," she returned tartly. "It was abduction and forced exile to a distant land."

"Close enough." She waggled a long finger at Anna. "Never say I don't know my charge."

"I never have."

Mrs. Culpepper set aside her drink. "Then you'll not be surprised when I inquire as to what has you out of sorts now?"

"I'm not—"

"You have been shifting in your seat," Mrs. Culpepper cut in and sniffed. "You know how I feel about shifting."

On the continuum of offensive behaviors, it fell somewhere between slouching and chewing with one's mouth open.

Mrs. Culpepper leveled a hard stare down the considerable length of her nose. "Out with it, child."

Anna scarcely refrained from rolling her eyes. "You can't intimidate me with that look anymore. I'm not twelve."

Mrs. Culpepper raised the stakes with the disapproving lift of one eyebrow. The sight of it made Anna want to laugh . . . and immediately do as she was told. It was a strange thing to be friends with one's former governess.

"Lord Dane is here," she admitted. Not because she'd

been pushed into it, but because the idea that Max's presence could be kept secret indefinitely was ludicrous.

"Is he?" Mrs. Culpepper leaned forward in her seat, her eyes wide. "Is he really? And you've spoken with him?"

"Yes." Anna frowned down at her sampler. "Things were a bit strained between us initially."

"Well, such a meeting is bound to be uncomfortable," Mrs. Culpepper returned, sitting up straight once more. The woman was never out of perfect posture for long. "You weren't *too* hard on the man, I hope?"

"Me?" Anna gaped at her friend. "*I* was the picture of decorum."

Mrs. Culpepper inclined her head in a mixture of apology and loyalty. "Of course you were, dear."

"*He* was exceedingly rude. He all but insisted I leave Caldwell."

"Did he, indeed?" Mrs. Culpepper sat even straighter and harrumphed. "Presumptuous devil."

"He was, quite," Anna agreed, feeling sufficiently mollified. "Fortunately, he has since apologized."

"I should certainly hope so. Did he provide an explanation for his abysmal behavior?"

"He was nurturing something of a grudge."

"Against you?" Mrs. Culpepper scoffed indignantly. "Outrageous."

"Not entirely," Anna admitted. "Though your defense is much appreciated. He says he called on me at Anover House not long after we met. Repeatedly. Mother sent him away, saying I wanted naught to do with him."

"Oh, good heavens." Mrs. Culpepper lifted her hand to her heart. "Oh, that *dratted* woman. I knew she could be petty and spiteful, but such malice . . . I'd never have guessed—" She blinked and some of the color she'd regained drained away. "You know I'd nothing to do with that. You must know—"

"Yes, of course." The idea of Mrs. Culpepper conspiring against her was preposterous. She was the only person on earth Anna had ever been completely certain of, the only person who'd never broken her trust. "The thought never occurred."

Mrs. Culpepper dropped her hand. "I ought to have taken you from that house years ago."

"This is *not* your doing," Anna argued. "The fault lies with Madame and Madame alone."

"She'd not have been able to do it alone."

"Very well, the fault lies with Madame and whichever maid or footman, likely gone on to other employment by now, aided in the deceit. It makes very little difference now."

It appeared to make some difference to Mrs. Culpepper. She pinched her lips tight, then grumbled, "I bet it was that Bridget Harbeck. She had a conniving air about her."

Anna couldn't begin to imagine what constituted a conniving air, but she knew an unhappy air when she saw it. Determined to see her friend's good humor and color returned, Anna swallowed her pride and set about drawing out a smile.

"I ran into a bit of trouble on my walk this morning," she said conversationally. "Nothing serious. Acquired a blister or two."

"I've a balm for that."

As Mrs. Culpepper had a balm for everything, Anna didn't see the need for comment. Instead, she paused a moment for dramatic effect and then . . .

"I came upon Lord Dane on my return. He insisted on carrying me back to the house."

"He . . . ?" Mrs. Culpepper's eyes went even wider than they had before. "Carried you? All the way to the house?"

All the way might have been ten yards for all Mrs. Culpepper knew, but Anna didn't see the point in spoiling her fun.

"All the way."

"Oh." Mrs. Culpepper let out a long, satisfied sigh. "Oh, that is *terrifically* romantic."

Anna smirked and leaned over to pat her friend's hand. "Never say I don't know my governess."

*A*nna kept Mrs. Culpepper company, reading and talk-ing, until the older woman professed a need for a lie-down. Abandoning the pretense that embroidery was holding her interest, Anna helped her friend become com-fortable, then headed downstairs to further investigate the house.

There was much she'd not yet seen, and if she was going to be at Caldwell Manor for days, she ought to know her way around. And if a particular gentleman should have returned early from the village, and if she should run into said gentleman, well . . .

She ran into Lord Engsly, who, obviously, was not the gentleman she'd had in mind. But she greeted him, and his offer to guide her down the hall of family portraits, with a smile.

She kept that smile firmly in place as he led her to their destination, even though being in his company still made her a little uneasy. This is what she wanted, she reminded herself, a chance to know her brother, and for her brother to know her. Spending time together was the only way she'd ever learn how *not* to be uneasy, and the only way he might learn to see her as something other than the illegitimate half sister to whom he'd promised a thousand pounds.

And it wasn't such a difficult lesson to endure, she admit-ted after a time. In fact, she found the experience rather enjoyable. It was fascinating, walking down the long, wide hall, seeing the faces of her ancestors for the first time— great-great-grandfathers and -grandmothers, long-dead aunts and uncles and cousins. She'd never seen so much as a miniature of her mother's parents; now suddenly she was surrounded by the images of family.

At the end of the hall, they came at last to the portrait of the late marquess, their father. Anna studied the painting with a keen eye, but saw no obvious similarities between her and the white-haired gentleman staring at her through cool blue eyes. Then again, she saw no obvious likeness between the late and current marquess either.

"The painting was commissioned five years before his death," Engsly told her. "He detested it. He accused the artist of adding ten years to his life and refused to pay. Gideon and I had to settle the account in secret."

"And yet he chose to hang it in the hall?" The man was either a cheat or exceedingly odd.

"No, I chose to hang it in the hall after his passing. It's an accurate portrait." His lips curved in a small smile. "And I wanted something for my money."

Anna had the feeling he wanted to poke at the old marquess, but she kept the observation to herself.

Engsly turned his attention from the portrait to look at her. "What do you know of him?"

"Very little," she admitted. "My mother said only that he had blue eyes."

"So he did." Engsly agreed, then pointed at the portrait of an earlier marquess they'd already passed. "You have our grandfather's eyes."

"Do I?" She made a second, closer inspection of the middle-aged man in the powdered wig and pink velvet coat with elaborate gold trim. There, beneath the scowling brow was a set of almond-shaped gray eyes much like her own. Well, she thought, with some amusement, the mystery had been solved.

"Handsome man," Anna declared and was gratified when Engsly laughed. "And whose eyes do you have? Not our father's or our grandfather's."

He gestured at the portrait of a woman wearing a white

gown in the classical style popular fifteen years earlier. "Gideon and I took after our mother in appearance."

Anna stepped closer to the painting. So this was the marchioness. Lady Engsly had beautiful black hair and eyes, and a pretty, quirked little smile that put Anna to mind of the *Mona Lisa*. Only friendlier. She was rather like Caldwell Manor, Anna mused. One knew one ought to be intimidated by the presence of such grandeur, but she was just so pretty. Perhaps it was she who'd had the shutters painted and the flowers planted.

"She's lovely," Anna murmured, then winced inwardly. Lovely was not the appropriate word to have used. Beautiful, exquisite—those were the adjectives one employed when referring to a marchioness. Particularly when one was speaking to her son.

Fortunately, Engsly appeared to take no offense.

"She was a lovely woman," he said gruffly, his eyes fixed on the portrait.

Anna heard love there, and a deep respect. Suddenly, she felt ill at ease again. No matter how welcoming he was, some part of Engsly had to resent the insult her very existence presented to the marchioness. Surely he wasn't wholly comfortable with proof of his father's faithlessness running about his mother's home.

She sidled away from the marchioness's portrait. This business of coming to know Engsly would need to be done slowly, she realized, and with great care. "I should look in on Mrs. Culpepper."

"Hmm?" Engsly turned to her, his face clearing. "Oh, yes, of course. I trust she is recovering satisfactorily?"

"She is quite nearly herself again."

"Excellent. Excellent. Well then . . ." He performed a quick bow. "Then I shall see you both at dinner."

Anna felt a knot form in her belly as she curtsied.

"We are quite looking forward to it," she chimed and

managed a credible smile until she turned about and walked away.

She was not looking forward to it.

The first time Mrs. Culpepper, Lord Engsly, and Max Dane gathered in the same room was going to be an unnerving event no matter the circumstances, but for it to occur at a formal dinner made Anna all the more anxious.

She'd never attended a formal dinner in her life. Oh, she knew the rules of etiquette required to participate as a dinner guest. Mrs. Culpepper had not neglected those lessons. But Anna had never been given the opportunity to use the skills, only practice them. She always took her meals with Mrs. Culpepper in the sitting room off her chambers.

Anna took a steadying breath and straightened her shoulders. There was no call to be worried, and there was every reason to be enthusiastic. Her very first formal dinner, and it wasn't at Anover House. This was wonderful, exciting . . . an adventure.

That's what she told herself as she reached her chambers, and throughout the afternoon and early evening as she kept Mrs. Culpepper company whilst training one eye and ear on the front drive. It's what she told herself as she dressed in her best gown of gold silk and headed downstairs for dinner, and it was what she repeated one last time when she saw Max, dusty and windblown, step in the front door just as she and Mrs. Culpepper reached the bottom of the stairs.

This was all but a grand adventure.

Max glanced up, caught her eye, and smiled. "Miss Rees."

Aware of Mrs. Culpepper's assessing gaze, Anna kept her shoulder's square and her voice steady. "Lord Dane, I am glad to see you returned safely. May I present my companion, Mrs. Culpepper? Mrs. Culpepper, Lord Dane."

She watched Max carefully for any sign of surprise or annoyance at having been introduced to a woman some might consider but one step removed from staff. But she saw only a gentleman greeting a lady with the polite regard he might afford any other guest. He expressed pleasure at their meeting, asked after her recovery from the journey, then begged leave to wash the dust of the road off before dinner.

Anna felt a ridiculous spark of pleasure and pride. Though she doubted he knew it, Max could not have done more to win Mrs. Culpepper's approval. The woman disliked presumed familiarity nearly as much as she did overt snobbery. Both were, in her opinion, highly disrespectful and therefore the height of poor manners.

Anna wasn't at all surprised when Mrs. Culpepper leaned down and whispered, "The boy has some potential," after Max had left.

But she was pleased, and with her confidence buoyed by the easy interaction, she found the first half hour of dinner a perfectly agreeable experience.

Max joined them only a few minutes late, changed and tidied, which Anna knew had been necessary, but thought was something of a pity. He'd looked quite dashing in his riding attire, with his cravat askew and his hair tousled about his handsome face.

Anna snuck a look over her bowl of pea soup and decided it was no hardship to see the man in his dinner attire either.

He looked up, met her eyes, and smiled, and she quickly looked away, embarrassed to have been caught watching him. Mrs. Culpepper and Engsly didn't appear to have noticed, but Anna resolved to remain focused on them for the rest of the meal, just to be safe.

Engsly led a light conversation throughout the meal, asking innocuous questions of Anna and Mrs. Culpepper, listening respectfully to their responses, adding a response here and there. Though it was hardly what she might call scintillating conversation, Anna was grateful for the ease of it. Her nerves diminished with each minute that passed without incident, and she began to grow confident that the meal would go off, if not splendidly, at least reasonably well.

Until Engsly asked, "Do you enjoy residing in London?"

"Yes, quite," she replied, mostly because it seemed the polite thing to say.

She was more than a little surprised when Max smiled slyly over the rim of the wine goblet he held.

"Is that the truth of it?" he asked. "And is there an aspect of town life for which you have a particular fondness? A favorite place in the city, perhaps?"

No sign of irritation was allowed to reach her face. But in her mind's eye she was glowering mightily at him and walking around the table so that she might deliver a swift kick to his shins. The blasted man knew damn well how rarely she left Anover House.

She only wished she knew if he was indulging in a spot of harmless teasing, or he had some other aim. Again her lack of experience put her at a disadvantage, but she'd be damned before she let her discomfort show. If he was teasing, then she'd only look a fool for becoming upset. If he wasn't teasing, she'd express her dissatisfaction with him in private.

She reached for her wineglass with a steady hand. "I confess, there is no place I feel more at ease than in the comfort of my home's own library. I have a great love for the written word."

Max's lips twitched while Engsly smiled broadly.

"Then we share a common interest," the marquess said. "Have you explored Caldwell's library?"

"No, I've not yet had the pleasure."

"After dinner, then. I think it will please you."

*P*leased, as it happened, did not begin to describe how Anna felt upon entering the library after dinner. She was astounded, enthralled. Even the fact that Max had declined to join them could not dampen her delight.

The Caldwell Manor library was the stuff of dreams . . . provided one's dreams were very grand indeed. It was simply enormous, its selection of reading material seemingly infinite.

All Anna could do was stand in the center of the enormous two-storied room and do her best not to gape. She was surrounded by books, shelf after shelf of them, more than a person could take in with a single glance, more than any one person could hope to read in a lifetime.

Next to her, Mrs. Culpepper murmured, "My heavens, what might we have accomplished with a library such as this at our disposal."

Anna nodded wordlessly. There looked to be books on every conceivable topic. At Anover House, Mrs. Culpepper had been forced to tailor Anna's education around the materials already made available in the large, but not particularly well-stocked library. As a result, Anna was poorly versed in subjects such as mathematics and British history between the fifteenth and seventeenth centuries. Alternatively, she had a very thorough understanding of geography and a phenomenal grasp of sixteenth-century Italian architecture.

She'd known at the time that much of the information she was acquiring would likely never be of use to her or anyone else. But she did so love the process of learning, of taking in the contents of a book and making them her own.

What a joy it would be to study here—she could spend weeks, months, even years and still learn something new every day.

Oh, how she *adored* this library. She felt her face breaking into a wide grin but hastily assumed a more appropriate expression. She might feel like an urchin in a sweet shop, but she would not embarrass Mrs. Culpepper or herself by acting the part.

As Mrs. Culpepper meandered off to inspect the cases at the far end of the room, Engsly gripped his hands behind his back and asked Anna, "Is there something in particular you might like? A favorite author or subject?"

All of them. Everything. "I've too many to name. This is . . . this is wondrous, my lord. I don't know where to begin."

"You might begin by addressing me by my given name and allowing me the same courtesy. We are family, after all."

The invitation drew Anna's attention away from the books. "Are you certain—?"

" 'My lord' is too formal for family, and Engsly was our father," he said by way of explanation. "I prefer Lucien."

Most people went the whole of their lives without being invited to address a peer of the realm by his given name. This was her second invitation in a single day. Anna decided to take it as a sign she was comporting herself reasonably well at Caldwell.

"Lucien, then," she agreed. "I'd be honored if you would call me Anna."

"Excellent." He bobbed his head, appearing most pleased with the development. "Excellent. Well . . . allow me to show you around a bit."

As fascinating as the tour of her family portraits had been, it could not compare to the thrill of being escorted about such a tremendous library. Lucien guided her in a loop around the room, showing her where to find particular subjects and authors, pointing out some of his favorite tomes.

"You're welcome to any book at any time, of course. Mrs. Webster has the keys to all the locked cases, if you'd like a closer look at anything inside."

"Truly?" Some of the cases were locked for good reason. The books behind the glass were extremely old manuscripts, beautifully handwritten works that were as fragile as they were valuable. She desperately wanted a closer look at them. "Some of them are irreplaceable." Likely all of them. "If you'd really rather—"

"I'll have Mrs. Webster give you any necessary keys."

Anna wasn't sure what to say to such an offer. She wasn't certain how she felt. It was such an incredible show of trust. The only other person to have shown that sort of confidence in her was Mrs. Culpepper.

"If I've made you uncomfortable," Lucien said in her ensuing silence. "I apologize."

"No, no," she was quick to assure him. "You've not made me uncomfortable at all." If he could trust her with his priceless manuscripts just to please her, she could damn well lie to please him. "I'm simply overwhelmed by the offer. It's exceedingly generous of you. Thank you."

"My pleasure, Now, if that's all settled, I'll leave you to continue your exploration of the library in peace." He bowed, turned to leave, then turned about again, looking slightly less sure of himself. "I hope . . . That is, I *very* much hope you will be comfortable here."

"I am certain I shall be." She wasn't at all certain. But in that very moment, standing amongst the books while Lucien smiled at her, she believed in the possibility of happiness at Caldwell Manor, and that was enough.

As Lucien bowed again and took his leave, Mrs. Culpepper came to stand beside Anna. "The marquess is leaving already? He's quite skilled at that."

"At leaving?" Anna looked to her friend, confused. "Does that require a particular skill set?"

"I should think our long overdue escape from Anover House should answer that for you, but what I meant was that he has a particular knack for knowing when it is best to be about, and when to give a body a bit of space. I think I may approve of him as well."

"He all but insisted we stay here." If that wasn't indicative of pressing company on someone, Anna didn't know what was.

"No one's perfect, dear, and he's not been hovering about you, has he?"

"No," Anna admitted.

Mrs. Culpepper nodded and continued to stare at the door through which Engsly had exited. "He shows good sense," she murmured.

Anna could all but hear the wheels turning in her friend's head. "What are you about?"

"Hmm? Oh, nothing of consequence, I was merely contemplating the happy prospect of an early bed. This evening has quite exhausted me."

Anna didn't believe it for a moment but arguing the matter would get her nowhere. When Mrs. Culpepper wished to remain silent on a subject, there was no convincing her otherwise.

"Would you like me to accompany you?"

"No, no. Stay here and enjoy yourself." Mrs. Culpepper gave her a peck on the cheek. "But don't wait too long to find your own bed, dear. This will still be here tomorrow. No reason to see it again through shadowed eyes. It's most unattractive."

Anna looked about her and sighed. "I can promise nothing."

Chapter 10

❧

Max watched Anna wander from shelf to shelf in the library, her fingers occasionally reaching out to brush the spine of a book, her expression one of complete engrossment—which explained why she'd still not noticed his presence, a solid five minutes after his arrival.

He'd walked in expecting to find Lucien, Anna, and Mrs. Culpepper. What he'd found was Anna, completely alone.

A gentleman would have quietly slipped back out again.

He'd made himself comfortable instead, leaning a shoulder against a bookshelf and folding his arms over his chest. And as he waited for her to notice him, he watched her.

It was a rare thing to see another person in a completely unguarded moment. He'd wager it was rarer yet to see Anna Rees in such a moment. The woman was as closed as a fortress. And yet here she was, exploring the Caldwell library in unabashed wonder and delight. She drew closer, not quite near enough to reach, but he caught a faint hint of her scent, or thought he did. And when she tilted her head to read the spine of a particular tome, he could see the candle-light bring out strands of dark copper in her hair.

She laughed softly to herself. The sound, low and smooth, sent shivers along his skin, just as it had four years ago at Anover House, and just as it had that morning in the open fields.

God, there was just *something* about the way the woman laughed. Made a man want to do all manner of things, most of them ill-advised, just to hear the sound again.

"Oh, to have a library such as this," she murmured, and he grinned. He liked knowing she was the sort of woman who laughed and murmured to herself.

"Is that really what you want?" he asked softly.

Anna started and spun around. And then, just like that, the Ice Maiden returned. Her expression became closed, her eyes shuttered. The transformation was so swift and so complete, it left Max wondering if she was fully aware of the change, or if it had become automatic to her. The latter possibility sat poorly with him for a multitude of reasons.

"Lord Dane." She smiled politely. "I'd not realized you were in here."

"Only just arrived," he lied.

"Oh." Her gaze danced around him, not quite meeting his own. "I thought you'd retired for the evening."

He shook his head. "Needed to look in on a horse, is all. Didn't you tell me once that your dream is to have a small cottage of your own?"

"It is," she said, a small furrow of confusion forming across her brow.

"You couldn't house even a fraction of a collection like this in a small cottage," he pointed out.

"I don't plan on taking any part of this collection."

"I meant you can't have a library." And clearly at least part of her dream also included books. The joy he'd witnessed just now had not been an act.

"Certainly, I can. Nothing like this, of course," she

conceded with a graceful wave of her hand at their surroundings, "but you'd be surprised how many books can be
fit into a small room. Shelves can be built in to the most
awkward of spaces. There's not a blank space of wall in my
chambers at Anover House."

He wasn't ashamed to admit that he'd pictured Anna
Rees in her chambers a time or two—or several dozen—
directly after they'd met. The fantasies had been perfectly
natural, highly diverting, and utterly devoid of book-
covered walls. Mostly they'd involved Anna in her prim
little night rail and wrap, and a bed of unlikely proportions.
They'd been great fun, those fantasies.

"Anover House has a respectable library," he commented
as she stepped closer to a bookshelf to inspect its contents.
"Why create a separate one?"

She glanced over her shoulder, appearing mildly amused
by the question. "Have you been in the library at Anover
House?"

"Yes, many times."

"Allow me to rephrase," she said dryly. "Have you been
in the library at Anover House for the purpose of perusing
the contents of its shelves?"

He thought back. There had been a clandestine meeting with Mrs. Pratt on his second or third visit to Anover
House. Then there'd been the evening when the card room
had grown overcrowded and the overflow had taken up
residence in the library. There had been a pleasant, if dis-
appointingly innocent, interlude with Mrs. Stoddington,
several instances of poking his head inside the room in
search of someone or other, and finally that fateful side trip
for the amber mystery drink the night he'd met Anna.

"No," he was able to say at last. "I don't believe I have."

"Anover has a library of respectable size, but its selection is less than ideal." She chose a book from the shelf
before her. "Besides, what's there belongs to my mother."

He watched the subtle movement of her eyes as she

opened the cover and looked over the first page. "And the books in your chambers are yours?"

"Yes, they were."

"Were?"

"Hmm?" She looked up and blinked. "Oh, *are.* They are." She gave him a sheepish smile. "I beg your pardon. I was distracted."

He stepped closer, took a quick peek at the book she was holding, and smirked. She wasn't distracted, she was playing coy by pretending a divided attention. "It's in Russian, Miss Rees."

To his surprise, she returned his smirk and patronizing tone in equal measure. "Ancient Greek, Lord Dane."

"I—" A second look told him the letters were, indeed, Greek and not Cyrillic. Clearly, he needed to spend more time in his own library. "So it is," he conceded, amused by his misplaced smugness and her cheek. "I beg your pardon. You can read ancient Greek?"

"Perfectly," she replied. "Now there's something else you know about me."

"There certainly is. How did you learn it?" *Why* had she learned it? It couldn't have been done voluntarily. No one in their right mind studied ancient Greek voluntarily. It was an obligatory hell reserved solely for schoolboys and historians.

"Books, of course. I learned all my languages from books."

All? "How many comprises all?"

Her eyes narrowed and looked to the ceiling, and he realized with astonishment that she was counting.

"Eight," she said after a moment. "Including English."

"Eight?" Good God, and he'd thought himself well educated knowing three.

"Mrs. Culpepper says I have a talent for learning language." Her lips curved in a self-depreciating smile. "Mostly, I've had time."

"Which languages?"

"French, German, Italian, Russian, Latin, and Greek."

"That's seven with English."

"Oh, ancient Greek and modern Greek."

"Impressive." And, for some reason, decidedly alluring. He had the strangest urge to ask her to say something to him in French. To stifle it, he spoke in Italian.

"Non tutti quelli che hanno lettere sono savi."

Anna's forehead wrinkled in concentration. "Not all . . . letters . . . something." She shook her head. "What does that mean?"

"I thought you spoke Italian."

"I can read it without trouble, but I must speak it slowly."

Because she'd learned it from books, he realized. Eight languages, learned entirely through books. It was an astounding achievement. "It's an old proverb. It means not everyone who is educated is wise, though that's not a strict translation." He smiled at her disgruntled expression. "Have you heard Italian spoken by someone else before?"

"A passing phrase here and there. Along with what Mrs. Culpepper managed in my studies. She's no more fluent than I." She closed her book and looked at him hopefully. "Will you say something else?"

"Vorrei poterti baciare," he said without thinking.

Anna bit her lip thoughtfully. "I . . . would like . . . something?"

I wish I could kiss you.

"Not quite," he told her and counted himself damned lucky that she'd not recognized the words. He hadn't meant to say them. "Can you speak any of the languages?" he asked, hoping to distract her.

"Yes, French and, to a lesser degree, German. I was fortunate to have Mrs. Culpepper for a governess." She stepped closer to him, eager. "Tell me what it meant."

"No." He shook his head. "I don't think I will as yet."

"Why not?"

Because not everything a man is thinking ought to trip off his tongue. "I am mad with power."

"Suit yourself," she replied and hugged her book to her chest. "I'll not beg."

"Certain of that?"

"Yes, quite."

He shook his head in playful disappointment. "Killjoy."

"So my mother has often accused."

That wasn't what he wanted to hear. "If this new friendship is going to work, you'll need to refrain from drawing comparisons between me and your mother."

Her lips twitched as she nodded. "Fair enough."

"Why didn't she raise you elsewhere?" he asked, hoping to draw her completely away from the matter of Italian and kissing. "Forgive my bluntness, but if the two of you were not close, why did you remain in the house?"

"Madame liked having a daughter about," she explained with a small shrug. "Someone to put in diamond dresses and show off to her friends."

Like a living doll, he thought, disgusted. "And yet she had no reservations about sending you here for your inheritance?"

There was a marked pause before she answered. "It is possible she did."

"She tried to stop you?"

"No. I wasn't being coy in saying it was possible, I meant it was possible but I've no way of knowing for certain. I didn't speak with her before leaving."

"She doesn't know you're here? Did you sneak out of Anover House?"

"Of course not. I'd never be so heartless . . . I left a note."

"A *note*?"

"You may wish to temper your criticism of me. She was taking laudanum for her injury before I left. Holding a rational discussion on the matter was out of the question."

"And if it hadn't been?"

"I . . ." She pressed her lips together a beat before answering. "I would have snuck out and left the note. She is often unreasonable, even irrational."

He added this bit of information to everything else he had learned of Mrs. Wrayburn in the past four-and-twenty hours. "Well, I am relieved I decided against paying her a visit today."

"You thought to go to London?"

"No, I went to London," he admitted, surprising himself. He'd no intention of telling her that, but he found he had no taste for continuing the lie about having gone into the village.

"I see." She tilted her head, her expression shrewd. "And did the contract meet with your approval or your expectations?"

"Both, as pertains to you. The first as pertains to your mother. I assumed she gave you the contract," he explained. "I suspected she might be lying to us all."

"Ah." She nodded thoughtfully. "Well, your trip makes sense, then. I daresay, I'd do the same in your place. But, no. Mrs. Culpepper and I . . . er . . . discovered it."

"Discovered," he repeated, amused. "I know what that means. You're not angry that I went to London?"

"When you said you were going to the village? No, not especially. Your reasons were sound. And you've told me now, haven't you?"

"I have." And he hoped she was telling the truth about not being upset. There were too many misunderstandings between them already. "I should have told you my intentions this morning."

"Perhaps," she allowed. "But our peace is new. We're bound to have a misstep or two, and I like that you've erred first. You're now obligated to forgive me when I make a mistake."

"Does Miss Anna Rees make mistakes?"

"They say there is a first time for everything."

Her willingness to make jests erased any concerns he had that she might secretly be harboring a little resentment. "You're truly not upset," he said, a bit awed.

"You were being protective of your friends," she replied. "There is nothing wrong in that."

"I am sometimes overly protective of Lucien and Gideon," he admitted.

"And why might that be?"

"Another time," he evaded. He wasn't opposed to telling her his history with the family, but he wasn't interested in telling it tonight. He wanted to learn more about her. "So, you found paperwork you were not meant to find and you left home without permission or even advance notice. Am I right in guessing that this is an escape from your mother?"

"Her world," Anna clarified. "Anover House, the demimonde. It is an escape from all of it."

"A world is greater than one person and one place. The demimonde has more to offer than what goes on at Anover House."

She looked decidedly unconvinced. "I assure you, if the demimonde offers it, it goes on at Anover House."

He wondered if she was jesting, or if she was naïve enough to believe it. Anover House, while very much a den of considerable infamy, was by no means the destination of choice for either the most depraved individuals of the demimonde, or the most interesting. Present company excluded, naturally. "Would you say all of those of the ton are the same?"

"I'd say near enough that I don't want anything to do with them either."

"You're stubborn in your views."

"Determined in my path," she countered.

It bothered him to hear it. The demimonde was his

world of choice, the ton his world of birth. To know she was looking to be rid of both made him nervous, and a little defensive.

On the other hand, it gave him greater insight into her determination to gain a thousand pounds from Lucien. She didn't merely want the money or feel entitled to it. Having left the protection and support of her mother, she needed it to survive.

"What role does your Mrs. Culpepper play in all this?" Did she encourage Anna's bleak views on society? he wondered.

"Oh . . . friend, travel companion—"

"Coconspirator?"

"That as well," she admitted with a soft chuckle. "She was the architect of our plan, to be honest. I'd still be at Anover House, were it not for her."

"Then I owe her a debt of gratitude."

She didn't blush, as many women of his acquaintance might, but her eyes darted away a second before returning to his. It was a start, he told himself.

But he wanted so much more. He wanted to kiss her.

The Italian phrase hadn't materialized out of nowhere. The desire was there. The urge to touch her had gnawed at him since he'd walked into the house and seen her walking down the stairs.

It seemed right to do it now, while she was surrounded by flickering candlelight and the books she so clearly loved. They were alone and hidden, and he badly wanted to pull her close and feel the warmth of her through their clothes, her mouth move beneath his.

But it wasn't the right time. Trust wasn't rebuilt in a day, and he'd be a fool to push things too far, too fast. Particularly as he wasn't at all sure where he wanted things to go.

Better for him to step away.

Better . . . but not easier. His brain produced a half

dozen excuses for his prompt departure, but not the discipline to put a single one of them to immediate use.

He stayed exactly where he was as a weighted silence stretched out between them.

His eyes dropped to her mouth.

Her gaze skittered away as her fingers played with the spine of her book. He imagined them sliding up the back of his neck to play with his hair.

Clearly, she was aware of tension building between them. But she wasn't running away. That was promising. Very, very promising.

But it changed nothing. He was going to put an end to the tension. Immediately. He was going to walk away so she wouldn't have to run. He was going to—

In the end, he didn't have to do anything. It was an upstairs maid, Abigail, who saved them both. After a polite knock on the open door and an equally polite apology for the interruption, the young woman crossed the room and handed Anna a small ring of keys.

"Mrs. Webster has said that His Lordship has said that you are to have this."

"Oh, right." Anna accepted the ring, looking far more composed than Max would have liked. "Thank you. I hope I've not caused an inconvenience."

"A few less keys to haul about is no inconvenience to Mrs. Webster. But it was kind of you to ask. Should I show you which keys go to which cases, miss?"

Anna's gaze shot to him briefly. "Yes, I suppose that would be wise."

Max tried not to resent the intrusion (they were keys and locks, for pity's sake, how hard could it be?) even as he acknowledged that it was all for the best.

"I believe I'll leave you to it, then," he said before Anna could follow Abigail to the nearest case. He gave her a small bow. "Good night, Miss Rees."

"Good night, Lord Dane."

If she was disappointed by his decision to leave, no sign of it reached her face. Her smile was polite, but distant. It irritated him no end.

Which is why he made a point of whispering in her ear as he brushed by her on his way to the door.

"Sweet dreams, Anna."

He'd never know if she had any visual reaction to his words, but he heard her breath hitch, and that was enough for him, for now.

Chapter 11

❦

$\mathcal{A}$s dawn broke over Caldwell Manor, Anna stood in her room, wiggling her bandaged feet inside her shoes.

"Quite comfortable, really," she murmured.

Mrs. Culpepper's balm and a good deal of time spent barefooted had done wonders for her blisters. With bandages and a careful choice of shoes, she was confident she could walk a little ways without further aggravating her sore feet.

And should they became a little aggravated . . . Well, she would live with it. It was too fine and sunny a morning to stay indoors, she decided and headed downstairs.

As for the rest of yesterday's mishaps, they were easy to avoid once a person knew what to look for. She'd keep her feet away from manure and out of streams, give a wide berth to sheep and shepherds' dogs, and limit her stroll to level ground.

A warm wash of early sunlight settled on her face the

minute she stepped out the back door Max had carried her to the day before. She blinked, clearing her eyes, and discovered Max himself leaning against the stone balustrade of the terrace and looking quite handsome in his black coat and buckskin breeches.

He looked even better when he smiled at her, his hazel eyes shining a bright green in the morning light. "I hoped you'd come this way."

"Good morning." Better than good, possibly the finest morning she'd had in years. "Rather early for you, isn't it? I thought the demimonde kept town hours, even in the country."

"I keep whichever hours suit me," he replied, straightening as she approached. "And it suited me to find you here this morning."

She rather doubted he'd risen at dawn and come outside on the off chance he'd meet her, but she appreciated the sentiment. "Are you for the village?"

"No, I'm for escorting you about the countryside. I assumed any woman so determined to have a morning stroll that she was willing to walk on wounded feet was determined enough to give that morning stroll a second try. And I thought perhaps you might like a guide. I promise to steer us away from raging rivers and man-eating beasts."

Good heavens, he really had risen early to seek her out. How lovely. "I should like that very much."

"Excellent, but before we begin—how are your feet?"

Anna looked down to the cloth boots peeking out from her skirts. "Much improved, thank you, but I shall have to stick to soft paths and dry earth for a day or two."

"Easily done," he assured her and, with a sweep of his hand, invited her to lead the way off the terrace.

They kept to a leisurely pace over the next half hour and kept conversation at a minimum. Max pointed out a low mound where a few large, crumbling stones protruded from the grass, all that remained of a small medieval fortress predating the Engsly estate. Anna asked after several intact outbuildings and a pair of songbirds, which Max professed to know absolutely nothing about.

Anna didn't feel the need to fill all the lulls in the conversation. There was so much going on around them, it seemed foolish to constantly speak on top of it all. Why go on a walk in the country if one wasn't going to take a moment here and there to appreciate the sight of a hawk soaring overhead or the sound of the wind in the trees?

She snuck a glance at Max. It seemed odd that they could go from mistrust and anger to comfortable silence in so short a time. Stranger still that it didn't seem *more* odd. It felt right, to be walking side by side with Max whilst the early morning sun warmed her back. It felt better than right, in fact. It felt perfect. Better than any daydream she'd ever had.

That sense of rightness gave her the confidence to break the silence and ask a question that had been niggling at her. "Were you poking fun at me at dinner last night? When you asked me about my favorite spots in London."

He gave her a quizzical look, though whether he was surprised by her question or merely the sudden appearance of that particular topic, she couldn't say. "Not at all. Only teasing a little. If I wounded your feelings, I apologize—"

"No. I wasn't sure, that's all. I've very little experience in making friends," she admitted, "and given our recent history . . ."

"You assumed I was looking to wound," he finished for her.

"I didn't know," she corrected. "In my defense, it's clear you'd been nurturing a fair amount of anger toward me for some time."

"I called on you no less than a dozen times. Pricked my pride some, as I explained—" He broke off unexpectedly and there was a short, weighted pause before he spoke again. "That's a lie. It did fair more than prick, and it was more than my pride. I was . . . notably disappointed. I was certain you would see me. I knew of the countless others you'd turned away, but we had met and you—"

"I'm sorry, others? What others?"

"The other gentle—" He stopped in his tracks, blinked at her blank expression, and swore. "Oh, hell. You didn't know about them either, did you?"

"Them?" There was a *them*? "Tell me."

He hesitated, clearly reluctant to speak. "I was not the first gentleman to pay you a call at Anover House," he said at last. "There were—"

"Others," she finished for him as a sick weight settled in her stomach. "Countless others."

"Well, not *literally* countless."

A brief pause followed that statement. "What a relief."

"Anna—"

She shook her head, cutting him off. She wasn't in the mood for platitudes. "These others who called on me, I suppose they were friends of my mother's, like you?"

"I'm no friend of your mother's," he said grimly, "but yes, I believe many first saw you at Anover House."

"Not likely to have seen me anywhere else."

"I saw you at the theater once," he offered kindly. "A year or so before we met."

It took her two seconds to figure out which one. *"The Magic Flute."*

"I . . . Yes, how did you know?"

"I've been to the theater twice in my life," she explained, dully. *"The Magic Flute"* is what I saw a year or so before we met."

"I'm not helping at all."

"You are, in fact. So many truths were hidden from me for too long." She thought about that. "Or I was hidden away from them for too long. Either way, you have helped to enlighten me, and for that I am grateful."

He looked away, clearly uncomfortable.

As she hadn't the first clue how to remedy that, she simply pushed forward. "Do you know the names of any of my callers?"

"I recall a few," he replied after a moment's thought. He gave her a peculiar look. "Are you wondering after someone specific?"

Was he wondering if she was wondering after a particular gentleman? She rather liked the idea of that. Pity she hadn't the experience to tell.

"I was interested in whether or not any of them were ladies. Not true ladies, of course"—a real lady would never visit Anover House, not even to retrieve a wayward husband or son—"but a woman—"

"Yes, I understand. And no, I don't know. I imagine a female caller would be loath to announce she'd not been received."

"It's different for the gentlemen?"

"For some. It . . ." He looked away again, cleared his throat. "It depends on the circumstances."

She waited for him to elaborate on that, then rather wished she hadn't when he met her gaze again and said, *"Anna,"* in *that* tone—that gentle, reluctant, awful tone that inevitably preceded the delivery of very bad news. "Why don't we find a place to sit?"

A place to sit? Good Lord, that was worse than the tone.

"I don't want to sit." She highly doubted whatever he had to tell her would be improved by an additional three to five minutes of dread, or however long it took them to find a proper seat.

Max reached out and took her hand in both of his. "Not every man is an arse. You do know that."

"I've some hope for it being true," she allowed and wished her gloves weren't quite so thick, and that he was holding her hand for reasons other than comfort.

"There was . . ." He squeezed her fingers gently. "There was a wager amongst a few of the gentlemen in London. A pool, if you will. A challenge."

"And the nature of this challenge?"

"A man could, if he wished, place five pounds in the pool before paying a call on Anover House. The first man to gain audience with you was to win the pool."

"I see." She saw red, specifically. But she pushed the fury down, where it wouldn't show. "And this pool is no longer in existence?"

"The wager was abandoned some years back. The participants were allowed—"

"How large was the pool before it was abandoned?" she cut in.

"I don't know."

She narrowed her eyes at him. If he knew of the wager, then he had some idea of how far it had gone. "How large?"

"I'd not followed it closely. I would estimate five, maybe six hundred pounds."

"Six hundred pounds," she repeated softly as fury melded with astonishment. She'd assumed "countless" was really only a dozen or so determined gentlemen who'd been denied her company at one of her mother's parties and thought to try their luck the following day. "I've turned away more than a hundred gentlemen?"

"No. Not at all," he assured her. "A gentleman was allowed to enter the contest more than once. Most made multiple attempts."

That was small comfort. More than a hundred times in the past, someone had called on her, entirely unbeknownst to her, and she'd turned them away. "Well, I've certainly earned my nickname, haven't I?"

"It would have been better applied to your mother," he muttered.

Anna couldn't argue with that. She wondered if Madame

knew of the game and took perverse pride in how high the stakes had risen. "How long ago did this contest begin?"

"Years ago, when you were . . . nineteen, perhaps?" His brow furrowed in thought as his gaze passed over her face, assessing. "How old are you now?"

"Eight-and-twenty, I think." And really, a hundred visits didn't seem quite so terrible when spaced out over the course of a decade. "Most believe me to be younger, but—"

"I beg your pardon," he cut in. "Did you just say you *think* you're eight-and-twenty?"

She withdrew her hand from his as the heat of embarrassment warmed her cheeks. She wished now that she'd thought to bite her tongue. For most people—certainly for men like Max—age was an integral part of one's identity, often inseparable from the milestones of life. Every well-bred man would remember that he left for school at ten, finished his studies at one-and-twenty, and reached majority at five-and-twenty. A girl might put her hair up at sixteen, make her debut at eighteen, and land a husband before twenty.

Anna had neither any of those experiences, nor the ability to know how long ago, exactly, she ought to have had them. It was embarrassing to admit she was missing that part of herself.

It was also too late to retrieve the words, and so she forged ahead, feigning indifference.

"My age was amended several times in my youth."

"And you're not aware of your original date of birth," he guessed and waited for her nod. "Your mother's idea, I presume?"

"Yes."

"She won't tell you your true age?"

"I think she would," Anna replied, finding it difficult to meet his eyes, "if she could remember it."

Max nodded philosophically. "I suppose that's not too

surprising, given everything else we've learned of your mother's character."

It wasn't, that was true, but Max's casual acceptance of the facts certainly was. "You're not surprised?"

"England is full of people who don't know their birthdays," he explained. "You're not the first I've met."

She'd wager she was the only one who wasn't an orphan, but if Max wasn't bothered by her odd circumstances, she wasn't going to force the issue.

"Does it bother you, not knowing?" he asked.

"Some, yes. I should like to have a consistent birthday, at the very least."

"A day to celebrate, you mean?"

She nodded, only a little ashamed to be admitting to the childish desire for a proper birthday party. "Mrs. Culpepper offered to pick a day for me, but it didn't feel right. One false birthday a year is enough."

*M*ax looked from Anna's guarded features to the stone façade of Caldwell Manor.

He'd wager that somewhere inside the house there was a letter from Mrs. Wrayburn to the late marquess announcing the birth of his daughter, and he'd wager that letter included a date. It was tempting to offer that bit of hope to Anna, perhaps propose a search of the attic or some of the storage rooms. But upon further thought, he decided to keep the notion to himself. *Most* women would have sent a letter to their newborn's father. There was no guessing what Mrs. Wrayburn had done.

Moreover, he wanted to turn the conversation away from missed birthdays and malicious contests.

Only he couldn't quite figure through how best to go about it. So much of Anna's life was foreign to him. He wasn't sure where to turn for safe ground.

He had experience with pampered ladies and sheltered

misses, earthy barmaids and worldly courtesans. Anna was none of those things. Or maybe a little bit of all of them. He'd never met a woman like her in his life, and while he generally sought out and enjoyed new experiences, in this instance, he wished for the wisdom of experience.

He wanted to know how to make her laugh again.

But Anna spoke before he could even make an attempt.

"About the pool . . ." she began hesitantly, and he suppressed a wince. No matter how much he may want it, it was foolish, and possibly even a little selfish, to think she could go from learning of the mean-spirited game to laughing in the course of a single conversation.

"What is it?" he pressed.

"Did you ever place a wager—?"

"No." *Thank God.* "Never."

She lifted a shoulder as if she didn't much care, but her eyes settled on something over his shoulder. "I'd not have held it against you, if you had."

"Liar." He certainly hoped she was lying. She had every right to think poorly of any man who'd placed a bet. She had a right to think less of any man who'd not protested the mere existence of the pool. He thought a little less of himself for not having put a stop to it until after they'd met.

"Well . . . I'd have held it against you less if you'd placed the bet before we met."

"And regretted it afterward?"

"That would help. But you never did?" She looked at him, finally. "Why not?"

And at last, he saw a way to lighten the conversation.

"I'd never place a woman at the center of a gamble," he told her and waited for her expression to turn to one of pleasant agreement, before adding with a mischievous grin, "their irrational natures make them far too unpredictable."

He was happy to see that pile of nonsense provoke a smile and a gentile snort from her. "That which cannot be comprehended by man must therefore be wrong."

"Beg your pardon?"

"Something Mrs. Culpepper said to me when I was younger. She is of the opinion that men are highly predictable creatures."

"Because we're rational?"

"Because you're simple," she corrected. "Women, she says, are complex. Too complex for the comfort of your average gentleman—"

"Being such simpletons."

"Exactly," she chimed with a point of her finger at him. "And how does the simpleton, particularly the arrogant, self-important sort, react to something he can't understand? Something that perhaps frightens him?"

"Generally, we'd prefer to shoot it."

"He ignores it," she continued on, ignoring *him*. "He renames it, belittles it. He makes it less than it is so that he may appear more than he is." She smiled, just a little. "Or he shoots it."

It wasn't the laughter he was looking for, but it was closer than he had a right to expect under the circumstances. "Are you in agreement with Mrs. Culpepper?"

"No, not entirely. My own experiences, limited though they may be, have led me to believe that everyone is prone to attacking what they do not understand, but I do think your gender is, on average, more predictable than my own."

"On that, at least, we can agree." It was utter rot, of course, but if it made Anna feel better to talk rubbish, he could wait to put forth a serious argument on the matter.

"Though only you view it as a compliment." She pursed her lips thoughtfully. "You told me on the night we met that you could talk the devil out of his tail."

"Did I, really?" He chuckled lightly. "My God, what arrogance."

"Do you know what I thought of that?"

"I can't even remember saying it."

"I thought, I imagine he would try. Because he is a man

and all men feel inexplicably compelled to reach for what they can't have. Even when they've no use for it and there is nothing to be gained by its acquisition." She made a scoffing sound. "The devil's tail. Honestly. What would you do with it?"

"You do realize I wasn't speaking in a literal sense?"

"Shoot it, probably, then mount it upon your wall so that others might admire your prowess." She shook her head in disgust. "My fate would have been no different."

"Beg your pardon?" Why would anyone shoot a tail? How was her fate tied into this?

"My gentleman callers, they were in search of the same thing."

They'd circled around back to that? Max shook his head, baffled, and willing to reconsider his personal opinion that men and women were equally predictable. "I don't think—"

"What would those gentlemen have done, had any of them gained my audience? Did they bring poetry along, just in case? Gifts of flowers and candies? Honorable intentions?"

"Doubtful," he conceded.

"Because they didn't care one whit for my company. They just wanted the tail."

There was a marked pause before he spoke. "You might wish to reconsider that analogy. It's . . . problematic. On any number of levels."

She gave him a bland look. Apparently, the varied connotations of tail had not escaped her. "It fits, on all of them."

"You're no devil, sweet."

"I am to them, or near enough." She looked down at her feet, toed at a small rock. "I was to you less than two days ago."

"I was wrong." It would eat at him for a long time, how wrong he'd been. "And I am sorry."

She shook her head. "What's done is done."

"Perhaps, but—"

She held up her hand. "No, please. Let's speak of something else. It's such a fine morning. I don't want to dwell on all this unpleasantness. I don't want to harp on about it."

She'd not been harping, but if she was eager to move on to other topics, he was more than happy to oblige. "All right. What would you like to discuss?"

"Tell me more about the Engsly estate," she decided after some thought. "How much of what we see belongs to the Haverstons?"

"Everything before us and more," he replied and offered his elbow as they resumed their walk.

He told her what he knew of the marquessate and Caldwell Manor, keeping up a steady stream of information—and possibly embellishing here and there for the sake of drama—until they returned to the house.

Anna parted ways with him at the bottom of a back stairwell, and as he watched her disappear around a corner, his mind mulled over the morning's events.

What's done is done.

The words were nagging at him. He agreed with them in principle. Certainly, he wanted them to be true for his own sake. But he couldn't help but wonder if what had been done could really be rectified with a simple, *Sorry, then.*

Time could restore what trust had been lost—morning walks in the sun, conversations in the library—every moment they spent together helped. But he wanted something more than a slow advance. He wanted a way to show her the conviction behind his apology.

A gesture was needed. And he had just the thing.

Chapter 12

⚜

Max knocked on Lucien's study door, and then walked in, not bothering to wait for a reply. "Why the devil are you holed up inside your study on this fine morning?"

Lucien looked up from his work and blinked in the manner of a man readjusting his focus. He glanced from Max to the mantel clock, then back again with a somewhat exaggerated expression of surprise. "Pardon?"

Max took his customary—and second-favorite—seat across from Lucien's desk, and ignored the implication that it was startling to see him up at such an hour. "What are you working on?"

"Oh." Lucien frowned down at the paper before him. "A letter to my aunt Gwen, explaining why I'll not be immediately bringing her new niece to London."

Max considered what he knew of Lucien's formidable aunt. "Best of luck to you."

"Thank you. Are you in need of something?"

"I am. You've a foxhound bitch, don't you? She has new pups?"

"I do," Lucien replied, relaxing back into his chair, "and she has."

"Will you sell one to me?"

"No, of course not."

"Excell . . ." Max pulled himself up straight. "I beg your pardon?"

"Your town house is no place for a foxhound," Lucien scoffed.

"Ah. No, it's not for me. It's for your sister."

"You want to buy a dog from me, to give to Anna?" Dark brows rose high on his forehead. "Why?"

"As a gift."

"A gentleman does not give a dog as a gift to a lady who is not his wife." He tapped the end of his pen against the arm of his chair. "A gentleman of sense wouldn't give one to his wife either."

"Do we really need to follow gifting etiquette here?"

"Unless you can provide a good reason why we shouldn't? Yes."

He could provide thousands, given time, but Max thought he could sum things up rather nicely with a simple, "It's idiotic."

Lucien, however, looked less than impressed. "Many rules are; we still have to follow them."

Not this one, not if he could help it. "Anna wants a dog. I want to give her one. Why should some asinine rule stand in the way of our collective happiness?"

"*Why* do you want to give her a dog?" Lucien pressed.

Max considered his next move carefully. With a bit of creative wording, he could avoid mentioning his past with Anna and still convince Max to sell him a dog. With a little more creative arguing he might be able to convince himself that he wasn't continuing a lie so much as retaining a secret.

Or he could just tell Lucien the truth. "I owe her an apology."

Lucien's face darkened as he sat up in his chair. "An apology for what? What have you done?"

"Nothing you need to work yourself into a fit over," he promised. "She's not angry with me." Anymore, he finished silently and waited for Lucien to nod before continuing. "Four years ago, I didn't merely meet Anna, as I previously . . . implied. I attempted to develop a friendship. I called on her on several occasions, even penned a couple of letters. Mrs. Wrayburn informed me, however, that her daughter wanted nothing to do with me. The experience left me bitter, I admit, and our first meeting after her arrival at Caldwell was a little contentious. I was something of a boor."

Lucien, not looking near as upset as Max had expected, waved an impatient hand. "Rubbish. You were uncharacteristically stilted perhaps, but that was only to be expected. I saw nothing boorish—"

"Not our greeting when she arrived," Max cut in. "Our first meeting, at which you were not present."

"Explain."

"You may put your dueling pistols away. I was less than friendly. I wasn't a knave." By some definitions, at any rate.

"Where did you meet?"

"In the hall," Max replied and felt only a little guilty for the half lie. Strictly speaking, they *had* met in the hall. True, the majority of the conversation had occurred in the billiards room, but that wasn't where they had *met*. More importantly, it wasn't something any of them would be better off for Lucien knowing.

"And what was said between you, exactly?"

"I questioned the timing of her visit. I expressed suspicion of her parental claims."

Lucien swore. "You had no right."

"Debatable. It's done now. I've apologized for it, and—"

"You should have told me she'd refused your attentions four years ago," Lucien grumbled.

"She didn't refuse me." God, that felt as good to hear as it did to say. "It was Mrs. Wrayburn's doing. Anna was never told of my visits. My letters never reached her. I . . . why the devil are you laughing?"

It was more of a chuckle than an outright laugh, but in light of Lucien's mood only seconds before it was . . . unexpected.

"You don't recall how Lilly and I were separated when we were younger?" Lucien asked.

"Your stepmother came between you. What does—?"

"She confiscated our letters without our knowledge and told me Lilly had run off to marry another man. I see some similarities, that's all."

"With the notable difference that I am not you, she is not Lilly, and we are not in love," Max countered, uncomfortable with the conversation's sudden change in direction. "All of this is immaterial. I am attempting to build a friendship with this woman because she is a Haverston. She wants a large-breed dog, and has for years. I want to give her one. We both want to make her happy. Will you sell me the dog, or not?"

"No—"

"*Damn it*, man."

Lucien held up a hand. "If you would allow me to finish? She may have her pick of the litter. The dog will be from *me*, as it is perfectly acceptable for a brother to gift such an item. You, however, may take credit for the gift in every other way. Tell her the reasons behind it, that it is an apology from you, that you convinced me to—"

"This is ridiculously and unnecessarily complicated."

"No, it's ridiculous and complicated and nonnegotiable." Lucien tossed his pen on the desk and grinned. "Welcome back to good society, my friend."

He didn't care for the sound of that. "It's only a visit."

Lucien's smile only broadened. "Of course it is."

* * *

Though he was eager to deliver his hard-won present, Max was unable to procure time alone with Anna for the remainder of the day. She spent the early afternoon with Mrs. Culpepper, late afternoon with Lucien, and the evening with everyone, which left him no choice but to postpone delivering his surprise until the following morning.

He waited for her on the terrace at dawn again and felt a jolt of pleasure when she stepped through the door, looked up, and smiled at the sight of him.

A man could grow accustomed to that smile, he thought, to that pleasure. A man could grow dependent on both.

Pushing that rather unnerving thought aside, Max offered a smile of his own. "Good morning, Anna. Ready for our stroll?"

He couldn't be certain, but he thought maybe, just maybe, she blushed a little.

"Quite ready. Shall we take a walk in the gardens? Mrs. Webster told me yesterday that her favorite clematis is in bloom."

"I don't know what that is," he said as they headed down the terrace steps, side by side.

"Nor I," she admitted with a light laugh. "But she spoke of it with such enthusiasm, it must be remarkable."

"I'm certain it is, but I've something else in mind for this morning. A surprise."

This time, there was no missing the color that rose to her cheeks. "Truly? What sort of surprise?"

"The surprising sort."

She rolled her eyes at that. "You must give me some hint. Is it a thing or a place?"

"Neither. But I will tell you that we are headed *there*," he said and pointed to the stables that sat not fifty yards away.

Her expression dimmed a little. "If you are after showing

me a horse, you are wasting your time. I don't know the first thing about them."

"It's not a horse."

"Oh." Interested once more, she fixed her gaze on the stable and bit her lip. "Is it something one typically finds in a stable—?"

"No, no more hints."

"Oh, but—"

"You can't wait twenty seconds to find out?"

"I could, but guessing for twenty seconds is more fun than not guessing for twenty seconds," she explained, and he wondered what it said about him that he both followed and approved of her reasoning.

"Very well, guess away."

"Excellent. Is the surprise animate or inanimate?"

"Yes."

She made a face at him. "Is it edible?"

"Possibly yes, probably not."

"Will I be able to—?"

"The answer is three."

"Killjoy," she accused, echoing his insult from yesterday.

"You'll thank me when you see what I've in store for you," he promised as they reached the open stable doors. Max took a deep breath of the dusty air when they stepped inside. He loved the scents of a well-kept stable—horse, leather, and hay. Or, as he'd thought of them as a young man at McMullin House . . . the scents of freedom. A quick saddle and ride, and he was at Caldwell with Lucien and Gideon.

"What am I looking for?" Anna asked.

"This," he said and brought her to the second stall on the right. There, on a pile of fresh straw, were the six foxhound puppies and their dam.

Anna gasped softly at the sight of them. Her face lit up with unabashed delight. "Oh. Oh, my. Oh, my *goodness.*"

"Foxhounds," he told her as he opened the stall door. "Lucien doesn't hunt, but he is fond of the breed. They're quite affable, good with other dogs, and . . ."

He trailed off when it became clear she wasn't paying the least bit of attention to what he was saying.

Eyes fixed on the dogs, Anna stepped into the stall and proceeded to make sounds only a woman could produce without complete mortification—coos and oohs and ahhhs—while the puppies scrambled over each other in a frantic bid to reach the visitors. They were all legs and ears and curiosity.

She knelt in the hay, reaching for them, and laughed when the puppies wriggled and squirmed under her stroking hands. The sound fell like music on Max's ears, but the sight of her so unguarded and happy was even better.

"They're so soft and warm." She rubbed the belly of one and laughed again.

"Choose the one you want," he told her.

She giggled as the puppy contorted itself in an effort to lick her hand without rolling off its back. "Oh, you are silly, aren't you? Just the silliest little . . ." Her hand stilled on the puppy. Her eyes shot to his. "What did you just say?"

"Choose which pup you'd like as your own."

"My own?"

"You wanted a hound," he reminded her.

"Yes, I . . ." She looked at the dogs, then back at him. "Are you giving me a dog?"

"For the sake of propriety, we are to say it is a gift from your brother, but . . ."

"But it's from you. You're giving me a dog," she said, and there was a notable catch in her voice.

"Well . . . more or less." For reasons that baffled him, he suddenly felt equal parts embarrassed and pleased. "It was my idea." He cleared his throat, fought off the urge to shift his feet. "I wanted another way to apologize for my earlier behavior. I hoped something more tangible than words might be in order. I remember you saying you wanted a hound . . . Something more substantial than your mother's lap dogs, correct?" He waited for her nod. "Well then, here you are."

"My own dog," she whispered in awe. "My very own hound."

He recognized her tone and expression as similar to what he'd seen and heard when she'd spoken in the library of having her own books, and he realized that this wasn't just about having a particular sort of dog, it was about having a pet all her own.

Her mother's library, her mother's gowns, her mother's dogs, her mother's carriages and friends and parties. There was no missing the disturbing pattern that had emerged over the past two days. Anna had been living as a guest in her own home.

Max found himself toeing at the loose hay at his feet while Anna fussed over the puppies. "You may take your time deciding which—"

"This one," she cut in, ruffling the head of a large female.

"Well, then. Excellent."

Her expression turned sheepish. "Did I do that wrong? Is there a right way and a wrong way to choose?"

"Probably, but I'm not aware of them, and I don't think they apply in this case. Any of these pups will do well for you, as long as you do well by them." He bent down to scratch at the chosen dog's back. "A dog such as this needs work. She'll not be content to prance about the house like a lap dog. She requires exercise and company. She wouldn't mind the companionship of other dogs."

She bit her lip, clearly worried. "Perhaps I should rethink this. I don't have a home of my own at present. I can't assume Mrs. Culpepper's sister will welcome a foxhound until I find a cottage, and—"

"You needn't worry on that score. She can stay here

until you've settled on a place of your own. I'll be happy to bring her to you."

"I can't ask—"

"Fine. Your brother, who has gifted you this dog, will be happy to bring her to you." He gave her an encouraging smile. "Stop worrying and enjoy the present, Anna."

She bit her lip again, but this time with growing excitement. "She really is adorable."

"She'll need a name."

"I'll think of something," she murmured as she played with the puppy. "Oh, you are a darling. You are. You most certainly are. Simply a darling."

They laughed as the little darling tottered over to attack his boot with a playful ferocity.

"Hermia," Anna said. "Her name is Hermia."

The name sparked a memory. " 'And though she be but little, she is fierce,' " he quoted, delighted at her choice, and with himself for making the connection to Shakespeare.

"You recognized it," she exclaimed, her face the very picture of astonishment.

He nearly made a flippant comment about everyone having seen *A Midsummer Night's Dream* at least once, even if it was only a performance offered by ambitious and bored family members in the parlor. But he bit the words back at the last second. It was highly unlikely that everyone, in this case, would include Anna.

"I have been known to open a book on occasion," he said instead.

"Well, I'm delighted you figured it out. I'm delighted with *her*." She played gently with the tip of the puppy's tale. "Am I to take her back to the house with me?"

"You can, if you like, she's well past weaned. But it might be easier to take things slowly. Why don't we start with a little walkabout?"

A furrow formed between her brows. "She'll not run off?"

"No."

She looked anxiously toward the stable doors. "You're certain?"

"She's too young to outrun us for long, and we'll not go far. To the edge of the woods and back." No more than thirty yards from the back of the stable. Just the right distance for the puppy and her nervous new owner. "It will be fun for the both of you, I promise."

Chapter 13

❧

*A*nna wasn't so much nervous about her newly acquired pet as she was thrilled, fascinated, and terrified.

The best part about having a dream was that it could be as far removed from reality as one liked. Anna hadn't thought of pungent manure and aggressive dogs in her daydreams of a country stroll because she hadn't needed to. It was just a dream, after all.

And when she'd dreamed of owning her own dog, she'd imagined wiggling tails and happy frolics in the fields. She'd not really dwelled on the fact that *owning* a dog meant that she would be *responsible* for a dog. But now she had to, and she found the notion fairly intimidating.

She'd never been responsible for another living thing in her life. Dear God, what if she failed?

Anna pushed the thought aside. It was less than useless to fear what she might do wrong instead of focusing on what she could do right. And what she could do right now was enjoy taking her new dog on a walk with Max.

With excitement edging out her anxiety, she found a bit of soft rope to use as a leash, but rather than risk frightening the puppy, Max scooped up Hermia and carried her outside instead.

Anna suppressed a sigh when they stepped out of the stable. Surely a sweeter picture had never been seen than that of Maximilian Dane standing in the sunshine with a squirming little puppy in his arms. *Her* puppy, she amended. Max Dane was cuddling the puppy he'd gifted her as an extension of an apology.

This, she decided, was worlds better than groveling.

She was almost disappointed when Max set Hermia down in the field, halfway between the stable and the woods. And some of her confidence was lost when it became clear that the puppy, though ungainly, was both plenty fast and not the least bit interested in accompanying them across the field to the trees.

Hermia sniffed the air, the ground, then turned tail and galloped back toward the stables. Well, Anna mused, at least she didn't have to worry about it disappearing into the countryside.

"Barn sour." Max laughed, then he looked at her, grinned and said, "Run toward the trees."

Anna dragged her eyes from the retreating puppy. "What? Why?"

"Trust me. Make it into a game. Show her it can be fun." And with that, he called out to the puppy, then turned about and headed toward the woods at an easy pace.

Without giving herself the chance to think better of the idea, Anna picked up her skirts and followed. She felt silly and awkward and absolutely giddy, running across an open field with Max Dane as if they were children at play.

Max looked over his shoulder as she gained on him. "You see?" he called out. "It's working."

Anna didn't need to look back. Hermia galloped right past her on her way to Max. He grinned at the puppy, then dodged left without slowing down to avoid trampling her as she ran directly underfoot.

And then, before she could call out a warning, Max spun forward just in time to collide with a tall, narrow, but evidently perfectly sturdy, young tree.

The accident was so abrupt, so jarring, that Anna simply came to a stop and froze, mouth agape, as Max stumbled back several feet, pressed his hand to his forehead, and let loose a peculiar string of half-curses.

"Sweet holy . . . Son of a . . . Bloody . . . *Bloody* . . ." He produced a long and decidedly angry groan and then finally, *"Damn it."*

And then all Anna heard was her own laughter. It echoed through the trees and set the puppy, now comfortably seated at her own feet, to barking.

She laughed until her sides ached and her eyes filled with tears. Because, God forgive her, she'd never witnessed anything so spectacularly hilarious as the impossibly urbane Lord Dane running headlong into a Scots pine.

"Oh . . . Oh, *Lord* . . ." She bent at the waist in a combined effort to put the rope around the puppy and to catch her breath. Only the first was successful on the initial try. It took two additional attempts to rein in her glee to the point where she could look at Max without risking another round of laughter.

He was still holding his forehead, but he was glowering at her, his expression one of promised retribution combined with begrudging amusement.

"I'm sorry," she gasped out. "I am so terribly sorry. Are you all right? Is the injury severe?" She could see for herself it wasn't, or she'd not have found it all so funny, but it seemed the thing to ask.

"Well enough," he grumbled and lowered his hand to look at his fingers. "Considering."

"You're not bleeding, are you?" She'd wager his pride was seeping out by the gallon.

"No."

"Shall I run back to the stable for assistance?"

"No." He swore again, but quieter. And this time, there was a bit of humor mixed in with the obscenities. "I've not done that since I was a boy."

This wasn't the first time? Anna couldn't say why that made it all even funnier. "Are you quite certain you're all right?"

"Yes." He looked at her, grimacing. "How bad is it?"

The skin above his left eye was a little red, but there was no sign of swelling. She doubted there would be. He'd not been going all that fast, really.

"The skin is scratched a bit, but not broken. I'd be surprised if it bruised."

"Hell." He prodded at the skin gingerly. "I will never live this down."

"*I'll* not forget it."

"It's not you who concerns me. It's the rest of Christendom." His lips twitched and he gave her a pleading expression that reminded her of why she'd once thought of him as adorable. "I don't suppose I could persuade you to tell a different story as to the origins of my bruise?"

"Depends on the story," she returned, willing to play along.

"Could we say I was wounded saving you from an animal attack?"

"What sort of animal leaves bruises about the head?"

"Feral horse?" he offered hopefully, making her laugh.

"You want me to tell people you were beaten by a horse?"

He tossed a disgusted look at the surrounding woods. "England has an appalling lack of dangerous animals."

"But no shortage of hazardous vegetation, it seems. Why not say we were set upon by brigands?"

"Can't," Max replied ruefully. "It would create too much of a fuss. Lucien would send out men to search for the villains. Villagers would take up arms. An extended and ultimately fruitless hunt for the criminals would ensue.

The pair of us would feel terribly guilty. Well, *you* would."
He grew quiet and turned his head, his eyes tracking through
the thin woods to the fields visible beyond. "Do sheep
stampede, do you know?"

The silliness of it all elicited another, albeit shorter, round
of laughter from her.

"You saved me from rampaging sheep?" she managed
at length.

"And the puppy. You mustn't forget to mention I saved
the puppy." He smiled and tilted his head as she continued to laugh. "You have the most . . . unusual laugh of any
woman I've ever met."

Her amusement faltered at the sudden shift of subject.
"You've heard me laugh before."

"And quite liked it, but I'd not heard you laugh quite so
freely. Nor so loudly. You laugh like a toddler."

She sputtered a moment, dumbfounded by the comment.
"I beg your pardon?"

"From here." He stepped forward and brushed his fingers across her abdomen, taking her off guard. "You laugh
from the belly. Part of why it's so low, I think."

His touch sent a shiver along her skin. She ignored the
conflicting instincts to both step away and move closer. "I
do not. It is not."

"No need to take offense. There's no greater laughter
than that of a small child. It's uninhibited, completely
devoid of artifice. It is the unencumbered, unabashed sound
of pure joy."

She pressed her lips together thoughtfully. "I don't like
anyone being hurt, but I clearly enjoyed your run-in with
that tree."

"Mm-hm. It's the surprise that did it, I think."

"But I'm not an innocent child."

"No, never that. Your laughter shares a few common
traits, that's all." He grinned at her. "Just as my humor does
on occasion. There's nothing wrong with either."

She felt herself smiling in return. "No, I suppose there's not."

Admittedly, if there had been, she'd likely still have let the matter go. She was in too fine a mood to go worrying over the fault in things. Why waste time on what might be wrong when it was so much more fun focusing on what was right?

And it felt ever so right to sit with Max in the grass and play with her new puppy. They tossed sticks for her to chase (which Hermia mostly ignored) and used the rope for games of tug-of-war (which Hermia mostly won) and otherwise spent the next half hour enjoying themselves immensely.

Such a simple thing, to sit in the sun, play with the puppy. Simple but not common, at least not in Anna's experience, and she was happy to see that Max, with all his experience and sophistication, seemed equally content.

When it came time to return Hermia to her family, Max once again carried her back to the stable. "Next time, we can bring some scraps to lure her into behaving on a lead."

Anna hid a smile at the words "next time" and "we," and stole a glance at Max as they stepped into the shadow of the stable. He'd given her a wonderful present, an unforgettable morning. She only wished she had something to offer in return.

Perhaps she did, she mused as Max set Hermia down with her littermates. "You know, if you'd truly prefer it, I could keep your mishap between the two of us."

He lifted a single dark brow as he walked out of the stall, closing and latching the door behind him. "That is a very generous offer."

Anna watched Hermia take three steps, then plop to the ground for a nap. "It can be . . . unpleasant, to be the center of unwanted attention. I hope I did not wound your feelings by laughing so hard."

"My feelings are far more steeled than that, love. My

pride, on the other hand, will require some restorative care. Tell me I'm handsome."

She laughed again and wondered if she'd ever had a day as fun as this.

He nodded at the sound. "I thought so."

"What?" she asked, turning from the stall.

"You've a lovely sense of humor, Anna. And, I think, a fondness for silliness."

She considered the events of the day and her reactions to them thus far. "It is possible I do."

And wasn't that a fine thing to learn about herself? How very unlike an Ice Maiden.

"I imagine there was little of it to be found at Anover House," Max commented.

She blinked at that, surprised by his insightfulness. "It wasn't common," she admitted.

Her mother's parties were terrifically obnoxious, nothing more. And Mrs. Culpepper, while a wonderful companion, was simply not a woman inclined to silliness.

Max nodded in understanding. "My childhood home was the same. I much preferred Caldwell Manor."

"Did you spend a great deal of time here?"

"I did." He glanced out one of the stable windows at the house. "Even after Lady Engsly passed and Caldwell became a less welcoming place. I still chose it over McMullin Hall."

"Did you know the first marchioness well?"

"As well as a child can, I suppose. I knew she was a marvelous woman, a true lady. She taught me how to laugh at my mistakes rather than define myself by them or turn myself into knots dreading their consequences. And she taught me how to find the humor in every situation . . . She tried, rather," he amended. "I was not as gifted a student as Gideon."

"I'd say you fare well enough." It wasn't every peer of

the realm who could laugh at himself for running into a tree. "She was very important to you, the marchioness," she guessed softly.

Max didn't immediately respond except to nod his head once. He turned from the stall and gestured her forward in an invitation to continue their walk. It wasn't until they were clear of the stable that he spoke again.

"You asked me once why I tend toward overprotective-ness where Lucien and Gideon are concerned."

Anna snuck a sideways glance at his face, but found she couldn't read his expression. "You said you would tell me another time."

He nodded, cleared his throat. "I promised Lady Engsly I would watch over her children. I made that promise to her on her deathbed."

He couldn't have been more than a boy at the time. "That was very selfless of you."

"She asked it of me."

"Asked it?" That couldn't be right. "How old were you, exactly?"

"Not more than thirteen."

"Good heavens." What sort of burden was that to put on a child? Pretty flowerpots or not, the woman was an idiot.

"You would judge her for it," Max guessed and shook his head. "Don't. She didn't ask for herself, or for her chil-dren. She asked it for me."

"I don't understand."

"It gave me a purpose," he explained. "It made me feel . . . trusted, valuable."

"Didn't you otherwise?"

"I was the second son of parents who felt they really only needed the first."

"They were wrong." In every way imaginable, they were wrong. "I am sorry your mother and father were not able to see your worth."

"Ah, well." He flashed her a crooked smile. "It's not an

uncommon story, is it? And in hindsight, I know I was valued as a friend by Lucien and Gideon, and as a brother to Beatrice, and even Reginald on occasion. But at the time, I'd felt rather . . . beside the point. One of Lady Engsly's last acts was to grant me a sense of importance until I was old enough to find it on my own."

"Which you've done with aplomb," Anna teased, thinking that perhaps Lady Engsly's request had not been wholly idiotic.

Max grinned at her. "Do you think?"

She laughed softly as a memory came to her. "Do you recall telling me I had to do what you said because you were a viscount?"

"Good Lord, no. I assume I shared that gem at Anover House?" He snorted in amusement. "I'm fair surprised you sat with me as long as you did, and that you wanted anything to do with me after. I must have been near unbearable, drunk as I was."

"To be honest . . . I found you adorable. Though I am glad to see you've tempered that vice in the years since. That kind of behavior wouldn't be quite so endearing if it occurred on any sort of regular basis."

His footing faltered. "Adorable."

"Yes, quite."

"I see. I honestly don't know how I feel about that." He repeated the word quietly, as if tasting it, then made a face as if he didn't care for the flavor. "You've not shared that sentiment with anyone else, have you?"

"Only Engsly," she assured him. "He's the one who told me you've tempered your drinking and—"

"*Only* Engsly? Good God, woman." He let out a pained laugh. "Between the tree and your professed opinions of me, I'll never hear the end of it."

He'd never hear the start of it, as she was lying. It was just so much more fun to watch him squirm than it was to speak of deathbed promises and heartless parents.

"Adorable?" he asked again, slanting her a pleading look. *"Truly?"*

"Oh, yes."

"Not handsome? Or dashing? Or wickedly charming?"

Oh, yes. "Sorry, no."

"Devilishly rakish?"

"You just ran into a tree."

"Right." He reached out and gently caught her elbow, stopping them in a small copse of trees where they were hidden from view of the house. His eyes settled on her, determined, and he took a purposeful step forward. "Right, then."

Before she could utter a word, he slipped an arm around her, strong and sure, and pulled her close.

"What are you doing?" she demanded, the question being, of course, entirely rhetorical. A blind man could see what he was about.

He bent his head, a wicked smile playing at his lips. "Remedying a misconception," he whispered.

And then he was kissing her, his mouth moving over hers in gentle demand.

It didn't occur to Anna to pretend maidenly affront. It might be wrong, irresponsible, and reckless, but in that moment, she didn't care . . . unexpected or not, the kiss was welcome.

Rather than pull away, she stood up on her tiptoes and kissed him back.

And she thought, *This is wonderful.* It was even better than the kiss in the nursery, because it was a kiss she'd never thought to have again. And of course, because sobriety and four years of maturing had changed Max from a boy who could turn over a girl's heart with charm and sweetness to a man who could devastate a woman with confidence and skill.

Anna grabbed handfuls of his coat and pulled him closer. She felt wicked and free and terribly impatient. As wonderful as the kiss was, she wanted more. She wanted him closer, his grip tighter, her hands moving over him faster. And she rather thought she was going to get what she wanted, which was why she was stunned when Max pulled his lips from her suddenly. He squeezed his eyes shut, his fingers briefly dug into her shoulders, and then he released her and stepped away.

Anna stayed where she was, breathless and dazed while Max planted his hands on his hips and bowed his head in the manner of one catching his breath.

She licked her lips, found them pleasantly tender. "Why did you stop?"

His gaze snapped up, hard and disbelieving. "You'd rather I hadn't?"

Yes. No. "I don't know."

He swore softly. "I'd rather I hadn't."

Then why the devil had he? "Well—"

"You should return to the house."

"I . . ." She blinked rapidly, trying to clear her head. Had she done something wrong? Was he already regretting the kiss? "Are you sorry?"

He looked taken aback by the question. "I'll beg your pardon, if you feel it's necessary—"

"No, not that sort of sorry."

"Oh. No." His features softened, just a little. "No, love. I'm not sorry. I'm not sorry in any sense of the word."

"Good." She squared her shoulders, tipped up her chin. "Good. Because I'm not either." And to prove it, she stepped forward and gave him a soft peck on the cheek.

She felt him go taut and still. His breath was hot against her cheek as the moment stretched out and the tension between them built anew. "It's time for you to go, Anna."

Pulling back, she took a careful look at him. His jaw was locked tight, his nostrils were flared, his breathing had not yet fully settled. He was, she realized, still quite wound up. And God forgive her, she liked knowing it.

Damned right he wasn't sorry about kissing her.

His eyes dropped to her mouth and stayed there. "Go inside now, Anna."

She nodded. She didn't want to leave, particularly, but if Max needed time alone, she could surely grant him that courtesy.

"Until this evening, then," she murmured and, with one last smile, turned and left.

M ax stared at Anna's retreating back and thought that *this* was what it meant to regret one's ambitions.

He was acquiring Anna's trust and friendship, just as he'd hoped. But they were coming along faster than anticipated, which was both a pleasant surprise and a worrisome development. He wasn't completely certain what he wanted from her yet. Nor did he have the slightest idea what she hoped to gain from him. And until he had a firm grasp of expectations, it was madness to continue forward at their current pace.

He was no longer five-and-twenty, foxed, angry at the world, and willing to propose after a half hour's acquaintance.

He was now nine-and-twenty, completely sober, and ready to pull a lady down on the grass like a maniac. *Then* propose to her.

Max dragged a hand through his hair. They needed time, the both of them. There was no need to rush things along. He wasn't off for the continent with his regiment. She wasn't besieged by suitors and marriage proposals.

He wasn't a bloody maniac.

But damn if he didn't love the taste of her mouth and that tantalizing warmth that had seeped through her gown to his hands. The rush of desire that had come the moment he'd touched her had taken him by surprise. The wave of need that followed had nearly swamped his control.

Max rolled the tension out of his shoulders. He didn't like losing control.

A little time and space to think things through before he pressed forward, that's what he needed. Two or three days to clear his mind and plan a sensible course of action.

Probably just the two, he decided, watching the seductive sway of Anna's hips as she climbed the terrace steps. He wasn't planning a military campaign, after all. Two days was plenty. More than, really.

Anna glanced over her shoulder just once, before disappearing inside the house.

Maybe one day was long enough. A solid twenty-four hours. That way, he'd miss dinner and two morning strolls. It was ample time to work things through to his satisfaction and, hopefully, everyone's benefit.

At the very least, it was time enough to shore up what was left of his self-control.

Chapter 14

✎

*A*nna patiently waited for Max outside the next morning, until pride told her it was time to go. Then she waited a little longer. Which was a mistake, because by the time she finally left without him, she wasn't merely disappointed that he'd not come, but also a bit put out with herself for having set such store by his company to start.

How foolish it was for her to have assumed Max would come. How foolish to feel so disappointed. They'd not officially made plans to meet. He'd not promised to walk with her every morning. Just as he'd not promised to attend meals.

He'd not come to dinner the night before, and Lucien had made only a cursory excuse for him. Max, she was told, was attending to business. Anna thought it distinctly unfair that a gentleman could get out of nearly any activity with the excuse of business. But she'd tried not to take Max's absence, or the irritating explanation given for that absence, personally.

It was difficult not to take his absence personally that morning. When a man avoided a woman after kissing her, it was unlikely to be anything *but* personal.

Unless, of course, he was simply being sensible. They both knew perfectly well that nothing could come of their growing attraction. He was still a viscount and she was still a courtesan's daughter. They were no more suitable for each other than they had been four years ago.

Maybe, in keeping his distance, he was being mindful of that fact and of her (admittedly questionable) reputation.

She'd really rather he wouldn't. God's truth, she wanted to be reckless. Just a little. Just while she was at Caldwell and just with Max. She'd spent her whole life being the Ice Maiden and she had the rest of her life to spend as a hopeless old maid. Right now, she wanted to be . . . she just wanted to be kissing Max Dane. And, more than anything, she wanted him to want that back.

How ironic that after years of wishing there were more gentlemen in her life, she now found herself wishing there was just one rogue.

Feeling dejected, but nonetheless determined to make the most of her morning, she stopped by the stable and peeked in on a sleeping Hermia before setting off to begin her stroll in proper. She'd not made it far, just to the end of the field where she and Max had played with Hermia the day before when she heard an odd, high-pitched laughter coming through the woods.

Anna stopped and cocked her head, trying to determine why it sounded so strange to her. The cadence of it was off, maybe, or the . . .

"Oh, no. No, no, no." It wasn't laughter she was hearing, it was the broken cries of a child. Horrified, she swiveled on her heel, cupped her hands around her mouth, and yelled back at the stable. "Help! I need help! In the trees!"

Praying someone had heard her but unwilling to wait and find out, Anna picked up her skirts and dashed into the trees, following the sound of the cries. Brush and branches caught at her dress and skin, slowing her down. More than once she tripped over exposed roots, nearly losing her footing. But at last, the woods opened again to pasture and, more immediately, a large pond.

At the center of that pond was a small girl. Visible only from the shoulders up, she was desperately clinging to a rectangular bit of wood and rope that may, or may not, have been the remnants of a raft. Only a portion of it could be seen above the waterline.

As Anna rushed closer, the child caught sight of her, and her young face became a heartbreaking mixture of terror and hope.

"Help me! Please! I can't swim! I can't swim!"

"Yes! Yes, I'm coming! It's all right!"

Anna reached the edge of the water and came to a sliding stop. The girl was in the very middle of the pond. Damn it, she'd no idea how deep the water might be. With an oath, she spun around again, her eyes scanning the ground in front of the trees.

"Don't leave me!" The child's voice took on a new edge of panic as Anna turned her back on the pond, searching. "Don't! Help me!"

"I'm coming! I'm coming, hold on just a moment longer!"

"I can't!"

Anna glanced over her shoulder. From the looks of it, she could. The top of the girl's blonde curls weren't wet. But she'd not have much longer than that moment. Whatever the child had been using to stay afloat was quickly disappearing below the water.

Damn it, where . . . ? "Yes!"

She found what she needed at the edge of the woods. A long, sturdy tree branch, still light enough for her to move. Half carrying, half dragging her find, she raced back to the pond and straight into the water.

The cool temperature of the water scarcely registered,

but the weight of it was impossible to ignore as it saturated her skirts and they pulled her down. Her feet sank into the muddy bottom of the pond. She lost one slipper, then the other. The branch floated atop the water, but it was a struggle, towing it behind her.

Her progress was maddeningly slow, and the farther she made it, the more the resistance of water and mud slowed her pace. It reached her waist, her chest, her shoulders, her neck, and then the bottom seemed to drop away.

"*Bloody* hell."

Just as Anna had feared, the water grew too deep for her to reach the child. One more step and she'd be in over her head.

But the child wasn't far, perhaps six feet away, and Anna could see that she was very young indeed, no more than seven or eight. The raft was almost entirely submerged now, and the girl was struggling to keep her hands on one slippery corner and her chin above the water.

Anna dragged the branch around and pushed it out before her.

Please reach. Please, God. Please, please, please let it reach.

The end of the branch stopped only inches short of touching the girl.

"Yes!" Anna felt a wash of hope. "Grab hold!"

The girl turned panicked eyes from the branch to Anna. "Help me!"

"Grab hold, love. It's all right."

"No!" The girl stretched one arm out toward Anna instead. "Help me!"

Damn it. Anna tried leaning forward, pushing the branch closer, but it was no use. "I can't reach you! You must grab the branch. You can do it. Go on."

Sobbing, the child threw out a small hand, grasping wildly, and somehow managed to take hold of the branch. "I have it! I have it!"

"There's a girl! Now take a deep breath, grab hold with both hands, and hold tight!"

By some miracle, the girl did exactly as she was told. Anna sent up a prayer the girl's grip was tight, then pulled on the branch. The child pushed away from the raft at the same time, and the sudden weight on the branch took Anna by surprise. For one terrifying moment, it threatened to pull her over the unseen precipice at her feet, but she was able to shift her weight and regain her balance in time. And then it was but a few pulls of the branch and the child was in grasping distance at last.

Anna grabbed the little girl's hand and pulled her into her arms. If she'd had the breath for it, she would have shouted with joy and relief. "There we are. Oh, there we are, darling. I have you."

Wiry arms wrapped around her neck and held fast. If the girl said anything, it couldn't be heard over the sputtering and sobbing, and the sound of Anna's name being shouted from the shore.

Anna turned carefully, moving away from the deep-water edge, and caught sight of Max charging into the water. Before she was halfway back to the shore, he was upon them, disheveled and winded, his handsome face set in hard lines.

"Anna—"

"Her boat sank," she told him and wondered if that sounded as ridiculous to him as it did to her.

He swung the crying, shivering child up in his arms as his eyes raked over Anna. "Are you all right? Are you harmed?"

Anna wasn't certain which one of them he was addressing, but she shook her head, figuring that worked either way. The girl didn't have an injury she could see, and her loud sobbing indicated that her lungs were free of water.

Max continued to stare at her. "You're certain?"

"Yes." She'd stood in water. What sort of injury was he

expecting? To be fair, she was feeling increasingly odd, as if she was becoming slightly detached from what was happening around her, but that scarcely qualified as an injury.

"Right," Max said, nodding. "Right, then. Let's get you back to the house."

With one arm holding the child perched on his hip, Max wrapped the other arm tightly around Anna's shoulders and ushered her toward the shore. Anna was grateful for the assistance. She didn't feel tired, exactly, but her legs did feel weak, as if she'd just finished a footrace. Of course, having never actually participated in a footrace, that might not—

"Anna?"

She glanced over and found Max looking at her expectantly and with great concern. He'd asked her something, but she'd not heard him over the splashing of water, the continued rush of blood in her ears, and the little girl's wailing.

"I'm all right," she said, figuring that would at least address his concern.

"What?"

Had she not been so out of sorts, she might have laughed a little at their complete inability to communicate. Instead, she reached up and squeezed his hand in reassurance, and waited until they'd reached dry ground to tell him, "I'm fine."

She wasn't sure he'd heard her (her voice sounded muted to her own ears) until his arm slipped from her shoulder, and he adjusted the little girl in his hold.

"What's your name, sweetheart?" He patted her back gently. "Come on, now. Take a deep breath. You're all right . . . There you go . . . Now tell me your name."

The child coughed, hiccupped, and after several tries, managed, "Cassandra."

"Cassandra?" Max pulled back to take a better look at the girl's face. "Cassandra Hughs? Mrs. Webster's grandniece? Jim Hughs's girl?"

She sniffled, hiccupped again, and nodded.

Max gave her a bolstering smile. "I've not seen you in ages. Grown a mite, haven't you?"

She took a ragged breath. "Aye, sir?"

"Ah, you don't remember me, then. I saw you last . . ." He thought a moment. "Two years ago, I'd say. You were but an infant then. Miss Rees, a proper introduction, if you please."

"What?" Anna blinked at him as her sluggish mind caught up with the words. "Oh . . . Yes, of course. Er . . . Lord Dane, may I present Cassandra Hughs. Miss Hughs, this is Lord Dane."

Cassandra's drying eyes widened considerably, presumably at the realization she was being hauled across the countryside in the arms of nobility.

Max pretended not to see. "Cassandra's father is the finest cabinetmaker in England. Isn't he, love?"

"Aye, milord," she readily agreed, awe of nobility forgotten in the face of pride. "Best there is."

"So I have told all my friends in London."

"London? Truly?"

"Truly," he assured her gravely.

Max kept up a friendly banter with the girl for the remainder of the walk home. Anna listened with half an ear, which was all she seemed capable of at present. Her mind was a jumble of racing thoughts, her body was simultaneously bursting with energy and completely exhausted.

Once or twice, she caught Max staring at her over Cassandra's head, a line of worry across his brow. But she didn't begin to understand the full extent of that worry until they reached the house.

A footman, who must have spotted them in advance, greeted them just inside the door. "My lord? Miss? Is everything all right?"

"No," Max snapped, surprising Anna. Apparently, he surprised himself as well. He winced and cleared his throat. "Beg your pardon, Perkins. If you would please, fetch Engsly and send for the physician."

"Aye, milord."

Anna looked at Cassandra. She didn't appear to be in need of a doctor, but she supposed it wouldn't hurt to have the girl looked over.

A great commotion sounded and Anna turned to see Mrs. Webster come bustling down the hall with three maids. The housekeeper's eyes grew wide at the sight of the two bedraggled adults and the little girl in Max's arms.

"Good heavens, is that . . . ?" She gasped, rushed forward, and all but snatched her grandniece away from Max. "Cassie! Gracious, child, what's happened to you?"

To Anna's bewilderment, the sight of a familiar face seemed to dissolve the composure Cassandra had managed to achieve in the walk back to the house. The girl wrapped herself around Mrs. Webster, buried her face in the woman's neck, and sobbed. Loudly.

"She had something of an adventure in the pond," Max explained over the noise.

"The pond? But she can't swim."

Anna reached out and rubbed the girl's shoulder. "She had a raft, I think, but it sank—"

"Raft?" Mrs. Webster scowled at the top of Cassandra's head. "That ridiculous bit of nonsense your cousin cobbled together with sticks and twine? Good heavens, what were you thinking? You might have been killed, you foolish girl."

Cassandra sobbed louder at the rebuke. Mrs. Webster gently patted her back. "You'll be lucky, you will, if your father doesn't take a belt to your backside for this."

"You'll see to it she reaches her parents?"

Mrs. Webster nodded and strode down the hall, scolding and soothing the young Cassandra all the way.

Anna bit her lip, concerned. "Her father won't really—?"

"No," Max assured her before turning to address the nearest maid. "Find Mrs. Culpepper."

"No, stop. I beg of you, do not tell Mrs. Culpepper of this. Not yet." There was no keeping it from her for good, of course, but a bit of stalling could be done. "She'll fuss. Terribly."

He didn't appear particularly pleased with her request, but nodded, then sent the staff in search of towels, blankets, brandy, dry clothes, and warmed milk whilst he ushered Anna into the nearest parlor.

"Light a fire," he instructed a maid as he settled Anna into a seat. "And make certain the physician knows he is to go to Hughs's home first and come here directly after."

"You mean to pay him for his care of Cassandra?" Anna asked. She shifted in her chair, uncomfortable in her damp skirts. "That is very thoughtful of you."

"And you," he replied. He accepted a blanket from a winded footman and wrapped it around Anna's shoulders.

How was it thoughtful of her? "I didn't think of it."

"I mean to pay him for his care of you."

"What? I don't need a physician."

"Then I'll have wasted his time and my money, but you'll have no reason for complaint. Here . . ." He handed her a small brandy. "Drink this."

She wrinkled her nose at the glass but expertly swallowed down the contents. "Oh," she gasped. "Oh, that is dreadful. I simply do not understand the appeal."

Max took the empty glass from her, set it aside. "You're not a stranger to spirits."

"No." Drink, like carnal relations between men and women, had been part of the Anover House education, as provided by Mrs. Wrayburn. When Anna had reached her (estimated) teen years, she'd been given a sampling of spirits, instructions on how each should be served and imbibed, and then told that she could help herself in the future. Without curiosity or the lure of rebellion to tempt her—and having witnessed firsthand what too much drink could do to a person—Anna had kept her distance.

"I'd rather I was." She made a face and reached for the tea someone had produced with remarkable speed. "Vile stuff, that."

But it served its purpose, warming her from the inside and settling the worst of her nerves.

She glanced at Max, took in his slightly paled coloring and the hard set of his mouth, and wondered if he might benefit from a glass as well.

Chapter 15

❧

$\mathcal{M}$ax wanted to drink the bottle, or at least from it, in great, long gulps.

But as that would render him even more useless in the current situation, he resisted the lure of oblivion and put his effort into caring for Anna. And into berating himself.

He had made it approximately twenty-one hours before seeking Anna out. At the time he'd thought himself weak and selfish for giving in to his desire to see her. Now he was trying to clear his mind of images of what might have happened had he not given in and sought her out.

Not that he'd been a particular help once he'd found her. Anna had been pulling the child toward her (albeit by the unlikely means of a stick) by the time he'd arrived. But he *could* have been helpful. If the child had been too heavy or too panicked and pulled them both under, he could have reached them in time to help. It was small comfort, but it was all he had.

Max grabbed another blanket and wrapped it around Anna's shoulders.

He ought to have been there to start. What had he been thinking, letting her walk about the countryside alone? Hadn't he been obligated to rescue her from Clover, then carry her back to the manor house the last time she'd gone exploring by herself?

She wasn't one of the village lasses, accustomed to the unique perils of the countryside. The woman had never before been out of London. Hell, the woman had scarce been out of her house. She damn well shouldn't have been out of this house without—

"Perhaps we *should* send for Mrs. Culpepper."

Max blinked at the sound of Anna's voice. Glancing down, he saw he had yet another blanket in his hands. "Am I . . . ?" God, he hated to ask. "Fussing?"

"Oh, yes." She nodded emphatically. "To be honest, I've never experienced the like, not even with Mrs. Culpepper. You do realize it's warm outside?"

He looked at the blanket in his hand, the two she had on, the fire in the grate, and the steaming cup of tea in her hands.

"You were shivering," he said defensively.

"Was I?"

Only a little, but he'd felt it when his arm had been around her, and he'd hated it. He absolutely loathed the idea of Anna being hurt or sick, in no small part because it terrified him.

"Shock can give a body chills," he told her.

"I don't feel chilled. I feel . . . Well, I do feel out of sorts as yet, but *not*"—she held up a hand as he stepped closer—"chilled."

He studied her face closely. There was a warm, healthy color in her cheeks. But that didn't stop him from wanting to wrap another blanket around her. "Elaborate on 'out of sorts.' "

"It's . . . I don't know. I feel . . . disoriented, as if everything is moving faster than I am." She grimaced and colored. "That doesn't make any sense."

"It does," he assured her. "Go on."

"And at the same time, I feel invigorated . . . wonderful, really, as if I could climb a mountain and not be winded at the top. It's quite strange, and not entirely unpleasant."

"Perfectly natural." As a soldier, he'd experienced something similar after every battle. The mind wasn't always able to convince the body that danger had passed. He set the last blanket aside. "You'll be yourself again after a good rest."

"Rest?" She looked stupefied by the very idea. "I couldn't possibly."

"You can try. We'll get you upstairs, you can change, lie down, and . . ." He trailed off and fisted his hands, frustrated. Good God, what was *wrong* with him? When had he turned into a dithering, incompetent nursemaid? "Right. Of course you can't rest." Just as he couldn't stop himself from reaching out to brush a damp lock of hair off her shoulder and straighten her blankets. "Have pity and distract me. Tell me why you were using a stick."

"Beg your pardon?" She took a sip of her tea and he waited, almost patiently, for the words to sink into her racing mind. "Oh, the branch. I used it to reach Cassandra."

"Five feet away?"

"The water grew very deep, very quickly."

"And . . . you . . . ?" His heart plummeted to his feet, and what hope he'd had of fully regaining his composure was lost. "Holy hell, you can't swim, can you?"

"No, of course not." She blinked and looked to him with a curious expression. "Unless the skill might be innate, like a dog?"

He shook his head, stunned and horrified.

"Well, then." She grinned at him. "No, I can't swim."

A string of vulgar invectives spilled involuntarily from his mouth.

"Yes," Anna chimed. "I said much the same. But only in my head, as there was a child involved."

"You could have drowned. You might have died."

"Oh, yes, I know." She blew out a long breath and grinned again, like a woman deranged. "I was *most* terrified."

No wonder she'd been shivering. No wonder she remained "out of sorts."

"And that . . . pleases you?" Bloody hell, he wanted a drink from that brandy bottle. No, on second thought, what he wanted was to scoop Anna into his arms and onto his lap, wrap a dozen more blankets around her, and then drink the bottle of brandy while the reassuring heat of her seeped through to ease the painful knot in his chest.

"Not at the time, no. But now, yes." She lifted her shoulders in a sheepish manner and said, "It isn't courage if you're not afraid," as if that might provide some clarity.

He squeezed his eyes shut briefly, opened them again, and found himself no less confused. ". . . Sorry?"

"Courage is doing what is needed despite one's fear. Without the fear, it's merely . . . fearlessness."

He wondered at his state of mind that he was beginning to follow her logic. "And it's important to you, to be courageous?"

"I should think it would be important to everyone. But yes, I am relieved to know I am not a coward."

He reached out to tuck a length of hair behind her ear and found the warmth of her skin as it brushed against his fingers immensely comforting. Not so comforting as the warmth of her in his lap would certainly be, but helpful nonetheless. "Why the devil would you think otherwise?"

"I didn't. Not really. I simply . . . I didn't know. One wonders how one might act in dire circumstances. I wondered quite a bit. But . . . I so rarely left Anover House . . ." She trailed off, shaking her head.

Max nodded, rubbed her shoulder soothingly. He couldn't tell for certain if she was embarrassed or still battling shock, but he understood what she was trying to say. Much of how a person defined himself was through his interactions with the world. When that world was very small, it probably felt as if the opportunities for definition were very limited.

"You might have asked me," he said, and with a quick glance over his shoulder to be certain they were alone for the moment, he leaned down to press his lips to her brow. It was even better than touching her cheek. "I could have told you how brave you are," he whispered.

"Thank you." She sighed and offered a smile that was both grateful and apologetic. "But it's not the same."

"No," he agreed. "I know it's not."

There were some things about him he knew to be absolute truths. He enjoyed travel. He'd been a good officer. He'd been a poor brother. He was demonstrably bad at games of chance. If he'd not been allowed to leave McMullin Hall, he might never have known these, and a thousand other, things about himself.

Having never left Anover House, there were a thousand things Anna had yet to learn about herself.

Max withdrew his hand from her shoulder and turned to busy himself pouring a cup of tea he didn't want. For the first time, he wondered if he should be considering pursuing Anna at any pace, or if that was tantamount to thinking of snatching a young miss straight out of the nursery, or catching a butterfly as it emerged from its cocoon.

His next thought was that he'd been reading too much mawkish poetry of late.

Butterflies, indeed.

Anna Rees was not a fragile curiosity, nor a child in need of coddling. In fact, in many ways she was better suited to navigate the world than some of the young ladies of the ton. She was clever, sensible, and perhaps most important, well educated. Life at Anover House had not left her a blank canvas. Her experiences there had been unusual, not less.

No, it wasn't definition she lacked. The sort of woman

she was, was clear and sharp as glass. What she needed was confidence. That would come—and sometimes go—with time, as it did for everyone. A person was constantly learning new things about himself, the good, the disappointing, and everything in between. Anna wasn't alone in that.

She had learned something new about herself today and it had bolstered her confidence.

He had learned something new about himself today and it made him uneasy.

Apparently, he was capable of fussing. Evidently, he was incapable of going four-and-twenty hours without seeing Anna Rees. Clearly, he was less motivated by loyalty than he was by irrational fear, because when he was kicked out of the room two minutes later so that Anna might change into dry clothes, the first thing he did was go in search of Mrs. Culpepper. And then Lucien.

A little fussing, he reasoned, never hurt anyone. If Mrs. Culpepper and Lucien could fuss until Anna agreed to spend the remainder of the day with her feet up, all the better.

Chapter 16

❧

The following afternoon, Anna made her way down a back stairwell, taking stock of her various aches and pains. Her legs were pleasantly sore from her morning walk. Her fingers stung lightly in the places where Hermia's sharp little teeth had taken hold in play. Her sides and cheeks ached from smiling and laughing.

Anna was certain she'd done more smiling and laughing in the past few days than she typically did in a year, and almost all of it had been with Max.

He'd been waiting for her on the terrace again that morning. Only this time, rather than start them off on a stroll, he'd offered to teach her how to swim. Which she'd thought was quite funny, until she'd realized he was entirely serious.

Though it was a sweet thought, she ultimately declined the offer. She wanted to learn how to swim, but she wasn't willing to take off her gown in front of Max (and anyone else who happened to wander by) and hop into the pond with nothing on but a thin chemise.

In fact, a rather intimate image had flashed through her mind at the time. Naturally, Max would have to remove some of his garments for swimming as well, and she'd had a surprisingly clear picture of what the man might look like with his muscled chest bared, and his tight breeches clinging to his powerful thighs . . . And she'd imagined how his eyes might darken when he looked at her in her thin, wet chemise. And, well, perhaps Max had some inkling of just how problematic that could all turn out to be, because he hadn't pressed the matter when she'd declined, other than to extract a promise from her that she would ask Mrs. Culpepper for lessons with all due haste. Anna had no idea if Mrs. Culpepper had the first inkling of how to swim, but she'd promised all the same.

A movement outside the window at the bottom of the steps caught Anna's eye. She stopped, stared, and felt her heart drop past her feet and straight through the floor.

A carriage and multiple outriders were coming down the drive.

"Oh, no."

Lucien had guests. Lots and lots of guests.

After a moment's panicked debate over whether she wished to hide and wonder who the visitors were, or find out who the visitors were and then hide, Anna made a dash for the front hall, arriving just as the first guests were coming inside.

Only she wasn't *in* the front hall, not in the strictest sense. She was in the doorway of a small room used for storage, in a hall just off the front hall, where she could see and hear everything that was going on in the front hall without being obtrusive.

Very well, she was hiding and spying. And for that she felt foolish, but not so foolish that she was tempted to leave her hiding spot. Particularly when Lucien stepped forward and greeted a smiling gold-haired woman in a dusty green riding habit.

"Winnefred! I'd not thought you'd come."

Anna's pulse leapt. Lady Winnefred Haverston. Good heavens, the rest of the family had arrived.

Lady Winnefred gave her brother-in-law a friendly kiss on the cheek and stepped back. "It's far easier on horseback than inside that dratted carriage. Though to be honest, my backside has not yet grown accustomed to sitting a horse for so—"

"Freddie," a new feminine voice chimed, "do allow me to greet my husband before you embarrass him into leaving."

Engsly's countenance brightened remarkably as a second woman stepped through the front doors carrying a small wicker basket. *"Lilly."*

Lady Engsly handed the basket to Winnefred on her way to enveloping her husband in a warm embrace.

Anna felt her brows rise at the sight. Her experience with the ton was limited, but even she knew that such open displays of affection between husband and wife were uncommon.

Lucien brushed a lock of black hair behind his wife's ear and pressed a kiss to her forehead. "I cannot tell you how relieved I am that you are finally here."

"Worried we'd been accosted by gypsies?" Lady Engsly inquired with a grin. "Forced off the road by highwaymen? Become lost?"

"All that and more."

Lady Winnefred snorted in a definitively unladylike manner. "We've made the trip safely dozens of times."

"Yes, but never before without me," Lucien pointed out.

"Your presence would have been superfluous," a masculine voice said from the door. "As is generally the case when I'm available."

Anna leaned forward in anticipation as the one person

she'd been waiting for came inside. Lord Gideon Haverston. Her second brother.

As he and Lucien swapped good-natured barbs, Anna studied him in detail, noting he had the same dark hair and eyes as his brother. He wasn't greatly taller than Lucien, but he was larger—broader across the chest and shoulders, and more notably muscled. He used a cane and walked with a slight limp, the result, she'd been told, of a wound gained during a great naval battle. For a time, her brother had been Captain Haverston.

It was strange to think on. What had she been doing in the moments this man had fought for his life amidst the horror of battle? Making a sampler? Conjugating the verbs of a dead language?

What on earth were they going to find to talk about?

Her eyes drifted over Lady Engsly's finery and Lady Winnefred's confident smile. What was she going to find to talk about with any of them?

Keeping his arm around his wife, Lucien jerked his chin at Lady Winnefred. "What is it you have there, Freddie?"

"A basket."

There was a telling pause before Lucien spoke again. "What's *in* the basket?"

"Oh, the usual sort of basket . . . ry . . . items?"

Lying, clearly, did not number amongst Lady Winnefred's talents.

"It's a cat," Lady Engsly said succinctly. "She stole it from a coaching inn."

Lucien didn't appear particularly surprised by the news. "Put it in the stable, Freddie."

"Told you," Lady Engsly teased.

Lady Winnefred made a face at her sister-in-law. "I didn't steal her, I rescued her. And she isn't a cat, she's a kitten. She can't fend for herself in the stable."

"You can't keep her in the house," Lucien told her.

"Why not?"

"My valet has a sensitivity to cats."

Lord Gideon looked over from where he was holding a quiet conversation with the butler. "Kincaid? No, he doesn't."

Lucien shook his head. "Kincaid is visiting his mother."

"What difference does it make?" Lady Winnefred asked. "I'm not asking your man to cuddle with Gwennie."

"Gwennie?" Engsly looked to the ceiling and groaned. "As in Aunt Gwen? I thought we'd done with naming farm animals after members of this family."

"She assures me it's an honor," Lord Gideon said.

"It is," Lady Winnefred assured him. "I quite like your aunt. And I quite like this kitten."

Lady Engsly laughed and patted Lucien's hand. "And I am quite sure your current valet's only sensitivity is to the process of removing animal hair from wool coats. Freddie, promise you'll keep Gwennie away from Lucien's coats and valet."

"I promise to do my best."

"Freddie," Lady Engsly said in a warning tone.

"It's a cat," Lady Winnefred reminded them. "They're prodigiously stealthy."

Lord Gideon narrowed his eyes at his wife. "Tell me you don't mean to keep it in our chambers."

"How else would I keep an eye on it?"

"Right." He took the basket from his wife and handed it to the nearest footman. "Tell the stable master to keep an eye on it."

Lady Winnefred scowled at him, but even at a distance Anna could see there was no heat in it. "He'll be keeping an eye on more than just the kitten in a minute. Where is your husbandly loyalty?"

"Off cavorting somewhere with your wifely obedience." He bent down and gave her a light peck on the lips. "I'm told they make a happy pair."

Lady Winnefred laughed, but what she said next was

lost to Anna, drowned out by Max's voice coming from down the hall.

"What are you doing in there?"

Later, she would feel keen embarrassment at having been caught eavesdropping by Max. At the moment, however, it was the fear of being caught by the Haverstons that concerned her. Her eyes darted from Max, to the front hall, and back again. Since they didn't appear to have heard Max, she slipped from her doorway, hurried over, grabbed him by the arm, and pulled him through a doorway into what appeared to be a small parlor.

"What the devil are you doing?" Max asked, laughing.

"Shhh." Anna peeked out and discovered she could still see a sliver of the front hall, provided she stood on her toes and peered over the top of an oversized urn. "The family is here."

"Gideon and Lady Engsly?"

"And Lady Winnefred."

"Really?" He peeked around the corner and smiled, then turned back to her. "Why are we in here whispering?"

"I . . ." She bit her lip and searched desperately for a way to answer the question without actually answering the question, because *I'm being a dreadful ninny* wasn't something she wished to share with Max.

"I don't know that we need to whisper," she tried. "I can't hear what they're saying, so it stands to reason they can't hear what we're saying, although they might have heard what you said as you were coming down the hall. You were quite loud—"

"Why are we hiding, love?" Max pressed.

"Right." Her eyes scanned the room, hoping for inspiration. It was not forthcoming. "Right. Well. Because . . . You see . . . I . . ."

"What is it?"

Her shoulders slumped in defeat. "It's nothing. It's ridiculous."

"It's not ridiculous if it's upsetting to you. And it must be exceedingly upsetting to you if I can *tell* it's upsetting you." He shrugged when she looked at him, a little confused. "There's no denying you can be a difficult woman to read."

"It's called maintaining one's composure. Mrs. Culpepper is a great advocate of maintaining one's composure." She twisted her fingers into the skirts of her gown. "She would be exceedingly disappointed to see me now."

"Come here." He took her elbow in a gentle grasp, pulled her fully into the small parlor, and shut the door. "Sit down."

"I don't want to sit." She wanted the option to move about the room if nerves overwhelmed her.

"Then stand," Max agreed. "But tell me what the trouble is. Don't you want to meet the rest of your family?"

"I don't know," she replied without thinking, then winced at her own answer. "Of course I do. I don't know why I said that. Only . . . Only I've never spoken with a real lady. I don't think I know how."

"Certainly you do. You speak with Mrs. Culpepper every day."

"It's not the same. She's family." She clenched her hands, frustrated. "That is, she is family I know. And she isn't good ton, like they are. She may have been at one time, but—"

"You do have some experience with the ton," he tried. "You've spoken with gentlemen. Here, and at Anover House if one is lenient in one's definition of a gentleman."

"That's different. Men are different. They're . . ."

"Adorable?" he offered.

"No, that's just you. They're simple. *Please*, don't be angry," she hurried on when one of his eyebrows winged up. "I only mean that it's an easy thing to converse with individuals who have but two or three interests . . . That doesn't sound any better." She gripped the fabric of her skirts in an effort to keep her hands steady. "Lord Engsly loves the written word and adores his family. I am certain he enjoys exploring many other topics, but his passion is for books and his family. And so that is what we discuss. It's simple. Moreover, if I forget myself and speak out of turn, he is a gentleman and makes no mention of it. What if Lady Engsly wants to speak of . . ." She racked her mind for something sufficiently awful. ". . . Draperies, or some such? What if she wants to discuss fashion, or likes to gossip? What if I forget myself with her and say something that sends her into a swoon? What if—?"

She broke off, unwilling to admit her greatest fear aloud.

What if they stare and whisper and hate me because I am the Ice Maiden of Anover House?

They could make her life a living hell. According to Madame, no one, absolutely *no one*, could cut to the quick quite like a true lady. The truer the lady, the deeper the cut.

"I find ladies to be most intimidating," she finished rather lamely.

Max shook his head, looking bemused. "You're the most intimidating lady I know."

I'm not a lady. "They've nothing to fear from me, and they know it."

"And you've nothing to fear from them."

"You don't know that."

Max stepped closer, took one of her hands in his. "I'd not let anyone hurt you," he said quietly and rubbed the pad of his thumb over her knuckles. "I know that."

A warmness settled over her, easing the tight knot of tension at the base of her neck. She sought for a proper response to such a lovely sentiment, but he didn't give her the chance.

"Besides," he continued. "We've already established you're not a coward."

"One may be brave under some circumstances and less so under—"

He squeezed her hand. "You're not a coward."

She wondered if there was any possible way to argue that point without implying that she was, in fact, a coward, but nothing came to mind.

"No," she agreed, almost reluctantly. "I'm not a coward."

"Excellent." He offered his elbow, just as he did in the morning. "Now, why don't we take a stroll to the front hall?"

Anna took a deep breath, then accepted Max's proffered arm and allowed him to escort her out of the room.

As they drew near the front hall, Anna could see that the Haverstons were laughing and talking over each other in the way of a loving family . . . And then they spotted her, and the happy chatter faded away, replaced by a tense silence.

The joyous family reunion had come to an abrupt halt. Because of her. Anna had never felt so much the intruder as she did in that moment.

Chin up, shoulders back, eyes straight ahead.

She focused on the soft material of Max's coat beneath her fingers, kept her face studiously clear of the fear she was feeling, and fixed her gaze on Lucien. He, at least, looked genuinely pleased to see her.

"Ah. Here she is." Lucien waved her forward. "Anna, come. Come and meet everyone."

She forced a pleasant smile as introductions and greetings were made.

Lady Engsly, Lord Gideon, and Lady Winnefred were clearly fond of Max, greeting him with genuine smiles and a bit of good-natured teasing.

Their reception of her was more subdued. Lord Gideon smiled the most, but also studied her with the most intensity. Lady Engsly appeared friendly but wary, and Lady Winnefred struck Anna as being equal parts inquisitive and uncomfortable.

They inquired after her stay. She asked after their journey.

The word "well," was once again put to poor use. It was like meeting Lucien all over again, only the awkwardness and uncertainty were multiplied. And she couldn't use weariness as an excuse to escape to her chambers.

Luckily, Lady Engsly made the excuse instead. "I do hate to point it out, but Freddie and I simply must retire for a bit. We are positively coated in dust, and most uncomfortable—"

"No, I'm not." Lady Winnefred shrugged when all eyes turned to her, the dustiest of all the travelers. "Uncomfortable, that is. I'm just famished."

Lucien gestured down the hall. "Mrs. Webster just sent a small repast to the breakfast room, if you—"

"Excellent." Lady Winnefred turned bright amber eyes and a wide smile on Anna. "Would you care to join me, Miss Rees?"

The invitation took Anna completely off guard. Apparently, she wasn't the only one similarly affected. Several sets of eyebrows winged up at once.

Fortunately, she saw only surprise and curiosity amongst the group, not so much as a hint of disapproval. *Unfortunately*, that left her without a reasonable excuse for not joining Lady Winnefred in the breakfast room.

"I should be delighted to accompany you," she lied.

She wracked her brain for an acceptable, inconspicuous way to invite Max along, but before she could come up with anything suitable, Lord Gideon asked for his and Lucien's company in the study.

Before Anna knew it, Lady Engsly had left for her chambers, a maid had been dispatched for Mrs. Culpepper, Lucien had declared that they should all reconvene soon in the breakfast room, and Anna was accompanying Lady Winnefred from the front hall.

Anna wasn't sure whether or not it was a blessing that the breakfast room was such a short walk away. On the one hand, it removed the need for any sort of conversation on the way there. On the other hand, she didn't have the time to come up with a suitable topic of conversation before they arrived, which left her making a beeline to the side table filled with cold meats and cheese the moment they arrived.

Lady Winnefred, on the other hand, appeared to have something else in mind.

A moment after stepping out the door, she leaned back out it again, looked both ways down the hall, then stepped back inside and blew an errant gold lock out of her eyes.

"I promised Lilly I'd be on my best behavior, but honestly, this is *ridiculous*. How the ton comes to know each other around all this denial of the obvious, I will never understand." And with that small speech, she planted her hands on her hips in a distinctly masculine fashion and asked, "Are you *really* Gideon's sister?"

Anna carefully set down the plate she'd just grabbed and turned to face her sister-in-law. "Yes, I am."

Winnefred bobbed her head. "Gideon insisted that Lucien's man could be trusted, but sometimes a person needs to ask for oneself. I hope you understand."

What Anna understood was that Lady Winnefred had essentially just taken her at her word. "I . . . Yes, I understand perfectly." She just hadn't expected it.

"Excellent, now . . ." Lady Winnefred leaned over to peak out the doorway yet again before coming over to join Anna at the sideboard. "What was it like growing up in Anover House?"

"I beg your pardon?"

"Amongst the wild ladies and wicked gentlemen." She picked up and began filling a plate of her own. "Was it terribly exciting?"

"I . . . No, not particularly," Anna replied automatically, then wished she hadn't. Nothing in Lady Winnefred's tone or bearing suggested she was interested in condemning. Rather the lady was merely inviting Anna to share a story or two.

And now the lady looked mildly disappointed.

Anna swore silently. Speaking of her life at Anover House was not ideal, but it was shortsighted of her to rebuff a friendly invitation. She sought for a way to satisfy Lady Winnefred's curiosity without horrifying her but couldn't come up with anything more substantial than, "It was quite loud on occasion."

Fortunately, Lady Winnefred seemed appeased by that. She nodded in understanding. "London seems always to be prodigiously loud to me. I much prefer the peacefulness of the country."

Anna's heart leapt at those words. Something in common. They had something in common. "I do as well," she returned, picking up her plate once more. "I've only been here a very short time, mind you, but I always knew I'd like the country more than town."

"I always knew I wouldn't like London, even before I'd ever visited."

Anna tried to recall what history she knew of Lady Winnefred, but couldn't come up with more than, "You're from Scotland, are you not?"

"In a roundabout sort of way," Lady Winnefred said. "I'm English born. When my father passed, I became ward to the late Marquess of Engsly. Lilly was a cousin to his second wife, recently orphaned as well and in need of help. We were taken to Scotland and left there."

Anna was caught off guard by that last statement, and the matter-of-fact tone in which it was delivered. She had an image of a carriage stopping just on the other side of England's border, dropping off two young women, and turning round again.

"Left there?"

"At Murdoch House, my farm," Lady Winnefred clarified, as she carefully selected a slice of roast beef.

Anna wasn't sure that was altogether better. "Alone?"

"Very much so. Though I think Lilly, being responsible for the both of us, felt it more than I."

"How old were you?"

"I was thirteen. Lilly . . . a few years older." She smiled impishly. "She doesn't like it when I mention her age."

"Good heavens. You were children."

"By some standards," Lady Winnefred returned and reached for a thick slice of bread.

Anna was floored by the realization that she had something very significant in common with Lady Winnefred and Lady Engsly. They too knew what it was like to be isolated from the rest of the world.

"That must have been . . ." Terrifying, she thought. Thirteen ought to be childhood by everyone's standards. "Difficult."

"Very, at times. But I'd not trade Murdoch House for the world. It's home."

Anna didn't have a response to that. Somehow, *I've traded Anover House for the promise of a thousand pounds and a friendly dog* didn't seem right.

Lady Winnefred jerked her chin at Anna's empty plate. "Are you not hungry?"

"What? Oh, right."

Rather than take a seat at the table, Lady Winnefred leaned a hip against the sideboard and waited while Anna filled her plate. "Tell me more of this Anover House. Is it true that the ladies really run about all day with the tops of their gowns down around their waists?"

Anna nearly dropped the fork she was holding. "Where did you hear that?"

"From Lilly, and she knows everything."

"She is mistaken." Anna caught Winnefred's fallen expression and took a risk. "Though perhaps not *entirely* mistaken. There are some women who, at some parties, are not averse to, shall we say, advertising their wares. But it's not done by all the ladies, and it's not done all day."

"I see. Have you ever—?"

"No."

Lady Winnefred bobbed her head, thoughtful. "I can't imagine being so bold. I'm no prude, mind you, but prancing about without one's clothing . . ." She tilted her head ever so slightly and squinted her eyes, giving Anna the distinct impression that her ladyship was envisioning herself naked at the breakfast table. "No . . . No, I don't think I could do it either. Should dearly love to see it, though. What a ridiculous sight it must be."

Anna had only caught sight of such a spectacle a few times. Ridiculous was the perfect description. "It's not an experience one wishes to repeat."

Lady Winnefred nodded, sent a wary glance at the door. "Lord, I'll never hear the end of it if Lilly hears of this conversation, but I *must* know . . . Do the gentlemen ever participate?"

Anna could scarce believe she was having this conversation with a lady. "Less often, but it has happened."

"Have you seen it happen?"

She'd once caught a glimpse out a window of a gentleman's bare backside as he'd dashed through her mother's torch-lit garden after goodness only knew what. But before she could tell Lady Winnefred the story, they were interrupted by a voice in the doorway.

"Has she seen what?" Lord Gideon inquired, eyeing them both when Lady Winnefred smiled at him without comment and Anna took an extreme interest in her selection of cheese. "Do I want to know what we're discussing?"

"No," the women replied in unison.

Anna glanced up in time to see Lord Gideon shrug lightly. "Fair enough. Just be careful Lilly doesn't hear of it." He looked to her and offered a jovial wink. "She lectures."

Anna felt a bubble of laughter catch in her throat as she shared a private smile with Lady Winnefred on their way to the table. They had a secret, she realized with growing wonder. A silly, harmless, even pointless secret, to be sure. But a secret nonetheless.

Perhaps she wasn't so inept at conversing with ladies after all, she mused. And as the afternoon progressed, she began to wonder if she might be able to get on well enough with all the Haverstons.

After filling his plate, Lord Gideon joined in their conversation, which had moved on to the delights of country living. Lady Winnefred happily extolled the benefits of residing on a farm while Gideon teasingly baited her by extolling the benefits of residing with a happy wife, even if it meant extra time and travel for supplies and company.

Lucien and Lady Engsly entered the conversation when they arrived minutes later, with Lady Engsly being a proponent of town life, while Lucien recused himself from the debate, declaring he couldn't possibly choose between the pleasure of agreeing with his wife or contradicting his brother.

When Mrs. Culpepper arrived, introductions were made anew and then, to Anna's great delight, the conversation immediately resumed when Lord Gideon asked Mrs. Culpepper her views on country versus town life.

Just like that, they had invited Mrs. Culpepper into their conversation, who appeared to take to it like fish to water. Or perhaps diplomat to compromise. She quickly agreed with Lord Gideon's claim that it was one's company that mattered, not one's location.

The lively debate continued with Max's arrival.

Whilst Anna's enjoyment of it dimmed considerably.

Max was quite vehement in his objection to residing anywhere but in town. Country estates were for visiting, he opined. London was for life.

It came as no surprise to Anna, of course. He'd made clear his thoughts on the subject before. But it was disheartening, nonetheless, to hear him voice a view of the world so incompatible with her own.

When he excused himself from the group soon after,

Anna discovered with a heavy heart that she was unable, or perhaps merely unwilling, to look at him as he passed.

It wasn't until Mrs. Culpepper leaned over and whispered, "Eyes straight ahead, dear," several minutes later that Anna realized she was staring at her plate. Anna sent her a smile that was half gratitude, half apology.

Now was not the time to be glum. She'd not let a divergence of opinion with Max ruin her day, and certainly not her success with the Haverstons. The laughter and teasing she'd spied in the front hall had returned. She wasn't adding much to the discussion, but neither was she detracting from their enjoyment of it, and that was a tremendous improvement.

Anna wasn't ready yet to declare that she'd been welcomed in by the Haverstons. But she'd not been unwelcomed. And that was a promising start.

Chapter 17

❧

$\mathcal{A}$nna could not recall a time when she'd ever been so desirous of a nap.

It was amazing, really, how a person might walk for hours about the fields and woods without exhausting herself, but a single hour amongst the lively Haverston clan and she could scarcely see straight.

Exhausted but pleased, Anna twined her arm with Mrs. Culpepper's as they walked down the hall toward their chambers. "What a day this has been."

"Indeed." Mrs. Culpepper patted her hand gently. "What do you make of your family?"

"We've only just met them, but they seem kind. What do you think?"

"I think they are men and women of honor."

Anna pulled back a little for a better view of her friend's face. "That is a very definitive opinion for so short an acquaintance."

"You forget, I was aware of your brothers' reputations long before meeting them."

"And you set great store by reputation?" Anna inquired, knowing full well the answer was no.

Mrs. Culpepper stopped them in the hallway between the doors to their chambers. "In this instance, with your family . . . Yes. Their reputation for being an honorable family was, and is, of importance to me."

Anna wasn't quite sure what to say to that. The sentiment was so unlike her friend. According to Mrs. Culpepper, reputation was rarely representative of a person's true character. "Why would you make an exception for them?"

"Because everything about them has the power to affect you." Mrs. Culpepper took a step toward her door. "I should like a word with you inside, please."

Anna wanted to take a step back. "You look dreadfully serious."

"It is a matter of some gravity that I wish to discuss. Inside, dear."

"Yes, all right." Only it wasn't all right, particularly. They'd had a lovely afternoon. What sort of somber business was there to discuss?

Mrs. Culpepper wasted no time in answering that question. Upon entering her chambers, she walked to the middle of the room, turned about, and announced, "The time has come for me to retire."

Anna stepped inside and closed the door behind her. "You are retired," she said slowly. "You left employment when we left Anover House."

"Allow me to rephrase. It is time for me to leave."

"Caldwell Manor?" Anna shook her head lightly, more confused than upset. "I've not received the thousand pounds yet. I can't leave."

"No. You *shouldn't* leave Caldwell, but that is another discussion." She caught Anna's gaze and held it. "*I* am leaving, dear. I am going to my sister's. She has been desirous of my company since her husband died three years ago, leaving her quite alone, and she is not as strong as she once was."

"Oh." Anna crossed the room and took her friend's hand. "Oh, Mrs. Culpepper, I am sorry. Is she ill? Why did you not—?"

"She is not ill. But we are of an age, dear."

"Of an . . . ?" Annoyed, Anna dropped Mrs. Culpepper's hand. "You are of the ideal age to be looking forward to a long and happy life."

"And so I shall," Mrs. Culpepper calmly agreed. "With my sister. I have kept her waiting long enough."

Three years, Anna thought. It was a long time for her to have put off the trip. "Why did you not say something before?"

"I would never have left you at Anover House and I'd not have cared for an argument on the subject."

"I'd not have—"

"Nor would I care to have an argument on the subject now," Mrs. Culpepper said sternly. "I have been waiting for the Haverstons to arrive so that I might take measure of the family as a whole. This afternoon has convinced me you are safe here at Caldwell."

Anna bit the inside of her cheek to keep from arguing and to keep calm. Why Mrs. Culpepper had kept her silence until now was not the problem. The fact that Mrs. Culpepper was determined to leave, that was a problem. It was on the tip of Anna's tongue to promise Mrs. Culpepper that she'd not have to leave alone. Surely Lucien could now be convinced to pay the thousand pounds.

But Anna couldn't make herself offer the promise. She couldn't leave Caldwell. Not yet.

Instead, she surprised herself by blurting out the rather childish and embarrassing confession, "I still need you."

Mrs. Culpepper's features softened. "This time was to come eventually, dear. You are too old for a governess and no longer in need of a paid companion. You've family now."

Anna wanted to say that Mrs. Culpepper had been more than a governess and companion. She'd been more than a friend. *She* was family. But the words caught in her throat. Mrs. Culpepper was many things—compassionate, clever, witty . . . and wholly uncomfortable with open displays of sentiment.

It would be inexcusably selfish of her to try to convince Mrs. Culpepper to stay. More, a fuss would accomplish nothing but to leave them both feeling doubly miserable.

Anna cleared her throat, finding it difficult to swallow past the lump forming there. "When are you to go?"

Perhaps something would happen before then to change Mrs. Culpepper's mind. Her sister might decide to remarry, or move closer to London, or—

"At dawn."

"At . . . tomorrow?" There was no possible chance of an engagement by tomorrow. "But . . . so soon." It was too soon. She wasn't ready.

"I did not want a long good-bye."

Anna opened her mouth, shut it. She didn't know what to say to that, what to do with it.

I don't want to say good-bye at all. I don't want you to go.

"I need . . . I should like a walk," she announced, and headed for the door. She had to get out of the room. "We'll discuss this later."

If Mrs. Culpepper had a response to that, Anna neither heard nor saw it. She was out the door and down the hall in the blink of an eye. A few minutes, that was all she needed. A few minutes alone to clear her head and calm herself. Or better yet, a few minutes alone with Max. If she couldn't argue the matter with Mrs. Culpepper, then she could talk it through with Max. It was bound to help.

Only Max wasn't available.

Lord Dane, a maid informed her, had left for Menning and was expected to return early tomorrow. Anna knew Menning as a town ten miles away, a halfway stop between

Caldwell Manor and McMullin Hall. Sadly, the maid had not been informed why His Lordship had found it necessary to hie off to another town.

Menning wasn't any larger than Codridgeton. It hadn't any attractions one couldn't just as easily find in Codridgeton.

Unless, of course, the attraction one sought had a specific name.

Anna didn't want to think about that, about Max's love of the demimonde, and the demimonde's love of excess . . . every sort of excess.

But now that she was thinking on it, she was forced to admit that it was naïve to have assumed Max didn't have a mistress. He might very well have several. For all she knew, he had a legion of them, scattered about the countryside and the various neighborhoods of London. Where was the fun in being moderate in one's excesses, after all?

He might have children as well, she realized. He might have dozens. He might . . .

Anna stopped in the hall outside the library and took a deep, calming breath.

She was working herself into a snit over nothing. Or quite possibly nothing. Either way, it was rash and unfair of her to presume there was *something*. Max might have been summoned by an ailing friend, for all she knew. Why assume the worst?

Why presume she had any right to care at all? They'd made no promises.

Anna shoved that thought aside. "One trouble at a time."

And right now, that trouble remained Mrs. Culpepper's immediate departure from Caldwell.

And right now, Anna was left with no other choice but to spend the next half hour in the library, feeling very much alone. And then, when she was confident she could do so with her composure intact, she returned to Mrs. Culpepper's chambers to help her friend pack.

Chapter 18

❧

The next day dawned all too soon, and with weather that was fittingly miserable. A steady drizzle had begun the night before and persisted into morning when it grew into a proper downpour.

Anna had listened to it pelt the windows in the front parlor as Mrs. Culpepper said her good-byes to the Haverstons, and now she stood under the sheltering portico and watched it soak the footmen loading Mrs. Culpepper's carriage.

Next to her, Mrs. Culpepper supervised the proceedings. "Your mother's staff might take a lesson or two from these fine people. Tremendously efficient."

Anna made a noncommittal noise that may or may not have been heard over the rain.

Mrs. Culpepper gave her a bolstering pat on the shoulder. "Here now, not so glum, dear. We are at the start of new adventures, you and I. When next we meet, we shall have such stories to tell."

Anna nodded, but said nothing. She wanted to be perfectly self-possessed for Mrs. Culpepper, the very picture
of composure. It would make things easier on both of them
and, better yet, make Mrs. Culpepper proud. But it was all
she could do to breathe past the damned, awful lump in her
throat. She'd hoped it would lessen with sleep, but it seemed
to have only grown during the night.

"Now then," Mrs. Culpepper pressed on. "Should you
need assistance for any reason—"

"I know." Anna cleared her throat, kept her gaze focused
on the drive ahead of her. "And should you need me—"

"Yes, of course." Mrs. Culpepper brushed at the sleeves
of her traveling gown. "And you must promise to write
faithfully or I shall know the reason why."

"I'll promise if you agree to take this journey slowly.
Stop at the first sign of illness and rest."

"Agreed. And you must come to visit as soon as you are
able."

The reminder that this need not be a permanent separation lifted Anna's spirits, if only marginally. "I should like
that very much."

"Whether or not you should like it is immaterial," Mrs.
Culpepper intoned. "You will come."

"I promise."

"Good. Well." Another pat on the arm. "Good-bye, dear."

Anna felt herself mouth the word, "Good-bye."

And then she was watching Mrs. Culpepper walk down
the steps and out into the rain.

It felt wrong, terribly wrong. This was not what Anna
had envisioned happening when she'd fled Anover House.
This was not something she had envisioned happening at
any time . . . Because it *was* wrong, she realized as Mrs.
Culpepper climbed into the carriage and a footman shut
the door behind her.

Mrs. Culpepper deserved better than this.

"Stop! Wait." Anna threw her hand up, dashed to the carriage, and threw open the door.

Mrs. Culpepper gasped as the damp wind blew inside. "Good heavens, child, what—?"

"I want you to know something." Anna's fingers curled into the wood of the door. "You were . . . You are . . ." She took a short, deep breath and met Mrs. Culpepper's eyes. "You are twice the mother Madame could have ever hoped to be. I love you very much."

Mrs. Culpepper blinked, twice, then did the unthinkable. She shifted in her seat.

"I love you too, dear. You are very much the daughter of my heart." She reached out and patted Anna gently on the arm, then sniffed and withdrew her hand, signaling the end of their sentimental moment. "Now off with you before you catch your death and hand me mine. Running out into the rain like a street urchin. Honestly. One would think I'd have raised a woman with more sense . . ."

Anna grinned at Mrs. Culpepper's good-natured lecture as she stepped back from the carriage, closed the door, and signaled the driver to be off. If Mrs. Culpepper had been a different woman, Anna might have returned to the portico with all due haste as a parting gesture of respect.

But Mrs. Culpepper had not been a typical governess in an average household.

Mrs. Culpepper had taught Anna how to stand in front of the condemning gazes and sharp, whispering tongues of her mother's guests without giving them the satisfaction of seeing so much as a batted eyelash. She'd taught Anna how to acquire an education without proper resources, or even permission. She'd shown her how to ferret out the secrets of her lineage despite her mother's lies and locked doors, and how to escape from a world that was little more than a well-dressed prison.

In essence, Mrs. Culpepper had taught her defiance.

And so Anna stayed where she was on the drive as the rain poured down, soaking her to the bone. With her heart in her throat, she tipped her chin up, squared her shoulders, and kept her eyes straight ahead, and to her everlasting delight, the last thing she heard before distance and the rain drowned out all sounds from the carriage, was Mrs. Culpepper's quick bark of laughter.

That, she thought, was a proper send-off.

Pity the fun of it didn't lift her mood for more than the time it took her to go back inside and change. By the time she reached the library, where she'd gone in search of distraction, the lump had returned to her throat.

And it had grown some by the time Max came striding into the library, a quarter hour later, wearing a wet overcoat and carrying a hat in his hand.

"There you are," he said. "I've been searching for you."

He couldn't have been searching for her for long. He looked as if he'd only just walked into the house. Anna turned from the shelf of books she'd been staring at without much interest.

"Mrs. Culpepper has gone," she told him, because she didn't much feel like making friendly chatter.

"Yes, I just heard." He tossed his hat on a side table, began to divest himself of his coat. "I'm sorry I wasn't here. I had business in Menning."

"Was she worth the trip in the rain?" she asked and immediately snapped her mouth shut, horrified. The ugly accusation had come out before she'd known it was there. "I'm sorry. I don't know where that came from. I had no right. I'm so—"

"It's all right. Forgiven." He set his coat next to his hat, peeled off his gloves. "I bought a horse for my niece, one of Reginald's daughters. A lovely little mare named Iris. I'd been after her for some time now. I stayed late because Mr. Hudson is an agreeable old widower who does not see enough company."

"I see." Well, it wasn't a visit to an ailing friend, but she still felt a fool. "I apologize, I do. I should not have rushed to judgment, nor presumed—"

He was quiet a moment, studying her. "I don't have a mistress."

"Oh. Well." What did she say to that? Good? Damned right, you don't?

"You don't believe me," he said softly, and she heard the first hints of frustration in his voice.

"What? Yes, I do." She took an awkward step forward. "Of course I do. I just . . . I wasn't certain what to say, that's all."

His eyes narrowed for a split second, and then all traces of irritation were gone from his features. He blew out a small breath. "You're a difficult woman to read, Anna Rees."

"I don't mean to be, not with you." But the lessons she had learned from Mrs. Culpepper were not easily put aside. Anna's chest tightened, and she blurted out, "She said we were embarking on new adventures."

To his credit, Max merely blinked at the sudden switch in topics, then walked around a chaise and set of chairs to stand nearer to her. "Mrs. Culpepper? I'd not have guessed her to be the adventurous sort."

"She's not, particularly. It's just something she used to say when I was younger and frustrated at being unable to leave Anover House." She found herself staring at a lower shelf of books and mumbling a little. "Every day can be exciting and fulfilling. Even if you fill it with dreams of adventures to come."

"Adventures like having a cottage of your own?"

Fearful he was poking fun, she shot her eyes to his face, but she saw only interest there, not an inkling of humor.

"Yes," she said quietly, dropping her gaze once more. The ball in her throat swelled. "But I never thought to imagine the cottage without her."

Max reached out, tipped her chin up with his finger. "Look at me a moment, sweetheart." The corners of his mouth turned down. "You're very upset about this."

"I've never . . . We've always been together. Since I was a little girl, she's been . . ." She tried to swallow, found it impossible. "I'm not sure what to do without her."

"You've not lost her, Anna."

It *felt* as if she'd lost her. She'd never been apart from Mrs. Culpepper for more than a night or two. And now it would be . . . She didn't know how long it would be until they met again. It could be weeks, months. The one good constant in her life growing up had been replaced with uncertainty.

She felt an errant tear slip down her cheek. Then another.

"Anna."

She shook her head as her vision began to blur and took a step back from Max. Oh, this was humiliating.

"I should like to be alone now," she choked out, "if it's not too much trouble—"

"It is." His arms slipped around her gently, pulling her close. His breath was warm in her ear. "I don't want you to be alone."

Clearly, she didn't really want to be alone. She stepped into the embrace, gripping the lapels of his coat and resting her forehead against the cool fabric of his waistcoat. For the next few minutes, she quietly cried out her heartache against his chest while he held her tight and whispered soothing nonsense in her ear.

"There now," Max whispered as her tears began to subside at last. "Better?"

Not at all. Her head hurt, her eyes burned, there was no getting air through her nose, and there was little chance she looked any better than she felt.

But she didn't want him to think his efforts weren't appreciated, or that she'd inconvenienced him for nothing, so she pulled away a little, to prove she was capable of standing alone, and nodded.

"Liar," he accused gently. Keeping a supporting arm about her waist, he led her to the settee. "Come here. Sit down with me."

Max sat down next to her, produced a handkerchief, and handed it to her silently.

Anna wiped her face with shaky hands. "I'm dreadfully sorry—"

"Don't," he cut in. His hand came up to brush a comforting circle over her back. "Not about this." He took the handkerchief back and brushed a corner of it gently across her cheek. "I have a younger sister. Did you know that?"

She sniffled, shook her head.

"I wasn't sure if Engsly had mentioned it. Beatrice Dane. You'd like her."

"We're similar?" she asked.

"Not the least bit," he assured her and smiled. "She's just exceedingly likable. Lively, charming, sharp as a whip . . . I suppose you do have some traits in common. My father married her off to a sixty-eight-year-old baron a week after her seventeenth birthday."

Anna grimaced but held her tongue. She found that sort of arrangement most unfair, but perhaps Max felt differently. She was willing to debate the topic with him later, but right now, all she wanted was for him to keep talking.

"I spoke out against it," Max continued. "But when my father made it clear he would brook no opposition, I let the matter drop. Because it was expected of me." Max set aside the handkerchief. "Two years later, she arrived at my town house with my newborn niece in her arms and a myriad of bruises on her face."

"Oh." Anna's stomach twisted at the thought.

"She'd been expected to deliver an heir."

Anna didn't know what to say to that. It was awful and disgusting, but according to Mrs. Culpepper, as common as arranged marriages in which the bride's cooperation was debatable.

"I'm sorry," she tried.

"Not as sorry as I, for having done nothing to prevent the match."

"But you helped her when she came to you with your niece," Anna guessed.

"I did," he said quietly. "Our options were limited. A divorce was out of the question, as it would leave my niece in her father's hands. Once again, I asked my father for help. Once again I was told not to interfere."

"But you did as you pleased."

Max's expression turned grim. "Not entirely, or I'd have run Beatrice's husband through with a dull sword and hung his rotting carcass from the nearest tree."

"I see."

"Beatrice wouldn't hear of it. She'd had her fill of violence. So, I hid her away. Someplace the blighter will never find her. Try though he does."

"You're certain?"

"She has a new name and a new life." A wistfulness entered his voice. "And the world is a very big place."

The world? Anna had assumed she'd gone off to Scotland or Ireland, or possibly the continent. She'd not considered the world.

"You've not been able to see her, have you?"

"Not in years." Max looked down at the handkerchief he was still holding. "It is no easy journey, and I can't risk leading her husband to her."

"I am sorry," she said quietly, wishing she had more to offer. "That must be very hard."

"It is always hard to say good-bye to someone you love."

Anna nodded, thinking it helped, however, to have the ear and shoulder of someone who understood. "Thank you for telling me of your sister."

"Of course." He leaned back into the corner of the settee. "I like to speak of her, truth be told."

"It doesn't make you sad?" Even thinking of Mrs.

Culpepper right now made her sad, and she wasn't nearly as removed from her as Max was from his sister.

"The why of it all does, yes. But then I remember that her husband is a very old man consumed by hate. He's not long for this world, I think."

And when he was gone, Beatrice would be free to come home. Anna wasn't comfortable wishing for the death of someone, but rather thought she might be able to make an exception for Max and Beatrice's sake. "Is all this why you became known as the Disappointment of McMullin Hall?"

"It was the start of it. When I took a moment to think on it, I found I couldn't arrive at a compelling reason to continue on, trying to please my father and his ilk. I never once found success in the endeavor, and no good had ever come from my efforts. I find it is better to please oneself than to worry over disappointing someone else."

"And it pleases you to spend your nights in the company of the demimonde."

"It does, yes."

Though she'd already known it to be true, she hated hearing it, which was probably why her voice took on an edge. "And your days sleeping off your excesses?"

"Not every day," Max responded calmly. "Certainly fewer than four years ago when we met. I had a point to make then, and the lost opportunities of my salad days for which to make up. But I do continue to enjoy the carefree life in London." He cocked his head at her. "Do you expect me to feel shame for it?"

She shook her head. She'd never thought of her mother's world as being carefree. It seemed a desperate and grim existence to her. "I suppose one's view of that world is dependent upon how one arrived there, and whether or not one is allowed to leave."

"I don't understand."

And she wasn't sure if she was capable of making him understand, but she had to at least try. "You're like a wealthy patron at a shabby tavern. You're only there because you wish it, and you may choose to leave at any time. That is not the case for everyone."

"Not for you."

"Yes, though I wasn't thinking of me, specifically. Do you truly believe that every fallen dove and merry widow of the demimonde left good society by choice? That every woman at my mother's parties wishes to be there? Some have been forced into that life, left with no other choices but to find either a protector or the workhouse. They are not living their lives as they see fit, nor do they deal a figurative blow to the strictures of the ton. They've merely traded trying to please people like your father and his ilk, for trying to please people like you."

She knew she'd gone too far almost immediately. Max rose from the settee, his face set in hard lines.

"I would never force my attention on a woman, nor would I ever sit idly by while someone else—"

"Of course not. That is not what I meant. You must know that is not what I meant."

"I'm not sure that I do," Max snapped. "God, you would make me out to be a lecher, a heartless jackal preying on the wounded and weak."

"That was not my intention." But now that she stood back to think on it, it did rather sound as if she thought the men of the demimonde were either predators of virtuous women or scavengers of the fallen, and all the women were helpless victims and prisoners. "I didn't mean to make it sound as if *all* the women of the demimonde were under duress." She searched for a way to smooth over her blunder, to make things easy with him again. "I'm sure there are many women who enjoy their positions in the demimonde. Women like my mother." She shrugged, found a tiny loose thread on the settee cushion and picked at it. "I only wished for you to look past the obvious."

"You wish to tell me what I should look at in my world, and how to interpret what I see?"

Her gaze snapped to his. "I didn't—"

"I am not in need of a governess, Anna. Are we understood?"

Anna said nothing. Somehow, they'd gone from point A to the number four in the blink of an eye, and she suspected it might be mostly her fault.

"Yes, I understand." She understood that he was furious and that she wished she could go back a few minutes and take the conversation down another path. She didn't want to fight with him, especially not today.

She watched him stalk off to the window where he looked out over the garden and dragged a hand over his face, then over to the sideboard, where he stared at a crystal decanter full of brandy.

Uncomfortable sitting while Max contemplated drinking spirits in the morning because of something she said, Anna rose and ran a smoothing hand down the waist of her gown. "I wish—"

Max cut her off with a gesture and turned from the decanter to face her. "It is possible you struck a nerve."

"Oh." She'd thought he'd been working himself further into a fit, not calming down. She really hadn't been expecting a concession. But now that it had been offered, she wanted to grab hold of it and demand more.

Look. Look at what you've been doing. Look at what's around you. How could wild parties in London be better than what was to be had at a place like Caldwell?

But she wanted that for herself, not for him. "I've not . . . I am not accustomed to having the ear of someone . . . someone like you."

"I'm sorry? Like me?"

"Someone who has influence over my world," she explained. "Mrs. Culpepper's authority in Anover House has always been limited. Madame's control is complete, and she has never . . . listened, as you do. I grew overambitious in my argument and thoughtless in its execution—"

To her surprise, Max cut her off with a short laugh. "For God's sake," he groaned. "Are you trying to apologize, Anna?"

"Oh. Well . . ." She shifted her feet. "Yes?"

"Then say sorry, love."

"Sorry."

"Forgiven."

Anna pressed her lips together in annoyance. She was happy to see he wasn't angry with her still, but it didn't sit well with her that her apology should be the end of the discussion. She shifted her weight once, twice, three times. And then she caved. "I'm not *wrong* in my point, you understand. I do think it important . . . *stop laughing.*"

"I can't help it. You are *astoundingly* tenacious. I could all but see you fighting back the argument." Crossing to her, he reached down and took her hand in his. "And I am very happy to see you feeling more yourself."

Anna swallowed her next argument. She *was* feeling better, because of him. Perhaps now was not the best time to press for a debate.

"I am feeling more myself," she agreed. She glanced at the window and saw that the rain had begun to let up a little. "And I think a visit to Hermia might be just the thing to cheer us both."

"I think that's a fine idea." He reached up to brush a loose wisp of hair from her temple. "Things will be easier with time, Anna, you'll see."

Chapter 19

✦

*A*nna was happy to discover that Max was right. Though she continued to miss Mrs. Culpepper, over the next week, her life took on a mostly lazy, comfortable feel. A new routine was established now that Mrs. Culpepper had gone and the Haverstons had all arrived.

The only aspect of this new routine Anna found unpleasant was seeing less of Max than she had before. He walked with her every morning, but he was often absent from meals or ready with an excuse for why he couldn't join the family for a trip to the village, or for conversation in the library after dinner.

At first, Anna was afraid she'd angered him more than she'd realized with her talk of merry widows and fallen doves, but he seemed relaxed and happy during the times they were together, leading her to believe that he was perfectly happy with her company, he was just seeking that company out with less regularity.

His reasons for doing so didn't become clear to her until

a miserably stormy afternoon kept the Caldwell Manor residents confined to the house and Lady Engsly had suggested a game of charades in the front parlor.

Halfway through the game, while Anna was occupied trying to decide if Lady Winnefred's wild hand gestures were an actual clue or merely a sign of amused frustration—her turn had gone on for some time—she felt the hairs stand up on the back of her neck.

Turning her head, she found Max standing in the doorway. He smiled at her, and as always when their gazes met, her skin warmed and her pulse sped up with pleasant anticipation. But rather than join in the fun as she expected, his eyes traveled over the laughing group, then returned to her for a moment before he'd quietly excused himself from the room.

That was when Anna realized that he was giving her the time and space so that she might come to know her family.

She thought it a remarkably thoughtful gesture. That didn't lessen her discontent at seeing less of him, but it did soften the blow. It also helped that he wasn't wrong in his assumption of the time she needed with the Haverstons.

It was no small feat, coming to know a brother and two sisters-in-law in so short a time. But it was achievable. Moreover, it could be good fun. Anna was happy to learn that no matter how dissimilar their origins, there were all sorts of places where two people might find common ground. Provided they were willing to look.

It was more easily done with Lady Winnefred with whom she'd already established a tentative friendship on the first day. Bold and occasionally a little crass, Anna rather thought one would have to work at finding a way to shock or offend the woman.

Lady Engsly was of a more subdued nature, but she seemed quite genuine in her interest in developing a bond with her husband's sister, and after an initial spot of fumbling about, they discovered a shared interest in embroidery and a common love of Shakespeare.

Lady Winnefred pronounced both to be the dullest topics on earth, but she did so with a smile. The teasing sort one reserved for friends and family.

The sight of it had made Anna want to crow.

Best of all, however, was how quickly she developed a rapport with her new brother, Lord Gideon.

Admittedly, it was difficult to imagine how one could not develop a quick affection with someone like Lord Gideon Haverston. He was exceedingly good-natured, quick with a smile and kind word, and quite possibly one of the most amusing individuals she'd ever met. Granted, the number of people she'd truly met was limited, but Gideon Haverston had a talent for comedy, there was no denying it.

He put that talent to use one late afternoon by giving Anna a second tour of the hall of family portraits, this one complete with long, amusing, and highly improbable stories attached to each picture.

"You are making all of this up as we go along," Anna accused after Gideon informed her that their great-great-aunt had run off to the Far East with a one-armed merchant.

"Not all of it. Great-Uncle Harold really did have someone else stand in for his portraits. He was obsessed with how he was to be remembered, and he wished to be remembered as tall and fair of hair. Instead, we simply remember him as the great-uncle without a portrait." He turned a critical eye on the portraits they were standing before now. "But, to be honest, I haven't the faintest idea who most of these people are."

"Weren't you made to memorize them like Lucien?" she asked on a laugh.

"Thankfully, no. But I did like to sit here of a rainy afternoon and imagine what they'd been like. They were all knights-errant and fair maidens when I was young, of course. A boy does like to believe he is the descendent of heroes. I grew more creative as I aged. For a time, that gentleman behind you in the walnut frame had eleven toes.

Great-Grandmother Elizabeth was really a blacksmith's daughter, secretly switched at birth."

Anna imagined him as a boy, studying the paintings, lost in his imagination. "I should have loved to have helped you create such stories as a child."

"I should have loved the company."

There was sincerity in his voice, and something else as well. A hint of sadness that surprised her. "You had Lucien and Lord Dane."

"I should have loved your company all the same," he replied. "Particularly for something like this. My brother and Max were not so fanciful as children. Funny that they should be more so as adults."

"Perhaps they felt they couldn't be."

"Exactly so," he agreed and sent her a curious look. "And what of you? Were you a serious child or a maker of tall tales?"

"Oh, I was most serious," she admitted. "Very dedicated to my studies."

"Were you happy?" he inquired softly.

Her gaze shot from a portrait of a plump young man holding a spaniel to Gideon's earnest face. She quite liked that they shared a fondness for silliness, though he preferred to call it a refined taste for the absurd, and so it came as some surprise to her that their conversation had taken a sudden turn into seriousness.

"Beg your pardon?"

"As a child in Anover House," he clarified. "Were you happy? There is little I might have done to help, as I'd have been a child myself. But . . . To know that I had a sister in need of help—"

"My life has been more comfortable than most," she assured him quickly.

"But not as comfortable as it might have been," he translated with a nod. "I apologize on behalf of our father."

"Unnecessary, but accepted, if you need it to be."

He frowned thoughtfully. "I don't, to be honest. I don't much like the idea of our father's sins being so easily forgiven."

"Shall I be angry with him a little longer, then?" She wasn't angry with him at all. It was difficult to feel a personal betrayal, having never met the man. But Gideon seemed pleased with the notion, and that had been the point of the offer.

"I would consider it a personal favor."

"The sort I might collect on in the future?" she teased and marveled a little at the wonder of being able to tease. She was constantly reminded of how much had changed for her in so short a time.

"You may assassinate the character of our next ancestor," Gideon offered. "How's that?"

"Make up a story, do you mean? I don't think I'd be much good at it."

"Won't know until you try. Give it a go."

Rather liking the idea, Anna did as suggested. She was not, as it turned out, a particularly gifted storyteller, but what she lacked in skill she made up for in enthusiasm.

She took turns with Gideon, slowly making their way down the hall, laying waste to the family tree. Anna might have been content to continue on for hours, but a young maid came hurrying down the hall, a letter in her hand and a flush of red on her cheeks.

"Beggin' your pardon, but a letter come for you, miss, while you were out with Lady Winnefred. I were supposed to give it to you earlier, but I plumb forgot." Round blue eyes shot to Gideon and back again. "I'm dreadful sorry."

"Oh, that's all right. No harm done." Anna took the letter eagerly. "Would you mind terribly if I read this now?" she asked Gideon sheepishly. "I have been most anxious for news from Mrs. Culpepper."

"Not in the least," he assured her. "I should be off, at any rate. I have neglected my lovely wife for too long."

She smiled her thanks, then hastily broke the seal and tore open the letter as the sound of Gideon's footsteps diminished down the hall. The first line pulled a gasp from her lips.

The letter was not from Mrs. Culpepper.

It was a summons from her mother. And it hadn't come from London. It had been sent from the Bear's Rest, Codridgeton's only inn and tavern.

No. No, no, no.

"Is everything well, miss?"

No! ". . . Yes. Yes, quite. A small surprise, that's all. Thank you, Mary."

Anna was vaguely aware of the maid dropping into a quick curtsy before leaving. Her eyes and mind remained fixed on the letter.

Her initial instinct was to simply write a declining note in return, but Anna knew that would never work. Madame had traveled all the way to Codridgeton to speak with her daughter; she'd not accept a letter in response. She was likely already chomping at the bit in frustration at having her summons ignored for so long. The stroll with Winnefred had been hours ago. Really, it was a small wonder Madame wasn't pounding on the front doors.

The image of her mother doing just that sent a chill up Anna's spine. She could not allow things to come to that.

Equal parts determined and afraid, Anna crumbled the note in her hand and headed for her chambers for her bonnet and gloves.

Chapter 20

❧

The Bear's Rest was a lively, well-kept establishment that held the dubious distinction of having burned to the ground and been rebuilt on the same spot on four separate occasions over the course of two hundred years. The last reconstruction had taken place less than a decade earlier, but Anna didn't notice the straight lines of the tavern's wood frame, nor the evenness of its wood floors.

She noticed but ignored the curious stares of its patrons when she entered alone and asked to be shown to Mrs. Wrayburn's room.

Anna waited for the maid who'd escorted her upstairs to leave before knocking on the door. It opened almost immediately, giving Anna the impression that her mother might have known in advance of her arrival.

"My *darling*." Mrs. Wrayburn limped gracefully out of her room, a whirl of bronze silk and sparkling jewels, with her arms opened wide, as if seeking an embrace. She wasn't, of course. That would be too, too gauche. She grabbed Anna by the shoulders instead and kissed the air next to Anna's cheek. "I was beginning to wonder if you would *ever* come. Come inside, darling. Come inside."

Anna allowed her mother to pull her inside the room, but she didn't wait for the door to be closed again before speaking. "What are you doing here, Madame?"

Mrs. Wrayburn closed the door with a jeweled hand and gave no indication of recognizing her daughter's cool demeanor. "At the moment, enjoying the comforts of this fine establishment. Bit more modern than one generally finds outside of London."

"Yes, it's lovely. What do you want?"

A hint of annoyance flashed across Mrs. Wrayburn's face. She'd never been as skilled at keeping her composure. She'd never had Mrs. Culpepper as a teacher. "Are we to dispense with the niceties altogether? Very well, I want you to come home immediately."

"To Anover House? Absolutely not."

"Of course to Anover House. It is your home, after all. And this little"—she waggled her fingers dismissively— "adventure of yours has caused us both enough embarrassment."

Anna tipped her chin up. "There is no embarrassment for me. There is nothing wrong in what I am doing. I was invited to Caldwell Manor by the marquess himself."

"Invited? By the Marquess of Engsly? Little liar. His sort has nothing to do with our sort."

I am not your sort. Should I take a thousand lovers, I will never be your sort. "Do you suppose I showed up at his doorstep unannounced?"

"Yes. And you must have something hanging over him to have kept you on all this time. What is it?"

Anna studied her mother a moment, seeking signs of drink or laudanum. "You know why he's kept me on. We share a father—"

"Oh, what the devil would he care of that? The ton is lousy with bastards of nobility. It means nothing to them."

"It means something to him. To them."

"You'd not have come here on the hope that it would. Even you've more sense than that."

Hoping to avoid any future ugliness, Anna hadn't mentioned in the letter she'd left behind at Anover House how she'd come to know of her connection to the Haverstons, only that she had. Clearly, however, the time for dissembling had passed. "My father promised to support any offspring that resulted from a union with you. The current marquess, my brother, wishes to honor that debt."

"What nonsense is this?"

"I found letters and—"

"Letters . . . Between Engsly and myself?" Mrs. Wrayburn gasped dramatically, brought a hand to her heart. "The ones in my sitting room?"

Anna nearly rolled her eyes. Her mother was fond of acting, but she was dreadful at it. "You already knew."

"I most certainly did *not*," Mrs. Wrayburn protested, badly. "How dare you go through my things?"

Anna was suddenly reminded of something her mother had admitted to whilst under the influence of the laudanum.

I lie for all sorts of reasons. Mostly for my own amusement.

There was no arguing with that sort of mind-set. "I also dared to find your contract with the marquess."

"The contract? . . . Oh, for Christ's sake. *That's* what you've over the marquess? The old contract? *Idiot* child. The debt was paid."

"It wasn't. I saw the letters. I saw the contract." She didn't mention the journals. If her mother wished to pretend outrage over that, she'd have to admit she knew of its disappearance.

"This is what comes from snooping about in my chambers," Madame chided. "A *new* contract was agreed upon.

He offered a lump sum of eight hundred pounds in lieu of an allowance and I accepted." She brushed a hand down her sleeve while a smirk danced on her lips. "Payment was delivered in full."

"No . . ." Anna took a small, calming breath. She would not let her mother's lies get the better of her temper. "I saw the letters and—I heard you. I *heard* you say the contract had done you little good."

"In keeping him. I didn't want the eight hundred pounds. I wanted your father, the heartless cad. He left the moment he became aware of my condition. Coldhearted, that one."

"You'd have made the perfect match," Anna bit off. "I want to see this new contract."

"It was an informal understanding."

"You came all this way to tell me a lie?"

"I came to fetch you home, as I said."

"No. Truth or lies, I'll not be returning to London." Now that she'd tasted freedom, sampled life beyond Anover House, she could never go back.

"But . . . Don't be ridiculous child, where do you think to go?"

"I have friends now, family who—"

"*I* am your family," her mother snapped. "You belong to me."

And there, Anna realized, was the crux of the matter. Mrs. Wrayburn was unwilling to give up one of her possessions.

"I am not a reticule or jeweled necklace, Madame, nor one of your lapdogs."

"For pity's sake, who has said otherwise? Oh, never mind. This is absurd. Take me to see Engsly, he shall be made to see reason."

Oh, dear Lord. The very idea of inflicting Mrs. Wrayburn on Caldwell Manor and its occupants was terrifying. "Not for the promise of ten thousand pounds."

Madame's brow lifted. "No longer good enough for you, am I?"

Anna took a steadying breath and squashed the urge to continue the argument. There was nothing to be gained from it, no possibility of compromise, understanding, or reconciliation.

It might be momentarily satisfying to confront her mother with every lie, every blatantly selfish bit of manipulation, but it wouldn't be worth the inevitable frustration that would follow when her mother simply denied everything.

She would never apologize for having sent Max away four years ago. She'd likely not even admit to it. Where was the sense in fighting for either?

Instead, Anna sought the cool, calm façade she had honed over her lifetime. "You may form whatever opinions of me you like and take them back to London in all due haste. What must I do to make you leave?"

"You are cold, Anna Rees. As cold and heartless as your father—"

"Indeed. Tell me what it will take, Madame."

Mrs. Wrayburn sniffed, her nostrils flaring. "Unlike you, I do not seek out family for payment. Either you return with me to London or I remain in Codridgeton. I daresay the Marquess will look upon your company less favorably if his precious wife is forced to make room for me in her parlor as well."

"I daresay the marquess could have you exiled to Australia if it suited him or his wife."

Madame brushed that concern away with a careless sweep of her hand. "Too much trouble for him. Easier to send you packing, which he'll do and quick once he learns the truth of things."

"Once he hears your lies, do you mean?"

"I thought it might come to this. Very well, if it is proof you require . . ." Madame trailed off dramatically and limped over to the bed to retrieve a stack of letters from a small leather satchel. She handed them to Anna with a smirk. ". . . Here it is then. All the proof you, or the Haverstons, could ask for.

Letters between the marquess and myself in which we discuss, and agree upon, the terms of the settlement."

Anna snatched the letters out of her mother's hands and opened one at random. To her shock, she discovered that it had been sent from Madame to the late marquess. "How on earth did you acquire these?"

"The previous Lady Engsly was happy to sell them back to me for a nominal fee," Madame explained with an indifferent lift of her shoulder. "My affair with the marquess was over long before their marriage, and she was in considerable debt. An opium eater, that one. Now . . ." She took the letters back, stuffed them back in the satchel, and handed the bag to Anna. "You have the night to explain things to the marquess. I want to leave for London by morning. Wear something decent. I can't be seen traipsing about the countryside with my daughter in rags."

Anna shook her head, baffled, horrified, and disgusted. "You *gave* me this gown."

"Not for you to wear in public. Some things aren't meant for the public. You don't see me traipsing about in my nightclothes, do you?"

Nightclothes? There was no response to that, only the growing worry that, perhaps, in her success at keeping her distance from Madame at Anover House, Anna had missed the indications that her mother was growing a little mad.

She stepped backward, toward the door. Her mother had always been odd, and more than a little mean. But this, all of this, was beyond the pale. "I'm leaving, now."

"Yes, of course. I said you could."

Anna stopped when she felt the wood of the door against her back. With the satchel gripped in her hand, she spun around and let herself out as fast as she could. The last thing she heard before closing the door behind her was her mother's voice.

"I expect to have those letters back, Anna. I expect you to bring *everything* back."

Chapter 21

❧

$\mathcal{M}$ax knew something was wrong the moment Anna walked into the library. She wasn't hiding and fidgeting as she'd been on the day the Haverstons had arrived, nor sad about the eyes as she'd been when Mrs. Culpepper left. She was stiff as a pole, and paler than he'd ever seen her.

A sick fear lanced straight through his belly. He reached her in three long strides and took her by the hands. "Something's happened. What is it?" His eyes raked over her form. "Are you ill? Hurt—?"

She shook her head stiffly. "No. It's my mother. She's in Codridgeton."

"Your mother," he repeated and gave the fear a moment to abate. This wasn't welcome news, but it was a far cry better than a few of the alternatives that had flashed through his mind. "You've had word from her?"

"I've spoken with her."

"You went to see her? In Codridgeton? Alone?" He

swore ripely when she nodded. "Tell me you had more sense than to walk there."

"I borrowed one of the carriages. It wasn't the best, and I'd have asked first, but . . . I didn't want to tell anyone where I was going. Besides, Lucien is out with Lilly doing"—she withdrew one of her hands to waggle it in the general direction of the outdoors—"whatever it is a marquess and marchioness do. Settling a dispute, or collecting rent, or I don't know."

"They're at a neighbor's. Sweetheart, there was nothing wrong in taking the carriage. You needn't have asked, except that you shouldn't have gone alone."

"I shouldn't have left her that blasted note, that's what I should not have done," she muttered. "And I shouldn't have taken Madame's carriage. We should have taken a mail coach. She'd not have been able to come after me so quickly."

"Why has she come? Not to wish you well in person, I presume?"

"No." Anna worried her bottom lip, clearly wanting, and not wanting, to tell him more.

He rubbed the pad of his thumb gently along her knuckles. "What is it, Anna?"

She looked at him, her fae gray eyes searching his face. "Can I trust you with a secret?"

You can trust me with anything. The words nearly tripped off his tongue. It was a neat and easy promise, and one he badly wanted to make, in part because he was so desperate to make her happy, and in part because he wanted it to be true.

But then he thought of Beatrice, standing battered on his front door step, and he was reminded that he was capable of failing those most important to him.

And so, in the end, what he said was, "Yes."

Because he could. If nothing else, he knew he could be trusted with a secret.

Fortunately, it was all Anna seemed to require.

"Madame . . . Madame says the Engsly estate owes me nothing." She shook her head. "Nothing. She gave me these." Her free hand shook as she reached into the leather satchel she had over her shoulder and withdrew a handful of letters. "They're letters from mother to the late marquess. The marquess's second wife sold them back to my mother. She says the proof is in here."

"All right," he said carefully and gently took the letters from her. There was a new catch in her voice that made him distinctly uneasy. "We can look through them together if you like."

"She'd not have given them to me if she'd lied about the contents." She stared at the letters with eyes that were beginning to shine. "My father settled with my mother. I came here under false pretenses and now—"

"No. You came here with information you believed to be accurate in every way. There is a considerable difference."

"Not considerable enough. Once Lucien hears of the truth, he'll . . ." She opened her mouth, closed it.

"He'll what?" Max pressed.

"I don't know. I don't know how he'll react."

"Clearly you believe he'll act poorly, else you'd not be so worried. You should learn to have a little faith in your brother."

Her brow lowered in annoyance. "That's ridiculous. How does one *learn* faith? That's a contradiction of—"

"*Have* some faith in Lucien," he amended. Good Lord, the woman did grow argumentative when she was upset.

"I do," she returned, but the strength of her conviction was diminished by a sheepish wince. "Truly, I do. Just . . . not as pertains to this. He'll have every right to be angry. I should have taken better care."

Max considered his response carefully. Anna was as tenacious in her misconceptions and worrying as she was in everything else. If she thought the discovery of a journal, a pile of letters, and a signed contract constituted having not taken enough care, it was unlikely she was in the mood to be convinced otherwise.

Clearly, a new approach was needed.

"Then don't tell him."

"I beg your pardon?"

"If it troubles you so, keep the information to yourself."

She looked horrified by the mere suggestion. "I couldn't possibly."

"Why not? It's your word against your mother's, isn't it? It was shortsighted of her to have handed you the only proof—"

"I am certain she didn't. She would have kept at least one letter mentioning the settlement, which is neither here nor there." She withdrew her hand from his. "I can't lie to Lucien."

"Certainly, you can. I do it all the time." He'd left out pertinent details recently regarding his past with Anna, which was hardly the same as lying all the time, but for the sake of argument, he was willing to lie a little bit right now.

"All the . . . ? He is your dearest friend. Does honesty mean nothing—?"

"I value the truth," he cut in. There was a limit to how far he was willing to take the role of devil's advocate.

"But you would toss it away so easily."

"No, I would be judicial in its application." And that was the truth.

"Semantics."

"Common sense. Everyone lies now and again. *Everyone*—" he stressed when she opened her mouth to argue. "You'd not insult a friend by pronouncing her new gown unappealing, would you?"

"Mrs. Culpepper doesn't have ugly gowns. She has exquisite taste."

Her literal interpretation threw him less than the reminder that Mrs. Culpepper had been her only friend.

"You understand my meaning," he said quietly.

"I do," she admitted with obvious reluctance. "But this is not the same. I'd not be lying to Lucien to spare his feelings, but my own. And I'd be cheating him out of a thousand pounds."

"He didn't invite you here for the thousand pounds, Anna."

"That would only make my stealing it that much worse," she muttered miserably. "*Damn* the woman."

He couldn't agree more, but he had the impression Anna needed more than easy agreement at present. "For telling you the truth?"

"For telling the truth now, of all times. She's always lied, why . . . Heavens, she could be lying now, couldn't she? I don't know why I didn't think of it earlier." She turned to him. "Those letters could be forged, couldn't they?"

"They could," he agreed. "Anything can be forged, but I can't imagine why she'd bother."

"For the same reason she bothered to come all the way here to deliver them. To make certain she gets back what's hers."

"I don't follow—"

"She wants me to return to Anover House," she explained. "My mother collects things for herself and *only* for herself. I think . . . I think she's come to retrieve a part of her collection."

"She doesn't own you."

"I know that. But as far as Madame is concerned, I belong to her as surely as the horses in her stables. And mother doesn't share."

He tried to wrap his head around the idea of that. The notion of ownership within a family was not uncommon, particularly when it came to men and their wives. Though they weren't married, he could admit to feeling quite proprietary toward Anna and could admit, privately, he wouldn't mind if she returned the sentiment. But this was clearly different, clearly uglier, and he couldn't quite find the sense of it.

"She shared you with Mrs. Culpepper."

Anna shook her head. "Madame paid Mrs. Culpepper to care for me. In her eyes, a governess could no more own the child she rears than a maid could own the silver she polishes. But a father, brothers, sister-in-laws . . . These are real threats."

"That sort of rationale baffles me."

"Yes, because it isn't rational." Anna's gaze fell on the leather satchel and she sighed. "In truth, I don't think she's lying. I want her to be but . . . she was too smug. Usually, when she's lying about something substantial, she becomes dramatic. Excessively dramatic," she amended after Max gave her a dubious look. The Mrs. Wrayburn he remembered had always been dramatic. "She makes great sweeping gestures with her hands, and lifts her voice, and embellishes her stories with the most improbable details. The tsar sends her love letters, you know."

"I didn't know."

"Mmm. On parchment with corners dipped in gold. There's an estate and a hundred serfs waiting for her outside of Saint Petersburg, should she want them."

"Charming."

"Sometimes it's two hundred. Sometimes it's not stories she tells, but promises. My mother makes the most wild promises when her mood is high and she's had too much wine at dinner. When I was younger, perhaps ten, she promised me a dowry."

"The thousand pounds."

"No. Five hundred." She blinked at that, then laughed suddenly. "Good Lord, even in the lie she cheated me."

"Anna—"

"She told me once that she didn't look for ways to hurt me, and I believed it. I thought her meanness originated from selfishness, not an actual desire to harm." She shook her head, her lips pressed tight. "I'm no longer sure that's true."

"I'm sorry," Max murmured, feeling angry and help-less. "I wish I'd not been so easily thwarted four years ago. I wish I'd persisted and found a way to see you, take you away from Anover House. I should have—"

"Don't be silly. You can't blame anyone but my mother." She blew out a short breath. "And I am likely overestimating and overstating her willingness to do harm."

"I'm not convinced of that."

"She's not a good mother, not even a particularly good person, but neither is she a monster."

He figured the best response to that was a noncommittal "hmmm."

"I never went hungry, or cold. I never feared the back of her hand, or the possibility of being forced to entertain one of her gentleman friends."

"The fact that she might have been worse doesn't make her better by default."

"Nor the fact that she may have been better, worse."

Max squashed the urge to continue the argument. The last thing Anna needed right now was a debate on just how awful her mother truly was.

"You know her best," he murmured.

"I'm not sure anyone knows—" She broke off and turned at the sound of light voices and footsteps hurrying down the hall past the library door.

"Lucien's returned," Max said and swore he heard Anna swallow. "He'll work in his study a bit before dinner. It's a good time to speak with him."

She nodded but stayed where she was.

"Do you want me to come with you?" he tried.

"Yes. No. That is, I do. I would very much like your company. But it wouldn't be right."

She looked at him, her lovely gray eyes worried, but her

lips curled into the faintest smiles. "You knew I'd never agree to keeping this secret from him."

"Yes."

"And you don't really lie to him all the time, do you?"

"You've decided to give away your secrets. I've not agreed to give away mine."

The smile grew, just a little. "Thank you," she whispered. "For everything."

Unsure of what else to do for her, he stepped close, slipped an arm around her waist, and pulled her in for a soft kiss.

There were other things he intended to do for her later, of course. Not all of her troubles would be solved after speaking with Lucien. And the anger roiling under his skin would not be appeased with inaction.

But right now, a moment more of comfort and distraction was all he could offer. Determined to make the most of it, he ran his hands slowly up her back, molding her to him, while he brushed his lips tenderly over hers, took small, careful tastes of her mouth, and otherwise walked that very fine line between stirring a gentle passion and courting a wild need.

All too soon, he felt the latter threaten to overtake them, and with a sigh of regret, he pulled away and pressed his lips to her forehead, then the warm skin of her cheeks.

"I'll be here," he whispered, "if you need me."

Chapter 22

~⚮~

*A*nna walked to Lucien's study with her heart in her throat.

She recalled the first time she'd learned the Marquess of Engsly was her brother, in the sitting room at Anover House, and she recalled the first time she'd seen Lucien standing on the portico, waiting for her. Both times, she had experienced a curious detachment from him, an inability to *feel* that he was her brother.

If he'd scorned her upon her arrival at Caldwell, it would have concerned her only in so far as what it meant for her chances of receiving a thousand pounds.

How drastically things had changed.

The idea of facing Lucien's scorn, his censure, made her feel physically ill. His good opinion meant something to her now. *He* meant something to her.

Her pulse picked up as she reached the open door to his study and saw that she had caught him just as he was taking a seat behind his desk.

"Lucien? May I speak with you a moment?"

He glanced up, smiled, and gestured her inside with one hand while the other pulled impatiently at his cravat. "Yes, yes, of course. What might I do for you?"

Anna stepped inside and took up position behind a chair rather than in it. She found that curling her fingers into the upholstered back helped to steady her. Probably, she thought, there were ways one might ease into a sensitive topic, but damned if she could come up with anything at present.

"My mother has come to Codridgeton," she heard herself say. "She is staying at the Bear's Rest."

Lucien slowly lowered his hand. His eyes turned sharp. "Is she? She made the trip to visit you, I presume?"

"No, not to visit, exactly. She . . . She came to . . ." She swallowed hard, tipped her chin up, and forced herself to finish. "She has informed me that I was mistaken in coming here. That I did so with false information."

"False information," Lucien repeated slowly. "You are not my sister?"

"What? Oh, no. That is, yes. *Yes*, I am your sister. I'm sorry, I should have made that clear immediately." Her fingers curled deeper into the chair. "And I should not have come. Your father and my mother entered into a separate contract regarding my care, the terms of which your father satisfied."

"My father did provide for your care?"

"Apparently, yes. I—"

"Huh," Engsly cut in with some surprise. "I'd not have thought him capable of it . . ." He frowned at a spot on the desk for a second, then shrugged. "Well, there's an end to that, then. I thank you for telling me of it. It is nice to hear something good about one's father from time to time. Will you still be going to Menning with Lilly and Winnefred tomorrow, or would you prefer to postpone that for now and spend the day with your mother?"

The extended apology she had prepared died on her lips. "I . . . Beg your pardon?"

"The trip to Menning? Lilly and Freddie wished to show you the ruins of the old abbey?"

"I . . ." She opened her mouth. Closed it again and shook her head mutely.

"I could have sworn they spoke of it to you."

"They did," she managed at last. "I only . . . We're not done with this . . . other business, are we?"

Lucien looked well and truly confused. "I'm sorry, I thought we were. Was there something else you wished to discuss?"

". . . No?"

"I'll take that as a yes. What's troubling you about this?" His eyes narrowed a split second before they went wide and he sat up a little straighter in his chair. "Is it the thousand pounds? Because it's still yours, if you need it. Or if you simply want it for that matter."

"It is?"

"You're my sister," he said with the barest hint of impatience. "If you need a thousand pounds, you'll have it."

As simple as that? Surely not. Nothing was as simple as that. "Oh . . . All right?"

He studied her a moment more, then swore under his breath. "It *would* help you to have the thousand pounds, wouldn't it? I apologize, I should have thought of it sooner. It has been a long time since I've been obligated to look to someone else for my own funds. I've forgotten the restraint that dependence puts on a person, and I've taken for granted the freedom in financial independence. I'll have my man draw up the bank note tomorrow. Then you may cease worrying about your future quite so much and enjoy Caldwell a little more. Sound reasonable?"

A thousand pounds tomorrow, she could scarcely believe it. She'd come to him expecting his disappointment and fearing worse, and now here he was, offering her a thousand pounds. "Yes. No. I don't understand. Am I to understand you want to pay money not owed to me *and* you wish for me to stay?"

"Haven't we been through this?"

"Yes, but . . . When you invited me, you were under the impression your father died in debt—"

Anna broke off at the sight of Lucien rising from his chair, his face set in hard lines. He looked, she thought, as he pinned her with a hard stare, every inch a peer of the realm . . . and not the dissipated, ineffectual sort that frequented Anover House.

"I do not invite debts to Caldwell Manor," Lucien informed her. "You are welcomed here because you are my sister. No contract, fulfilled, nullified, or anything in between will alter that. Are we clear on the matter?"

She nodded but barely found her voice. "Yes."

"Are you certain? Because I've no interest in having this conversation again."

"Yes. Yes, I'm certain."

He nodded once, caught his hands behind his back. "Good. Now, I do not know your mother, only vaguely of her, but I am beginning to suspect, by the extent of your misgivings, that she did not bring this information to Codridgeton for the purpose of enlightening you or protecting you. Am I correct in this assumption?"

"Yes."

"She'll be gone by tomorrow."

Anna came around the chair. A giddy relief was growing inside her by leaps and bounds, but it was not enough to squash her fear of anyone from Caldwell being thrown into the same room as her mother. "That won't be necessary. I'll send her off tomorrow."

"Anna, I can't—"

"Please. She's my mother. It's for me to do."

"Is she a danger to you?"

"Only to my peace of mind," she assured him.

He considered it, and her, for several long moments. "Very well, but you'll take two footmen with you."

"Yes, of course." Just not into the inn itself. Whatever ugliness Madame might spew would not be allowed to land on *anyone* connected to the Haverstons.

"And you'll inform me if she gives you any more trouble."

"Yes," she replied and prayed he'd not make her promise to anything specific. The odds of Mrs. Wrayburn agreeing to leave without making trouble in the form of the aforementioned ugliness were slim.

"Good. Then, as I believe I informed you earlier . . . There's an end to that."

Max considered and rejected the idea of asking Anna if she wished for direct assistance in dealing with her mother. There was every possibility she might say no, in which case she would be all the angrier that he had decided to assist anyway.

The woman needed to learn there was more to independence than trusting no one and doing everything for oneself. No one did everything for himself. A tailor didn't weave his own cloth, a blacksmith didn't mine his own ore.

And Anna would not be sending her own mother packing, which was why, immediately after he saw Anna leave the study arm in arm with Lucien, he left for Codridgeton on horseback.

Besides, begging permission was generally less successful than begging forgiveness.

And his mission tonight would be successful.

It was quick and easy work to learn which room belonged to Mrs. Wrayburn. The owner of the Bear's Rest, Jim Alden, had known him since childhood; his wife had been particularly fond of Beatrice.

"Don't need my help in finding it," Jim grumbled inside the tavern. "Pair of gargoyles standing right outside the door. Mr. Ox and Jones, they calls themselves. I don't like 'em. Where does she think she is, she needs protection like that? St. Giles? She'll start rumors the Bear's Rest ain't safe—"

"I could have them gone by tomorrow."

The innkeeper's eyebrows lifted near to the top of his head as he realized Max hadn't come for a social call. "Could you now?" He flicked a glance upstairs. "Can you see to that without breaking me walls?"

The inn's construction was fairly new, the walls still sturdy. "Possibly."

"Give it a go, then."

Max didn't give Jim a chance to reconsider. He took the back stairs two at a time and, just as Jim had complained, immediately identified which room belonged to Mrs. Wrayburn by the two intimidating-looking men lounging outside her door.

Max recognized the men from his visits to Anover House four years ago. The short, stout fellow with the arms of a blacksmith was Ox. The lanky man with the look of a weasel was Jones.

Though Ox appeared the more imposing of the two, it was Jones that posed the real threat. He was fit, fast, and quick to draw a knife.

Max rolled the tension out of his shoulders as he approached. He clenched and unclenched his hands.

If possible, he'd talk his way into the room. If not . . . Well, he'd not mind a little battle. Seeing Anna worried and hurt had set his blood to boiling, and since he couldn't land a blow on Mrs. Wrayburn for it, he'd settle for Mrs. Wrayburn's men.

"Evening, lads," he offered as he came to a stop, placing himself closer to Jones than Ox. "Tell your mistress Lord Dane is here to see her."

"Mrs. Wrayburn ain't takin' callers." Ox straightened from the wall, sniffed mightily. "Milord."

"She'll make an exception."

"I don't—"

Max cut Jones off with a sharp look. "You may step inside and inform her of my presence, or I can stand here and shout it loud enough for her, and the innkeeper, to hear. Which do you suppose your mistress would prefer?"

Jones took a small step closer and, as expected, drew his blade. "You won't be botherin' her."

Max eyed the knife coolly. It had been some time since he'd engaged in physical combat, but not so long he didn't remember the basic elements, the most crucial of which being the element of surprise.

And men like Ox and Jones, accustomed to fending off the occasional inebriated and belligerent houseguest—most often with just the threat of violence—were fairly easy to surprise. A drunk dandy was easy to intimidate or overcome. A former soldier willing to fight a little dirty, less so.

Before Jones could think to raise the knife, Max shoved a shoulder into his chest, knocking the man back into the door, which gave Max just enough time and room to deliver a quick right jab to Ox's nose, followed by a kick to the knee that sent the man crumpling to the floor with a pained cry.

"My leg! You ruttin' bastard! My leg!"

With Ox out of the fight, Max spun around to face Jones again, just in time to dodge a swing of the man's blade.

A quick lunge, grab, and violent twist of the wrist, and Max took possession of the knife and sent Jones to his knees with a pained cry. Another twist, this time taking the arm around the back, and Jones was completely immobilized, except for his mouth, which he used to howl in protest.

Which is when Mrs. Wrayburn opened her door, took in the scene before her with a careless glance, and sighed.

"Unhand my man, please. I still require his presence for the trip home."

Max looked down at Jones, watched beads of sweat pop out on the man's forehead. Then he studied the skillfully carved ivory handle. "You pay your men well. One would think they'd be more work to dispatch."

"They function well enough as deterrents. Typically." She eyed him from head to foot, slowly. "Your desire to see me must be substantial."

"I'm not here for me." He pocketed the knife and let go of Jones. "Help your associate into your chambers and stay there."

To their limited credit, both men turned to their mistress and waited for her nod before dragging themselves away, snarling and swearing.

Max waited until the men disappeared into their room before following Mrs. Wrayburn inside. She swept through the room before him and immediately took up a pose next to the cold fireplace. She didn't appear the least unnerved to be in the company of an armed, angry man she scarcely knew. Max wondered if the confidence was a sham or if she'd fooled even herself into thinking she could control every situation.

"Lord Dane." She drew his name out as if tasting it. "My goodness, I've not had the pleasure of your company in some time. Not since you came sniffing about at my daughter's heels. Such a sincere, adorable little puppy you were."

"Ah, fond memories, those." He matched her pleasant tone and casual manner as he took up his own position in the center of the room. "I remember the days as well. We were so much younger, bit less lined around the eyes, bit more gullible."

"I've never been gullible."

"Shortsighted, then."

"I've not—"

Max decided he wasn't in the mood for banter. The few hits he'd landed on Ox and Jones had barely taken the edge off his anger. "You thought you could keep her locked up forever, didn't you? Thought the truth would never come out."

"We are speaking of Anna, I presume?" Mrs. Wrayburn rolled her eyes. "Locked up, indeed. You are every inch as gullible as you were four years ago to believe that."

Max decided he wasn't in the mood to beat around the reason for his visit either.

"Go back to Anover House, Mrs. Wrayburn."

She blinked rapidly. "Heavens, you are blunt. Rest assured, I've every intention of returning, my lord. *With* my daughter."

"That will never happen."

Full lips curved into a mocking little smile. "You're still angry I sent you away all those years ago, aren't you?"

"Not angry, no," he lied. He was going to be angry about that for a good long while. "I just don't like you."

"Because I turned you away?"

"And a myriad of other reasons, some of which I'm sure I've yet to learn."

"And some of them may warrant your censure," she agreed easily. "But I'll not apologize for sending you or any other man who came sniffing at my daughter on his way. Drunks and libertines who would have turned Anna into a whore. She was better than that. She *is* better than that. I was right to do all in my power to protect Anna from—"

"From the very men you invite into your home? The home you'd not allow her to leave?" Max scoffed.

"She is safest with me. I am her mother. Who else would care—?"

"You missed your calling as an actress," Max cut in. His patience was nearing an end. "And this debate is closed. You'll leave Codridgeton at first light, or you'll pay the consequences."

"The . . . ?" Mrs. Wrayburn's mouth fell open and a

short, harsh laugh emerged. "What consequences, you ridiculous boy? You're but one man. A viscount, to be sure, but not a particularly influential one, and I've a half dozen peers in my pocket at any given time. There is nothing you can do to me." She threw her shoulders back and spoke with great pride. "I am the most popular woman in all of England."

"No, you are the most infamous woman amongst London's demimonde," he corrected. "At present. And you've been fortunate in your competitors. Mrs. Fisher? Eliza Tomlison?"

Her lips pressed together in a thin line. "Do you imagine them lambs?"

"I imagine they've not a fraction of the influence in all of society as someone like, just as an example . . . Lady Engsly." He saw the tiniest flinch, knew he'd hit his mark. "London adores that woman. Your modiste, I'm sure, would be happy to have her, even if it meant forsaking you. Your staff would flee to her employ in the blink of an eye. What gentleman would attend a ball at Anover House when Lady Engsly has decided to hostess a last-minute party on the same night?"

"You would hide behind the skirts of a woman?"

"One does not hide behind a sword, Madame. One wields it."

Mrs. Wrayburn had so much to say about that, it took several seconds of rage-induced sputtering to sort the words out.

"This is outrageous." She sputtered a bit more, then seemed to land on a thought she could get a proper hold of. "By God, this is *her* fault. The ungrateful little brat. So like her father, takes what she wants without a thought for anyone else. She's had her own way for years, doing whatever she likes while I work to see she has food in her belly and a roof over her head. I ought to have taken a strap to her years ago." She shook a bejeweled finger at him. "I am still her mother, you know. She's mine. She will always be—"

"She will *always* be the acknowledged half sister to the

Marquess of Engsly and Lord Gideon Haverston and respected friend of Viscount Dane. More importantly, she is a grown woman who will have nothing more to do with you. You have lost this battle, Madame. You've no ground to stand on here. Fall back—"

"I don't need your ground," she spat, and her eyes darted toward the wall that separated her room from her men's. "You have your sword. I've weapons of my own."

His blood went from boiling to ice cold in the space of a heartbeat. He wanted to believe Mrs. Wrayburn wouldn't strike out at her daughter in anger, that she was, as Anna had implied, a woman of empty words. But he wasn't willing to risk it.

"You'll not have the chance to use them in London. You'll be out of Anover House by month's end." After he convinced Anna to return to London with him, the last thing either of them would need or want was to be looking over their shoulder for her lunatic mother. "Bath has a thriving society. You'll do well enough there."

Mrs. Wrayburn's eyes grew almost comically round. "Bath? *Bath*? Are you mad?"

"Did you really think you could make a threat such as that and I'd do nothing?" he asked coldly. "Month's end, Madame, or I'll see to it there's not a door in Britain open to you, not a gentleman in England willing to take you on."

"You can't do that. You'd not—"

"I assure you there is no limit to the devastation I will inflict upon you should you misplace one hair on Anna's head."

"You would lay hands on a woman?"

That hadn't been the sort of devastation he'd had in mind, but he'd rather Mrs. Wrayburn worry he might be capable of violence than Anna discover that her mother truly was.

"Harm her, Madame, and I will *end* you." How she wished to interpret his meaning was up to her. "Have I made myself clear?"

He didn't bother waiting for her answer. As far as he was concerned, the conversation was over. Mrs. Wrayburn would take herself off to Bath, or he'd see to it she was dragged there. It made very little difference to him.

Naturally, Mrs. Wrayburn still had quite a bit to say on the matter, and her fury followed him to the door. "She's mine! Do you hear me?! I *made* her! No man will *ever* take what's mine!"

"End of the month," he called over his shoulder before stepping out into the hall and closing the door behind him.

A thin screech and the sound of glass breaking against the door was the only response.

Chapter 23

❦

$\mathcal{M}$ax returned to Codridgeton before first light. He watched from across the street as Mrs. Wrayburn's carriage pulled away from the inn just as the first grays of dawn appeared on the horizon. And then he turned his horse around and rode back to Caldwell where he waited for Anna in the front hall.

She came down the stairs not ten minutes later, a yellow-and-blue bonnet in her hand, and the shadows of a sleepless night beneath her eyes. She smiled when she saw him, but not the way she did most mornings.

"Good morning, Anna. I thought you might come this way this morning."

"I'm headed out to see my mother."

"About that . . ." Max took her elbow as she stepped off the stairs and led her into the front parlor. "She's not there. She's gone back to London. For now."

"Gone back?" Anna pulled her arm from his grasp. "I don't understand. Why would she—?"

"I left her no choice."

"You . . . ?" He watched, caught between fascination and concern as all emotion was wiped from her face. "You went to see my mother?"

"Last night," he confirmed. "After we spoke. I'd have told you of it directly after, but you went straight to your chambers after dinner."

"I see. Well . . ." She took a noticeable step back from him. "I should like to hear of this meeting now, if it's not too much bother."

"Right." Just how angry, he wondered, was she? "Would you care to sit first, or—?"

"No."

More than a little angry, evidently.

Max gave her a quick but thorough accounting of what had happened at the Bear's Rest, omitting only the scuffle in the hall and Mrs. Wrayburn's most blatant threat of violence. The fact that there was now evidence Mrs. Wrayburn was a monster where her daughter was concerned was simply not something he could bring himself to tell Anna. Most people spent their adult lives with copious illusions about their parents still intact. Anna should damn well be able to keep one.

For her part, Anna listened quietly until he was finished, then said simply, "You should not have gone. It was for me to do."

"Anna, I couldn't ignore—"

"You might have *asked* me at the very least," she cut in.

"I should have," he agreed, hoping a quick apology would soften her displeasure. "I apologize."

"That was very quick." Her eyes narrowed in suspicion. "You knew from the start it was wrong."

"No. Not at all." He'd known from the start she'd not like it, which was entirely different.

"You knew I'd not like it," she bit off.

Damn. "It occurred to me that might be the case," he

admitted, catching his hands behind his back. "And I will apologize for being presumptuous. But not for protecting you."

"I didn't ask to be protected. I wanted to do it for myself."

"And I *needed* to do something for you."

"Why?"

"Because . . . that's how things are done," he tried, frustrated. "Because I wanted to, that's all. Because . . ." He swore, looked away and back again. Bloody hell, he hated conversations like this. "Because I failed to do something, anything, for you four years ago. I needed to do this for you—"

She cut him off by holding up a single finger. "Am I to understand that you'll not apologize for having done something wrong, because you did that something out of apology for something you did four years ago that *wasn't* wrong and does not require an apology?"

"No . . . Maybe . . ." Good God, he could feel his left eye want to twitch. "Say it again, but slower."

She dropped her finger. "I take back what I said about men being simpler. You made this all much harder than it needed to be."

"*I* made it harder? I'm not the one demanding an apology for being aided in a time of need. Playing knight-errant and rescuing the fair maiden is as simple a ritual as rituals come. The knight slays the dragon, the fair maiden climbs down from her tower, gifts the daring knight with a token—"

"And marries the wealthy landowner two counties over, yes," she drawled. "Tradition as old as time. I'm not a fair maiden."

"And I'm no knight-errant, love. But I did what I know was right and I'll not apologize for it." This time, it was he who held up a finger for quiet. "I *will*, however, concede that it was bad form to keep my intentions from you. I should have discussed them with you before going to the inn, not after." And by discussion, he meant argue, because he'd still have left for the inn, with or without her blessing. "Do you think you can forgive me—?"

"It's not that simple," she snapped, surprising him. "You want it to be, but it's not. The dragon you slayed was my mother."

He shook his head, baffled. "Do you feel I was too hard—?"

"No. It's nothing like that. It's . . ." She sighed deeply. "You feel as if there was more you should have done four years ago. I fear I will always feel as if there was more I should have done today."

"I see." And he did—for the first time since the argument had begun, he understood the real origins of her anger. He'd not merely removed a danger, he'd stolen a chance for her to discover something else about herself, a way to prove herself. He'd stolen a way to define who she was and where she stood in the world.

Bloody hell.

He felt like a thoughtless oaf. And yet . . . "I'm not certain what to say. I couldn't have let you return to the inn alone. I couldn't."

"We might have gone together."

He considered that. "Would you have agreed to wait in the carriage?"

"What? No, of course not."

"Hmm."

"Max—"

"What if something happened to you?" he bit off. "You may have the courage to face your mother and the likes of Ox and Jones, but I can't promise to sit idly by while you do so. I've played the passive fool before and lost a sister for it. I'll not repeat—"

He broke off, embarrassed to have brought that particular past failure into the conversation.

For the first time since he'd brought her into the parlor, Anna took a step toward him. "This is different than what happened with your sister," she said. Her voice was gentle and careful now, and that made him feel all the worse.

"Yes, I know." He waved his hand dismissively. "It's irrelevant. I should not have brought it up."

"It's not—"

"May we speak of something else?"

She didn't want to; he could practically see the argument sitting on the tip of her tongue, but to his relief, she simply nodded and asked, "Did you say my mother brought Ox and Jones?"

He hadn't meant to let that slip out either. "Yes."

"I didn't see them."

"They've a room of their own. And it would've behooved Mrs. Wrayburn to keep them hidden during Anna's first visit.

Her eyes darted away from him. "She brought them along for protection, I'm sure."

She wasn't sure. He could see it in the way some of the color had drained from her face. She was envisioning the other reason her mother might have brought along two burly men—to secure an uncooperative passenger for the return trip to London.

So much for illusions. It grated to have taken that from her after all. And yet it felt very much like the right thing to do. Very much like what she was asking from him now—to be protected less and supported more.

He could give her that. He still wasn't going to tell her about the mention of weapons—that he would take to the grave—but he could make an effort to give her at least some of what she wanted.

"She's gone now," he said and wished he had something more to offer.

Anna sighed once, straightened her shoulders a little,

and gave him a small smile. "Yes, she's gone. And we, I think, have wasted enough time in arguing over who ought to have sent her away . . . Thank you for going to the inn."

"You're welcome. If—"

"But *never* do something like that without my knowledge again."

He opened his mouth, then closed it again when he was hit with the sudden, unexpected urge to laugh. She'd offered him an olive branch and a slap on the hand at the same time. Damn if the woman wasn't the most tenacious individual he'd ever met.

There was no way around it, not without running away or letting the debate drag on indefinitely, he had to capitulate.

"Not without your knowledge," he agreed and decided that small surrender was worth it when he saw her smile.

Chapter 24

❧

*A*nna felt better leaving the parlor than she had entering, but her disagreement with Max still managed to cast a gray pallor over the rest of her day. Careful to keep up a cheerful demeanor, she wasn't pressed to answer prying questions from any of the Haverstons during their trip to Menning or at dinner upon their return. But it hadn't been the easiest thing, keeping her mind on her family and a smile on her face.

It didn't help, particularly, that Max had chosen to adhere to his recent routine of disappearing for the day. She was certain that a bit of time spent doing normal, everyday sorts of activities with Max would have helped to put their disagreement squarely behind them, and both of them at ease.

But Max did not come to Menning, or to dinner, or to the library after dinner for a game of cards or chess. Nor did he come to the library after the Haverstons had sought out their own beds and Anna had stayed up, hoping Max might seek her out now that she was alone.

He hadn't, and as Anna stood in her chambers and pulled a pin from her hair, she scolded herself for having hoped otherwise. She really needed to stop putting herself into positions where she was left waiting about, hoping Max might make an appearance. Honestly, if she needed to see him so badly that she was willing to sacrifice her pride for the privilege, she could bloody well just fetch him herself. Or send someone with a note. At the very least, she could—

"Miss?" A soft knock sounded on her door. "Miss, are you awake?"

Recognizing the voice as belonging to Mary, the maid, Anna hurried over and opened the door. "What is it? Is something the matter?"

"No, not at all," Mary whispered. "Lord Dane has requested your company on the back terrace."

"Does he?"

"Aye, miss. You're to dress and follow me, if you would please. Quietly."

Had such a request come from a man at Anover House, Anna would not have thought twice before declining the offer. She only hesitated a split second before accepting this one, and only because she'd just spent a half hour waiting for him in the library.

"I'm already dressed," she pointed out and began re-pinning her fallen hair. "Lead the way."

Anna followed Mary downstairs and outside, and found Max was waiting for her on the terrace as promised. Along with a dozen members of the Caldwell staff, all carrying lanterns, baskets, or crates, and all whispering and smiling excitedly.

"What on earth—?"

Max stepped forward and grinned. "You came."

She heard a distinct hint of relief in his voice. It did wonders for her mood. "What is all this?"

"A moonlit picnic," he explained. "I thought you could do with a bit of cheering."

"Oh." Oh, that was lovely. "I appreciate the sentiment, and the effort, I do, but, did you wake all these people for this?"

"Of course not. They were already awake."

"At your request?"

"Demand, actually. I threatened termination of employment and immediate removal from Caldwell Manor."

She sent him a dry look. "That's not funny."

"It is a *little* funny," he countered. He stepped up and took her arm gently. "Stop fretting and come along. I offered a pretty penny to anyone willing to assist. And I supplied them with a picnic of their own."

"Ah." And once again, *lovely*. No wonder the staffed looked so cheerful and excited, this was an adventure for all of them. Anna glanced over her shoulder as she and Max led the way off the terrace, and wondered if it was anyone else's first moonlit picnic but hers. She could guess by how well and how quickly Max had planned the affair that it wasn't his first.

"You've held a midnight picnic before."

"It's not half past ten," he reminded her, and offered no further comment.

Which she took to mean . . . "Always with a lady?"

He shrugged. "It's not so much fun to go on a picnic by one's self."

"No, I suppose it wouldn't be," she agreed and let the matter go. The women in Max's past didn't concern her particularly. He wasn't with them now.

The group didn't go far from the house, just to a clearing on a small hill that was blocked from view of the house by trees and outbuildings. Barely a five-minute walk, but once out of sight of the house it felt like another world. The landscape retreated into the dark and the star-studded sky filled her view. There was something almost magical about being there, in the moonlit meadow with Max. Though it was unlikely, given their lack of privacy, Anna allowed herself to consider, just for a moment, the possibility that Max might find a way to take advantage of that magic and steal a kiss before the evening was over.

At Max's direction, the staff set up his and Anna's picnic at the top of the hill, and another for themselves at a discrete distance. Close enough to keep an eye on the couple, and hear a request for assistance, but far enough away to keep the conversations of both parties private.

After having her offer of help rejected, Anna made herself comfortable on the blanket amongst the various baskets of goods. There was wine and cheese and fruit, plates and silverware, and even an extra set of blankets.

"You've thought of everything," she commented.

Max took a seat in front of her, his knee a hairbreadth from where her hand rested on the blanket. It was a curious sensation, that almost touching. She had the strongest urge to reach out and close the tiny distance between them. She moved her hand to remove the temptation. Attraction was all well and good, but one simply could not go about touching men's knees on a whim. Particularly with a crowd of people looking on.

"I've one more surprise," He told her. He reached into a basket sitting behind him and pulled out a long, brass tube.

"A telescope," Anna gasped, delighted.

"It's not terribly powerful, I'm afraid, better suited for nautical purposes, but you can see the moon well enough." He handed her the telescope and then set about making them plates and pouring the wine. "Gideon and I used to do this when I came for visits, sneak out to look at the stars, when we were eleven or thereabouts." He gestured at her with a goblet. "Ah, there, you see. Not all my nighttime forays into the wilderness involved a lady."

"Just all those you engaged in after the age of eleven." She smiled a little at the thought as she turned the telescope over in her hands for inspection. "Sneaking out of the house as a boy. You must have given your mother fits."

"Everything gave my mother fits. I once saw her weep over undercooked peas. She was a woman of significant emotional bent. My nighttime escapades, however, went unnoticed."

"You were stealthy," she guessed.

"Yes. And, before my break with my father, quite eager to please. I asked Lady Engsly for permission in secret."

"Did Gideon know?"

"I hadn't the heart to tell him. He so rarely defied his parents." He tapped the end of the telescope. "Go on and try it. There's not a better spot I know of to view the moon and stars on a clear night."

Anna put the telescope up to her eye. She saw nothing but darkness at first and then . . . "Nor a better spot to see into that woman's house."

"What?"

She handed him the telescope. "See for yourself. Just off to the left there, through the space in the trees."

He aimed the tool in the direction she pointed and looked. "You're not supposed to be looking ahead of you. You're . . . Good God, that's Mrs. Mitchell's cottage. You can see straight into the window."

"Yes, I noticed."

"Huh." He lowered the telescope. "All those nights we spent out here and we never noticed. Mrs. Mitchell is a fortunate woman."

She turned appalled eyes on him. "You'd have spied on her?"

"We were eleven-year-old boys. Of course we'd have spied on her. Particularly as it is Mrs. Mitchell. She's something of a mystery in Codridgeton. Married once at the age of seventeen, widowed and childless at nineteen, she remains a lively, amiable, and very pretty woman at six-and-forty. But she's never expressed even a sliver of interest in any of the men who've come calling on her. And there's been no shortage."

"How do you know this?"

"A man hears things, here and there."

She accepted the telescope from him once again, and this time took care to aim it at the sky before looking through the eyepiece. After a bit of adjustment, the moon loomed large and brilliant (if still rather blurry) in her vision. "Amazing," she whispered and made a note to ask Lucien to borrow the telescope another time.

As spectacular as the moon appeared when magnified, it could not hold her interest nearly so well as the man sitting before her. She lowered the telescope and set it aside. "Perhaps Mrs. Mitchell was madly in love with her husband and simply cannot fathom replacing him in her home and her heart."

"It was an arranged marriage and he was thirty years her senior."

That didn't discount the possibility of love entirely, but it did seem less likely. "Maybe the men who call upon her are lacking in some way, or maybe she is faithful to another love from whom she is separate—a soldier in a distant land, or a diplomat. They might conduct their love affair by post."

"Poor devil."

"I think it rather sweet." She smiled at the thought, then shrugged when another occurred to her. "Or it could be she prefers the company of a woman."

"She has many female friends, certainly, but—"

"No, not that sort of company. The carnal sort." She fought the urge to squirm when he silently lifted one dark brow. She should not have suggested such a thing? "I beg your pardon. It wasn't my intention to offend. I assumed as a visitor to Anover House you were aware that such proclivities existed. I shouldn't have—"

"Oh, I'm aware, and I'm not offended. Surprised, that's what I am. I find you endlessly surprising."

"I was raised in that house," she reminded him.

Max set her plate before her on the blanket. "I thought you were sheltered from much of its doings."

"I was sheltered from its guests. Not from the knowledge of what went on, what *goes* on, between them. My mother kept me removed but . . . well informed. She is of the opinion that nothing tempts curiosity like ignorance and nothing courts disaster like curiosity."

"I can't believe I'm going to say this, but I find myself in agreement with your mother. Of course, it would have been wiser to have raised you outside the house, away from the need to educate you on rakes and libertines—"

"Like you?"

He shook his head lightly. "I'm no rake, sweetheart."

"Of course you are." She gave him a quizzical look. "Aren't you? You told me you weren't a gentleman."

"By the standards of some, I am not," he agreed easily. "But the fact that there are some rules I'll not follow does not mean there are no rules to which I will adhere. I don't mind disappointing the likes of my father's old friends, but it shouldn't follow that I am actively seeking to become an ogre. I'm not a despoiler of virgins. I don't seduce married women or dally with respectable misses and—"

"Just women like me?"

He blinked at that but said nothing for a long time, and she realized he was choosing his next words with some care.

"I have nothing but the highest regard for you, the greatest respect," he said at last. "I'm not certain what it is, exactly, that you are doing, but let me assure you . . . I am not dallying."

What a wonderfully romantic thing to say, she thought, her heart beating a little faster. If it hadn't been for the lack of privacy, she might have kissed him then and there. And it was on the tip of her tongue to say she wasn't dallying either, but she bit the words back.

She spent every morning strolling through the countryside with him. She sought him out for company and conversation at every turn. She'd kissed him twice, and rather hoped to add to that number. Even now, she was sharing a picnic with him beneath the stars.

And she did all this knowing it was leading nowhere. She wasn't a lady, and this wasn't a courtship. Eventually, it would be time for her to go.

What was she doing, then, if not dallying with the man?

What were they both doing?

"That wasn't meant to make you sad," Max murmured.

Anna shook her head. She didn't want to be sad, there was nothing to be gained by it. If her time with Max was limited, then it was all the more important she make the best use of every moment.

"I'm not sad," she replied and almost believed the lie. "Merely thoughtful."

She was lying.

Max knew that Anna would never be an easy woman to read, but he liked to think he was beginning to recognize the signs of certain moods. Certainly, there were some things she was no longer able to hide from him completely. And he knew she was lying.

He'd rather have known why. Why the devil would a sentimental confession from him make the woman sad?

That wasn't at all flattering. Nor promising, considering he had other sentimental confessions planned for the night.

"What are you thinking?" he asked, hoping to draw her out.

"I was thinking of . . . Oh, all sorts of things. Mrs. Culpepper. My mother. It has been a trying few days."

He murmured an agreement and tried to decipher if she was still lying or not, and what he might do about it either way.

"Have a slice of apple," he suggested and felt like an idiot. Because, really, he ought to have been able to come up with something more helpful in the moment than fruit.

But she seemed to appreciate the effort. Smiling, she accepted the slice and took a small bite from the end. "Let's speak of something cheerful. Tell me something I don't know about you. Tell me about your nieces."

He hesitated, still concerned, but ultimately decided that it was in his best interest to cheer her in whatever way she preferred. "I confess, I do not know them as well as I ought. My sister-in-law is not overly fond of me, and I find we are all happier if I do not force my attentions on the family for any length of time."

"But you bought your niece a horse?"

He lifted a shoulder. "I am kept apprised of their interests."

"By the dowager viscountess?"

"No, by the greatest viscount that never was."

"Beg your pardon?"

"My cousin, Mr. William Dane. He runs the estate for me while I'm away, which is to say, he runs the estate. He came to me three years ago in hopes of borrowing the money to purchase a commission—the plight of a third son of a second son, I'm afraid. I've known William since infancy. He's a good man, a fine leader with a head for business and a talent for diplomacy. I asked for his assistance in running the Dane estate and he gladly accepted." He popped a grape in his mouth and spoke around the food. "My involvement became unnecessary some time ago."

"He sounds a competent man."

Max nodded. "The Dane family has never been so well

off. The tenants and staff have never been as happy. Even my difficult sister-in-law cannot find fault with the man, and I assure you, Lady Dane could find fault with Everlasting Paradise. The viscounty should have gone to William."

"What would you do, then?" she asked, reaching for her goblet of wine.

He watched her lips touch the rim as she took a sip. It was a small, simple act, but one he found incredibly sensual. "What do you mean?"

"If you hadn't the responsibilities of a viscount, what would you do with yourself?"

"Exactly what I do with myself now, only more often. Drink, lounge about"—he winked at her—"seduce beautiful women."

"Liar," she accused on a laugh. "You're not half as wicked as you would have people believe. You've already told me you're not a rake or libertine. You're certainly not lazy."

"Know me so well, do you?" he asked and wondered what she would say if he told her that, while he may not go about seducing women indiscriminately, he was plenty eager to seduce her, specifically.

He could show her wicked. He was coming out of his skin with the want to show her how much fun it could be to be fully, unapologetically indecent.

Which was why, he thought with a quick glance at the group on the other blanket, he'd brought along half of Caldwell Manor as her chaperone.

"I believe I know enough that I might make a respectable guess at what you might do if you were truly free of all constraints," Anna said. She took another sip of wine, then set down her goblet. "You wouldn't return to a soldier's life, I think. You resigned your commission before becoming Lord Dane. You haven't the patience for politics. The church wouldn't have you. I wonder . . ." She tilted her head. "What is it you do with yourself when you're not thumbing your nose at the ton? When no one's watching?"

His lips curled up slowly at her question, then he waggled his eyebrows in the most ridiculously suggestive manner he could manage.

Anna gasped, clearly caught between horror and amusement. "That is *not* what I meant."

"I know." He laughed. "But I do so appreciate that you knew what *I* meant. You really have had an unusual education. Was there nothing your mother left out?"

"How would I know if something was missing if she didn't make me aware of its existence to start?"

She had a fair point. "Your own personal research? I imagine the library at Anover House wasn't short on material of a . . . let us say explicit nature."

"Oh, well, if everything there is to know about such things can be found in the books on the subject that my mother possesses, then, no, she didn't leave anything out."

"Does she possess a goodly number of books on the subject?"

"Oh, yes," she assured him. "Stacks and stacks of them."

"I should have spent more time in that library."

She laughed and shook her head. "The best ones were kept separately as part of my mother's private collection."

"Dare I ask what makes a book one of the best?"

"Artwork," she said succinctly.

He considered that. "As in the inclusion of, or the quality therein?"

"Well, quality is so subjective . . ."

"Indeed. What was the title of your favorite?"

It was impossible to tell in the dim light, but Max got the impression Anna blushed a little at the suggestion. "I'll not tell you that."

"Why not?"

"I don't know," she admitted on a laugh. "I just don't care for the idea of it. Knowing you'll look at it knowing *I've* looked at it."

"I already know you've looked at it," he pointed out.

"Yes, but you don't know what 'it' is."

Well, now, this was interesting. "Are we speaking of a specific it? A favorite bit of artwork in a favorite book, is it?"

"I didn't say that."

"Near enough. What's it a depiction of?" He laughed when she sniffed and turned her head. "It would've been titled, being in a book. What's it called? Tell me."

"Not for all the naughty artwork in England, milord."

"What about France? The French have created some spectacular—"

"Yes," she said coyly. "I know."

*T*he drawing Anna was thinking of wasn't particularly wicked, not so far as drawings in Anover House went. It was a colored sketch of a young man and woman embracing in a sun-dappled garden.

Her embarrassment was not in the nudity portrayed . . . well, not all the embarrassment . . . it was in the sentiment. The couple were entwined in each other's arms, lost in each other's gaze, seemingly oblivious to the world around them.

For Anna, the picture was a sweet bit of ink and imagination that epitomized every silly romantic notion she'd ever had about falling in love. And it was that silly romanticism that embarrassed her. It was always a little uncomfortable to admit wanting something you knew you couldn't have.

"I think we should return to our original topic," she declared. "What it is you would do, were you free to do anything at all. I would guess—"

"You may guess all day and not land on the answer to that," Max cut in. "So, let us strike a deal. I shall tell you what I would do, were I completely free, and you will tell me the name of this book with—"

"*No.*"

He sighed quite dramatically. "Very well. I'll tell you what I would do, and you can tell me the same."

It hardly seemed a fair trade, as he already knew that what she *would* do and what she was *going* to do were the same thing—purchase a cottage for herself. But if Max hadn't thought of that, she wasn't going to enlighten him. "Very well, you first."

"It's quite simple for me. I would be a man of business."

She sent him a bland look as she reached for a bit of bread. "Oh, do be serious."

"I assure you, I am in earnest."

She took a second glance at his features and saw that there was no hint of teasing or humor on his face. Good heavens, he was serious. "But if business interests you, why leave the running of the Dane estate to your cousin?"

"Because that's not the sort of business that interests me—crops and rent and politics." He shook his head. "I would do something else. I would be in trade."

"Trade?"

"Are you shocked?"

"Yes, rather."

"Because it's unseemly for a man of my station?"

She thought she heard a touch of defensiveness in his voice, but she couldn't say for certain. "No, because it requires a considerable level of dedication, above and beyond simply not being lazy. You told me when we first met that you didn't dedicate yourself to anything because it was entirely too much work."

"I was lying," he admitted. "I wasn't about to admit to the lady I was hoping to impress that I wished to be a man of business. I wasn't that drunk."

Anna was certain that, for as long as she lived, she would never understand how it was the inebriated sorted out their priorities. Drunk enough to offer marriage, but still sufficiently sober to keep his secret? It was baffling.

"Why do you wish it?" she asked.

"Because what you have is what you've earned," he explained. "And because what I might earn would be mine, not tied to an estate. And because I'm damned good at it."

"You engage in trade now?"

"You're sworn to secrecy."

"Yes, of course."

He nodded and reached for his wine. "I've made a respectable sum in the past six years. All under the name of Mr. Jeremiah Blackwater."

"You've an alias? In earnest?" She broke out into delighted laughter when he nodded. "Oh, that's *marvelous*. I've never met someone pretending to be someone else before."

He tipped his goblet at her. "How would you know?"

"You have a point," she conceded. "But why do you have one at all? You've never expressed a care for the opinions of the ton before, why care what they think of this?"

"I don't, particularly. But my nieces could suffer for it." He shrugged, as if a little embarrassed to have been caught caring. This was not, she realized, as easy a conversation for him as he would like to pretend. "It is one thing to remove oneself from good society. It is something else to drag four young girls along behind you. The eldest will make her debut in a few years."

Anna considered that—an uncle with a reputation for excess would do little to harm his niece's chance at a good match. An uncle who sullied his hands in trade would hardly render her a pariah, but there would be whispers and ridicule. Some doors would be closed to her, some gentlemen out of reach.

She smiled at Max, pleased with him for a dozen different reasons in that moment. "You see? Not half as wicked."

"I'm glad you think so. It will make it easier to gain your cooperation when I ask you to marry me."

Surprised by his careless words, and not a little hurt,

Anna's gaze snapped to his. "Don't jest about such things. It's not—"

"Why should I jest?"

"Are you . . ." She studied his face, found it difficult to read. "Are you being serious?"

"Perhaps." He took a sip of his wine, eyed her over the rim of his goblet. "And if I was? If I was to request your hand in marriage tonight—?"

"I would say no, of course," she cut in as her heart began to hammer. "I cannot believe we're having this conversation."

"You can't be that surprised," he muttered, lowering his glass. "It's not the first time."

It was the first time he'd broached the subject of marriage while sober; that was close enough. "And my reasons for saying no haven't changed."

He cocked his head, remembering. "You said no because you wanted the cottage and the hound."

"Yes, and because I didn't want to be a member of the demimonde or the beau monde."

"Why not?" He set his drink aside, visibly irritated. "Why do you give such weight to the opinion of others?"

"I don't—"

"Why do you bind yourself to someone else's narrow definition of respectability and honor? Why should it make a difference to you?"

For her, it wasn't a matter of being considered honorable or respectable, it was a desire for people to stop considering her altogether. But aside from that, it pricked at her to hear him speak so casually of respectability and honor, as if a woman might toss them away with all the care one might show an apple core.

"It's all well and good for you to say," she retorted. "You don't *have* to care for your honor. You're a viscount. In the eyes of society, you were born honorable. You've honor to toss away. Huge, unending quantities of it."

"That's not entirely—"

"What's more, you can get it all back again if you wish. A bit of good behavior, a few words of atonement, and suddenly your antics were but youthful indiscretions." She waved a hand that wanted to shake. "Boys will, and all that. You're reformed now, redeemed, welcomed back into society with open arms."

"That's certainly not—"

"Do you suppose a woman like me will be allowed the same courtesy?" she pressed. "Do you know *any* woman who's been allowed to completely free herself from ignoble origins, or a lady who's been allowed to redeem herself after a fall?"

He didn't answer, though whether it was because he couldn't come up with a response or he was merely tired of being interrupted, she couldn't say.

"No," she answered for him. "There is no redemption for a fallen woman, nor acceptance for the daughter of a well-known courtesan. She is a spectacle for life."

"A spectacle," he repeated slowly. "That's it, isn't it? This has less to do with what others say than the notion they're speaking of you at all. You don't want the attention."

"Yes, that *is* it," she eagerly affirmed. She wanted so desperately for him to understand. "I loathed attending my mother's parties. I hated being stared at, whispered about, being made the subject of speculation and wagers, and no end of jests, I'm sure. I don't want to be a spectacle. I want to be like everyone else."

"No one is like everyone else—"

"Don't," she cut in. "Don't play with my words. This isn't a game."

"I don't mean to make a game of it. Anna, look at me." He waited until she lifted her eyes to meet his. "I don't want you to be like everyone else. I don't want you to be like anyone else. You're perfect just as you are."

Irritation melted away as pleasure warmed her from the inside, out. *"Max—"*

"Marry me, Anna."

Anna suppressed a groan as pleasure gave way to hollow longing. Oh, how she loved the idea of spending the rest of her life with Max. But oh, how she loathed the idea of being a viscountess. Just the thought of playing the part of Lady Dane in London made her stomach turn and her palms sweat. She'd not be just a spectacle amongst the demimonde then, but amongst the ton as well. She'd have gone from the Ice Maiden of Anover House to the Grasping Whore of McMullin Hall.

"We can't marry, Max, you must know that. I can't go back to London. I won't."

"You . . ." Max's mouth thinned to a hard line. He glared at her, then swore once, gained his feet, and strode five feet away to glare at something in the distance.

Wishing she had some way to make things better, Anna watched him drag a hand through his hair then come back and stand before her with his legs braced apart and a determined glint in his eye. "Fine. *Fine.* A cottage it is."

"What—?"

"But something closer to Caldwell Manor and McMullin Hall than next to your Mrs. Culpepper," he grumbled. "I'll not spend days in a carriage to visit the only other country gentlemen I know."

Anna stared at him in astonishment. He meant it. He truly meant it. He would forgo London and stay in the country with her.

It was an astoundingly selfless, wondrously romantic offer. Oh, not *nearly* so wicked, she thought, and it was on the very tip of her tongue to say, *Yes, yes, a thousand times yes.* A life in the country with Max. A lifetime together to take walks and share meals and read quietly in the library or perhaps play a game of chess. It would be a dream come true . . . for her.

It would be his nightmare.

"You'd perish of boredom within a year," she said quietly. And before that year was up, he would resent her for his choice, and she would think less of herself for having accepted his offer. She knew what it was to be well and truly trapped. He was the last person on whom she would wish such a fate.

"I wouldn't. I'd—" He snapped his mouth closed and looked away. They both knew he would, or at least knew enough to fear he might.

Despite that knowledge, Anna was disappointed. A part of her, a small irrational and hopelessly romantic part of her, had hoped he might put up a convincing argument.

I'll never grow bored, not with you. You will always be enough for me.

But instead he looked away from her, and Anna wished she could curl up into a ball to ease the ache inside her chest.

Max's next question nearly startled the ache right out of her. "Are you dallying with me?"

"What? No." The denial came automatically, because it just seemed so absurd, the notion that *she* might be playing with *him*. But it took only a moment for her to realize she had answered in haste. "I don't think so."

"You don't *think*—?"

"It is not my intention. I . . ." Now it was her turn to look away. "I care for you. I wish to be with you, for more than just today and tomorrow, but I cannot see my way to how. If that means I am dallying—"

"You wish to be with me?" Max cut in.

"Yes."

"Well." Max's stance visibly relaxed. "Well then, this changes things."

"It does?" No, it didn't.

To her complete astonishment, a smile began to form on his face. "You want to be with me."

"Well, yes, but—"

"Then you'll be with me," he declared. And with that, he resumed his seat on the blanket.

Anna stared at him, caught between horror and reluctant admiration at his capacity for arrogance. "Max, it doesn't work like that."

"We'll make it work. We'll figure it out."

Figure it out? Isn't that what they'd just tried to do? Didn't they just fail? "I'm not sure—"

Max took her hand, squeezed it gently. "I want to be with you now, here on this blanket, under these stars. Do you want the same?"

"Yes."

"Then let's be together, and not waste a minute more of this beautiful night worrying about tomorrow."

Anna considered it. She was more than happy to end a conversation she'd not wanted to have to start. And he wasn't asking her to do anything she'd not already been doing since their first walk—namely, ignoring the fact that they had no future together. And so, when Max offered her an encouraging smile, she couldn't see any reason not to smile back.

Except that she didn't feel like smiling, particularly. She did it, for him, and for the hope that they might regain some of the enjoyment and easy companionship of earlier. But in truth, Anna knew things weren't going to be the same again. Not tonight. Quite possibly never again.

Chapter 25

*A*nna returned to her chambers as the clock on her mantel struck one. Sighing, she dropped into the soft chair next to the fireplace and reached for the laces of her boots.

My God, what a day. So much had transpired between the time she'd woken up to now that she wasn't sure how long it would take to sort it all through in her mind and come to some sort of—

A soft tap sounded on the glass of her balcony door. Her hand froze, her head turned. Surely not . . .

And there it was again.

"Pebbles," she whispered, straightening. Someone was throwing pebbles at her balcony doors.

With a small, baffled sort of giggle, she rose from the chair and threw open the balcony doors, letting in a soft whoosh of fresh air. She stepped outside, peered over the iron railing, and discovered, without much surprise, that it was Max standing below.

He grinned at her and said, "Good morning, Anna," in the exact same tone that he'd said, "Good night, Anna," less than ten minutes ago.

She shook her head, laughing softly. "What on *earth* are you doing?"

"Romancing you." He tossed aside the remainder of his pebbles. "Tell me I can come up."

"Up? You mean climb up? Absolutely not. You'll break your neck. Go inside and use the stairs. I'll meet you in the hallway."

"That's not romance. That's just sneaky."

"It's sensible."

"Sensible?" he echoed, clearly disgusted. "To hell with that, I'm coming up."

"Max, no, I . . . Oh, for . . ." Caught between amusement, irritation, and fear for his safety, she watched as he made his way up the uneven stone face of the house. "Serve you right if you fall and break your head, and don't think for a moment I'll . . . Good Lord, you *are* agile, aren't you?"

The man was scaling the side of the house with remarkable speed. Within moments, he was parallel to the balcony. Then it was just a matter of grabbing hold and climbing over the railing, which he did with the easy grace of a cat.

Anna couldn't help but notice that Max's display of uncommon physical aptitude left her keenly aware of her own body. Most notably, the tingling sensation she was experiencing from head to toe. Attraction, she mused, was a strange and wondrous thing.

It was also something best kept under some control. Pushing her admiration for his climbing accomplishment aside, she scowled at Max. "You might have hurt yourself, you know."

Max brushed dirt and mortar from his hands and clothes. "It's not that far of a drop."

"Far enough when there's a perfectly good door on the

other side of this room. Was it absolutely necessary you take the risk—?"

"Yes." He gave his coat one last brush and stepped close to her. "I don't like that we argued." He smiled ruefully. "Again. But I do like grand gestures."

"Yes, I've noticed," she said and smiled in return. "I'm beginning to like them myself."

"And I hate that in the midst of our arguing and then trying to move past all that arguing, and because of all the staff about . . ." He brought a hand up to cup her face. "I lost my chance to kiss you in the moonlight."

"I hate that too," she whispered, a second before he brought his mouth down on hers.

It was a sweet kiss to start, a gentle and romantic kind of kiss. The very sort Anna had imagined passed between her embracing couple in the garden.

Max's arm slipped around her waist. Her arms twined around his neck, and for a long, wonderful while, there was nothing in the world to her but the two of them. There was only the heat of Max's strong body pressed to hers, only the taste of him upon her tongue, only his scent of coffee and clean soap surrounding her.

There was only Max, kissing her.

Slowly, however, the kiss changed. The tingling feeling Anna had grew into an ache, making her restless. Suddenly, *only* kissing Max was no longer enough. She wanted so much more.

She pressed closer to him, and let her fingers slide up his neck to slip into his hair. Max shivered once and began to move. His hands roamed over her possessively, down her arms, across her waist, up her back. His mouth broke away from hers to travel across her jaw, nip lightly at her ear.

Anna heard her own ragged gasp, then a long sigh as Max trailed kisses down the sensitive skin of her neck.

This, she thought vaguely, *this* explained in a way even

the most detailed lectures could not, why there were so many fallen women in the world.

Eager for the taste of him again, she urged his face back to hers and captured his mouth for a kiss that wasn't quite so sweet now. It was determined, even desperate, a searing battle of tongue and lips that Anna hoped would go on forever—

Max pulled away with a ragged breath. "Enough."

Anna shook her head. It wasn't enough. She wanted so much more. Everything she could have from him, all the things she shouldn't take. Her hands slipped down between them to dig into the soft fabric of his coat, pulling him back. "Come inside," she whispered.

His hands caught hers and trapped them against his chest. "I didn't come here for that."

"I know." That made the invitation all the easier. "Come inside, anyway."

The invitation, it would seem, was all he needed. His arms banded around her again, his mouth came down to move strongly over hers. And once more, Anna's world narrowed down to her and Max and the passion that built between them.

She would never be able to fully remember how they went from standing on the balcony, to standing inside, nor how it was that she was able to divest him of his boots, coat, and waistcoat, or when it was, exactly, that he'd pulled the pins from her hair and undone the buttons of her gown.

A part of her knew what they were doing was wrong. Well, all of her knew it was wrong, but there was only that one small voice in the back of her head that was still audible over the roar of blood in her ears.

It wasn't terribly difficult to silence it. This was just like the kiss in the nursery, only more, she reasoned. There would be no other gentleman callers for her. No other passionate kisses in the moonlight. There would be no other Max. And so she would have this one experience.

She would take advantage of him this one night. She would take the risk for herself.

She tried to hurry things along by stepping out of her shoes, helping him divest her of her gown and stockings.

She heard him whisper, "Slow down, sweet," but she shook her head and urged him toward the bed.

Probably, it was not the done thing for a woman to be so aggressive. No doubt it was not expected of most virgins. But to hell with expectations. She wanted Max, and she wanted him now, before either of them could change their minds.

*M*ax bent, slipped his arm beneath Anna's knees, and hauled her off her feet.

God, he did like the weight of her in his arms.

He laid her on the bed, slipped out of his shirt, and tormented himself by slowly lifting Anna's chemise over her head, exposing the heated skin beneath inch by inch.

"Beautiful," he whispered and drew his hands over her slowly, purposefully, in direct contrast to Anna's frantic movements and his own raging instinct to take as much as he could as quickly as possible.

He needed to slow them both down. Particularly her. Anna's hands were everywhere, brushing down his back, up his arms. Inquisitive fingers speared through his hair, explored his chest. It was more enthusiasm than technique. And it was devastating. Everything about the woman destroyed him.

The enormity of his want for Anna was something he'd never experienced with another woman. No fine lady, innocent miss, merry widow, or experienced courtesan had ever tempted him the way she tempted him. But if they kept up at their current pace, it would be over too soon for the both of them.

He caught her wrists, pinning them gently against the

mattress, and took her mouth in a slow and gentle kiss meant to settle them both.

This was Anna. This was the woman of his dreams, the object of his fantasies, the woman he would make his wife. He wanted to make the night last, if not forever, at least long enough to leave no doubt in her mind what it meant to him, how important it was for him to please her. How much she was needed.

Which was not going to happen in a ten-minute romp atop the counterpane.

Anna arched beneath him, tugging her arms. "Let me go."

"I will." He bit gently on her bottom lip. "Wait."

"But—"

"Trust me," he whispered, knowing it was no small thing he asked of her. "Please."

When she sighed and relaxed beneath him, he kissed her again, softly, then set out to earn that trust. He explored every inch of her body, tasting and touching, looking for anything that pleased her, everything that made her gasp and shiver.

He brushed his palm along the sides of her breasts, watched her arch her back and shudder. He bent his head to flick his tongue across a taut nipple and listened to her sweet moan, felt her fingers dig into his shoulders.

Slowly, steadily he built the heat between them, removing the last barriers of clothing and inhibitions until there was only the slide of skin on skin, and she was twisting with need beneath him.

"Max."

His name spilling from her lips was more than he could take. *Now,* he thought, dragging her legs up to wrap around his hips. With a groan of his own, he pressed forward into the wet heat of her, moving past resistance with a long, steady push. His hands dug into the sheets as the sharp pleasure of being inside her washed over him in waves.

It felt like heaven.

Less so, evidently, for Anna. She gave a short cry of pain and went utterly still, except for her hand, which delivered an open-palmed slap to the side of his head.

He scarcely felt it, but he was keenly aware of her obvious discomfort. Bloody hell, he should have taken more care.

Desperate to soothe, he sought a way to apologize, to make things right again. "I'm sorry. I'm sorry, love. I should have . . ." He wasn't all that sure what he should have done differently. He'd never bedded a virgin before. "I should have warned you. Told you what to expect."

She blew out a small, jagged breath, then reached up to stroke his hair. "It's all right. It will pass."

"I—" If he'd been capable of it, he would have laughed. The woman was comforting him. Because of course she'd known what to expect. She was the daughter of Mrs. Wrayburn. The experience was new, and this particular part of it was unpleasant for her, but none of it came as a surprise.

Anna brushed a lock of hair off his forehead. "I'm sorry I hit you. I didn't mean . . . Have I ruined this?"

"No, love." He bent his head, brushed his lips across her brow. "No."

"Kiss me again?" she whispered.

"Sweetheart, you don't need to ask." He settled with his lips just a breath away from hers. "Take what you want."

In that moment, Max was willing to offer anything she wanted, anything she cared to demand or take for herself.

As Anna cupped his face in her hands and brought his mouth to meet hers, Max sent up a small but heartfelt prayer that what she would ultimately want was him. All of him. The good, the wicked, the gentleman, and the scoundrel.

God knew, he wanted every part of her in return. But he would start with this, he thought—the long, soft lines of her, the feel of her under him, around him, and the delicious relief of sensing her begin to relax.

He moved tentatively, gauging her reaction to a nicety—her indrawn breath, the flutter of lashes, the short sigh of pleasure. Emboldened, he set a slow and gentle pace and watched the blush of desire return to her cheeks.

When he was certain, absolutely certain that there was only pleasure for her, he closed his eyes and gave himself over to the wild ecstasy of moving inside her. There was only Anna, warm, beautiful, incredible Anna, and the overwhelming sight of her lost to passion and searching for its peak.

Her gasps turned to cries, those cries grew higher in pitch. And when at last she came apart in his arms, Max wrapped them around her tighter, buried his face against her neck, and gave in to his own pleasure.

Chapter 26

❧

*A*nna woke alone, turned her face into the soft beam of sunlight filtering around the drapes, and smiled. Max had left before dawn, waking her with a soft kiss on the forehead and a whispered something in her ear she couldn't make out but was quite certain was lovely. Pity he'd not been able to stay and whisper it to her again when she was fully awake.

With a sigh, she rolled out of bed and began to wash and dress, noticing a number of unfamiliar aches and pains. She was just finishing pinning up her hair when her eyes fell on the leather satchel her mother had given her, lying atop the vanity. Anna fingered the leather strap, considering. She could burn the letters now, and probably should out of respect to the late Lady Engsly.

But before she could do that . . . Anna picked up the satchel and upended its contents onto the vanity. She wanted to know what else might be in those letters.

She picked one at random, but a rap at the door pulled

her attention away before she could so much as open the letter.

"Come in," she called, assuming it was a maid.

It was Max who appeared in her doorway. "You really ought to ask who it is first. What if there were other guests in the house?"

"Max, what—" She hurried across the room, grabbed him by the arm, and dragged him inside, shutting the door behind her. "What are you doing? What if someone saw—?"

"If there was someone about to see, I'd not have knocked." He slipped an arm around her waist and pulled her close. "Come here," he demanded with a smile a moment before he took her mouth in a short, but tremendously sweet kiss. Pulling back, he touched his lips to the tip of her nose. "I've been wanting that since I left."

Anna felt heat rise to her cheeks, and wished her education on carnal matters had included some hint on what a woman was to say to a gentleman after all else was done.

"Good morning," she tried. It was better than nothing.

Fortunately, Max seemed to like it well enough. His hazel eyes danced with humor and affection. "Good morning. I thought . . ." He trailed off and scowled when he saw what she was holding, then noticed the mess on the vanity. "Are you reading those?"

"I was about to. I thought they might contain information of interest. Perhaps my birthday?"

His gaze snapped to hers when she mentioned her birthday, and the scowl immediately disappeared. "Right. Yes, of course." He held out his hand, waggled his finger. "Give it here. I'll read them for you."

"What, all of them?"

"No, five, and then I'm sure I've better things to do."

Anna rolled her eyes, bit the inside of her cheek to keep from smiling. "We can read them together. But not here. If a maid or one of the Haverstons were to come . . ."

"The library, then. Five minutes."

He didn't give her the chance to argue. He planted another quick kiss on her lips, then released her and sauntered out of the room.

Anna didn't give him a chance to be diverted by *business*. Immediately after his departure, she gathered up the letters into the satchel, waited for a count of thirty, and then ten more, so as not to seem too eager, then made her way to the library, where she discovered Max was already waiting.

How lovely.

They settled on opposite sides of the settee, spread the letters out on the cushions between them, and slowly began to make their way through the pile. Anna couldn't help but notice how cozy it felt, sitting across from Max quietly going through papers while a soft breeze ruffled the drapes of the open windows. Well, cozy until one gave a thought to what those papers were, and why she was compelled to go through them. Then it became a bit odd, a little disheartening, and—

"You're nine-and-twenty."

"What?" Anna's gaze shot to Max's. A jolt of excitement sent her heart to racing. "You found it? You're certain?"

He certainly looked certain, and tremendously pleased with himself. "Only your age so far, but it's a start. Listen to this . . . 'My dearest Engsly, it is with a full heart that I announce the birth of our daughter, Anna Rees.' " His eyes scanned a little further down the page, then he sent her an apologetic look. "She doesn't mention a specific birthdate, I'm afraid, but the letter was sent only a few weeks after my own birthday."

"May I . . . ?" She held out her hand, took the multi-paged letter and read the pertinent passage. "I'm nine-and-twenty. That will take some becoming used to."

"It's not so very great an adjustment. You'll become accustomed to the ear trumpet in no time."

"You're an arse."

"On occasion, when I think it will make you smile."

"No," she said smoothly. "Not just then." She scanned the remainder of the letter while he laughed, her eyes flying over the next page, and then the last. "I've lost more than a year of my life. How odd. I feel as if . . ." She trailed off as her eyes landed on a particular passage in the letter. "There's a date . . . Good heavens, this letter was sent well after my birth."

"What?"

"There's a birthdate. An actual date of birth, and it was weeks before she wrote this letter." She turned the pages over, double-checking the date at the start of the letter before returning her attention to the remainder of the letter's contents. They weren't particularly enlightening. "My mother apologizes to the marquess for her tardiness in writing, makes excuses—illness and what have you. Wonder what she stood to gain by waiting? I suppose . . ." Her head snapped up as a certain realization dawned on her. "Good Lord. I'm older than you."

"No, you're not," Max argued, sounding suspiciously defensive. He took the letter from her and looked it over. "Huh. So you are."

Anna craned her neck a little and stared, a little bemused, at the letter. In a matter of weeks, she would turn thirty and he would still be nine-and-twenty. How very odd.

"I'm nearly two months older than you," she murmured and looked up in the long silence that followed to discover Max's expression was one of mild disgruntlement. "You don't like that."

"I didn't say—"

"Well, you'll grow accustomed." She ran her tongue over her teeth and smirked. "We'll find you a set of short pants while we're out for my ear trumpet."

He glared at her. "Very clever."

"I rather thought so." She blinked at his scowl. "It doesn't truly bother you, does it?" She should have considered the possibility before making a jest of it. She'd heard men could become sensitive over the silliest things.

He chuckled softly, and Anna had the impression it was mostly at himself. "No, sweetheart. I'm happy for you. You've a birthday."

"I do, don't I?" She stared at the letter, ridiculously happy with it. After all these years, she finally had a birthday to call her own. "I can't wait to tell Mrs. Culpepper of it." In fact . . . She lifted apologetic eyes to Max. "Would you mind terribly—?"

"Go write your friend," he invited, standing to help her put the other letters back in the satchel. "I've business to occupy myself with for a time."

She didn't need a second invitation. With a grin, she grabbed the satchel, her proof of a birthdate, and was out the door.

*M*ax didn't have a single bit of business to see to that morning, but saying he did was much better than saying he didn't, which implied he had nothing to do but wait about until Anna was done with *her* business.

In short, he lied to save his pride.

And now he was stuck looking for something to do so he might keep that pride. Which was why he went looking for Lucien in his study, and why he didn't mind, particularly, when Lucien said, "I was just about to go looking for you," without looking as if he much wanted to see him.

Apparently, word about the picnic had only just reached the study. Pleased with the timing, Max took his usual seat across the desk. He'd clear up any misunderstandings, correct any misinformation Lucien had received, and by the time he was done, Anna would likely be as well.

"I imagine this is about last night?" he began. "Allow me to—"

Lucien, evidently not in the mood for allowances,

slammed a hand on his desk. "You took Anna out of this house, at midnight, without my permission. What the *devil* were you thinking?"

"It wasn't quite that late," Max returned and felt a flicker of annoyance. "And I don't need your permission, and neither does she."

"Damn it, man, I thought your presence here might help ease her transition from your world into mine, not entice her back into the ways of the demimonde."

"I'm not enticing her back into anything." Just toward himself, Max amended silently. "We had an army of staff present. There was nothing—"

"She needed a proper chaperone."

The annoyance was growing into outright irritation. An army of anything qualified as a proper chaperone. "What, exactly, is your point of contention? That I didn't ask her to bring along Lilly and Winnefred?"

"Yes. Or myself or Gideon. Someone else should have been there. That is the only way your little outing would have approached acceptable. I've fine staff, Max, you know that—"

"The finest," he agreed easily.

"But they're human. They'll talk. A midnight picnic was not an appropriate outing for a young, unmarried lady."

"Anna is a woman grown, not a silly miss taking her first bows. Why don't we allow her to decide what is appropriate for her and—"

"No one person sets the standards for good behavior."

"That's for good society to do?" Max scoffed and shook his head. "She is the illegitimate daughter of a courtesan, raised in a home one small step removed being a fully-fledged brothel. The ton will never accept her as one of their own. You *know* that."

"She needn't continue to be the subject of rumor and scandal either," Lucien countered.

"Her mother is famous. She will always be the subject of rumors. Neither of us can change that. At least let her make use of what advantage she gains from it."

"What advantage?"

"Freedom."

Lucien shook his head. "She's not you, Max."

"Not in the least. I could acquire the good opinion of the ton, if I cared for it. I don't."

"Anna can—"

"No, she can't," he bit off. "Damn it, man, you *know* she can't. And you'll not offer false promises or bully her into begging for something she can't have. I'll not allow it."

Lucien reared back in his seat. "You'll not *allow* it?"

"Correct." He'd not had to take a stand against Lucien on anything in the past, and never dreamt he'd have to go against him on a matter involving family, but he'd be damned before he let Max send Anna off to court the good opinions of people who would as soon skewer her as look at her. "Let Anna decide her own path. We shouldn't even be having this discussion without her."

"Shouldn't be having . . . ?" The anger in Lucien's face disappeared as he trailed off and sat down slowly. "Do you care for her, Max?"

What sort of question was that? "Why else would I be spending time with the woman?"

"To offer her a sense of the familiar at Caldwell Manor because I asked it of you." Lucien tapped his finger against the arm of his chair, his gaze speculative. "How much time, exactly, have you been spending in Anna's company, how much do you care for her, and why haven't you informed me of either answer before now?"

Nearing the end of his patience, Max spoke before thinking. "I've not counted the minutes, none of your damn business, and—because it is none of your damn business."

"I am her brother."

Max opened his mouth, shut it, and took a calming breath. Without a doubt, it was Lucien's business, but he wasn't going to hand the man that victory outright. "Are you looking for me to seek permission to court her? Very well, may I court your sister?"

"No."

"What? Why the devil not?"

"Permission to court my sister for your mistress? Are you mad?"

Insult fled as quickly as it had arrived. "Ah, no, not for my mistress. My wife."

Lucien digested that information in the time it took him to blink once. "Permission granted."

It took Max longer to digest Lucien's response. "I . . . Well. That was a very sudden change of heart."

"My oldest friend wants to make my sister a viscount-ess. I'd be a fool to object. You've given due consideration to the ramifications of such a choice, I assume?"

"The few that interest me."

"Fair enough. Tell me how I can be of assistance."

"All right," Max said slowly. Nothing about this meeting had gone the way he'd expected. "Allow me to court Anna my way."

Lucien swore under his breath and dragged a hand through his hair before leveling a hard stare at Max. "Do you realize what you're asking of me?"

"I am asking you to trust me." Suddenly uncomfortable, he began to pick at a loose thread on the seat of his chair. "You know I'd never . . . You know what this family means to me."

"I do." Lucien, looking equally ill at ease, nodded and busied his hands and gaze with an ink blotter on the desk. "Very well, proceed as you see fit." He stopped fiddling and jabbed a finger at Max. "But know this, one word of complaint from her and I won't hesitate to call you out."

Max's shoulders relaxed at the exceedingly masculine and therefore infinitely more comfortable threat of violence.

"You loathe the practice of dueling."

Lucien shrugged. "I've never wanted to shoot anyone before."

"Unbearable as a brother, just as I said."

"Say whatever the devil you like, just remember who's the better shot."

Chapter 27

❧

$\mathcal{M}$ax kept Lucien's warning in mind as he set out to woo Anna over the next few days. He didn't believe for a moment that Lucien would call him out for a duel under any circumstances. But neither Lucien or Gideon would hesitate to beat him to a bloody pulp and then ban him from Caldwell Manor. Max could take a beating well enough (and damned if holding Anna in his arms wasn't worth the risk), but banishment was not a punishment he could so easily dismiss.

He'd lose his chance to court Anna altogether. And he'd lose Lucien, Gideon, Mrs. Webster, and . . . Hell, he'd lose everyone and everything that meant anything to him.

And so he was careful. Far more careful than he'd been the night of the picnic. He was forced to take his pleasures in experiencing the small things—a touch of her hand, the meeting of knees as they shared a bench, the brush of arms as they passed by in the hall. And he discovered that, when one paid attention to them, there was a great deal of pleasure to be found in those little touches.

Not every moment that passed between them was innocent, of course. Max wasn't above stealing a kiss or two (or ten) on their walks, or in the shadowed recess of a hallway—just a brief meeting of lips, an excuse to cup her face in his hands and torment himself with the taste of her.

Lucien wouldn't approve, but neither was he likely to take too much offense. And if he did, well, Max figured he could always remind Lucien of his courtship with Lilly. No man cared to be a hypocrite.

Max smiled as he urged his horse into a gallop along the road from Codridgeton to Caldwell. All in all, things were coming along brilliantly. With a little more time and patience, he could win over Anna and they—

Max never saw what knocked him out of the saddle. There was a blur of movement in the trees along the road and something hard slammed into his side. The force knocked him off balance just as his mount veered to one side, and the next thing Max knew, the hard road was rushing up to meet him.

The force of impact knocked the air from his lungs, but with some luck and quick reflexes, he managed to protect his head and roll when he hit the ground, avoiding the sort of abrupt collision that could easily break bones.

Still, it was jarring to be knocked bodily from a moving horse. Even as he pushed himself to his knees, the world spun around him in a long, nauseating circle.

A dark form rushed at him from the side, with a heavy boot aimed at his midsection. Max threw himself out of the way at the last possible second, then scrambled to his feet just in time to take a fist to the jaw from a second assailant. He stumbled back, instinctively throwing a forearm block to escape the next blow, and took quick stock of what he was up against. There were two men, and although both were masked, they were easy enough to recognize.

Ox and Jones. Bloody hell.

Max dodged a lumbering charge from Ox and managed
to jam an elbow into the man's lower back as he stumbled
past, then spun and ducked as Jones swung at his head.
Lashing out with his own fist, he was rewarded when knuckles connected with nose, and Jones howled in pain. He
stepped forward to follow up with another attack, only to be
knocked sideways by a glancing blow from one of Ox's ham-
sized fists, a gentle reminder that he would have to fight this
battle on two fronts.

He did his best to cover both, landing blow after blow,
but he took almost as many hits in return. When his left eye
began to swell shut from an unfortunate collision with Ox's
right elbow, Max realized he needed to bring the fight to a
close or lose any hope of victory. He dodged a swipe of
Jones's new blade and turned quickly, catching the man off
balance so a swift kick sent him sprawling. The knife clat-
tered across the rocky road into the thick grass and Jones
scrambled after it, allowing Max to finally give Ox his full
attention.

He beckoned the big man forward in a taunting gesture
and was not surprised when his opponent lowered his head
for another bull rush. Slow learner, Mr. Ox. But this time,
instead of just dancing out of the way, Max ducked under
the massive arms that reached for his throat and got a proper
hold on one. He gave that arm a firm twist as Ox's own
weight and momentum carried him forward to the ground.
There was a sharp snap and a bellow of pain.

"My arm. Rutting bastard broke my arm!"

Abandoning the search for his knife, Jones rushed forward and grabbed Ox's other arm to drag him backward.
"Shut *up*, man."

It was tempting to taunt them, to let them know he'd
recognized them before Ox had opened his mouth. But it
was smarter to say nothing.

Particularly as the injury to Ox seemed to have put the

men off any further violence. They backed away, Ox cradling his arm, then turned around and bolted into the trees and, no doubt, their waiting horses.

Max stood where he was for a long time after they left, willing his wavering vision to steady. As the intensity of the moment passed, so did the worst of his dizziness, and at last, he was able to walk the distance down the road to collect his horse and pull himself up into the saddle.

The ride home would always remain something of a blur, as his only real thought had been to stay on the horse. And his brief journey from the front drive to the front parlor would also remain a blur simply because of the amount of noise and movement that accompanied it. One footman spotted him climbing the steps to the portico, and by the time he was taking a seat on the settee, a dozen members of Caldwell staff were buzzing around him like flies.

Max breathed a sigh of relief when Lucien strode into the room and took command, sending most of the staff away on errands. Then he poured Max a glass of brandy, pulled a chair close to the settee, and took a seat.

"Anything broken, you think?"

Max finished the drink in a single swallow, ignoring the sting of his split lip. "Oh, that's better." He set the glass aside and gingerly prodded the most tender spot on his rib cage where Ox had landed a particularly brutal blow. "No, nothing broken."

"Tell me what happened."

"Mrs. Wrayburn's men."

Lucien went very still. "You're certain?"

Max nodded, then wished he hadn't. "Mother of God, that hurts."

"I hadn't realized she was capable of something like this." Lucien swore viscously. "I let Anna confront her at the inn. She asked and I—"

"No, I went."

"You did?" Lucien slumped in his seat, sighed heavily.

"Thank you. Thank you for that." He dragged a hand down his face. "Think she's become desperate, stupid, or mad?"

"She's not stupid. Desperate and mad are possibilities." She had to have known the risk of discovery was high, if not inevitable.

"Do we tell Anna?"

"Tell me what?" Anna's voice floated in from the hall, cheerful and light. "What are the pair of you doing? Mrs. Webster said you needed . . ." She trailed off and visibly paled as Lucien moved aside and she got her first look at Max's face. "Oh, my Lord. Oh, my God. What happened to you?"

"I ran into a bit of trouble."

She rushed to him, sank down beside him on the settee. "Trouble? What sort of trouble results in this?"

"It's not as bad as it looks."

"Have you sent for the physician?" She spun on Lucien. "He should have a physician."

"I don't need a physician. It's a spot of bruising, that's all." He took her hand gently. "I'm fine, Anna."

"You are *not* fine," she snapped, and he wasn't sure what surprised him more, the sudden anger or the tremor he heard in her voice. "You're a terrific mess and I'll know the reason why. Right now."

Well, this was . . . rather nice, Max decided. Anna was well and truly worked up over the state of his well-being, or lack thereof. She was *fussing.*

Lucien looked from Max, to Anna and back again, then rose from his chair. "You're obviously in concerned hands. I'll just see what's delayed the physician then, shall I?"

Max would have rolled his eyes if he could have been sure Anna wouldn't see it. The physician hadn't arrived because the physician hadn't been sent for. If nothing was broken, there wasn't a point.

"Did you fall from your horse?" Anna demanded. "Is that it?"

"First off, love ... only drunkards fall from their mounts. Everyone else is thrown. And no, I wasn't thrown." He was knocked off, most likely by a large stick or rock, but he felt strongly she didn't need to know that sort of detail. "I met with a pair of unsavory men on the road from the village."

"Someone did all this to you?" she whispered, aghast.

"A pair of someones," he corrected. "It took two of them. And I assure you, they're worse the wear for it." He flexed his right hand into a fist and took grim pleasure in the ache and sting of his swollen knuckles. "I broke at least one nose today."

"Broke a ... ?" She glared at him, clearly appalled. "They might well have killed you. You ought to have given them what they were after and been done with it. Was it worth protecting a few coins and a cravat pin? What if they'd had a gun, you fool? Or a knife?"

"They had a knife."

Too late, he realized he shouldn't have mentioned the knife. Anna's gray eyes went from wide to saucer-sized; her skin paled.

"You shouldn't have fought them. You should have given them your purse. You—"

"They didn't want it."

"Your horse then, or whatever it was they were after."

"You don't understand, love." He took her hands, gently brought them to his lap to hold. "They weren't highwaymen, Anna. They weren't after my coin or my horse. They were after me." He rubbed his thumb over her knuckles. "It was Ox and Jones."

"Ox and ... My mother's men?" She pulled her hands away slowly. "My mother did this?"

Max had never wanted to lie so desperately in his life.

"I believe so, yes."

"Oh, no. I knew she could be ... But I never thought ...

I *never* . . ." She shook her head, her eyes shining. "This is all my fault. I should not have—"

"Stop it. I'll not hear it." The morning was rotten enough without having to witness Anna flog herself for her mother's crimes. "There is nothing you have done that you should not have done. This is Mrs. Wrayburn's doing."

"But—"

"*Only* her doing."

"And her men."

"I . . ." If he could have done so without hurting himself, he might have laughed a little "Yes, fine, *and* her men. You always have to be right about something, don't you?"

"I don't like to think I was wasting our time in arguing."

"My practical Anna," he murmured. He reached up to brush the backs of his fingers across her cheek, ignoring the throb and sting of his knuckles.

When he would have dropped his hand, she caught it by the wrist and held it against her cheek. "Why would she have done this?"

Max chose his words carefully. "Because she imagined she could get away with it."

She'd done it as revenge, and it had been directed at both of them. Mrs. Wrayburn may not have been close with her daughter, but she knew Anna well enough to know she'd feel some level of responsibility for what happened.

Provided, of course, that what happened could be traced back to Anna's mother, which was fairly easily accomplished when one dispatched a pair of idiots like Ox and Jones.

No, Mrs. Wrayburn wasn't stupid. Mad and desperate, however, remained on the table.

"I think," he said, "that it would be futile to look for the rationale behind an irrational act, don't you?"

"I suppose," Anna murmured, clearly, and not surprisingly, unconvinced. She brought their joined hands down to her lap. "What will you do, now? Will you bring charges against her?"

"I will if you like, but I'd just as soon avoid a lengthy, public trial." And any criminal proceedings involving not only a viscount and the infamous Mrs. Wrayburn, but also Mrs. Wrayburn's illegitimate daughter, the Marquess of Engsly's new sister would be wildly sensationalized and on the tongues of every member of the demimonde and beau monde alike.

Max could live with the bother of it all, but it would be a considerable inconvenience for the Haverstons and, more importantly, a living nightmare for Anna. "How do you feel about exile to a distant land?"

Anna's gaze settled on his battered face. "She should go to prison."

His heart twisted at the words. No one should be forced to wish such a fate on her own mother. And he'd be damned before Anna went from being the daughter of the Mrs. Wrayburn to the daughter of *that* Mrs. Wrayburn—the mad lady in prison. All of which was probably neither here nor there. "The truth is, if she's not left the country already, she will once she hears I was able to identify Ox."

"We can't punish her at all?" Anna demanded, outraged. "She does this to you and—"

"She'll pay a price for it," he promised. "Either she'll be forced to spend the remainder of her life quietly hiding in some obscure corner of the continent—"

"Lord, would she hate that."

"Exactly. Or, and I believe this the more likely outcome, she'll reestablish herself in Paris or Rome or some other fine city, with the expectation we'd not bother chasing her across the channel."

"I'll bother."

He could see from her face that she would certainly try, and damned if he wasn't touched, and just a little amused, by the sentiment. Not every man could claim his own knight-errant. "Thank you, love. I believe I'll join you in that quest. Together we can banish her to somewhere less accommodating."

"Can it be somewhere cold? She does so hate the cold. Greenland, perhaps. Or Newfoundland."

"Kabelvåg, Norway."

She blinked, twice. "That is . . . very specific."

"It's a lovely fishing village where I've some investments, and a gentleman overseeing those investments who can be persuaded to keep an eye on Mrs. Wrayburn after her arrival."

"Norway it is then." She nodded once, then once again, as if trying to convince herself of something. "Tell me about these investments of yours while we wait for the physician."

"As to that . . ."

"Oh, for . . ." Her shoulders slumped and she gave him an annoyed and slightly patronizing look. "You didn't send for the physician, did you?"

"It's just a few cuts and bruises. I don't require—" He broke off when she stood up abruptly and stalked over to yank on the bellpull. "What are you doing? Stop that."

She yanked the pull again. "You made me see the physician because I'd stood in a bit of water. You can damn well suffer his company because of this."

*A*lthough Mrs. Webster and all the Haverstons offered to take on Max's care until the physician arrived, Anna refused to leave Max's side.

In truth, there was little she could do for him, even with all the help provided. The best she could manage was to bully him into lying back on the settee and letting her place a cool, damp cloth over his swollen eyes.

She studied his battered face, willing away the injuries. She wanted to brush her fingers along every inch of the marred and broken skin and watch it heal beneath her touch. How she wished he would allow her to apologize. She may not have sent the men who'd attacked him, but she was the reason they had come.

Life had taken on such a lovely routine, she'd almost forgotten that Caldwell wasn't home, that her last name wasn't Haverston. She'd begun to think of her past less and her future more, and in doing so, she'd stopped giving adequate attention to the consequences of her actions, past and present.

She should have known there would be a cost for leaving Anover House, and an even higher one for defying her mother by not returning.

Today was a reminder that there were almost always hidden costs to the choices one made. It might be weeks, months, or even years before they came to light, but eventually they would. And there were other consequences that weren't hidden, exactly, but all too easy to brush aside, or ignore all together, until it was too late.

The Haverstons would likely have children of their own soon. What would her presence in their lives mean for their future? The acknowledgment of an illegitimate aunt or uncle wasn't so rare an occurrence, but an illegitimate aunt who happened to be the daughter of a famous courtesan who had mysteriously disappeared from the country at the very height of her popularity and directly after her connection to the Marquess of Engsly was discovered . . . that was bound to be mentioned.

And what if Madame took it into her head to cause more trouble before she could be found? What if she was angry enough, or mad enough, to target Lilly and Winnefred? What if she blamed . . .

"Oh, my Lord! Mrs. Culpepper!"

Max tore the cloth off his eyes. "What?"

"What if she sent someone after Mrs. Culpepper? She knows we left together. She knows—"

He pushed himself into a sitting position. "Does she know where Mrs. Culpepper has gone?"

"I don't know." Anna wasn't sure her mother was even aware that Mrs. Culpepper had a sister. "She could find out, surely."

"Maggie," he called out to one of the maids. "Fetch His Lordship, if you please." His voice was calm and steady, but there was an underlying thread of steal. "I highly doubt your mother sent out more than one band of ruffians, but we'll send someone out to check on your Mrs. Culpepper, just to be safe."

Chapter 28

✣

*J*t took a full two days to receive word back from Mrs. Culpepper.

Anna read the letter from her friend with relief at first, then with interest and then, as she reached the end of the pages, a heavy but determined heart.

Mrs. Culpepper was happy to report that both she and her sister were whole and hale and had neither seen nor heard from Mrs. Wrayburn. As for Anna's other inquiry . . . yes, there was a cottage available for purchase in the area that would be suitable for her needs.

Mrs. Culpepper then went on to strongly encourage Anna to think long and hard about what her needs might be before committing to anything.

Anna, however, had already thought long and hard, and had made up her mind. All that was left now was to tell Max she was leaving Caldwell Manor.

The physician had promised a full recovery, as nothing vital had been damaged, and already there were signs

Max's wounds were beginning to heal. The swelling about his face had decreased dramatically, and he was able to move about the house without grimacing, or having to hide his grimacing, as Anna expected to be the case.

Still, it pained her to see his myriad cuts and bruises, knowing she was at least in part responsible for them, and as she shared a game of chess with him in the library that evening, she found it easier to stare at the board than to look at him.

"You are very quiet again tonight," Max commented. He'd made similar observations over the course of the last two days. Anna had put him off with vague excuses of being tired and assurances that she felt fine.

But now . . . She glanced at his battered face and away again. Now it was time for the truth. "I've been thinking . . . The time has come for me to leave, I think."

"Surrendering so quickly? You've a chance yet." He gestured over the small table. "Use your queen. You always hold on to her too long—"

"Not the game, Max."

*M*ax looked up from the board, took in Anna's expression, and set down the pawn he'd been holding.

"Caldwell Manor," he said, mostly in the hope that she'd correct him.

"I received a letter from Mrs. Culpepper this morning. There is a cottage available not far from her own new home."

Devil take the woman. "She has asked you to come?"

"No. She was simply reminding me that I have options."

"Those options include remaining at Caldwell."

"Indefinitely?" She shook her head. "I've been a guest in my own home my whole life. I don't want that—"

"You're not a guest here. You're family. The Haverstons must have made that clear by now. Lucien—"

"I was family at Anover House as well," she pressed on. "It's different, I know, but the fact remains that this isn't my home. I have very little control over anything here. That's not to say I don't like it here. I do. I like it here very much, but . . . Now, with the London season over, the ton will be headed to their country estates or visiting friends. I understand Lady Engsly very much enjoys being a hostess."

"Is that what this is about?" he asked gently. Caldwell Manor would no longer be a refuge from everyone else in the world. "Would it be so awful, attending a ball or dinner party every now and then?"

"Yes . . . I don't know," she admitted. "I don't want to know. I don't want to take the chance at being the evening's entertainment."

"There are advantages and benefits to taking that risk. Dancing, laughter, music. We could waltz together, you and I." He reached for her hand, only to have her pull it away.

"Max, don't."

Panic began to bite at him, little nibbles he did his best to ignore, or at least shove aside with reasoning. This was merely a conversation, he told himself. She was just expressing her options aloud, that was all. Nothing had really been decided upon yet.

"All right, you won't stay at Caldwell indefinitely. But you needn't choose a solitary life in a cottage either. You have options, as your Mrs. Culpepper pointed out."

"It won't be solitary. I'll have Mrs. Culpepper to visit, and—"

"*Anna.*"

"We cannot always have what we want," she said stiffly.

Max studied her face, the shadows under her eyes, the way she refused to meet his gaze. "You mean this? You *truly* mean to leave?"

"Yes." Her hand came up to pick at the wood at the edge of the table. "I think, perhaps, tomorrow—"

"Tomorrow?" Panic was immediately eclipsed by anger.

He pushed away from the table and rose. "Tomorrow? Just like that? You didn't think to give me any time, any chance to—"

"To fight with me over my choice?" She shook her head without looking at him. "There's no point in our arguing. We knew where this was heading from the very—"

"No, *you* knew. You assumed. I asked for your hand. *That* is where I thought this was heading." He swore, stalked the short distance to the window while Anna spoke at his back.

"You know we can't marry," she said quietly. "I can't live amongst the demimonde; you can't live a quiet life in the country. Our families would face censure. You—"

He spun around and cut her off. "Our families are insulated by titles, wealth, and power. They will emerge unscathed, I assure you."

"Your nieces—"

"Would be forced to marry men who would show respect to my wife. I am fully comfortable imposing that limitation."

"It is not that simple. Young men have limitations set on them by their own families. A perfectly wonderful gentleman may be forbidden by his father to court one of your nieces, because of me."

Max brushed that away with an impatient wave. "If the gentleman feels the hand of my niece is not worth the courage it would take to find his own way, then good riddance to him."

Anna closed her eyes briefly. "You are oversimplifying things."

"No, you are making things worse than they are, than they have any need to be. You spend so much time worrying over what society might make of you, you don't stop to consider the opinions and desires of those who matter."

"That is not true," she snapped. She lifted her gaze to meet his, finally, and rose from her seat. "I *am* considering them. For pity's sake, *look* at you. Look at what my own mother did to you."

Max took a few hesitant steps forward as anger and heartache battled for supremacy. Never before had he wanted to shout at, shake, and soothe someone, all at the same time. "You are not to blame for your mother's actions, Anna. You must know that—"

"I do know it. Just as I know that it would be irresponsible of me to ignore the reminder that there are all sorts of consequences for my own actions. Some of them are only possibilities, yes. And perhaps, where our families are concerned, they seem greater to me than they truly are." She held up a hand before he could seize on that small capitulation and run with it. "But some of them are real, some of them would be inescapable, and some of them I know well enough to be certain I have not exaggerated them in my mind. I *am* a source of gossip and scandal. I *would be* a target for derision in London. I always have been."

"If the talk bothers you so terribly, we'll stay clear of it. I am not asking you to return to Anover House as the Ice Maiden. I am asking you to share a home with me as a viscountess." How could she not see the difference in what her mother had forced on her and what he was offering? "Invite your own guests, make your own friends, attend the balls *you* want to attend. Start your own bloody rumors, if you like—"

"There will *still* be whispering and—"

"Devil take the whispers," he broke in. He dragged a hand through his hair, frustrated and hurt beyond measure. "God, you give up so easily—"

"I don't. I am trying to make the inevitable easier for us, but that—"

"I don't want easier. This isn't bloody inevitable, it's your bloody-minded choice and it damn well shouldn't be *easy.*"

"Please stop shouting."

Max bit off an oath. He hadn't realized he'd raised his voice, and now that he did, he found it difficult to lower it again. To regain control meant to let go of some of the anger, and that meant leaving the door open once more for panic, and worse, old fears and insecurities.

Anna was leaving. He wasn't needed. He wasn't even wanted. Because he wasn't enough. She had her cottage in the country, her Mrs. Culpepper, and her disdain for all things London. Why would she need him?

"If you are determined to run away, I cannot stop you, and I'll be damned before I beg you to show a little courage."

"I am *not* being a coward," she snapped. "I am being reasonable and sensible and *honest.* And I am trying to be mindful of what my choices would mean for all of us, but if all you can see in that is a coward, then . . ." She angled her face away, pressed her lips together in a hard line. "Then clearly we do not understand each other as well as we imagined."

He said nothing. There didn't seem to be any words left.

"I think . . ." Anna said quietly. "I think it would be best if we said good-bye now, instead of drawing this out and—"

"Good-bye, Anna." His voice was stiff and sounded hollow to his own ears. "Godspeed."

He bowed without looking at her, turned, and left the room. If she said good-bye in return, he didn't hear it. He bloody well didn't want to.

Chapter 29

❧

M ax stood at the window of his chambers and watched
as a carriage was brought round to the front of the
house. The dawn had come gray and cheerless, with thick
clouds sagging low over the hills and the smell of rain
clinging to the air.

He wouldn't stay for this. He'd decided the night before,
as he'd sat alone in his room, nursing a brandy and his
anger. He wasn't going to be around to see Anna run off to
her cottage, her new life, without him.

She could bloody well watch him ride off to London . . .
Well, to McMullin Hall, really, but she didn't know that.
Let her think it was to town where there were plenty of
ladies who might welcome his affections. Lovely, sophisti-
cated, wickedly willing ladies . . . who didn't interest him
in the least, but she didn't need to know that either.

It was ridiculous and infantile . . . but there it was. He
was willing to be ridiculous and infantile. He was willing
to try anything that might fill the aching hole in his chest.

And so he too borrowed a carriage and, having no need to pack, left Caldwell Manor just as the footmen were finishing loading Anna's carriage, and just as the first small droplets of rain began to fall from the darkening sky.

The trip to McMullin Hall would be quicker on horseback, but to ride through the rain and mud seemed impossibly forlorn. And he wasn't forlorn. He was bloody miserable.

He'd lost Anna. Or, more accurately, she'd let go of him. She'd rejected him outright. And holy hell, that *hurt*. It sat on his chest like a boulder, tore at him as he'd never imagined a refusal could.

Worse, there was no sweeping that sort of rejection away. He couldn't just say, *To hell with her. To hell with all of it.*

Because he was already in hell, so it was rather like inviting her along, and she'd already declined the offer of his company.

It was maddening. How could she choose a life of isolation over a life with him? How could a woman speak of courage and adventure and then toss aside both to hide away in a cottage? A damned *cottage*, for God's sake.

What the devil was she going to do there? Embroider all day? Was she going to spend the rest of her life reading, or taking walks, or having picnics, or playing with dogs, or . . .

Max shifted in his seat, uncomfortable with the realization that he was listing the things she'd been doing at Caldwell. Activities he'd either joined her in or enjoyed watching her perform.

He tried to push the thought aside and focus on his anger, but the hours and days spent with Anna filled his head. She'd looked content embroidering with Lilly in the parlor, and at home with a book in her hands in the library, and perfectly happy walking in the fields and woods with him.

With some reluctance, he turned his mind to thoughts of

Anna in London. It wasn't the first time he'd done so. He'd imagined her in his town house dozens of times—in his bed; at the table for breakfast with the early morning light shining through the drapes; holding court at a dinner party or salon filled with poets and artists and scholars, carefully selected men and women who would appreciate Anna's wit and intelligence. In short, he had imagined Anna in *his* London, in the world he wanted to give her.

He had not, he was forced to admit, given as much consideration to the London Anna feared, to the consequences she was certain were inescapable. She had argued, more than once, that she couldn't possibly reside in London without inviting stares and whispers, and yet not once had he pictured her in situations where she might have to endure those stares and whispers.

He made himself picture them now—every trip to Bond Street, every ride through Hyde Park, every visit to the theater, any and every foray outside the house held the potential of turning her into a target for ridicule and scorn. He saw her in his mind's eye, visiting all those places, doing all the things that he took for granted as part and parcel of living in London. And she wasn't smiling. She was cold and aloof, once again playing the Ice Maiden to save her pride.

Max swore ripely as much of his anger turned inward. Anna *would* be miserable living in London. She would be every inch as trapped as he might feel playing the country gentleman.

Damn it, he should have listened to her more carefully. He should have spent more time considering what she needed, instead of trying to convince her that he knew what she really wanted.

Amazingly, he could see now that what she needed was exactly what *he* needed. Freedom. They'd simply taken different steps to obtain it.

He'd embraced the demimonde and welcomed the ton's

censure and disdain. She'd turned her back on society altogether.

There were benefits and disadvantages to both approaches, and it had been the height of arrogance to assume his approach was the better, the smartest, the exclusive road to happiness. *Their* happiness. Because, clearly, no one was happy at present.

And it had been a pretty piece of outright stupidity to have expected her to set aside, in the course of a few short weeks, the fears and needs created by a lifetime of living in Anover House, simply because he told her she should.

I could talk the devil out of his tail.

Anna was right. Men were outrageously arrogant creatures.

Strangely, the more he went over things in his mind, and the more he realized how shortsighted he'd been, the less convinced he became that all hope was lost.

There had to be hope. He had to be able to fix this. What was the bloody point of realizing you'd been wrong-headed if you couldn't make things right again?

What was the point of anything, if he couldn't make things right with Anna?

"Stop!" He banged on the ceiling. "Stop the carriage! Turn it around!"

*A*nna stared out her carriage window at the wet and dreary countryside that rolled by. Soggy as her pillow, she thought ruefully.

She brushed impatiently at a tear that slipped down her cheek. One would think after having spent the better part of a night weeping into that pillow, she'd have run dry. Yet somehow the view out the carriage window was blurred, not by the day's gloomy light and halfhearted rain that pattered on the roof, but from the seemingly endless reservoir of misery that welled up inside and filled her eyes.

She wanted to turn the carriage round again. Only there was no point. Max had already left for London. He'd left while she'd said her own good-byes to the Haverstons.

Leaving them had been painful as well, and exhausting, as Lucien and Gideon had tried their best to convince her to stay on, then dragged a thousand promises from her to visit regularly and write often and accept a shockingly generous allowance before they agreed to let her go. The pain of saying good-bye to them, however, was dulled by the more acute wound of her parting with Max, rather like procuring a nasty cut and not really feeling it for one's head being on fire.

Anna swiped away another round of tears as the carriage lurched in a rut.

This was not how things should have ended with Max. She'd known they couldn't be together from the start, how could she have been so ill-prepared for the end? How could she have bungled it so terribly?

Surely there was something she might have done differently, something that would have allowed them to part as friends. Now there would be no word from him, no letters or visits. It certainly would not be Max who brought her Hermia.

Anna shook her head, resolute. It was for the best that their separation was quick and thorough. What would visits do but torment them both? What ridiculousness to think they could go from lovers to friends the way a lady might change from a ball gown to an old night rail.

One could not take one's feelings on and off for the sake of convenience and easy good-byes.

If one could, she wouldn't be so damnably in love with Max.

She brushed away the next tear, took a ragged breath. She was in love with Max. It was surprising how natural it felt to admit it, rather like admitting one had lungs or a heart. Perhaps because a part of her had always known she loved Max. Just as all of her had known that, in the end, it changed nothing.

Love wasn't a vital organ, for pity's sake. She could live without it. Surely. Maybe.

God, she honestly didn't know if she could. It bloody well felt as if something vital had been removed—ripped clean out of her chest.

And while the sensible, pragmatic side of her insisted that sometimes love was simply not enough, the rest of her—and the painful hole in her chest in particular—demanded to know why the devil it shouldn't be.

Why *couldn't* love be enough for her?

It was enough for other people, wasn't it? To hear her mother tell it, the road to Gretna Green was thick with fools who chose love over all else. Many of them, Anna thought with a new kind of discomfort, likely facing obstacles greater than her own.

She heard Max's words from the night before.

If the gentleman feels the hand of my niece is not worth the courage it would take to find his own way, then good riddance to him.

She wasn't that gentleman, of course. The circumstances were entirely different. She *had* found her own way. Just as Max had found his. Their ways took them in opposite directions, that was all.

Because she hadn't the courage to find another way.

Anna shook her head at the unbidden thought but found she couldn't break free of it.

Other people found a way. When it mattered, when something was worth it, they found a way.

Why hadn't she? Was she that afraid of a few more stares and whispers? She'd managed before. She'd stood in the face of them for years because it had been necessary. Couldn't she do it now because it was necessary in order to be with Max?

She was aware of her stomach tightening at the thought

of returning to London, but rather like saying good-bye to the Haverstons, the discomfort seemed . . . more manageable now compared to the pain of losing Max forever.

So, why on earth had she chosen the most painful path for the future?

"I'm a fool," she whispered. "I've been a coward."

But maybe she could fix it, she thought with dawning determination. Maybe they could find another way together. She had to at least try.

She stretched up to pound on the ceiling. "Stop! Stop the carriage!" Ignoring the misting rain, she stuck her head out the window to shout at the driver. "Turn us around! Quickly! We need to catch up to Lord Dane!"

Anna withdrew herself from the window and blew out a long, hard breath. She was doing it. She was really going to chase after Max, all the way to London if need be.

As it happened, it didn't need to be. The driver had turned the horses around and taken them no more than five minutes down the road before the carriage rolled to a stop.

"What on earth?" Anna stuck her head out the window once more. They couldn't possibly have caught up to Max so quickly.

But there, stopped and facing her in the middle of the muddy road, was Max's carriage. For the space of a few heartbeats, she simply stared at it, caught between elation, fear, and simple astonishment.

He must have been coming for her. It was the only thing that made sense.

Then his carriage door flew open and Max bounded out, breaking the spell. He came striding toward her with a determined air, and without another thought, she threw open the carriage door and jumped down into the mud and sprinkling rain.

She hurried to meet him halfway, and then . . . stopped short, as he did, suddenly unsure how to bridge the last six feet that separated them.

She didn't know what to say to him. She'd not thought that far ahead. It should be something eloquent, something unforgettable and apologetic and very, very convincing, and—

"I love you," she heard herself say. "I am completely, utterly in love with you."

Max went very still, except for his hands. She watched them clench and unclench at his side. Please, please, please, she thought, let that be a good sign.

She kept her own hands gripped in the material of her skirts while the air backed up in her lungs. "I thought . . . I thought you ought to know, because—"

"We should travel," he cut in suddenly.

"I'm sorry?"

He took a cautious step forward. "We can go to Europe, if you like, or the Americas. That's excitement enough for me and you can be free of the gossipmongers—"

She moved closer as well as hope began to fill that hollow spot in her chest. "I don't need that. I want it, I do, but I'll give it up. I'll stay in London if that's what you need, or—"

"We can try everything. Every continent, every country, every damn city and town, if we want. Why not?" He stepped closer, near enough that she was certain he could feel the longing that came off of her in waves. "There's a place for us, Anna. I know it. We can try the country and see if it suits us, then London if we decide it doesn't. Maybe Scotland. Freddie swears by the Scottish countryside. Paris or Rome or Boston after that. We can emigrate or travel indefinitely. We'll look—"

"And if there is no place for us?" The question slipped out before she could bite it back. "If there is nowhere we can both belong?"

"I don't care. I don't care if I spend the rest of my life searching for the perfect place. I don't care if I die having never found it . . . as long as I'm searching with you. As long as the last thing I see on this earth is you. This . . ." At last he stepped close enough to touch. He took her face in his hands. "This is what I need to be happy. This is where I belong. I love you, Anna Rees. *You* are all I need."

She opened her mouth to speak, but yelped instead when the sky, so doggedly determined to leak all morning, decided to open up at last and let loose a great flood of water.

Max laughed as they were both instantly drenched from head to foot. He pulled her into his arms, lifted his voice above the roar of the sudden downpour. "Will you travel the world with me, Anna Rees?!"

She heard her own laughter over the sound of the rain. "Yes! Absolutely, yes!" Her fingers dug into the sodden fabric of his coat. "Will you take me to Gretna Green, Max Dane?!"

She felt, rather than heard the groan that originated from deep in his chest. "Yes. By God, *yes!*"

He bent his head and kissed her then, and the gray world around her spun away, taking with it the last vestiges of doubt. He loved her. She loved him. Whatever came next, whatever adventure awaited them, they would meet it together.

Epilogue

❧

The marriage of Viscount Dane to *the* Miss Anna Rees was the talk of London for months.

Theories as to how the grasping little minx had landed the dashing rapscallion (and whether or not it was in some way connected to Mrs. Wrayburn's sudden emigration to Norway) were bountiful. Speculation as to where the viscount had run off to with his new bride after the nuptials was rampant.

Society had seen neither hide nor hair of the happy pair. They were believed to be making a tour of Scotland, but only the Haverstons and Dane's cousin, Mr. William Dane, knew for certain, and they remained annoyingly tight-lipped on the subject.

Terribly bold of the girl to have reached so far above her station, it was said. Foolish of the viscount to have so carelessly tossed aside his responsibility to the title, they whispered. Probably, they'd run off to the continent in shame, it was agreed.

The whispers ballooned initially, but tapered after a time, and then somebody heard that Lord Truch's daughter had been caught sneaking out her window to meet with a merchant's son in her own garden, and talk turned to that. And then, three weeks later, turned again when Eliza Tomlison was caught attempting to set fire to a rival's home in a pique of professional jealousy.

By the time Lord and Lady Dane returned to London, a full year after their nuptials, they were no longer the talk of the town.

There were still whispers, as was to be expected. But before there was even a chance of the talk becoming widespread, the pair moved on to Caldwell Manor to welcome the birth of Lord Engsly's first child, a daughter, and then to McMullin Hall for his cousin's marriage, and then . . . And then all but their closest friends stopped paying attention to what the couple was doing. They were seen about here and there—at the theater, an exclusive dinner party, Lord Dane at his club and Tattersall's, and their names popped into conversation from time to time.

Have you heard Lord Dane's sister has been made a widow at last? I do wonder if she plans to return home.

But for the most part, the pair was no longer so interesting as to require particular attention from society. It was last noted that the couple had purchased a moderate country home outside the village of Menning, but that they were planning a trip to Venice, or possibly Rome.

What did it matter, really, when everyone who was anyone was talking of something else.